MW01147190

THE COUNCIL OF THE DEAD

GLORIOUS MISHAPS

K.A. ASHCOMB

LIQUID HARE PUBLISHING

Copyright © 2024 K.A. Ashcomb

All rights reserved.

Published by Liquid Hare Publishing 2024

Riihimäki, Kanta-Häme, Finland

This book is sold subject to the condition that it shall not, by way of trade or otherwise, be lent, resold, hired out, or otherwise circulated without the publisher's prior consent in any form of binding or cover other than that in which it is published and without a similar condition including this condition being imposed on the subsequent purchaser. Under no circumstances may any part of this book be photocopied for resale.

This is a work of fiction. Any similarity between the characters and situations within its pages and places or persons, living or dead, is unintentional and co-incidental.

ISBN 978-952-69026-7-8 (Paperback)

ISBN 978-952-69026-8-5 (eBook)

Contact K.A. Ashcomb: k.a.ashcomb@gmail.com

Follow K.A. Ashcomb's blog: https://ashcombka.com

Cover Design by K.A. Ashcomb

Edited by Emily Nemchick

ALSO BY K. A. ASHCOMB

For the loving memory of my father, Kari. I would have loved to keep you around for a little longer

PRINCIPAL CHARACTERS

Town Hall

Petula Upwood, necromancer, current mayor of Necropolis

Dow, mysterious secretary for Mayor

Mrs. Maybury, politician, the Union of the Undead leader

Her, Petula's cat.

Elvira, receptionist for Mayor

Mr. Colton, bodyguard for mayor

Cruxh, police officer, ghoul, husband to zombie Mrs. Mayburry

Harriet Stowe, Prime Minister of Leporidae Lop

The Coven

Henrietta Culpepper (Mother), Head of Witches Coven

Eurof Culpepper, Henrietta's husband

Imogene Granger, Henrietta's secretary

The Council

Otis Thurston, necromancer, inventor of the Bufonite machine

Percy Allread, hexer, Monster Hunter, works for the Council

Mr. Crowen, Necromancer Council's representative

Alvira, vampire, Percy Allread's handler

Ichor Pod, Otis's lawyer

Elmer Spooner, the Council's internal investigator

Laura Devlin, the Council's internal police

The newspaper
R. E. Porter (Raul), reporter
Maximilian, editor (Raul's boss)

The needlepoint group
Ida Mortician, banker
Annabella Sepulcher, lawyer
Lattice Burton human resources manager

The prison
Silas Philpot, prison doctor
James Hardrick, warden of the Necropolis' Reformatory for the Criminally Insane and Other Offenders
Karin Rotbell, body guard

The Ghoul City
Gwerrusxh, Mother of all ghouls
Sirixh, Cruxh sister and Gwerrusxh daugther and the leader of the Differs Soul Party
Philomena Lace, witch doctor, living in the Ghoul City

Others
Kraken, diety, lives in sea near Necropolis
Madam Sabine, Leader of the Church of Kraken

PROLOGUE

The sea billowed against Necropolis's shoreline. The restlessness of the city seeped into the waters, stirring Kraken. It cocked its head towards the landmass where belief kept its ancient copper blood flowing fresh and young. As always, there was misery and death. So it always was with the two-legged creatures who sent their gifts to the sea. Behind them, the city was hungry. It waited for its cut of flesh and bone to feed its soil.

Kraken's tremendous body swayed against the flow of the tides as it surfaced.

There on the cliff overlooking the ocean stood a man, waiting for it. The man had been there every night, tempting Kraken. He didn't believe in the gods. He wanted the city for himself, fighting to make Kraken release its tentacles from Necropolis. The man had no trust in it or any of its kind.

The sea was getting colder, yet the air was still warm. The eternal mist swallowed Necropolis, leaving only Kraken and the cliffs visible. Here and there, the lights of the houses glimmered through the thick, moist air. Kraken still saw every wall, every home, every inhabitant, and heard what they whispered in the wee hours of the night. It sensed what they hungered for. It was what every being hungered for—to exist, to be loved, to be valued, to do—yet their hunger could never be satisfied. It slipped from their fingertips as soon as they touched it. Like a curse, they were doomed to roam the land in search of meaning.

The man sensed it too.

Necropolis shivered between the two of them. A person in its own right, wanting nothing more than to exist into eternity, forever growing.

Kraken dived, leaving the man on the cliff.

Their fates would be sealed with death. Whose, was for the flux of time to show.

Chapter One

THE GAME OF LIFE

Life comes with sticky situations. The kind that will define the person and the future to come. Such is the nature of the game of existence. Even on a minuscule scale, existing isn't a simple, straightforward thing. Take, for example, a common earthworm. It isn't only you-know-who that lurks in the mornings to catch the worm. There are beetles, ants, you name it, making the path between A and B shaky at best. It's the same thing with bigger creatures, like humans. Humans are especially peculiar in this regard. They have come up with novel, social ways to hunt each other, starting from victim blaming, moving to mortgages with fine print, and ending up with things like nuclear bombs used as the last Hail Mary.[1]

Not that Necropolis had yet seen destruction of the nuclear variety, but that time would come, if you believed in determination. Souls were another thing. The last necromantic war almost ripped the fabric of the entire cosmos apart. It was stopped only by the grace of the Necromantic Council. But this wasn't about wars. This was about souls and hunting others with fine print. Not the mortgage kind. No.

Otis Thurston knew all about the fine print and the rules he was supposed to follow, and which he was accused of violating. It was what had

---

1. A Hail Mary worthy of what, no one actually knows.

landed him in the prison cell of his own making. Otis measured the room, pacing from the door to the back wall. Nothing had changed in the past month. It was still small and necromancy-proofed. The guards weren't fooled when he turned himself into a rat or an otter. His shapeshifting abilities, along with his necromantic ones, were no use against the Necromantic Council. They knew how to keep their prisoners imprisoned and awake.

Otis guessed this place—the room with a bed, washing bowl, a desk, and a small shelf where he kept books and trial papers—was a fitting cosmic payback. Not that he thought the cosmos was interested in payback or that what he'd done was bad. He had been curious. There was nothing wrong with that. The Council should be celebrating his discovery of how souls could be used to power machines rather than locking him up here to be forgotten. Machines like the Bufonite, which could make anything out of nothingness, would revolutionize life as the Necropolitans knew it. Okay, Otis agreed that on some moral level, it was unseemly to trap a living soul inside a machine and make it serve the whims of others, but a lot worse things had been done in the name of science, or for that matter, in the name of freedom and money.

The Council didn't agree. They would make him pay for his brilliance with his life.

And with his sanity. The Council deliberately kept him awake and had done so for days with perpetual light and Kraken-damned noises. Even when he closed his eyes, everything glowed a sickly orange. Otis hated witches. With necromancy, you knew what you were getting, but with witchcraft, it was anyone's guess what curses would be sent after you. Foul business, the whole witchery thing.

Otis paused and leaned against the desk. His heart was beating fast, like it had done for days now. He was ready to beg the witches to come in and give the Council the Bufonite. He bit his lip, drawing blood, tasting the iron. His silence was the only thing keeping the Necromantic Council from inflicting a fate worse than death. He was a necromancer, after all. No necromancer had a restful afterlife or a resurrection. Too dangerous to have a necromancer milling around as an undead. He would give anything to die for a second or two, even for fifteen minutes. Just to shut his eyes and be at peace... and then pop back up.

"Witches." Otis gripped his hands tighter against the wooden desk. The Necromantic Council more than happily employed the Coven's witches to do their dirty work, keeping necromancy as a gentleman's game and witches one step closer to a full cackle. Otis pushed himself up and started pacing again, trying to ignore the constant shrill sound getting higher every minute. He roared against it but only ended up coughing on the floor, his lungs about to give out. Otis lay there on the floor, curled into a ball.

The Council was at fault here. Their outdated rules were turning Necropolis into a backwater where brilliant minds went to die. They were making an example out of him. No necromancer was allowed to leave and practice outside Necropolis. No necromancer was free to think on their own. Otis spat out a mouthful of blood, still remembering the fairytale drilled into him and every necromancer and every Necropolitan alive: how the Council had saved them; how it existed to serve Necropolis and prevent future necromantic wars from happening. What a lie.

"Control freaks," Otis shouted, crawling towards the bed and burying his head in his hands as he got there. "Just let me sleep."

The lights went out, and the shrill screech was gone, but his ears were still ringing.

Otis blinked, waiting for the noise to start again. The witches hadn't grown a conscience just like that. Not here, not inside the Council. It wasn't exactly known for its kindness.

He drew the covers over him.

Otis waited for the noise or the sleep to come, but his mind was as much of a dick as other people could be. Thoughts kept spinning inside his head, replaying how everything had happened, how he was still alive thanks to his ability to be jovial and make friends. He had been caught in Threebeanvalley by the Necromantic Council's Monster Hunter, Percy Allread. The man had dragged him back here on a ship. Otis had made buddies with the crew, who had made sure the word of his arrest got out. Now the Council couldn't keep him or the machine as their dirty little secret; hence the public trial to come. Otis's only way to freedom was the moronic undead lawyer, Ichor Pod,[2] and to hope that the court wasn't corrupted. Fat chance in Necropolis, where the laws were already skewed towards the powerful and where everyone saw it as their moral duty to take bribes. Otis was sure his lawyer was in the Council's pocket. Who wasn't? The Council and its anonymous board owned the city. So it was and had always been. Everyone knew it.

He wasn't getting out of this alive or sane. The only thing he could do was to wreak as much havoc as he could against the Council. He had the perfect weapon for it: the Save the Otis Group, as the newspapers had christened the crowd outside the Council protesting his arrest. Somehow the self-centered Necropolitans had managed that. The whole city questioned the Council's right to detain him. They were even asking for more freedoms for the necromancers. Otis had become a martyr. His friends on the boat had done him a solid. If he could only speak to the group, he could be free, but he was only allowed to speak to his lawyer. The boring, dry undead who made Otis question fate, destiny, and the whole lot. The stupid man had let his life amount to spinning papers.

---

2. There was nothing moronic about Ichor Pod. He was the most sought-after lawyer in Necropolis. There were even rumors that he had been around when the first laws were written. But that was just a rumor, if you asked him. Not that he ever denied it that hard. Perception and all that.

Otis rubbed his eyes and turned onto his right side. The sting made him moan. That and the fatigue all over his body were getting to him. The lights would soon come back. So would the noise.

Maybe it was a blessing that he couldn't get his word out? He had become this mythical hero rather than the Otis he was. He wasn't exactly one of those people you would call inspiring or lovable. Charming, yes. Self-centered, definitely. Jovial at best. But lovable, modest, and noble, no. He didn't give Kraken's ass about making things better for the other necromancers. He only wanted to screw the Council over, and if that meant he got a cult created around him, even better. According to his lawyer, he had become enough of a nuisance, having forced the Council to hire a public relationship manager. Which meant that if they did their job right, the best outcome for Otis would be a martyr's death. And they were doing their best. Most likely, it was one of those charmers—a witch—good with their tongue.

Otis turned again. He hated the Council. Necromancy shouldn't be about following the rules and acting like a good little boy. It had always been about ultimate anarchy. The middle finger to the gods who thought humanity was made to die. Necromancers should be allowed to tamper freely with the line between death and life. Who cared about the cosmos or wars? At least, with freedom, there would be excitement, which was severely lacking when you were stuck following the Council's schematics. Who wanted to be a slave to forms from A to H with endless numbers attached to them?

Otis opened his eyes. Tears flowed out, but he couldn't feel them. His eyes were swollen and red. The burn scar on his forehead ached. The one he had gotten saving the life of the Council's hunter during the fiery explosion back in Threebeanvalley. Everything would be easier if he had let Percy Allread die. The man's witness statement was already floating around the city, and Necropolis didn't care about proof. Rumors were enough to sentence a man. Otis could still see the fire that had destroyed the first machine and taken Levi Perri's life. Everything glowed bright orange and yellow. He barely registered the door to his cell opening. He had no strength to lift his head and greet his interrogators. They could carve him, poke him, and tear him apart; he wouldn't protest. At least then he would finally be put out of his misery, released into the endless sleep.

"Mr. Thurston," a solemn voice stated.

It was his lawyer, the undead man in the best black suit money could buy, with pinstripes to prove it.

"Mr. Pod," Otis greeted, keeping his head down and his eyes shut. "What's new?" he asked, more out of the need to have a conversation than the expectation of getting something useful from his lawyer. You could say he had lost all hope.

The thing was that there's always hope. It's just that Otis couldn't see it. The trouble was that once you lost hope, you were pretty much a goner. It was as simple as that. Meaning needed to come with life and life with meaning. And if Otis had paid attention beyond his misery, he might have heard the stories embedded in the walls of the old library which was now the Council's headquarters. The walls whispered about heroic escapes with dragons, heroines, and damsels included. All Otis had to do was harness their power to escape. Such was the power of stories. They shaped the world even for silly reasons like power. You just needed to utter them aloud and everything was altered, human affairs put into perspective. And stories were just that, images of the world to be believed in. Otis didn't notice any of it. It was the ego thing that all too often got in the way.

He pushed himself up to greet his lawyer, putting his trust in legal writing. A story in its own right. A different story, though. One without knights and dragons, but definitely with terrifying monsters and tragic endings.

Petula swirled her shoulders back, trying to stretch her chest after being hunched over her desk in the Town Hall the whole day. It would be easy to think that as a tyrant[3] she was the freest person in the entire universe, but that would be a misconception. The same applied to mayors, presidents, and anyone dependent on others' support. The ugly truth was that no living creature was free. There was no escape from the fact that as long as you were alive and here in Necropolis, even past that, you darn well needed others, or at least a very effective way to say, "Good morning, and please bugger off.[4] "

The needing others part was only the beginning of the trouble. As time went on, and the complexity of the society or the tyrant's circles expanded, things got even trickier. It all became a juggling act, where you had to keep all the eggs in the air and be happy with their flight paths, or they would come crashing down and beat you to death. That was what Petula had been doing all day: shifting papers to keep the eggs from murdering her.

Though the legal clauses were already killing her with every word added. Petula pretended that a good night's rest would fix it. It never did. The tasks piled up on her desk, threatening to one day collapse and create a massive hole in the fabric of space and time. She kind of hoped that day would come. Being stuck perfecting the art of being a mayor was a thankless job

---

3. Or something of the sort.

4. Which you rarely hear tyrants saying, especially the please part. But Petula had found it a very efficient way to get things done. You could say she saw anything social, involving other people, as a necessary obstacle. Ghouls were a different matter entirely. She kind of liked them. They had poetry in their souls and knew how silly humans were, and most importantly they got things done. In Petula's book, humans were as nutty as a fruitcake.

with no hope of escaping other people. All a tyrant, or a mayor[5] in her case, could do was to trust the institutions built around them and the company they kept while knowing well that, given the opportunity, every single one wanted to stab them in their back. Of course, the whole knowing part depended entirely on how inflated their ego was, and with someone insane enough to take the job of a tyrant, their ego was most probably as inflated as the stock market. They might mistakenly see adoration and friendship where there was none.

Petula was painfully aware of all this, despite not being an actual tyrant. She could be if she wished. It was her right as the lawful ruler of Necropolis. Not that being mayor was a picnic either. She served by the grace of the people, the Town Hall Council (including the Necro Democratic Alliance, the Union of the Undead, and the newcomer, the Differs Soul Party), and, as she had come to understand, by the grace of the business community, including banks, and the inescapable Necromantic Council. Also, there was nothing like a Bureau of Acquisitions to take the tyranny out of leadership when asking for a pen. Lastly, there was the Church of Kraken and Madam Sabine, whose religious power had squirmed into every aspect of the city. All of them wanted to have their say in how things should be done, how Petula should act. Minta Stopford[6] had left behind a mess of half-finished proposals and laws to convert the government's arcane methods of relying on the top necromancer's despotism into Frankenstein's democracy.

Petula was now *the necromancer* with wings cut and a headache to prove it, with no personal free time or friends to call her own. And there was still a rule in place that any necromancer could come and challenge her to a duel to the death. To top it all, Mrs. Maybury was still around. The leader of

---

5. As she preferred to be called.

6. The former mayor and a very wise woman, who knew when to take her exit and enjoy her hard-earned freedom and solitude.

the Union of the Undead and her husband Cruxh, a ghoul, lurked behind her with their novel ideas about politics and policing. And she had yet to identify the contents of the vial Cruxh had given her.

In all this, all Petula wanted was some peace and quiet to read a book, which was all she had wanted ever since turning three. But if she locked herself in her room, if she didn't participate in the charade they called politics, people would suffer, and she didn't like suffering. A fact she had regretfully come to realize about herself. She'd started to care.

Caring led to sacrifices, long hours, heartburn, and lunacy, where she actually thought she could make a difference. What was even worse was that Petula had come to know the rules of politics were not so different from the schoolyard's unwritten laws. Gossip, friendship packs, betrayals, alliances, hatred, bitterness, the social hierarchy of the hormonally imbalanced humanoids, and much, much more. She had never been good with schoolyard rules. She had always been the one who stood in the farthest corner, ready to set the whole yard on fire if anyone approached.

But amongst all this, there was Dow... Dow, who never left her side. Dow, who kept her safe. Dow, whom she was sure heard her thoughts and visited her dreams. A weaker person would go insane with him always lurking around, unable to distinguish where one person started and the other ended. Petula was sure that was all the man desired: her to be a vessel for him. Before her it had been Minta, and before that, Kraken only knew who. For now, she was his prized pet. For what purpose, she wasn't entirely sure. There had to be an end game. With people like him, there always was. And the people part was questionable. Petula hadn't quite been able to pin down what Dow actually was. Not human, though. Far from it.

Still, if he thought she was some docile creature to be molded to his liking, he was a fool. She was no puppet and never would be. She wasn't under any illusions either. What Dow did was not actually evil. He was not some shadowy man who steered the world to serve his needs and desires for power and money. He actually believed there was a way to create a perfect city. It was just that Petula thought such beliefs were harmful. The obsession with perfection blinded a person, allowing them to justify anything for the cause. This way of thinking could only end in totalitarianism, where no one had room to think or breathe.

Petula had started to notice she had no room to breathe or think. So she fought back with her extracurricular activities. She lifted the orange tabby off her lap, receiving a dirty look from the cat. Both of them knew who was in charge here, but one of them had to go on pretending it was them.

It was time to leave. But as always, Dow stepped in, sniffing out her plans to call it a night and sneak out of the office to a meeting of the like-minded.[7]

"Ma'am," Dow greeted.

"Petula," she corrected.

"There's that," Dow said, carefully stepping in as if in search of booby traps.

If he didn't stop calling her ma'am, there might be.

"I was about to leave and go home to change. I have the usual meeting with Mrs. Culpepper," Petula said. The usual meeting was her needlepoint group with Henrietta and a few other ladies. Dow disapproved of her association with the witch. Not because Petula was making friends. He'd asked her to play nice with others, and she had gone and done that. But because she'd happened to make friends with the leader of the witches, the Mother of the Coven. Those were some dangerous friends to have as a necromancer, especially if you asked the Council. Plus, Petula was sure Dow hadn't found a way to worm his informants into the circle. Yet he hadn't intervened.

Dow slightly changed his posture. There was no mistaking what that

---

7. Or somewhat close. She had yet to find anyone with a mind quite like hers. And it was exhausting.

meant. He didn't believe for a second that all those brilliant minds sat in Mrs. Culpepper's garden to stitch.

"What is it?" she asked.

"It has come to my attention that the Necromantic Council will sentence and execute Mr. Thurston next week. They are expediting the process as we speak. We need to prepare ourselves for what will follow." Dow took Petula's gray wool jacket from the coat rack.

"Hmm," she let out. He would be the first necromancer executed publicly since Minta took over from Oliver the Great. There was no mistaking that the Necromantic Council planned a public display of its power over the Necropolitans and over her. She wished she had months left to prepare, but all the pressure from the Save the Otis Group had rushed things forward. They were starting to lose the minds of the necromancer. The Council couldn't have that. If Petula ever wanted to be free, she would have to act now. But the Council played dirty. And it did actually serve a purpose. If the Council ceased to be, who knew who would fill that void? The banks? Madam Sabine and her Kraken followers?

Petula grimaced. "Thank you, Dow. We will discuss this tomorrow. Now I truly must leave. I don't want to be later than I already am."

He helped her shrug on her jacket. "Are you sure, ma'am?"

"About what?" Petula bit her lower lip, trying not to snap at him.

"That your group takes precedent over this?" Dow stepped away from her when all the chivalry was done.

"Of course it doesn't. But there's nothing I can do now. We will wait for tomorrow and contact the Council to negotiate. Of course, I want to stop the unnecessary execution, but we both know the evidence is piled against Mr. Thurston... to our and his dismay. And we can't really argue against the Council's rule: no necromancers abroad, least of all a practicing one. The rule is in place for a good reason. No one wants the necromantic wars to return."

Dow's face would appear emotionless to a casual observer, but Petula had learned to read the man. He didn't quite believe her. Especially her words about not arguing against the Council and doing it for good reasons. Yes, she thought some of the rules were open for interpretation, but Petula didn't want a repeat of the necromantic wars either. The last time had nearly destroyed Necropolis and killed thousands of people as nations had gone against nations with their necromancers and undead armies. It was only through the cooperation of the oldest necromancer families that total destruction had been avoided. Even the idea of what would have gotten loose if the wars had created a tear between the worlds of the living and dead was unfathomable. That something might have wiped out all life. That didn't dampen her desire to remove or re-organize the Council as it was. It was an antiquated institution that was rotten to its core.

"Now, if you'll excuse me. I'm going to be late." Petula walked to the tabby and scooped it into her lap. The cat gave her one of its looks, judging her. Sometimes she was sure the tabby was in cahoots with Dow, but that would be paranoid of her. Still, the cat seemed to ally with her secretary more often than with her, even when she never saw them near each other. This circled back to paranoia and why it was not fun to be the leader in Petula's book. A couple of years ago, she didn't need to think in terms of friends and foes or question the very fabric of physical laws when considering what things could be listening in. Now even the coat rack had ears.

Necropolis's constitution still gave her permission to turn into a despot. There was that.

"Of course, ma'am. I will fetch you your coach." Dow made his exit.

Before he left, she said, "I expect you to find me everything there is to be known by tomorrow morning. I will be in at five a.m." Somehow, she had to fix the Otis problem. She knew it. He knew it. But she wasn't going to let it stop her from leaving now. There was always a good reason to stay a little longer.

"Ma'am." And he was gone.

"Don't look at me like that. I couldn't help it," Petula said to the tabby eyeing her. Petula lost the staring contest and looked away. The cat settled into her embrace and let her take it with her. Sometimes she left it behind at the Town Hall, but only when there was enough hunting to be done. Otherwise, the cat traveled back and forth with her. Despite everything, she enjoyed the cat's company so much that she'd started to consider giving it a name. It couldn't continue to be It, or Her, as Petula said when she was feeling extra affectionate. But somehow, she never got around to giving it a name. The cat didn't seem to be one for titles. She couldn't blame it. Names gave others control over you. And it wasn't only old superstition to think so. Here in Necropolis, names and curses were entwined.

Petula stepped out of her office, regretting it instantly, as there were more unmovable objects in the world than just Dow. Mrs. Maybury came at her at full steam, and Petula couldn't run or hide. She had been spotted.

Crit, Petula thought. Maybe she could use the tabby to distract the undead woman. But all three of them knew there was no escape. *Oh well*, Petula thought. There went the possibility of having a bath before meeting the needlepoint group.

CHAPTER TWO

ALL ABOUT THE NECROMANCERS

I t was good to be home. The atmosphere was just right in Necropolis. The usual mist hung around as Percy Allread made his way to the Necro Botanical Gardens to see Mother. The Witches' Coven was a huge complex not too far from the university. Unlike the Coven, the monstrous university buildings had become the symbol of all things Necropolitan. But unlike the university, the Coven's gardens were the most visited attraction in the city. Also, witches, or hexers, as he was, had their own department at the university. It was mostly centered around the gardens, where the head witch, Mother, ran the Coven. The witches didn't actually have a head witch in the same way that the Necromantic Council was in charge of the necromancers. The head witch was elected with a democratic vote—one witch, one vote. It was done every seven years. The position had first been bestowed upon Henrietta Culpepper eleven years ago. Usually, the Mother or Father stayed until they died or were killed. Still, democracy was involved.

Henrietta ran the Necro Botanical Gardens along with the Coven and taught the newer witches about the use and compounds of the plants. Percy had always respected the older woman. That was why he'd also voted for her the second time around. Percy had an inkling why she'd summoned him, fittingly, in this witching hour.

The walk across the city at midnight invigorated him enough to push past the gloomy thoughts of being summoned. He listened to the distant howl of a wolf. His specialized Monster Hunter ears told him it was an ordinary wolf and not one of the were-kind. It was in the tone. The richness of it. Percy instinctively reached for his sword belt, making it easier to seize his short blade under his long leather jacket. He almost laughed as a group of Kraken devotees passed him at the next junction. It was clear who would be the biggest threat here. The devotees snarled at him as he circled around them.

This was what a city should feel like. Not like the always sunny Three-beanvalley with its false pleasantness. Here, hatred and anger were on display, shown but seldom acted upon, making interactions more honest than multi-meaning smiles.

It was good to be home.

Percy relaxed his hand from the blade's hilt.

He had gotten home six months ago, bringing Otis Thurston with him to be imprisoned. Soon after, he had been taken off his undercover assignment at the Worthwrite Bank of Necropolis Ltd and gone back to accounting for the Council, waiting for his next assignment abroad. He was unsure if he could be employed as an actual hunter ever again. He'd become notorious for arresting Otis. Blasted in all the newspapers. Maybe he could go back to work as a Monster Hunter when the dust settled. But it wasn't only Otis making the transition difficult. He had killed a necromancer overseas, Cathy, whom he had been sent there to arrest. It had been self-defense while trying to capture her and force her to come back home. It was just that... it was just that all Cathy had tried to do was make an honest living with her talents as a necromancer in a new, blooming city. The whole thing didn't sit well with Percy anymore. She had died, fighting hard against being brought back to Necropolis. She had begged him to let her be. All she had done was wake up the dead for short goodbyes or to divulge where they hid their pennies. That was all, and now she was dead, and her face followed him around.

And Otis hadn't wanted to come back home either. Why?

Percy squeezed the hilt again.

Otis wasn't the same. He had used living souls to make his machine. He'd let his demon friend hunt and kill for him. Otis was guilty. They were demanding capital punishment for him in the newspapers. That didn't feel right.

Percy hated the word feel. It had nothing to do with decision-making.

Percy dodged another passer-by, stepping into the street gutters. Rainwater splashed his boots. It had been pouring hard all day. The early December kind of rain: cold, chilling to the bone. Just the way he liked it. Percy made his way past a woman in a dark hood. She smelled like a witch.

Percy tipped his hat.

She nodded in return.

He turned left from the next corner, finding the colossal iron gates to the botanical gardens in front of him. The yard had turned brownish and dead from the changing season. The tall trees had dropped their leaves all over the ground, and in the distance, someone had tried to rake them into piles. Percy followed the paved path past the huge glasshouses. The sight of the buildings gave him a sense of awe every time. They had been built around twenty years ago. The rumors said they were based on a plant with monstrous leaves that could carry a grown man. The witches had borrowed its capacity to turn its delicate frame into something strong. The metallic frames supported the wide glass that curved over the ceiling, creating another layer for the trees to grow tall. Wesley Epith, Henrietta's mentor and former head witch, had been behind the design, securing funding for the place. The legend went that Wesley had come up with the plan during his travels abroad. Some distant, exotic places where leaves grew as wide as a small coach and trees as high as the tallest buildings in Necropolis. Percy hadn't seen anything like it on his travels or in Threebeanvalley. There, the growth was stunted by the harsh sun without enough moisture for the trees to grow tall and proud.

A homey yellow light shone past the conservatory inside the huge five-story Gothic stone building that spread even wider than it was tall. The Coven. A center for research and all the students. Percy walked around the greenery and was sure he heard the iron gates closing behind him independently. If there had been someone with him in the yard, he would have sensed them. Percy always had his hexes up. They ricocheted off their targets, mapping every tiny change in the fabric of reality. His hexes were telling him that the yard was empty except for the trees and a few adventurous birds and squirrels. Inside the first glasshouse, someone was working amongst the flowers and plants, but he needn't be concerned by them. They were too immersed in their work. But the house he was heading into was full of life, as had been the streets he had come from. Some of that life had followed him here, but that someone didn't dare step into the compounds. They weren't brave enough to violate the witches' sanctuary. Not when the gardens were closed to the public, and the little gift shop by the iron cage had its doors shut.

The door to the main house opened as Percy stepped onto the porch, again on its own. A simple movement spell to impress un-witches, and only to be seen here. The witches' talents were heavily monitored and regulated. Percy was only free to use his curses as a sanctioned Monster Hunter, and by the grace of the Council. And he could only use them freely when engaged in hunting down renegade necromancers. By and large, basic alterations were allowed, but bigger spells had their magic clipped. The Necromantic Council didn't allow any excess use of power in the city, including the dead variety. Everything had to be controlled in the name of preventing unnecessary altercations. In Percy's case, as a hexer, he was forbidden to curse his opponents to pave his way to the positions he wanted. Killing with brute force and other more subtle ways was allowed.

Welcome to Necropolis, Percy thought. Not that he minded. It was best for everyone. If you set your sights high enough, you could get away with murder.

Still, some of his former classmates argued that the decision-makers thought too little of their citizens. That the Council's insistence on enforcing rigid rules and treating everyone like children to prevent individuals from using others as their toys or jeopardizing the whole city with their reckless behavior was moronic. They were the ones who were naïve. In his line of work as a Monster Hunter,[1] Percy had learned that nothing was that simple. He had seen people do horrendous things to others in the name of curiosity. Laws and rules were there to defend those who couldn't protect themselves.

This hadn't always been so. There had been times when it was better to learn a spell or two to protect yourself. If you didn't, what you got was what you deserved. His grandma told tales of the good old wild Necropolis, and his mother said that under Oliver the Great, things had been better for the witches; however, mysterious deaths had been an everyday occurrence. Both his grandma and mother would have taken the mysterious deaths over having their powers monitored and regulated. Every witch had to be registered with a full account of their name, talents, family relations, and academic scores. The Coven ran the registry, but the Council and the Town Hall had access to it.

Percy stepped in through the open door, surprised to find Mother herself waiting for him in the foyer. The older woman seemed nervous. Not that most people could detect such a slight difference in her behavior. Usually, she was composed, almost relaxed to the point of making anyone question if she took the situation seriously. But now, her pose was rigid

---

1. The sanctioned special force the Necromantic Council used and the city employed.

and formal. She wore simple olive-green walking trousers and a blouse. Henrietta was a robust, towering witch who commanded any space with ease.

"Good evening, Mother." Percy used the archaic honorific and bowed.

"Mr. Allread," Henrietta sighed. "I'm glad you could meet me at this hour. I have arranged tea for us in the parlor. If I remember correctly, you take it with a drop of milk and honey?" The last remark was more like a statement than a question.

"You do me honor, Mother," Percy said. He took his hat off.

Mrs. Culpepper frowned and gestured towards the door. "You can leave your jacket and hat on the stand behind the door."

Percy wasn't sure how he'd offended her. "Thank you, Mother." There was the wince again. But he couldn't call her anything else. It was customary.

He took his outer coat off and hung it on one of the hooks on the stand full of capes and hats of all colors and sizes. He turned to face Henrietta once more and followed her into the parlor with a sickening feeling this was about Otis Thurston. Everything had been about the necromancer ever since he had gotten home.

Inside any institution there are liminal spaces between what is, what has to be, and what could be. In the Coven, those spaces were always in flux. No witch could agree on the future of things or the perception of now. But still the plants got planted, the cakes baked, and the tea served. The uncertainty and certainty of change never got in the way of doing. That was witches for you. That was what made Henrietta love the Coven and its ancient Gothic house with stone walls and the always creaking floors. Doing made everything more bearable. She guided Percy into the parlor, watching the man's rigid formality. He was a hexer.

"Mother," Percy said as he took a seat at the table laden with tea, herb biscuits, and honey cake made by Judika, the Coven's cook.

Henrietta didn't care for all the Mother business. She was never meant to be a Mother. She was meant to do research abroad, but then Wesley had gone and died. And here she was, leading the Coven and making sure the always-bickering witches got things done in a city governed by necromancers. Wesley had insisted as much. He had sent her a letter before his death, begging her to come back. He'd known he was going to die; that he would be killed. The death notice and the letter had arrived on the same day. Henrietta had packed everything up, even her husband Eurof, and come home from the Amanita Islands, a paradise so rich in peculiar plants, flowers, mushrooms, and wildlife that she had never wanted to leave. A place where research never stops. If she shut her eyes, she could still see the tall trees climbing high towards the sky and hear the bird calls. But that wasn't here. Here she worked tirelessly to make the gardens flourish in the dismal Necropolis landscape, where she had no escape from politics. All she did was attend meeting after meeting to convince others to see her point of view and pass new clauses upon the existing ones to secure the witches' freedom from the Council and the Town Hall. All of which left a bitter taste in her mouth.

Henrietta took her place opposite Percy. "Tea?" she asked.

"Let me, Mother," he said, reaching for the porcelain cups.

"Don't be silly. You are my guest." Henrietta got up and poured the tea, offering his with a drop of milk and honey.

"The honey is from our gardens. Remind me to give you a jar to take home with you."

"That's too kind of you—" Percy began.

"Please, call me Henrietta. All these formalities make my head hurt. I might be past my youth, but I'm still too young, not to mention too vain, to care for being called Mother by every person I encounter." She sat back down. She drew the honey cake to her and sliced two huge pieces, offering a plate to Percy.

"If that is what you wish, M... Henrietta," Percy said.

"Old customs are old customs, and while they have their uses, some became outdated a long time ago. So, Percy, how do you find it to be back home?" Henrietta pushed her pastry fork into the decadent cake. The right balance of sweet and sour on her tongue made her linger in the sensation and savor it. There was a hint of orange blossom in the cake. Henrietta had always been a savory sort of person, but Judika's cooking transformed a person. What the cook did in the kitchen was magic.

"I'm happy to be back home, Mo... Henrietta." Percy stopped himself. He followed her example and took a forkful of the cake.

Henrietta observed his every move. He didn't seem to be transformed. There was no pleasing everyone. Henrietta sighed. He was as the reports described him. Henrietta reminded herself again that the man was a hexer and he had to carry the rules with him. He wouldn't make this easy.

"Good, and is everything to your liking?" Henrietta set down her plate with the half-finished cake. She hadn't meant to eat so much with one mouthful.

"Everything is to my liking." Percy hesitated.

Henrietta watched as the man debated silently what to say. She had clearly hit a nerve.

"With all due respect, Henrietta, I would prefer if you asked me what you want to ask." Percy lowered the plate, having barely touched the cake.

Henrietta smiled. "Ah, yes. Clearly, I have gotten too accustomed to these social dances one has to do. But yes, let's not pretend this is just a social call. As the Coven, we want your full account of the events that transpired in Threebeanvalley with Mr. Thurston and this machinist they call Levi Perri. Also, we would like to know about this machine... what was it called..."

"The Bufonite," Percy supplied.

"Yes, the Bufonite. If I understand correctly, this machine was created using necromancy and is highly powerful, yet it didn't survive an attack by...?" Henrietta gave Percy an opening to elaborate.

"By the Luddites."

"Yes, the Luddites, and as I gather, they are a group fighting against the mechanization of the workforce?"

"That would be correct, Mother. But unfortunately, no, I cannot give you all the details of what the Bufonite was and how it came to be. I don't have all the details. And what little I know..." Percy stalled.

"You are not permitted to tell," Henrietta offered.

"Yes, Mother. All I can say is that Mr. Thurston used necromancy to make it."

"That's all?" Henrietta asked.

"I'm afraid so, Mother. Mr. Thurston is the only one who can answer your questions." Percy gave a dry smile. A smile which told Henrietta he wanted to say more but couldn't. There was no point in speculating on what he left out.

"Such a shame. Then tell me, do you think the Council should own such a machine that the rumors state can produce anything out of nothingness?"

"It's not for me to say." Percy shifted uncomfortably on his chair.

"But you have thought about it," Henrietta persisted.

Percy said nothing. The man let the silence do all the talking. Or so Henrietta suspected. If the Council had ears and eyes inside the house, as they undoubtedly did, the man couldn't incriminate himself.

"What about your thoughts on the machine? Should one like it exist if it truly can conjure matter out of nothingness?"

"Mother, all I can say is what I witnessed."

"And that is?"

Percy looked around.

"People willing to hurt others to obtain the machine, Mr. Thurston ending up back here imprisoned, and the machinist Levi Perri killed in the fire. It seems like calamity follows it."

"I see. Thank you, Mr. Allread." There was no point in pressing on. "Now, let's not let a good cake and tea go to waste." Henrietta reached for her cup and took a long sip, keeping her eye on Percy the whole time.

Percy followed her example. After they finished the tea and took a second helping of cake, Henrietta sent Percy home with the honey from the Necro Botanical Gardens as promised. She even gave him a parcel to take home containing herb biscuits and honey cake. Percy had tried to refuse, stating it was against the Council's rules for employees to take gifts, but Henrietta was having none of that. He was her witch and under her jurisdiction.

Henrietta watched Percy walk across the yard from the parlor window. He was soon swallowed by the misty rain, leaving behind an empty garden. Humans were more complex creatures than plants. Humans complicated their lives unnecessarily and then wondered what had gone wrong. Plants didn't do that, as far as Henrietta knew. Which, in her book, had no bearing on their intelligence. It had taken humans years to master the glasshouse, and plants, especially ferns, had evolved their sturdy structure to withstand the wind millions of years ago, doing the impossible. And when they had evolved, they hadn't brought devastation with them. Devastation like that which followed the Bufonite, as Percy had graciously warned her. She had already gathered as much. The Bufonite in the wrong hands would be dangerous. Anything manmade often was. Deadlier than oleander, which could kill a person, containing a lethal amount of cardiac glycosides, known as oleandrin and nerine—symptoms ranging from vomiting to seizures, and the ultimate one: death. The Council was the last entity in Necropolis—heck, make it the entire world—Henrietta wanted to have a machine deadlier than oleander.[2]

Publicly, the machine was condemned as a dud. But a dud which caused the whole world to come to Necropolis. A machine Mr. Thurston had built as revenge against the Council, as the papers wrote. Otis had apparently sworn to show Necropolis what they could do with their rules. Henrietta didn't believe any of what was written. The Bufonite was real, and the Council wanted it. And now every necromancer who saw themselves as a tinkerer and had a basic understanding of how the glowing skulls worked had gone full steam ahead trying to replicate the machine. None had yet succeeded, as far as Henrietta knew. So Mr. Thurston had become a desired acquisition. She'd heard rumors that the Worthwrite Bank of Necropolis LTD had hired a lawyer, claiming that as Percy Allread had worked for them during the arrest, Mr. Thurston was theirs to keep. And the Church of Kraken insisted that the man was theirs, as his soul belonged to Kraken. Henrietta wasn't sure about the logic behind that. One thing was sure: Henrietta's only hope was to get Otis released and hope that, in the meantime, he didn't cave in, or the Council would own the world and there would be no room for the witches to exist.

"Mother," came from the door.

Imogene, her assistant, stood there, looking highly apologetic. Her curls flowed beautifully over her shoulders. She wore a cotton dress with an apron over it. She bit her lip nervously, as she always did.

"Yes?"

"Your needlepoint group is here. I took them to the glasshouse. I set your things there as well." Imogene clutched the hem of the apron. She tried not to look Henrietta directly in her eyes, gazing down at her black shoes.

"Thank you, Imogene. I'll be there shortly."

"This arrived for you." The witch took a letter from her pocket and

---

2. That grew in the back gardens. Only accessible for the most loyal of witches.

handed it to her.

Henrietta frowned at the handwriting on the letter addressed directly to her and not to the Coven. She opened it and read the short note. It was from her spy in the Council. They were going to execute Mr. Thurston, and soon.

"Is everything all right?" Imogene asked.

"All is fine. You may leave me now," Henrietta said.

"Yes, Mother." The girl turned around and walked away, her long red hair following her in a swirl.

CHAPTER THREE

SIGN YOUR NAME HERE

There were those institutions that guarded the truth, but whose truth and what kind of truth was still up for debate. Truth about the state of matter was easier to state objectively, or so many thought. But the truth about force, interaction, and state of being was an entirely different matter. These came with variables and change. Still, there was an expectation that some sort of facts needed to be stipulated and held static. Any deviation should be condemned.

Raul scratched his head as he looked at the new typewriter the newspaper had bought and wondered what on a corpse worm he was supposed to do with it. It was a monstrous thing, taking up half of the space on his messy desk. The thing looked like it was willing to bite his fingers off if he got too near its keys. Raul didn't want to have anything to do with it, and it wasn't like he had the excess time to master it. Paper and pen were enough. Those things had been around long enough to demonstrate that they weren't out to get you. Raul scratched the back of his head. He desperately wanted to have a drink, but he'd sworn off drinking. He looked at the glass of water on his desk and took a sip. It wasn't the same. Ale or a shot would make his thoughts clearer, but that one ale would lead to another, and he would find himself in the gutters, as always, wondering how he got there.

Raul turned his attention to the buzz over tonight's deadline. Everyone was yelling over the thundering of the downstairs printing press. His piece would have to be out by midnight, and he hadn't started it yet. He had been covering Otis Thurston's imprisonment and how the Town Hall, or more like how Petula Upwood, had handled it. Their beloved mayor had stayed silent thus far. Both sides accused her of sympathizing with the other. What he'd gathered about their necromancer leader was that she didn't take sides. She took her side. He just had to figure out what she was planning.

The Town Hall and Dow Spurgeon had refused to give him an interview. He needed that interview. There was only so much he could cover about the Save the Otis Group or the standard reply the Council gave. It wasn't enough. He'd tried to get an interview with Mr. Thurston as well. The Council had told him to contact the necromancer's lawyer. What a pointless exercise that had been. To keep his articles interesting, he'd enchanted everything with the mood of the city. It was a real thing. Something the Council and the Town Hall couldn't deny and should be cautious of. People were getting restless. They would explode if and when Otis was hanged. He had written as much. If he pushed his pieces even further, there was no saying how he could alter the minds of the people. Raul was sure he could even force the Council to change its policies. It had to, if this went on.

But he had been followed for the past couple of weeks. And they weren't masking it, meaning someone was sending a message. They couldn't kill him straight off. He was the beloved newspaper reporter everyone loved to hate, yet everyone followed his articles. The golden boy who got away with coming into work drunk as a Kraken worshiper after a religious orgy. That was another entity in the city trying to keep him off its grounds. The Church of Kraken. But he had seen what went on in their ceremonies. There were human sacrifices, for starters. He'd reported as much; that had gotten him on their enemy list.

Raul's hands shook as he pushed the paper into the typewriter. He stroked the first key, and it let out a loud click. The cold metallic pedal was oddly reassuring under his finger. He pushed another letter, and soon he found that he had written an entire piece about the Church of Kraken sniffing around the machine and Otis. It was all hearsay, and he couldn't print it. But he knew it to be true, just like everyone else did. He just had to get an inside source to make it factual. He might know someone: Agatha Wicks, the second in command in the Church. Raul had heard she was being banished from the city to some remote island to bring its inhabitants the word of Kraken. What he'd gathered was that Agatha had grown her own following, and Madam Sabine wasn't happy about it.

"Mr. Porter," a voice said behind him.

His editor towered over him. The tall man with a hairline that had followed the stress level of the job tried not to squirm in front of him. They had been friends ever since college, and clearly, Maximilian had things to say, and he didn't want to say them aloud. The man looked at Raul like he didn't know what to do with a mangy dog with puppy dog eyes and foam dripping from its mouth. Raul Emerett Porter restrained himself from smelling his armpit, but he was pretty sure he stank. He hadn't taken a bath for a fortnight, and it was starting to show.

"What have I done now?" Raul asked. He had usually done something. Holy corpse worm, he'd made the man suffer. Not only as the top editor of *Necropolis Times*, but also as the closest friend a man could have. He had dragged him out of several establishments where they served drinks on tap and had a bouncer to collect the payment.

"You have to be careful. Just that. I got another note from the Council." Maximilian rubbed his temples as if to drive away the demons inside him.

"They are always coming at me. This is no different than any other time."

The editor sat on his desk and looked down at Raul, whose chair had lost its height a few years back. Raul couldn't remember what had happened, but there had been drinking and betting involved at the office's Midsummer party.

"This time, it's different. They are not messing around. All the newspapers have gotten the warning, and most of them have obeyed. You know what the Council can do."

"Yeah, yeah. But you still want me to write the story, don't you?"

Maximilian glanced at the piece Raul had just written, taking it in his hands, and shook his head. Both of them knew that a piece like that would sell. That it would fuel the speculations and plunge the city into further turmoil. If people and, most importantly, the elite knew that the Church was also making a play to get Otis and the machine in their possession, there was no saying what kind of war would be on the cards. Raul was sure that the machine couldn't be useless, as the Council's official statement claimed. The one they had also printed in the *Necropolis Times*. But it was bogus. The city wasn't going bonkers for nothing.

Raul didn't care about the machine. He knew he should. Clearly, everyone wanted it. Even the banks and the city's business community were putting pressure on the Council to be part of making the machine. There was no way this was going to end nicely. There would be bodies, blood, and tears all around. Just what a good reporter loved. It was just that he had seen his fair share of those things, and his stomach wasn't up to it any longer. He'd rather be standing to the side, preventing all the bloodshed from happening. But he was the only one. All around him were creatures of every sort willing to either fuel the fire or go along with the line fed to them. Both sides were making the city even more mad.

"We can't print this." Maximilian lowered the Church of Kraken piece back to the table.

"No. It was just an exercise of thought."

"Keep it that way. We don't need Madam Sabine coming at us like last time. The paper barely survived her."

Raul grimaced. He had almost bankrupted the newspaper with the litigation following his Church of Kraken ceremony story. Not to mention, he had barely survived the fanatic followers who had shown up at odd hours of the night to stare at him through his window and followed him everywhere he went. He had to leave the city for a month to let things blow over.

"I would burn it," his editor suggested.

"I will." Raul took the piece and crumpled it, tossing it into the furnace not far from him and the other writers' desks. It landed among the other papers there, ready to be tossed away.

"So?" Raul asked.

"I need a good one for the front page. You have four hours, or I will give the spot to Sandy."

Raul made a face. Sandy was a brilliant writer, but she was boring as Kraken shit and made her pieces as political as she could. She had agendas, and Raul didn't like that.

"Then I better get to it." Raul stood up, taking his jacket from the chair and his hat from the table.

Maximilian nodded, and when Raul was at the stairs leading down to the front door, the man shook his head. You could say he was just waiting for the day Raul was found dead in some ditch and their new keen police officers had to figure out which of all the possible reasons had gotten him there.

Raul was happy to be out of the stuffy office and away from the constant thumping of the printing press. Here on the streets of Necropolis, the howls and the wails were more soothing than any other noise Raul had ever known in his life. But once again, as his feet hit the ground outside the paper, the familiar pattern of steps followed him. It was the sound of someone pretending not to be there but making sure they were noticed. Raul didn't even bother to glance over his shoulder to see the petite woman in black following him. She had become a permanent fixture attached to his shadow.

So Town Hall it was. He wouldn't get anything out of the Council. And he needed a response from the mayor anyway. His sources said that Otis's trial had been moved up to next week and that a noose was already being made for the occasion.

Raul glanced at the coach parked next to the paper, but tonight he felt like walking. This was the best hour to be around and about. Necropolis came alive in the darkness. He stepped aside from the usual pickpockets and madmen hunting the careless tourists. Holy corpse worm, he loved this dark, Gothic, gargoyle-ridden city. The month he'd spent in the countryside, hiding from the Kraken cult, had bored his mind to tatters. Here, everything pulsed with life with all its deformities, making the words in his head shine. The walk was too short for his liking. The Town Hall's manor-like appearance soon loomed over him. The colonial-style building with the white walls, the dark wooden window frames, and the weeping willows was meant to be more civilized than the previous castle where Oliver the Great had spewed his madness over everything. Power was power, however you tried to disguise it. He made his way into the Town Hall, which never slept. There was always someone around to conduct their business or petition this and that from its bureaucrats, who worked tirelessly in shifts. But one thing was constant, and that was the old woman at the front desk.

"Elvira." Raul tipped his hat to the woman, who sucked her teeth as if she was drawing all the joy out of any person daring to enter the building, engulfing them in misery.

She gave him a dry smile.

Raul had heard that the woman didn't let anyone past her, but somehow she always let him loose in the building, never asking why he was there or with whose permission. She was no mortal woman, but he didn't have time to figure out who or what she was. There were more pressing stories to write. One day he would come back to the mystery behind those judging eyes.

Raul headed upstairs to where the mayor's offices should be. He took two steps at a time, feeling his stiff knees ache. He never got to the second floor. There came a distinctive cough behind him. Raul slowly turned around to face Dow Spurgeon.

"Good evening, Mr. Porter," Dow said. "To what do we owe the pleasure?"

"Mr. Spurgeon." Raul took his hat off, drawing his notebook and pen from it.

"Hunting for a story?" Dow smiled a thin smile that would make any living soul shudder.

Raul took a step back, disliking that his entire body went into goosebumps.

"That's my bread and butter, Mr. Spurgeon. And the public has a right to know the truth."

"Aaah, yes, the truth. One thing that never rests on the lips of those who like to sway the minds of others."

"You don't believe in truth then?" Raul flipped the notebook open.

"Believe? No, Mr. Porter. I don't believe in anything. I know."

"Then what do you know about the Council moving up Mr. Thurston's trial?"

"That's not my department, Mr. Porter. That's the Necromantic Council's jurisdiction."

"Then what's your department?"

"I'm a secretary, Mr. Porter. My department is scheduling appointments for the mayor. And I happen to know that there isn't one in her diary with your name on it."

"You can't damn a man for trying."

"No, I can't. But I can advise a man on how not to get himself hurt. It's nasty business, this tress and passing; who knows what lurks in the shadows. This is an old building that doesn't look kindly on those who have no business in it."

"Are you threatening me, Mr. Spurgeon?"

"I wouldn't dare, Mr. Porter. Just passing on those things you might call facts. Let me escort you out." Dow showed him the stairs.

Raul took two steps down and said, "You are only hurting her with your silence."

Dow looked Raul straight in the eyes. The yellowish eyes of the man seemed to grab him from his chest and read his mind. For a while, the man said nothing. Dow just controlled the moment for a long time with his quiet, slow breathing. Then, when Raul was ready to give in and tell him where all the bodies were buried, the secretary released him.

"You might be right, Mr. Porter. Silence is a very unnatural thing in this world of ours. People don't like it. But you ask for a reaction to a complicated situation where there's no truth to speak of, just different narratives tailored to all sorts of motives. I think you have a sense of our mayor, or at least so it reads. If that is true, you know she isn't one to buy into the stories readily told. She wants the truth both of you seem to think exists. So silence is the only thing the Town Hall can give for now. But I'm pretty sure that somewhere in this building you can find Mrs. Maybury, Frederick Kilborn, and Sirixh, for that matter. They might be more willing to speak to you, it being campaigning season soon, and who knows who's gunning for their spots as party leaders."

The cunning little Kraken shit, Raul thought. "Eventually, she has to talk. Sooner rather than later, before the trial. And I want an exclusive."

"As you wish, Mr. Porter. The Town Hall has an excellent relationship with your paper."

Dow let him walk off on his own. He headed down the stairs to find Mrs.

Maybury. She always gave the most vivid interviews a reporter could hope for.

It takes a humanoid to find a way to punish their own kind. The question of whether it's done for the good of all or the bad of the individual is up for debate, hence the existence of the class who make a living out of arguing. A class no one wants to hang with, but they seem to be a good idea when things go down the shitter.

Otis straightened his messy hair, aware how wild he must appear. From the uncomfortable looks his lawyer, Ichor Pod, gave him, or at least as uncomfortable as an undead could muster, Otis knew he was right. Then again, the undeads weren't widely known for their range of expressions, or for caring. It was all the formaldehyde and muscle rigidity and the afterlife part kicking in. So Otis could be wrong. Not that any of it mattered that much. The lawyer had seen a lot worse. Still, Otis made an effort and sat on the bed.

"Your court date has been set," the man stated as solemnly as always, making Otis wonder what good it did to bring the dead back to life if they made such a mockery of living. Living should be a constant celebration, moments being seized, life not wasted sitting behind a desk combing through laws to find loopholes. But he guessed he should be happy to have a lawyer of such long experience. If anyone knew the laws inside out, it was the stiffs from the beyond. "I have the papers here for you to sign." The man opened his briefcase, pulling out the most boring-looking papers Otis had ever seen.

Otis groaned. "So when is it?"

"Next week, December the eighth," the man said without straining a muscle.

For a moment, Otis's arms went limp. He had been waiting for this day to come, and now it felt like a cosmic-scale mistake.

"Seven days? And?" Otis let out as he squeezed the rim of the bed. Feeling something tangible between his fingers made the room less sway-y.

Ichor Pod offered the papers to him. "And you will be sentenced to death."

The room began to sway, and a lot. There was a tight ball inside Otis's stomach, and it wanted to come out.

"Isn't there something you can do?" Otis stuttered. "Isn't the trial supposed to find whether I am guilty or not, and aren't you supposed to argue on my behalf?"

"Normally, yes, but in your case, Mr. Thurston, there's no doubt about your guilt. They have witness statements of your activities in Threebeanvalley. Not to mention the deeds you committed here to get there. I'm speaking about you faking your death. That alone would land you a long prison sentence. I can argue that you did all of it out of self-preservation, but such arguments won't hold against the evidence, or common sense, or the fact you broke several laws by doing so, I'm afraid. The only thing we can do now is settle your affairs and see that you leave the world with everything in order. As both of us know, they won't resurrect you due to your crimes and because you are a necromancer." Ichor Pod pushed the papers closer to him, waiting for him to take them and scribe his name on the marked line.

The room kept spinning, and the papers in the lawyer's hand made Otis want to puke. He looked up into the dead eyes of his lawyer. The man had no sympathy left in him. That was what death did to you. It took away the importance of life. To the lawyer, his death meant nothing. Maybe only a failure in defense, if he wasn't already working for the Council.

"You could try to discredit the witness," Otis groaned. "Percy works for them. He's biased. There should be an independent inquiry... And they have to hear my defense and witnesses at least..."

Ichor Pod shook his head. "There are no witnesses on your behalf. I have looked. All I can find is your ex-coworkers saying they wouldn't put it past you. They don't seem to like you, Mr. Thurston."

Otis ignored the last remark. "This isn't justice," he protested. "This is an absurdity. Percy is a liar, and, and..."

"Mr. Allread is a highly respectable member of the Witch Covenant and the community, not to mention the Monster Hunter Force and the Standards of Accounting. For me to discredit him would take a miracle."

"You haven't even tried," Otis wailed. "Who knows what skeletons the man has in his closet?" Otis knew he sounded desperate. He was.

"Is that how you want me to spend my hours assigned to you? I can try to find out if he does indeed have skeletons in the closet if that makes you happy."

Otis knew sarcasm when he heard it. No one in Necropolis cared about a few transgressions. They were basically encouraged, making Boy Scouts seem like the devious ones with their goody-two-shoes attitude.

"No," Otis let out. There was only one option, and both he and the lawyer knew it. He would have to give them the Bufonite in hopes the Council would make him disappear into some cozy little room to make another machine for them. "Then get me someone willing to hear what I have to say about the Bufonite. Not some low-level clerk. The real deal with power over my destiny."

"I'll do my best. But I still need you to sign the papers." Ichor Pod pushed the papers closer to him once again.

"What if I don't?"

"Then the trial will be stalled until the judge orders it to start without your consent and my representation."

"I can't see any harm in that. Doesn't it let me keep my head for a day or two longer? Maybe even a month if the court's docket is full?"

"It doesn't work that way, Mr. Thurston. You are making this unnecessarily difficult for yourself."

Otis snorted. "It's like you don't want to defend me, Mr. Pod."

"Sir, I have repeatedly told you that your defense is my utmost priority, and I take your charges seriously. I have done my best to have you acquitted. I'm on your side. I haven't lied to you once, and I have done my due diligence to find any loophole to free you, even though you have not made that easy with your unwillingness to cooperate. So if you truly want to stay alive, I will do what you ask and try to get a deal with the Necromantic Council. But to assure them of your genuine attempt to reconcile, I need something concrete. Signing these papers is the first step." The lawyer handed him a pen from his breast pocket.

Otis took it and the papers and signed his name on all the lines at Ichor Pod's instruction.

"And tell the Council this is no way to treat a prisoner," Otis said as he thrust the pen back into his lawyer's undead hands.

"You wish to make a formal complaint?"

"That too."

Otis slumped back on the bed when the lawyer left. At least the Council was kind enough not to put the lights back on. He fell asleep too tired to care about silly things like dying. What did it matter? He knew what waited for him in the netherworld.

CHAPTER FOUR

THE POWER OF CONVERSATIONS HAD

P ast the institutions, the laws are the people, who come with opinions and demands. You cannot escape them however hard you wish for it. They make everything spin. Petula almost did escape, but just for a fleeting moment. Petula was starting to regret ever stepping out of her office. Unlike Otis, she was rather satisfied in confined spaces. Then again, she didn't have a beheading looming in her future.[1]

Petula watched Mrs. Maybury coming at her full steam ahead. She backed into her office, which was bare of any traditional weapons. The one that used to be over the desk, the spear, was gone. Minta had taken it with her. Underneath it were the two statues where Jeremiah and Ona's spirits had once been trapped. Petula had sent them both to the netherworld. It would have been extremely cruel of her to keep them locked in the statues for an eternity to wait for erosion to run its course. And the more modern weapons—reason and legal jargon—were unusable against Mrs. Maybury. Petula had never managed to get away from the woman by claiming to have other duties. The only trick she'd found to work was being friendly and sounding as pleasant as she could.

---

1. At least not according to Dow.

Petula bit her lip when Mrs. Maybury finally shambled through the open door.

"Mrs. Maybury, to what do I owe the honor?" she said. If Dow was there to hear, he would have been feeling a little bit nostalgic, hearing the exact same tone Minta had always used with the undead woman. The tabby on Petula's lap dug its nails into her arm. It had learned not to hiss, but the cat was ready to act if necessary when it saw a predator.

"Don't you honor me, girl," Mrs. Maybury snapped.

Oh good Kraken, Petula thought. One of those moods. The undead woman had only two modus operandi. One was suspicion, when nothing annoying was happening. The other one was anger, with a whole lot of I-told-you-so, when something annoying happened. There might be a third mode, but Petula was sure that was reserved for Cruxh and Cruxh alone.

"Then what can I do to help?" Petula asked, sounding a lot like Minta would have again. This time Dow was there to hear it. But he'd be damned if he was going to come in and do any rescuing. If there was one person in the known universe who had an effect on Mrs. Maybury, it was Dow Spurgeon. But it was not his place to intervene. There would forever be someone like Mrs. Maybury in every office, in every family, and they ruled with fear and sheer disregard for anything other than their own opinions. Petula would have to learn.

"It's I who am here to help you, girl. I like you. You are a welcome change from what we had before." Mrs. Maybury shambled to the couch next to the window where the silhouette of the weeping willows loomed. She slumped on it, refusing to say Minta's name. Petula hadn't heard the undead mention the former leader even once, as if it would summon the demon[2] back. "But you are doing no favors for anyone letting steam into our city. My boys—"

---

2. According to Mrs. Maybury.

Petula rewired her thoughts, going through every conversation she'd had with the woman and then arriving at the one that had never been finished, as a duchess of some sort had interrupted them.

"Let me stop you there. It was not only I who voted for modernization. You know it's not the Town Hall's job to stifle new inventions the business community makes. They have the right to offer new services. You can't deny the mix of necromancy with new world inventions has been a welcome boost to our economy—"

"I see no boost! It's the undead who fuel our economy. With steam, they are making the old businesses obsolete, and at what cost? Rents have risen, jobs are hard to come by, and I'm sure, for the first time in ages, we are losing more citizens than are moving in. It's that cursed Threebeanvalley luring them away with their shiny, useless gadgets."

"Yes, I'm sure you are right. But change is happening, and we can try to obstruct it or adapt. If we choose to adapt, we'll be in control rather than playing catch-up with every step we take."

"I still vote for obstruction. What about when they learn to power corpses with steam, or better yet with lightning? You will be out of your job with nothing to offer for the market. We need new laws before our way of life is destroyed." Mrs. Maybury crossed her arms, ready for another fight.

"I would think steam-powered corpses would suit you. They would mean more freedom for your kind. No need to pay for the necromancers," Petula said, regretting her choice of words instantly. Mrs. Maybury was only looking out for everyone in her own way. The undead woman wasn't a bad person. It was just that it was her way or no way at all.

Mrs. Maybury leaned forward. "You don't seem to understand what I'm trying to say. I thought you had some sense, but it seems I have misjudged you."

Petula leaned away from the woman and wanted nothing more than to point out that such argumentative tactics were no arguments at all. They were just fallacies people pulled out when they were losing. But resorting to the laws of logical arguments and pointing out emotional pleas as failures was an even bigger prick move. It showed the other side was unwilling to consider basic human needs, indicating that the other side's logic had a restrictive understanding of life and the universe in general. Logic was a simplification, cutting out the chaotic bits some people couldn't handle. If she listened carefully to Mrs. Maybury, she could hear more than annoyance. The undead woman was concerned. The steam engines were challenging her worldview. And if Petula dismissed that, she would indeed not understand what the undead woman was trying to say.

On the inside, Petula stomped her feet on the ground and yelled, "*Why me?*" She didn't want to be dealing with any of this or be the bigger person and actually hear Mrs. Maybury's concerns. Still, the alternative would lead to unfruitful arguments where logic could never win. So no, she could not retort by pointing out logical fallacies, as she would only lose the conversation and gain nothing.

"I think you are right, Mrs. Maybury. We have no clear understanding of what and how this will impact us. If we want to be on top of the situation, we need to know how the steam engines will impact our economy and customs." Petula meant every single word she said, and she understood only now that she actually did. She had been so willing to miss a crucial point.

Most importantly, her words disarmed Mrs. Maybury. The woman uncrossed her arms. "Good. That's all I want. I'll visit the university and see if those bright minds can put the money we give them to better use than they are now doing. We need information if we want to get rid of all this fuss."

Petula stared at the undead woman with astonishment. She'd never expected such words to come out of Mrs. Maybury's mouth. She couldn't help but be amused by the way they were delivered. Petula agreed with the woman's assessment of how research was done at the University of

Necropolis. Meandering fools. But necessary fools nevertheless.

"Yes. We should reserve a grant for the study and see that it gets attention when it's ready. But it has to be unbiased, looking for both the good and the bad."

"So be it," Mrs. Maybury snarled, showing her blackened teeth.

"Ma'am," Dow interrupted them. "The coach is ready."

"Yes, thank you, Mr. Spurgeon. I'm ready." Petula took better hold of the cat, who had calmed down. An attack against the undead woman had been assessed as unnecessary.

"Good night, Miss Upwood." Mrs. Maybury got up and headed out. It would have been too much to ask her to call Petula "mayor" or anything else that showed respect. The undead woman never did that. Either she was a girl or Miss Upwood. The first one was reserved for when the woman wanted to command or insult her. Miss Upwood came only when she had done well in her eyes. It was a rare honor.

"Good night, Mrs. Maybury." The undead woman was gone before she responded. She left without saying what she had come to say. That Mrs. Maybury had dealt with the reporter for her, but Petula shouldn't keep stalling. And that she should keep her guard dog on a leash. But Dow had come.

Petula peered down the empty hallway. Mrs. Maybury could be as quick and silent as Death when she wanted to be. Mostly she lumbered more slowly than a snail, so as not to miss all the mistakes the world had to offer.

"So?" Petula asked Dow.

"So what?" Dow responded.

"You know. You heard the whole conversation. Don't lie to me. Did it go well?"

"Better than I could have done, ma'am."

Petula sighed and followed Dow out of the office. The meeting with Mrs. Maybury was proof that the duties of a leader never ended. Only when her head hit the pillow did Petula have some escape, and even then all the issues from the day sneaked in.

It would be lovely to think that it was the collective that mattered; that the madness of a single person couldn't sway the whole nation. Or to some, it was the other way around, where they found solace in one person being able turn the tide. Henrietta collected her poise, glancing out from the parlor window. She wasn't sure which one she hoped for. Otis was ready to crack, according to her sources. Thus far, the man had endured all the pressure the Council was putting on him, but the letter clearly stated that he was at a tipping point, especially with the upcoming execution. She needed to get him out and soon. Just when she had been making headway with the mayor on the Coven standing on equal ground with the Council. Now every moment of her waking life was consumed by the Bufonite and Otis, and not the future of her witches. The Council and its power-hungry bureaucrats would turn everything into form seven-hundred-seventy-two if she let them. No one would survive their grasp, turning Necropolitans into mindless drones.

Henrietta closed her eyes as she folded the letter back into her pocket. The house creaked and moaned around her, reminding Henrietta not to believe in first impressions. In a place like Necropolis, ghosts and demons could always be the cause, yet, like everywhere else, it was usually the temperature and moisture making the house complain. The old wood was like that. Here in Necropolis, people saw ghosts and nasty spirits everywhere, but not Henrietta. It was the basic laws of nature that governed everything. Something she taught to her witches. The newer witches loved the idea of old houses, spirits, and Ouija boards. Hungering for them. But it was a different matter to dream of communing with the spirits or sensing the future than to actually do it. Those who were gifted were tormented not only by the questions of sanity and insanity and reality and illusion, but also with the meaning of it all.

Henrietta remembered the olden days when she'd first set her black leather boots in this house. Back then, they still worshiped the old gods naked. The memory made her smile. Her generation had done everything to fight for freedom from such constraints, and now the newer ones wallowed in nostalgia, seeking corsets to make their waists smaller than sixteen inches, painting their long nails black, and frolicking outside without a thread on. A good hiking outfit would serve any botanist better. Plants weren't exactly indoor creatures. Nor were witches.

Henrietta opened her eyes and headed out of the parlor. She was fashionably late. Some customs were too good to be thrown away.

Necropolis's moist, cold air welcomed her as soon as she stepped out of the old stone building. A light already shone inside the glasshouse, and from the sound of it, all the other women in the needlepoint group had arrived. Henrietta carefully drew the back door open, trying not to tamper with the perfectly controlled climate. As she stepped in, she instantly felt at home. Here the air was hot and humid. The smell was rich in soil. It felt like Amanita. Her husband's home. Her home. It reminded her of all the exotic places she'd visited, all the insects she had seen, the flowers, the trees, the mushrooms, soil, all of it. She could get lost in the sensation. She had almost been able to get lost in the world, but the Father of Botany had asked her to come back and step into his shoes. He had shown her what a good leader did and what a good botanist could create. He should be here and not her. Wesley had been made from strong stuff and they'd killed him. Henrietta felt a twinge in her heart.

She stood there under the tall trees shrouding the ceiling and next to the underbrush's steaming life, listening to the chatter coming from the needlepoint group composed of influential women. The chatter fused with the chirping of crickets. If Henrietta looked closely at the soil and leaves, she would see other bugs keeping the ecosystem functional. Without them, the place couldn't be. A fact she reminded her students of at every turn. It was too easy to let your own expertise and actions blind you. At best, a botanist was a facilitator. She would never allow her students to forget that. It was what Wesley had taught her. It was what she continued to teach.

Henrietta stepped out, seeing that the mayor was still missing from the group. But others were already there, and as Imogene had promised, the food and drinks had been set out. So were the yarn and fabric, and Henrietta's personal basket and needles.

"Good evening, ladies," she said, taking her place in the circle.

"Mrs. Culpepper," Lattice greeted her. Others followed her example. Lattice Burton worked as an office and human resources manager at the biggest newspaper in Necropolis, the *Necropolis Times*. She was the head of their ethics committee.

Ida Mortician greeted Henrietta by looking down her nose. Ida was more witchy than any of the witches working for the Coven despite not being a witch. The woman was a banker and member of the Stopford Committee, which monitored the city's economic systems and proposed laws for the Town Hall to go over and implement if necessary. Ida corrected her velvet gown, letting it be known that Henrietta was a travesty. Despite the hostility, they got along fine as long as Henrietta remembered the woman had gotten her hopes crushed and was forced to live as an ordinary mortal in a city full of peculiars.

The last member of their group—their little revolution against the Council, or a needlepoint group, if anyone asked—was Annabella Sepulcher. She was a reborn undead woman who worked at the Church of Kraken under Madam Sabine. She was highly respected, and before she'd died, she had been a lawyer. Annabella didn't bring the Church into their discussions. She was here because Henrietta and Annabella were old acquaintances, and as a lawyer the woman had held great power in the city.

All of the women in the group were remarkable in one way or another. Annabella had changed the constitution, arguing that equal rights for women were a vital cornerstone for Necropolis to succeed. She had done that back in the Oliver the Great days. A miracle in itself, since if their former tyrant thought you were a nuisance, it was a one-way trip to the gallows. But Annabella had been in the right place at the right time, the so-called early days of their former leader, when he had been more flexible with his rule and not as paranoid, mad, and leached by the vipers he'd surrounded himself with. The days the streets had flowed with blood.

"Have any of you heard if Miss Upwood is coming?" Henrietta asked, nonchalantly reaching for the needlepoint pattern she'd started last time.

The group's hierarchy was delicate. The mayor outranked them all, but they met on Henrietta's turf, allowing her to have a say in how things were organized. One peculiar thing was that the mayor didn't seem to mind Henrietta taking the lead. She was disinterested in the social hierarchy to the point that it made Henrietta and the rest uncomfortable.

Everyone shook their heads.

"So she'll be here?" Henrietta settled back in her seat, crossing her legs and laying the frame on her lap.

"As far as I know. Has something new happened?" Lattice asked.

Another delicate thing within the group was determining what to tell and what to keep to oneself. All of them knew more about something than the others. And all of them knew that knowledge could alter realities. Still, they had a joint agenda. All of them wanted to chip away at the Council's hold on the city. But there would come a day when she might have to save herself from the others, especially from the mayor. The young girl was a mystery. Henrietta couldn't quite figure out why Petula wanted to lessen the Council's rule. She was a necromancer, after all. As far as everyone knew, she was the poster girl for the Council. Everyone adored her despite her personality defects. Petula wasn't what you might call affable. She was impolite, direct, sharp, and intelligent. Henrietta always felt uncomfortable under the necromancer's gaze, which stripped her naked. Still, Henrietta liked her. Anyone who knew their stuff got her respect. The young girl had learned to defend herself and quickly in a city full of goblins.

"Not at such. We'd better wait for Miss Upwood." Henrietta gave a smile to Lattice.

Lattice was there because the Council messed with her writers, according to her. She didn't like it one bit when they sent their memos about what topic to write about and what not to, and she had to pass on those assignments and hear the complaints. There was a more personal story behind it, but Henrietta hadn't been able to fish it out, yet. Not that anyone needed a personal story to question the ultimate rule of the Council. Of course, they did an important job sniffing out necromancers hiding overseas, ready to raise their own army of the dead.[3] But here in Necropolis, the Council had spread their rule too wide, worming their way inside the family table. They even dictated the Coven's jurisdictions and how they should handle their witches and hexers. Not to mention, the Council thought the Coven was a buffet where they could pick and choose the workers they wanted to do their accounting and hunt down renegade bogeymen.

There came a polite cough. Henrietta looked up and saw the mayor standing there. She was facing the door, yet she'd missed Petula coming in.

"Good evening," Petula said. She waved her hand before anyone had time to pop up to curtsy. This happened every time. Petula refused to let others grovel in front of her, yet the others had to pretend to try. "I'm sorry I'm late. I was held up by Mrs. Maybury," she said as if it should explain everything.

---

3. A secluded jungle was an ideal spot to start. Big, crowded cities worked too, as no one really noticed you. You could argue it was one of the core reasons for the fall of the psyche.

It did.

"Speaking of which, she would be a splendid addition to our group," Annabella said.

Everyone looked at her, horrified.

"You know it as well as I do. She holds great power in this city, and she has battled against the Council more than once. She's relentless, and..." Nothing more had to be added.

"You might be right. With her on our side, we could speed up the process, but she's also a target. The Council keeps a close eye on her," Petula countered, which was unlike her. She usually sat there quietly and showed only a little of her thoughts.

"At some point, we have to include her," Annabella protested. All of them knew she was right, and her statement had nothing to do with the solidarity amongst the undead.

"Let's leave that for later." Henrietta defused the situation. "We have more important things to talk about. I had a visit from our friend Percy Allread, and..."

"And?" Ida snapped.

"And he gave us nothing solid to go on. He will give a testimony against Mr. Thurston. I see no way to change his mind. He's all about protocols." Henrietta made her first stitch of the day. She might as well get some needlepoint done. Plus, it was sensible to have something to show. Otherwise, people got overly suspicious, and when it came to the opposite sex, especially those in power, they couldn't even begin to imagine you could stitch and talk at the same time. Smoking cigars and thinking what pieces to move on the checkerboard was fine when talking about state business, but stitching took up one's entire mental capacity. Either way, the stitching made rebelling all the more pleasant, especially with cake and coffee on the side.

"We don't need him. Like I said last time, we have the public ear, and we just need to play that against the Council," Annabella stated.

"And what? Play nice? Yes, the Council's support is at its lowest ebb, but people are ever so ready to go back to their oblivious existence." Ida stopped stitching and locked eyes with Annabella.

"Is that so?" Annabella stuck to her guns. Not many outside this room could do that against Ida. The banker could be spookier than the horrors from other realms when she wanted to be. Now Ida was trying to stare the undead lawyer down.

"Is the machine even real?" Lattice interrupted, trying to head off another full-blown battle between Annabella and Ida. You would think they were mortal enemies, but Annabella was Ida's godmother, and outside this place, they met every week to have tea and a chat.

"As far as I can tell, no," Henrietta replied. She could feel the mayor's eyes upon her. Silent and all-seeing.

"Then what's this fuss about?" Lattice asked and unknowingly stuck her tongue out as she made a stitch.

Everyone ignored the last remark.

"Then what do you suggest?" Ida asked, still keeping her attention on the undead lawyer.

"To wait and see how this plays out."

Ida made an "aha" sound as loud as she could.

The reason why Ida was in their group was still a mystery. One day she had been there, and no one had thought of a good reason to say no. Maybe it was because of her godmother. Every little girl should be blessed with Annabella as their guardian. A brilliant woman who, like Mrs. Maybury, had taken the Council to court several times. Once she had almost won the case, but then the judge chickened out.[4] The message was loud and clear: no one went against the Council. At least until now. The Save the Otis Group was too visible. So visible that even the most loyal newspapers had written about it and the trial, speculating what it meant for Necropolis and all necromancers. It was partly down to Lattice's brilliance and connections. Her writers loved her to bits.

"Mr. Thurston's trial is set for next week, December eighth." Petula spoke, and as she did, even Ida went silent.

Henrietta could almost pull off a similar effect. Almost.

Annabella was about to answer, but Petula interrupted her. "While I agree with Annabella about not putting the delicate balance between necromancers in jeopardy, I have to say, Ida is right."

The last statement rippled through the circle, with everyone holding their breath. The mayor seldom took sides or supported anything coming from Ida.

"The time is right now. We won't get a better chance to weaken the Council's hold on us. It's not like we are trying to destroy them. All we want are answers and accountability." Petula opened her long woolen coat and let the worn-out fabric drape over her seat. "I agree we have to use finesse when trying to achieve change. There Annabella is right. So, I propose we continue what we are doing on all our fronts. Lattice supporting reporters, Ida funding the Save the Otis Group, Annabella organizing and giving them counseling, Henrietta giving public statements and speculating what cooperation with witches and necromancers could look like on equal ground, and me speaking of the matter in the Town Hall. But Otis will soon be sentenced, and we all know that is going to be in the Council's

---

4. He had given a half-assed explanation about why the Council had the right to accuse a reporter of writing a defamatory article questioning the structure of the Council. Said reporter had ended up paying a hefty fine to avoid serving prison time.

favor. We need to stop the unnecessary death, and all of us have to find a way to go about it. So I have decided I'm going to meet the Council and demand to meet Mr. Thurston." Petula leaned forward, took her needlepoint from her bag, and began to stitch.

"I have to agree with the mayor," Lattice jumped in.

Others nodded too, Ida less eagerly, as she had her heart set on a rescue mission, or more like a full-frontal attack with all the horses, catapults, and horde of beasts she'd hired as security for her bank.

"What about you, Henrietta? What do you think? You have been quiet all this time," Petula asked.

Henrietta was startled. She noticed the mayor had used her first name. Oh, she had given her permission to do so—it was only customary—but this was the first time Petula had used it, and ever so casually.

Henrietta cleared her throat and set the needlepoint frame on her lap to give herself time to think. "The mayor is right. We all play our parts within legal parameters. The Council is waiting for that one slip to give it permission to attack us directly. I guarantee that the Council is clueless about what happens inside these walls. A meeting with the Council and Mr. Thurston would make a difference, and it might stall..." Henrietta paused. "...it might relieve the pressure they are putting on Mr. Thurston. I'm sure they are using everything in their power to get the Bufonite for themselves. I fear we don't have time on our side. I'll draw up a proposal for a witch committee to be set up in the Town Hall; that might be a worthy distraction."

The mayor kept looking at her silently. Then the girl took up her needlepoint and began to stitch.

CHAPTER FIVE

THE UNCOMFORTABLE UNIVERSE

D oing the right thing in a system composed of arbitrary rules set by time and non-relevant circumstances was almost impossible. The only thing left was taking action for action's sake and hoping that what followed wasn't as bad as it could be. Percy was meant to uphold his duties, but others kept changing the rules for him. He should head to the small, cramped, and cheap place he called home—all he could afford as a civic employee. Even the overseas commission with additional hazard pay didn't make him rich enough to live in a decent place.

All of this followed him there too. His mail carrier gave him dirty looks for all the invitations hauled to his address. Newspapers, social and financial institutions private and public wanted to see him. There were requests for him to attend banquettes and luncheons in his honor. Everyone wanted to get on his good side in hopes of getting their hands on the machine. The summoning to the Coven had been the lowest point. He, as a hexer, depended on their moral guidelines, and now even they wanted to use him. Percy tensed his leg as he took a long stride forward. The little puddles rippled underneath him. The rain was coming down hard, as it had a habit of doing in Necropolis.

Percy lifted his gaze to see the dark clouds covering the city. Whatever was going to happen to him, it was better for it to happen here in Necropolis. Here, his bones knew how to act. He would have to report this[1] to the Council. Percy glanced behind him at the road leading to the Necro Botanical Gardens and then to his lodgings. He sighed and headed to the Council's headquarters. His only hope for normalcy was for Otis's trial to come quickly. In the meantime, he had to keep his head down and his mouth shut.

Percy drew his jacket's collar up and stepped past a puddle. The night was tangible, and it made his heartbeat sound fast. Whatever he thought about all of this didn't matter. It was not his place to say if Otis belonged in jail or should be executed. Yet he feared that justice wouldn't prevail.

His hexes jolted him awake. Something or someone was there, just on the periphery of his steps. Percy listened to the rain dropping down on his leather jacket and wide-rimmed hat. He spread his hexes wide. They ricocheted from the stone houses to the metallic fences and back to him, coming up empty. Usually, the streets of Necropolis in this beautifully wicked hour were filled with creatures of all sorts. Someone had driven them into hiding. He had been too distracted by all the politics to notice.

He should have stuck with the rules and regulations. They kept him functional, as they did with any system in place. The politicians should leave the clerks like him to get on with it, but the politicians made a fuss about nothing and everything, not understanding it was the clerks like him who kept societies' wheels turning. But politicians learned soon enough that while you could change an organization's goals, you couldn't get the organization to alter its tasks. The beautiful line about objectives and duties was just that—a beautiful line. Accounting still had to be done, money allocated, and supplies ordered. But politics were there to stay, to Percy's

---

1. A funny misconception people had in a sticky situation that there was no other choice than to do this or that. There was always a choice. But it was convictions, values, and limited sight making the options seem scarce and people feel stuck, favoring the path of doom.

dismay.

He continued down the street, keeping the hexes up. That was all he could do. It was healthy to stay paranoid in Necropolis; it wasn't wise to stay put and attract only Kraken knew what lurked in the night.

Something tugged at his hexes again. Percy made a sharp turn at the end of the alley and continued all the way to Necrology Street without being attacked. Not that this meant anything. He looked up at the Council's headquarters standing amongst the other tall buildings. The Necromantic Council's headquarters stones shone beige and gray under the arches of its windows. The little eternal symbols on the glass reminded everyone that the Council wasn't going away, but the government might.[2] This was where the city happened. Where everything was defined. They used to announce the dead and the newly undead here. You could read the public rosters just outside the Council's building next to the Ministry of Public Works and Home Ministry, watched over by its gargoyles. Around the buildings the lamp posts cast shadows against the walls, making the irregular click of heels against the cobblestones sound even more sinister. In the middle of it all, the Save the Otis Group huddled under their tents, keeping out of the rain that came down hard, as if to punish them for going against the Council.

Percy looked at the lunatics who thought they could alter the inevitable with slogans and persistence. He then spread his hexes over them and past them to sense whether whoever had tugged his hexes earlier had followed him onto the Council's turf.

They had, and boldly so. The commotion outside the headquarters was enough to hide them from a careless onlooker, but not from Percy. Their soft feet padded against the cobblestones, and he heard it as clear as day. Most likely a werewolf.

---

2. They always did.

Percy flexed his muscles. His right hand ached as the burn marks from when he'd rescued Otis caused his skin to stiffen. He hoped that the wolf wasn't stupid enough to attack him here. Any werewolf knew there were consequences to an unsanctioned hunt in Necropolis—consequences involving silver and tongs. Percy reached for his blackened sword and listened to the wolf's breathing. But it never came. It disappeared into the shadows, and the hexes lost its tracks. Percy doubted the wolf had just been on an evening trot after a hard day at work. Werewolves were the best trackers in the city. Some did employ vampires for their espionage, but vampires were harder to motivate and even harder to keep loyal.

Percy turned his back to the streets and headed into the headquarters. Two witches guarded the huge wooden doors. Percy showed his badge to the witches, and the doors opened for him. Percy took the stairs up to the second floor and turned left, feeling unusually anxious. He pushed past it and headed right at the next junction, walking past the long corridor of small offices containing a handful of employees. His handler was in the fourth to the right. He paused behind Alvira Calhoun's door, and before he knocked, the door creaked open, accompanied by the strong smell of tobacco.

"Come in," came a gasping voice.

Percy stepped in.

Alvira sat behind her desk. The vampire looked as pale as always. Her loose silver hair framed her face. There was a full ashtray in front of her with a lit cigarette. Alvira grinned when she saw him. "How's my hero?"

There was that. This wasn't the first time someone in the Council had called him so. Most thought he'd done some great deed by not only dealing with his initial assignment, the necromancer Cathy, but also seizing someone who hadn't been detected by the usual precautionary methods—the spiritual feelers—the ones who sensed the mood changes in the ethereal realm and reported back. They were just a rumor everyone thought to exist.

The Council had them locked in their basement. It wouldn't be the first lie to become public knowledge, nor the first truth.

Percy groaned, closing the door behind him. He was no hero. Otis had been an accident, and the glory in many aspects belonged to Rose Pettyshare. Yes, he'd defused the spirit infestation the necromancer had unleashed, but any hunter in his situation would have. But here he was, being called a hero, with a medal to prove it. After all this, Alvira had started to behave more like his publicist than a handler. Percy didn't like any of it. Though he was glad that the balance of bitterness was still there. His coworkers hated him, especially those at the accounting office. The Council didn't exactly encourage cooperation. It liked to keep its employees sharp and competitive even in the mail room.

Alvira ignored his snort. She rummaged through her inbox, huffing as she did. "Here," she said and handed him a letter. "It's an invitation from Mr. and Mrs. Cunningham to attend their gathering and share all the wonderful stories about your travels abroad. They have eligible daughters, I have heard."

Percy lowered the wrapped honey and the cake he had been given to the desk and took the letter from his handler. He glanced at her from under his eyebrows, holding it.

"Don't give me that. It's a great opportunity. Who knows how far you can take this? They are aristocrats with a nice title of something something, I can't quite remember what. But that's not important. It might lead to a seat in the Town Hall and then the board of some institute, and before you know it, you are running things. Or if you wish to become a socialite, you can. The Cunninghams are willing to take you under their wings." Alvira leaned back, and her legs floated on the desk. She didn't even pretend to have to use her muscles.

Percy shook his head. "I'd rather not." He handed back the letter.

"Hang on to it in case you change your mind. It's never a bad idea to make friends in high places." The vampire smirked. "So, what can I do for you tonight?"

Percy folded the letter into his jacket pocket and said, "Mrs. Culpepper, the head of the Coven, sent for me, and I saw her no more than an hour ago. I came to give my report of the encounter."

Alvira squinted her eyes and swung her legs down. "I see. Must I get the forms?"

When Percy said nothing, Alvira let a slow, wheezing breath out between her fangs. He tried not to succumb to Alvira's usual tactics; she treated him like her ticket out of this office. More than once, she'd offered to come to the banquets and public events with him.

"So what did the old hag want?" Alvira asked as soon as she had found a pen and the proper papers. She took the tobacco off the tray and put it between her lips. She didn't even take a drag. It just hung on her lifeless lips.

He recounted the entire encounter, finishing by saying, "I think a werewolf followed me."

"You think, or you know?" Alvira narrowed her eyes, making Percy regret even mentioning the incident.

"Think."

"Do you want me to add it here?"

"Whatever you think is right."

"That's all?" Alvira asked.

"Yes. I wanted the Council to know right away." Percy wasn't exactly sure who the actual Council was; who decided the guidelines he followed and the directions the entire organization took. There was talk of the old families, the board, but no one was sure. Sometimes, late at night, the question gnawed at him. How could he work for an organization whose head was invisible? How could he trust the decisions made and follow them? Then he reminded himself of the duties the Council held and fell asleep.

When Alvira had finished the report, she looked ready to throw him out. Percy stood up and headed home to sleep, taking the honey and the cake with him.

The odd occasions when the systems actually worked were the little, blessed liberations from the clutches of a moody universe out to get you. Then again, the more saddening thought was if the universe actually cared or not. Otis had long ago accepted that the universe didn't care about him. He had to do all the caring himself.

He was astonished to find himself standing outside his prison cell, his feet and wrists shackled by enchanted metal, feeling somewhat shaken after having slept eight hours straight and finding out that his undead lawyer had done his work for once. Otis let the witches escort him through the Council's headquarters by way of the secret passages. Being up and about felt good. He let them take him into a small, cramped office and push him to sit on a chair in front of a tiny man in a suit without a single joke. His lawyer took a seat by his side.

The room was a sad excuse for an office. There was a tiny window at ceiling height, letting in just enough light to make him feel depressed. The place was more miserable than Otis's prison cell.

"Thank you for coming, Mr. Thurston and Mr. Pod. You may call me Elmer Spooner. If you would disclose why you have asked to see me?" the tiny man in a suit asked. The man looked uncomfortable, as if he wasn't used to having people in his office. Otis hadn't quite decided yet what the man did and who he was. He was Elmer Spooner, but what did that mean?

Otis tilted his head and looked at the goblin-looking man, wondering if he fit the profile of someone running the Council from the shadows. Who knew if Elmer Spooner's appearance was just that, an appearance, and underneath the goblin beat a cruel heart.

"I'm willing to speak about the Bufonite and how it's made in exchange for my freedom," Otis said.

Elmer Spooner harrumphed. "Then I'm afraid you have come to the wrong department. My duty is to go over the procedures the Council makes and evaluate their legality. I was under the impression you had a complaint about how your imprisonment has been handled?"

Otis squeezed the chair's armrests. He should have guessed this was just another method to torture him. Otis glanced at his lawyer.

"You asked me to put forward your discomfort regarding your treatment," Ichor Pod said without blinking.

"And this you managed to arrange?" Otis snarled at the undead man.

"It's a start," Ichor Pod said.

Elmer Spooner looked highly apologetic.

Otis looked at the goblin and then back to his lawyer. The two men were spitting images of each other if you stripped away the surface and found the bureaucratic core. They would have a field day with each other. Otis wondered if he could zone out and picture himself somewhere else. Somewhere with a deep blue ocean and girls with no clothes on. A thing which could be arranged if there weren't two witches inside the room. He felt their eyes burrowing into the back of his head, looking for an excuse to frog him up.

"So how can I help you, Mr. Thurston?" Mr. Spooner nervously glanced at him and then the witches at the door.

Otis snorted. This was justice, then. Corpse worm shit, he would make this fun. What could they do to him that they hadn't already tried? He put on a serious face and said, "With everything. My rights as a prisoner haven't been respected."

The man took a pen out of his desk and opened the folder in front of him. "Could you be more specific?"

"If you want. My right to see my family has been taken away." Otis smiled. Oh, he was going to make Elmer write until his hand went numb.

The man coughed and drew another file from under the existing one. Otis saw his name on all of the forms. "As I have gathered, your mother is dead, and your father is missing. You don't have any other known living relatives."

"Does that change anything in Necropolis? A seance with my granny or pap would do wonders for my spirit. Being isolated in my room, blasted by the constant lights and noise, only getting a break when meeting my lawyer or after a rare chat with the guards, is inhumane treatment. All against the rules Minta Stopford established early on in her reign, I have to say. Such acts are also against the International Convention on Human Rights, including all other sentient forms from spirits to vampires. I demand to have my voice heard. That's another thing. I have been silenced. My letters have been read and intercepted. I have the right to communicate about my sentencing and seek an outside opinion. The Council has also kept me misinformed about my trial and when it will happen. Nobody has consulted me about such matters. Next week's trial is an execution without proper due course."

Elmer Spooner hand-scribed as fast as possible, paraphrasing Otis's statements and adding numbers and clauses behind every item listed.

Otis's lawyer coughed and shifted his weight next to him. "If I can remind you, Mr. Thurston, prisoners do not have full constitutional rights. Yes, they are protected against cruel and unusual punishment, but the Council arguably acted for the safety of the public—" That was as far as Ichor Pod got.

"Excuse me," Elmer interrupted him. "I have to cut you short there. Mr. Thurston has the right to make his complaints heard. Such are the laws and rules of imprisonment, and I won't have anyone silence my client while they are in my chambers." The man corrected himself nervously, glancing at the lawyer then at Otis, and lastly at the witches. When Ichor Pod nodded, the man proceeded. "Now, do go on, Mr. Thurston."

Otis wanted to laugh. Mr. Spooner was a dark horse.

"I have been denied an opportunity to go outside and exercise," Otis said, knowing well he was stretching his argument thin. No one in Necropolis willingly went outside into the harsh, cold sea air, let alone to exercise. He got his inspiration from James Hardrick's reformatory ideas, which he had read in the news. The man thought that being outdoors was one way to elevate prisoners' spirits and make them better citizens. A worthy shot.

And not a futile one. Elmer Spooner wrote it down more than happily and managed to find a number to back it up.

Otis continued listing all the tiny things, from the food to the coldness of his room, the hours he wasn't permitted to sleep, and being forbidden to practice his necromantic powers, which he considered to be his religion. The last got a rise out of both Ichor and Elmer. The lawyer almost choked on his tongue, and Elmer broke the tip of his pen and had to hurry to replace it. From there on, Otis kept telling tales. When they were done, Elmer looked like his head was spinning, and the always stoic Mr. Pod was angry. Or it could be that a parasite was passing through his system.

Soon after, Otis was ushered from his chair and out of the chambers. But before he left, Elmer Spooner stopped him, grasping his hand to shake it. It was more of a ploy to pull him closer.

"Mr. Thurston, I'll make sure your words will be heard," he whispered and let go.

Otis wasn't sure if he'd heard the man correctly. It didn't matter; he was ushered out and marched back to his prison cell. All around them, the stories left there by the long-gone books whispered to Otis about how he could escape the old library. He heard none of them. He was too preoccupied with his own thoughts. He followed the labyrinth-like corridors and small alcoves, seeing the odd clerk here and there who was permitted to use the secret passages. They glanced at him curiously but turned their gazes away when the guards grunted. He stopped along with Ichor Pod outside the prison door to wait for the witches to let them in. But Mr. Pod didn't follow him.

"Mr. Thurston, if you don't mind, I'll leave you for now. I have to go over your files and try to contact the Council board to arrange a hearing about the Bufonite, as you wish."

"Of course. And thank you, Mr. Pod." Otis reached out to shake hands with the undead, but then he remembered what he was doing and stopped himself. Everyone in the corridor was astonished. It wasn't unusual for the living and dead to touch each other, but it was avoided if possible. Not for fear of transmitting some horrible disease, but because old beliefs die hard.

"Yes. Good, good, good," the lawyer stuttered and made an excuse to leave.

Otis waited for the witches to secure the room and get their spells ready, and only then did he step in. He sat on the mattress as the witches removed his shackles. He had tried to coax out their names. He had been refused. If he was back in Threebeanvalley, there would have been at least some form of jovial banter about the weather. Here, as soon as his shackles were off, the witches left and sealed the door with their protection spells.

Otis stared at the door and wondered if anything good would follow his meeting with the small goblin man, Elmer Spooner. Maybe he had kept his soul intact in this miserable place. All Otis could do now was pray to the old god of the necromancers, Old Man Death, and wish for some sort of miracle. It was just that he had no faith in the gods or the system. What was left was his talents, but if he was honest, he needed help from the outside world. His talents could get him only so far. So the stars had to align for him to escape, and Otis was pretty sure that they didn't even know he existed.

CHAPTER SIX

A FRIEND OR A FOE

B ut then there was the present, with all the diminutive details to be ignored or get lost in. The Necro Botanical Gardens were intoxicating. The exotic smells were sweet and overpowering. Like nothing Petula had experienced before. Sometimes she felt like lingering in the hot, luscious air, to search for necromantic uses for the plants. Commonly they served a sacrificial function. Burning lavender gave the dead peace, wolfsbane guided the spirits, and the deceased's favorite aromatics coaxed them out, but Petula was sure there had to be more ways to use them.

Petula bent over to put her yarn, unfinished work, and needles back into the basket. She almost laughed, picturing what she must look like in her old wool coat, hurrying through the night while clutching the woven bark basket with strings and needles sticking out. *There goes our mayor.* Not that she could do any hurrying through the night. Dow forbade her to go anywhere unaccompanied. Petula was sure he had his guards even on the roofs and in the bushes, ready to defend her.

Petula stood up. The stitches had been stitched and what had to be said had been said, and it was time to go home. Henrietta looked at her the way she always did when she wanted her to stay behind. But not to have a chat with a friend. Petula just couldn't make friends. She just couldn't. It was not only the mayor in her preventing her from befriending someone.

She had never learned how to be herself around other people. She was somehow made wrong. Of course, this situation was delicate in more than one way. There was too much to lose if she said too much. Sometimes Petula wished she could just make one friend in life. Agatha had almost been one, but—Petula didn't want to think about it.

"Miss Upwood," Henrietta said when she returned after seeing the others out. If Dow were here, he would advise her to prepare for the worst. Or at least, prepare to fight the old witch. She was a necromancer, after all, and Henrietta was a witch. Petula couldn't be bothered. That was the thing. In her weakest moments, she sometimes entertained the idea that dying wasn't as horrendous as others made it out to be. What was so wrong with closing your eyes and not hearing, seeing, and feeling anything? Petula sighed. Her sheltered life as the mayor, confined to politics, had taken a greater toll than she'd noticed.

"Do call me Petula," Petula offered. She was sure it had come out too coldly. Why couldn't there be warmth in her voice as there was in her sister's? She liked Henrietta, after all.

"One doesn't know how to act in these situations." Henrietta smiled.

"No, one doesn't. Sometimes I feel like our modern Necropolis isn't as modern as we like to think. All these rigid social hierarchies hold us back. Do you know what Mrs. Maybury proposed today?" Petula asked.

"Do tell me."

Petula couldn't quite tell if the woman meant it or not. "That we keep the machines out. Those coming up from the new continents. I was ready to dismiss her, but she was right. They'll change our city's landscape and maybe render us, the necromancers and witches and other power users, useless. Who knows? But I'm not sure if I oppose it or not. The world has to change, and Necropolis with it."

"Hmm. There's food for thought. Being in your position is more complex than I... imagined." Henrietta again gave her a confusing smile.

Friendliness or politeness, Petula couldn't tell.

"Working with people always is." Petula crossed her arms. "But you didn't ask me to stay behind to talk about Mrs. Maybury."

"No, gods forbid."

Petula wondered if she should defend the undead woman. While Mrs. Maybury was annoying—and no one could deny that—she had other qualities which made her worth having around. One of them was her tenacious nature and willingness to alter the world according to her beliefs. Not many could claim to have influenced the lives of others as Mrs. Maybury had. There had been bad policies, but there always were. The future was hard to see and even harder to master. Not to mention conflicts with distinct ideologies and personal needs. That seemed to be the nature of human affairs. Or at least humans made it out to be. Petula hadn't yet decided if it was the fault of political mechanisms or the human mind. Anyway, she had gotten too used to Mrs. Maybury being around.

Petula gave a smile. "She's something, but I have come to see her as an ally worth having. And she does care. More than others think."

Henrietta stiffened. "Of course, she does. She has done wonderful things for the rights of the undead and women as well."

"Indeed," Petula said. "Again, we are getting off track. What can I do for you?" She uncrossed her arms.

Henrietta observed her as Petula would have done in her shoes. The woman clearly wanted to uncross her arms as well, but she couldn't let Petula notice she was mirroring her gestures.

"Yes," Henrietta said after a while and let her hands drop by her sides. "Last time you were here, we discussed witches taking part in Town Hall decision-making as the Council does. You offered to look into the Constitution and see if it has to be put to a vote or whether the witches have a right to be part of the Town Hall."

Petula smiled. One of those stalling smiles Dow had taught her. Or more like the tutor had, the one Dow had found to teach her all about manners, rhetoric, and vocal tones.

"I have looked into the matter as I promised I would. It's not straightforward; the Council has the right to veto many of the decisions made. Including this one. While technically I'm part of the Council as a necromancer, I'm under their jurisdiction as well."

She'd tried to choose her words carefully. The whole structure of Necropolis was bizarre, outdated, and twisted so that there was no making sense of it. She was a tyrant by right. She could command the Council by right. But none of that was so when it came to the customs. The Council decided what went, who led, and what people could do and say. During Oliver the Great's era, things had been the same, but they had worked behind the scenes, controlling the city, despite Oliver the Great's tendency to execute those who disagreed with him. But a man like that was easy to keep happy.

"Of course, but if you..."

Petula wondered if the woman truly understood what she proposed. Petula already had a target on her back for inquiring after the matter. Not that she wasn't already on the Council's naughty list, but open opposition was another thing entirely. They were, and most importantly, she was, already putting pressure on the Council over Mr. Thurston's case. While she supported Henrietta's proposal and thought witches should be part of the government, this was not the time to start a war with the Council on all fronts.

"I'll see what I can do." Petula interrupted Henrietta. "But for now, we should concentrate on my request to visit Mr. Thurston."

The witch didn't look satisfied.

"I'd better leave then," Petula said.

"I'll let you out through the back door. I already locked the one in the front. You can't be too careful nowadays. Some of our plants are one of a kind, and keeping them alive alone has turned out to be tricky. I would even say impossible. The trouble is that cross-pollinating them with other plants will bring worthy hybrids, and current movements in botany frown upon this. They say purity should be upheld. But how can you keep purity when there's nothing to back it up? Plus, mixing heritages can strengthen the plant's chances of survival. Unfortunately, not everyone can see that. Of course, I'm not saying plants shouldn't be protected and cultivated. They should. But there's a line…" Henrietta suddenly became quiet. "Do forgive me. I sometimes get carried away."

"There's no need to apologize. I find it fascinating what you can do. I, when it comes to anything green, am hopeless. They tend to die on me."

"I can't quite believe that." Henrietta held the door open to her, letting in the cold, damp air.

It chilled Petula to the bones. "Even I can be clueless."

"As can all of us." Henrietta closed and locked the door behind them.

Petula tied her jacket tighter around her and made her goodbyes. She headed to the path where her coach was already waiting. A weasel-looking man greeted her as she approached. He was always there with her wherever she went. The man was Dow's most trusted associate. The man waited for her instructions ever so patiently, holding the door open until she told him where to go. Petula opened her pocket watch. It was too late to go back to the office and request an audience with the Council.

"Take me home, Mr. Colton."

"Of course, madam." The weasel-looking man winked and shut the door behind her.

It's debatable whether truth matters or not, especially on a societal level. Perceptions sway reality, not to mention values and organization of

thought. Raul was back at the office. He had barely gotten there in time
to meet the deadline. Mrs. Maybury had babbled on and on about how
Necropolis was being taken over by the new techies—her term for those
who had sold their souls to all things mechanical. She perceived the whole
business of mechanizing Necropolis as a threat to its existence. It had taken
Raul's sanity and the darkness of his hair to get Mrs. Maybury to speak
about Mr. Thurston and the situation facing the city. In the end, he'd
managed. She had given him more than he could have hoped for. She hadn't
actually gone with the election card as Dow had proposed. Mrs. Maybury
had spoken her mind.

Now he watched as Maximilian and Lattice Burton argued behind the
glass windows of the editor's office. He couldn't hear what was being said
above the thumping of the printing press, but it didn't look good. It never
was when Lattice made an appearance. Raul had come to detest her, despite
how much others loved her. There was something about her that made him
second-guess her motives.

"Raul, come here," Maximilian shouted from the door.

The other reporters pretended not to pay attention as he got up and did
as he was told, but when the door shut after him, the room exploded with
chatter. Raul glanced through the window, seeing his colleagues quickly
turn their attention to their typewriters.

"Mrs. Burton says we cannot print this," Maximilian stated, standing in
front of the huge windows running the length of the office. The man had
always had a flair for the dramatic.

Raul said nothing. He stayed near the door, leaning against the frame,
waiting to get this over with so he could go home. None of this mattered.
Everyone pretended the news was somehow imperative. It wasn't.

"We really can't. It's inflammatory—"

"All said by Mrs. Maybury. The undead has a right to her opinion," Raul
said quietly, forcing them to concentrate on his words.

"She has," Lattice started carefully. "But what she states about the Council having purposefully tortured Mr. Thurston without results cannot be verified. We need facts, or else they'll come after us."

"She looked very certain about it, and I did use words like *Mrs. Maybury alleges* when I wrote about her suspicions about the Council no longer needing to pretend to be in the shadows if they controlled the Bufonite. They could dictate their terms, and others would do as they were told. When she hinted that the ancient, powerful, wealthy families controlled the Council and used it to alter society so they could keep harvesting resources, money, and organs, I think I used *she paints the picture of*... and finished it off with facts about one percent owning ninety percent of the city's economy. All facts and all legal."

Raul couldn't help but smile. Of course, he knew they wouldn't print it. Mrs. Maybury had gone after the Council, and hard. Still, it was the truth. Everyone knew it. Mrs. Maybury had just stated it aloud. She should know. She and her fellow politicians took campaign money from the Council. And clearly, Mrs. Maybury hadn't gotten her share since she decided to speak out, or she had finally grown a backbone—or bought one.

"This reads like a conspiracy theory, Mr. Porter. We have to rely on the truth rather than cherry-picking facts to fit your narrative," Lattice said.

Raul laughed aloud, remembering what Dow had said just a few hours ago. "There's never one single truth, just different narratives tailored to all sorts of motives," he said aloud and shook his head. Dow was something else. "Do as you wish. Print Sandy's piece," Raul added and took a cigarette case out of his jacket, opened it, and lit the cigarette. Lattice and Maximilian watched in silence. "It's more fitting for tomorrow's paper. This is already yesterday's news, and you are right, it's just a narrative."

Lattice and Maximilian glanced at each other in disbelief.

"I'm glad you agree with us, Mr. Porter. We all want the truth to be printed and for our newspaper to survive."

"Indeed."

Raul waited for Lattice to gather her things and leave. She took the article with her and pushed it into the furnace in the center of the office. Everyone watched as she did, including Raul and Maximilian from the window. Then the woman walked off downstairs, heading to Kraken only knew where.

"I'm sorry..." Maximilian started.

"Don't be. It was a bad piece. She was right about that. But not why. It was too hastily drawn, and there were no facts. Just as she said, conspiracy theories." He left out the fact that it was one everyone believed in, yet no one did anything about it. What could they do? It was just how the world was organized and how it would always be organized. But he wasn't everyone. He was going to prove it, and then Lattice could suck it.

Maximilian had one of his "Raul, I'm concerned" expressions on his face.

"I'm truly fine. It's just one article, and a shoddy one at best."

"I would offer you whiskey, but..."

"Yeah, yeah." Raul waved a hand in the air. It had been their ritual when things didn't go well. Maybe not the best way to stay functional in this business. "I'd better get some sleep."

Another worried look passed across his friend's face. The man said nothing as Raul left to collect his jacket and hat. He was actually planning to go to bed and sleep, and tomorrow he would find his way into the Council headquarters and get the facts he needed.

CHAPTER SEVEN

MADE FROM THINGS THAT BREAK

Nature didn't need institutions. It just did its thing. Nature woke Henrietta up to the pale sun shining through the crack between the thick velvet curtains. There was no intention behind it. Just an occurrence happening on its own. Henrietta turned to her left to find the bed empty. As always, her husband was up before the birds. Most likely, he would be locked in his study, and it would be late in the evening when she would see him again. They had become two strangers. She spent all her time in the garden or running the Coven and he... She wasn't sure what he did. In Amanita, he had been a representative of his town. They had met her first day on the islands when she'd traveled there to study the native plants. He had been everywhere, smoothing her interactions with the locals and the government.

Henrietta was sure he'd grown to resent her during all these years here. Necropolis was dark compared to the nature-engulfed town where Eurof was born, always filled with strong sun, colorful flowers and people, and laughter. Here, laughter was a sign of menace rather than friendship.

Henrietta sighed and turned back to her right side, watching the pale light.

She loved Eurof with all her heart. That hadn't changed, but both of them knew this wasn't working. Now the Necro Botanical Garden's greenhouses were full of the plants they had brought with them and the students busied themselves with their cultivation, Eurof's initial efforts to help with the transition were no longer needed. He was only in the way, as his knowledge about plants, flowers, mushrooms, trees, bees, insects, soil, air humidity, and light was limited. Then he had taken it upon himself to grow oyster mushrooms to feed the Coven. Even that she had taken away from him. She felt her stomach tighten when she remembered assigning the task to a junior witch. Years later, she understood it had been his way of contributing.

Eurof's only official function was to assist at the annual black rose festival. A festival that flooded the gardens with people from all over the world coming to watch the roses bloom and buy their own to give to their paramours. Black flowers had become the symbol of mystery and eternal love. All the young and not-so-young were crazy about them. Henrietta and the Coven purposely kept the story of their symbolism alive. They were a great source of money and attention for the institution, keeping the more practical research going.

Henrietta swung her legs to the floor, letting her nightgown flow over her bare shins. She watched her ankles and saw the dry skin around her bones. There was a mint salve on her nightstand, but she couldn't be bothered. Not today. She got up, took a little pouch bound with string from the nightstand, and hung it around her neck. Then she walked to the windows and pushed them open, letting in the chilly morning air to freeze the cold room even more.

Outside, the winter birds were chirping loudly. Already preparing for the long, cold days to come. Henrietta walked to the washbowl and cleaned herself in the lukewarm water, which felt horribly icy against her skin. She hurried to dress so as not to catch a cold. She had this bizarre mix of love for the rawness of the chilling air and desire to be warm under the covers. Her husband laughed at her, how she couldn't make up her mind; how she unnecessarily tortured herself, as they had a perfectly functional furnace. But she'd said the cold built character. She would only get used to being pampered and comfortable.

She dressed in practical woolen trousers and a flannel shirt. If she was heading into town, there was a more appropriate outfit in the closet. An enchanted black governess frock, the sort of outfit the public liked to picture the head of the Coven in. Today, she didn't have to leave the Coven. She would go over the annual finances later. Usually, there was nothing major needing her attention, as her financial counselor, Lottie Letcoffin, was adept and thorough. Still, sometimes there were missing receipts. Those would come back to haunt her, and she didn't like to leave a mess for her future self to sort out. Then there was the matter of Petula and the Council. Henrietta took a deep breath and headed out, no more than a few steps from her bedroom door before duty found her.

Imogene waited in the hallway, standing on her tiptoes, appearing to have been there for a while. The student had made herself indispensable, always hurrying to be of service and taking care of day-to-day matters for Henrietta. The things that gave Henrietta a headache and kept her away from her plants and bugs. Gardening was never solely about flowers. That was what most people got wrong when they pictured cultivating the magnificent plants that could cure all ailments. The critters came with it, as they were forever joined together. Find a bloom, and you know there's some special insect to pollinate it. It had taken the great masters of botany a long time to understand this, as who in their wildest dreams could imagine a moth with a tongue twice as long as its body. Through thorough observation, such a strange creature had been found, and the bloom of Dendrophylaz lindenii, the ghost orchid, held no further mystery. The masters' hypothesis was proved right. But it wasn't just about bugs either. It was about money too. Money had to exchange hands for the gardens to thrive.

"Imogene," Henrietta greeted.

"Good morning, Mother." The young girl bowed deep.

Henrietta had corrected Imogene from bowing and using that name too often to care to repeat her distaste for all the deferences. She'd never asked for them, but some seemed to crave the courtesies to give the head witch mystery and power. Henrietta had come to realize they made those who yearned for control, order, and security feel safer in this chaotic world. Henrietta searched for the right words to ask Imogene what she wanted this time. She didn't want to appear ungrateful. Imogene had more than once saved Henrietta's day from turning catastrophic. She didn't have to find the right words. Imogene thrust an envelope into her hands.

"This came for you, Mother. I thought you should see it straight away."

Henrietta frowned and took the letter. Then she saw why the girl had been so anxious. There on the letter was the red signet of the Council. It wasn't unusual for the Council to send letters, but they usually came in thick envelopes with requests for cooperation or reports of joint tasks. This was a small one and was personally addressed to Henrietta.

"Thank you, Imogene."

Henrietta broke the signet, and Imogene nervously stood there, clutching the black apron over her dress. The spots where her knees were already had thick soil stains. She had been in the gardens. Henrietta was jealous. Her days stretched too long into the night for her to wake up at dawn and be with the plants. Imogene would go a long way. She was brilliant when it came to botany. Henrietta was even considering taking her fully under her wing and molding her to be her successor as Wesley had done with her. But Henrietta wasn't sure about Imogene's past. She was her mother's daughter, and Ruby Granger came with the girl. The woman did everything in her power to undermine Henrietta's lead. Then there was the fact that Henrietta suspected Imogene could never leave Necropolis. It was imperative to do field research somewhere else than here. It showed strength of character and the ability to bring something new to the table, and travel to exotic lands opened your eyes like nothing else. Henrietta had become a real witch and naturalist abroad, gaining a better understanding of the whole ecosystem. Now she could draw her powers from the plants as easily as they sucked the moisture out of the air. Plants helped her shape reality to her liking. Henrietta brushed the pouch hanging from her neck. She always carried soil and seeds with her.

Henrietta opened the Council's letter. There was an invitation for her to see someone called Wallace Crowen, an office manager, at the headquarters at two o'clock, and if that time didn't suit her, she was asked to send a new, more suitable time. Also, if she wanted to have a representative with her, she was welcome to do so. The letter also informed her that this was just a meeting to clarify some details. Her hands trembled as she folded the letter again.

"What is it, Mother?" Imogene asked when the silence got too much.

"Oh, nothing important. Just the Council being the Council. Now, is breakfast still being served?" Henrietta gave Imogene a weary smile.

"I saved you a plate."

"Imogene, what would I do without you?"

The young girl followed Henrietta down the stairs to the dining hall. It was a big room that could easily hold a hundred students. But it never did. The Council had somehow managed to control even the number of witches allowed to study at the university under the Coven's care. Some of the witches coming to Necropolis were refugees from countries that saw witchcraft as antisocial behavior. There were mere children in this house who had been tortured with fire, water, and metal just because. Now, they might never become full members of the Coven because the Council saw charts as divine. So, the room never bloomed to its full potential.

Imogene had indeed saved a plate for her. It was left in her spot. Henrietta snatched it and headed to her office after giving Imogene orders to get on with her studies; otherwise, the girl would trail after her the entire day.

Henrietta nibbled the food while she walked to her office, her thoughts looping around the Council's request. Her mind instantly jumped at doomsday thoughts,[1] but of course, this could be just an inquiry about the Coven's day-to-day business. She highly doubted that. They had to know of her involvement with the Save the Otis Group, or perhaps this was about her refusal to send them more hexers. Too many had already died on their overseas missions.

Henrietta drew her study door open and stepped in. A huge desk waited for her. Behind it rose three high windows with zigzagging wood paneling. Around the room were flowers, soil, seeds, and insect specimens. Some alive, some dried, and some inside test tubes. Her favorite one was on the windowsill. It was a small terrarium with a lizard inside it. The lizard was native to Amanita. It was a Leopard Gecko. She had fallen in love with the nocturnal animal, the little spotted yellow dragon-lizard. It should be sleeping in its hideaway. Last night, after the needlepoint group, Nestor had kept her company with its constant chatter on her shoulder as she went over the garden's acquisition forms.

Henrietta headed to her desk and flipped open her schedule book. She could easily visit the Council at two o'clock. She sat down and penned a letter telling them she could meet at one.

Now that she thought about it, the summons had to be about her having asked Percy Allread about the machine. She'd expected some form of retaliation, but to be requested to enter the belly of the beast full of clerks, accountants, and lawyers hadn't crossed her mind. It should have, as what the clerks, lawyers, and accountants did inside that building was real magic. Their ability to multiply papers, procedures, and employees was

---

1. You know, those nasty little buggers that invade your head without asking permission and shake your underlying belief in the goodness of the world, other people, and yourself.

spookier than anything she as a witch could do. And office managers were the scariest of the bunch. They constantly had to come up with new, clever ploys to seem important and busy.

Henrietta took a concentrated pause and massaged her temples. If the Council managed to constrain her, to make her abolish the group, or accused her of treason for talking to her own hexer, then the needlepoint group's only hope was Petula. The necromancer had to deliver. Henrietta drew her pen station closer and began writing instructions for Imogene on what she should do if something were to happen to her.

There should be solace in order. It should shield one from the uncertainty of life. It could, but for order to function, it demanded belief, as disorder, chaos, change, and death had a habit of sneaking into perfectly laid plans. Often the chaos dribbled in from outside, but on rare occasions, the disturbance began from inside, at first with doubt, then with restlessness, and finally with a collapse.

Percy was back at his desk the next morning, having gotten only a few hours of shut-eye. He looked at the ledgers detailing the upper management's lunch expenses. His heart wasn't in it. Usually, the pattern the numbers created lulled him into this meditative state where the line between his skin and the world of arithmetic fused into one. Not today. Last night echoed inside him, making his whole body feel hollow. He couldn't shake off the feeling something wasn't right. Percy forced himself to focus on the sums.

"Mr. Allread?" a joyless voice asked behind him.

He turned in his seat to face an undead man standing behind him. He wore a plain black suit and a gray bowtie, clutching a folder under his arm. The first finger on his right hand was missing, but otherwise, the man was well preserved. He even had a thin head of hair, which had been trimmed short and combed back. His dull eyes seemed to follow Percy's every movement, reminding Percy that any undead had the ability to kill you with their bare hands. It was easy to forget such a thing in a city that had more undead than those alive.

"Yes, how can I help you, sir?" Percy stood up and bowed. He expected the man's folder to contain more expenses to be added up, ignoring his intuition insisting this wasn't the case.

"Could you come with me?" the undead asked.

Percy was about to say he was in the middle of his calculations, but he stopped himself. Instead, he said, "Just give me a second, sir." He closed the ledgers, drew the desk drawer open, and put his unfinished work there, locking the ledgers securely away. He slipped the key into his vest pocket. The undead observed Percy's every move as he followed the Council's protocol to the letter.

The undead grunted.

Percy followed the man out of the office past his fellow accountants. He could feel their eyes on him and hear their whispers. He wasn't sure if they thought he would get a raise and recommendation or be sacked. Everything had been off-balance ever since he got back to the accounting department.

They passed his manager's booth. The woman eyed him. Prior to everything that had happened with Otis, Percy had barely existed at all to the woman, and now she despised him. She'd made it loud and clear. Percy had always preferred the sense of not existing. He had never been one to make a fuss about himself. He left that to more capable hands. His twin sister, Margot, had always preferred to be the star of the show. He had been her shadow until they had been separated after their mother's death. She had been taken by their grandpa and he by their grandmother to watch the sea. They were briefly joined together at the Coven. But even there, their paths had been different. She was more gifted with omens and he with hexes.

The undead took him out of the accounting department. Percy made as little noise as he could going up the stairs to the upper, upper floors, where *the Council* met. Percy tried not to think about the direction they were heading and followed the man in silence. The undead pushed two huge mahogany doors open, letting him into a dimly lit room. The dark, heavy curtains were drawn shut, and Percy had to blink several times to see that human shapes were sitting around an oval table.

The undead guided him to the front of the room. He could barely see anything, but he noticed that the figures seated at the table had covered their faces with hoods. Percy realized he was looking at *the board*. He'd never heard of anyone working for the Council being summoned up here.

"Take a seat, Mr. Allread," the undead said, indicating a chair just behind him.

"I'd rather stand, if that is fine with you," Percy replied.

The undead grunted, and Percy heard murmurs going around the table.

The undead retreated to the doors, drawing them shut. With his hexes, Percy detected that the man had stayed in the room. He didn't dare to send them further to get a better feel of the board members. It would be sacrilege.

"We can begin," someone said. It sounded a lot like a man. Percy hung on to any piece of information he could get to make sense of this, even though this particular detail didn't give him any clue what in holy Kraken was going on. But his mind hungered for something to latch on to. Otherwise, the room was a dark pit. The only light that had crept in was from the opened doors, and now they were nailed shut. The trained hunter in him waited for his eyes to adjust to the darkness. The instincts molded to protect the institution he loved.

Percy said nothing. He waited for them to speak so he could respond accordingly. If they sanctioned him, so be it. The Council was in the right.

"We appreciate all you have done," a new board member started. This one sounded androgynous. Sometimes this meant an undead, as their speech pattern changed as social expectations stopped influencing the pitch of their voice, but it lacked the usual gasping tone of the dead. Again, the tiny details did him no favors.

The person continued, "But you have left us in a pickle. You see, Mr. Allread, you have become quite notorious. Again, I have to stress that the board values your efforts to stop the machine and to bring Otis Thurston here, but at the same time, we here at the Council honor obscurity as our modus operandi. It's what keeps us alive and functional. We are the body of the Necromantic Council. You included, Mr. Allread. We are not individuals. We serve."

Percy waited a little longer to see if they would continue. He wasn't sure if it had been a threat or not. He was here to serve. The Council was right. He had become notorious. But clearly not notorious enough not to be here. Maybe Alvira had been right in suggesting that he attend all the social gatherings he had been invited to.

"Yes," he said. He could hear a slight gasp. "I mean, yes, I'm here to serve. As for the notoriety part, I..." Percy wanted to say he was helpless against all the attention he was getting, but helpless wasn't a word he wanted the board to associate with him. "I want nothing to do with the publicity I have received. I have refused to give any interviews or attend any social events I have been invited to. It's harming my ability to do my work as a hunter. I just wish Mr. Thurston hadn't mentioned me personally in his initial statement. His word shouldn't have gotten around."

Percy kept staring into the darkness. He wasn't good at this. He had never taken part in office politics, and now he had been pushed in the deep end for having done his duty. But the board knew best; he had to trust them.

"We trust you to keep it that way," the man who had spoken first replied. "What worries the board as well is that we heard Mrs. Culpepper contacted you."

"You are correct, sir." Percy put his hands behind his back. He could work with this. He knew he had done the right thing in reporting the meeting with Mother.

"And?" The man corrected his posture. He was third on the left, closest to the door. There were six altogether.

Percy glanced at the undead who'd escorted him here. If any emotions were at work inside the man, he didn't let them show.

"Mother wanted to know about Mr. Thurston's arrest and the machine he was creating overseas," Percy replied, despite knowing the Mother part could offend. But it was the correct term.

The man took a deep breath in. "Yes, we saw the report. What we would like is to hear it in your own words."

"As soon as I arrived at the Coven's Necro Botanical Gardens and entered the main building, I was greeted by Mother. She escorted me into the tea parlor, offering me refreshments. After the niceties, she asked me about Mr. Thurston and the machine. I declined to speak about the matter as politely as I could. Then I left and came straight here to report the events." He left out the wolf part and the cake and honey he had taken with him. Not sure why.

"That was all?" the androgynous voice asked. The person to whom it belonged sat farthest from him, on the right side of the table. Almost in the corner. Percy instantly recognized a kindred spirit who was used to covering all the exits. It was the spot Percy would have taken, given that there was no fear of gargoyles coming crashing through the windows.

"Yes." Percy unclasped his hands behind his back and let them fall next to his body, showing his open palms to the board.

"Thank you, Mr. Allread. That's enough. We advise you to continue doing what you are doing, not giving any interviews or accepting any invitations. Also, we would consider it an act of loyalty if you refrained from going to the Coven for the time being," the androgynous voice said.

"Yes, sir," he said, despite the boldness of the request. It was Percy's given right to visit the Coven. A witch without other witches was a disaster waiting to happen. It was the others who kept you away from cackling and poisoning apples. As a hexer, he was in the most danger of letting corruption pull him under. The only way Percy had kept his sanity and integrity was by following the rules. Otherwise... He didn't even want to think what would happen if he let his curses do all the talking.

"Mr. Crowen will show you out."

And that was it. The undead instantly appeared next to Percy, startling him. The undead guided him out through the same doors he had come in, taking him back to his desk, observing Percy closely the whole time.

"Mr. Allread," the undead said, nodded, and turned to leave.

Percy watched the man go, seeing the other accountants glancing at them. They clearly wanted to ask questions, but no one did. Percy wasn't exactly comfortable with casual conversations, and everyone knew that. Others seemed to enjoy the activity, constantly sharing what their daughters and sons were up to, what they ate for dinner, and who they went out to have a pint with. All of which made him uneasy. He understood it served a purpose. Studies showed that gossip and chatter increased productivity. Still, somehow it felt against the rules. To him, the room and the gaze of his manager demanded quietness. Percy drew the key out of his vest pocket and pushed it into the drawer's lock. He paused. His hand froze there, unable to turn the key. He could still sense some of his coworkers' attention on him, as if waiting to see if he would go mental. Percy expected Garry from two booths over to have a bet going. He always did. Percy drew the key out, slipped it back into his pocket, and stood up. The silence of the room carried that observant pressure of unspoken thoughts. Percy took it all in. The outside world didn't define him. His values and tasks made him who he was, and he would act according to them. He walked out of the room, maybe more stiffly than he normally would have. His manager followed him with her gaze but didn't intercept his flight. The room exploded with noise as soon as the door shut after him.

He got up one flight of stairs and turned left at the doors where Alvira's office would be. All around him were the gentle rustle of papers and the susurrus of conversations. He barely paid attention to the clerks going past him. He had to see her. The door to Alvira's office was open, and the vampire was on the floor gathering papers. Her office looked ransacked.

Alvira narrowed her eyes and hissed when she saw him. "You did this!"

Percy braced for the anger to come, kneeling to help the vampire clean up her office.

CHAPTER EIGHT

WHAT DOES THE TYRANT DREAM?

I f it was up to the individual, everything would be a lot simpler, even down to the model of the wheel. Annoyingly, it was proposed that it shouldn't be up to the individual, especially when it came to the government; nor was it about the individual. It was about the many, making everything a whole lot more complicated.

Petula turned to her side, watching the pale sunrise, wishing she could just go on sleeping. The thin curtains swayed as the cold got into the building from the single-paned windows. Petula could feel her breath. She drew the blanket over her. Any second now, a maid would come in to heat the furnace and draw her a bath. Then she would have to go back to the Town Hall, and everything would start all over again.

If it was just her, things would be different. But the Council existed, Henrietta and the Coven wanted more, and somehow she had to fit the people into that equation. If she thought herself already dead, maybe she could feel free to do as she pleased. It wasn't so far from the truth. There would come a time when a necromancer came to challenge her to a duel, and she wouldn't be prepared.

Petula shut her eyes and massaged her temples. A governmental resurrection service might balance out the control the Council had over the city. It was something Minta had already started, but it had been forgotten in the basement. She penned a visit into her mental calendar. A visit she would make just before meeting with the Council.

She pretended to sleep as the maid carefully opened the door to her room. She kept her eyes just open enough to see the girl lay her walking skirt, white shirt, waistcoat, and laced boots on the armchair next to the copper bathtub. Lastly, the girl laid her white undergarments and a corset on the clothes. Petula wondered if the maid had added new fine stitching to them. A skull here, a bone there, and a coffin here and there. She watched the girl work her way around the room, taking trips in and out of the open door, carrying in the bathwater. In the past, Petula had insisted on helping. That had upset the order of things, and she'd stopped.

Petula let her mind wander into the calculations of her experimentations, especially to the vial Cruxh had given her. The only thing she'd proved thus far was that the black liquid, the essence of ghouls, wasn't demonic. Cruxh had been relieved to hear that. But she needed more time if she were to find out what it truly was; not to mention time to practice necromancy. It baffled her how Dow, or anyone else for that matter, expected her to continue to be the best necromancer there was to stay alive as their mayor if she couldn't read and practice the latest findings.

"Miss," came a careful voice.

Petula yawned. Even though she had woken on her own, she still felt as if she hadn't slept at all. It had been the sleep of one who had too few hours in the day to be and do. The cat was curled next to Petula, and she eyed the maid as if she'd disturbed its rein. Petula scratched Her on the back of its neck. The spot it liked. Her closed its eyes and permitted Petula to get up to let the maid help her into the bath. There was something to be said for being immersed in hot water. It was poetry for the soul, especially with a good book. If there was something Petula was never willing to give up, it was this. She wasn't made for living rough at the monster hunter camps as her predecessor had been. Sometimes she wondered if her bookish smarts were a lousy substitute for the wit and strength of Minta Stopford. She had been reading the woman's plans for Necropolis, and the department for governmental resurrection services had been just the beginning of how Minta was going to free the city from its predators. But everything that's perfect will end. Petula had learned the constant flux of human nature made sure of that.

The maid helped her up from the bath and wrapped her in a linen towel, drying and dressing Petula. Petula's ghostly white hair was combed, and the loose front curls were tied up with a black velvet ribbon. She was ready. She ate her breakfast during the coach ride to the Town Hall. Petula had her tea in a blue porcelain cup with a golden rim. She nursed it between her hands, watching the city pass by. This was her home. Those were her people. She, damn Kraken, was going to be a tyrant for them.[1]

"Ma'am." Dow bowed once Petula got out of the coach.

"Dow," she said, handing him the cup, and strode into the building.

The secretary took it without blinking. "Mr. Porter visited us last night..."

"Let me guess, he wants me to give him an exclusive interview."

"Yes, ma'am."

"Haven't we spoken about all this ma'am stuff?"

"I think there was a mention of it at some point."

"Good, keep that in mind."

"If you wish, ma'am."

Petula glanced at her secretary. The man looked back with a straight face.

"What else?" Petula asked.

"The Council has summoned Mrs. Culpepper to its offices."

---

1. Not that they asked her to. Also, some might say that such thoughts were condemned to fail. Who was anyone to know what was good for others? Not without listening, and perhaps not without walking in their boots. Imagination could be ever so limited.

"Why?" Petula could feel her heart racing.

"The letter was sealed."

"I see," Petula said, not believing anything could be sealed from Dow.

She shifted her focus from the secretary to the older woman minding the front desk.

"Good morning, Elvira." Petula nodded. The woman sucked her teeth and nodded back. Petula wasn't sure what to make of the woman. She'd tried her biscuits once. They were as hard as cobblestones. You could build an entire house with them. Petula grimacing had made the woman shine with happiness. A stormbringer of misery, that was what her coworkers said about her. But she happened to be Petula's strombringer, guarding the front door against unwanted pests. And sometimes Petula thought the woman liked her. Every time she baked a new batch of biscuits, she made a special effort to save Petula a serving. Petula had heard the others in the office hid theirs inside flowerpots and filing cabinets, and some took them home and buried them in their back gardens for fear of Elvira's scorn.

Today there was no tin.

Petula turned her attention back to Dow. "Summon Mr. Porter. It's high time I give him that interview he so desires. Get me a meeting with the Council. Tell them I want to meet Mr. Thurston."

"As you wish, ma'am." Again, there was no expression on the secretary's face. "Do you want me to draw a statement?" Dow added.

"No, I'll be fine. Make sure Mr. Porter is here before the noon paper. And make sure my time to meet with the Council is at three, not before."

"Ma'am?"

"Dow, I need this."

"As you wish, ma'am."

Dow handed her the penned itinerary and stepped aside.

Petula continued to her office, dropped the itinerary on her desk, and left it there to be ignored. She took out Minta's outline for the resurrection services. She read it through three times, corrected the assumptions she didn't agree with, wrote her own opinions into the margins, and then transcribed the new proposal. Petula glanced at the pocket watch she drew from her waistcoat and frowned. It was time. Before she could put it back, Dow was at the door.

"All set?" Petula asked.

"Mr. Porter is here, ma'am."

"He was fast." Petula stood up and smoothed her skirt. "Hand me my coat."

"Ma'am?" Dow asked.

It was too late to change her mind now. She thought about being already dead and felt a whole lot less restless. "A field day," Petula replied.

"I see." Dow helped her slide the thick woolen coat on.

Petula glanced at Her sleeping on the couch under the window. The cat looked content. So she left Her there and stepped out of the office. Mr. Porter waited downstairs, as was customary. Not too far from him, Mr. Colton—the weasel-looking man, Petula's personal bodyguard—kept a close eye on the man. A man who had tossed around words like ineffective, elitist, and bookish when describing Petula and her decision-making. She remembered, and clearly, so did Mr. Colton. If given the go-ahead, she was certain the bodyguard would cut him open. Petula was sure he winked at her just so she would nod and let him loose.

"Mr. Porter," Petula greeted, ignoring the weasel-looking man.

The reporter jumped up from the couch, instantly alert. He scanned her from head to toe, confused.

"Follow me, Mr. Porter. We are going out," Petula said as if it would explain everything. She heard Dow grinding his teeth, or she thought she did. Not that anyone else in the room would have detected the slight change of tone in the absence of noise coming from her secretary. But she had spent enough time with the man to know what his silences meant. Mr. Colton wasn't happy either. His whole posture tensed as he observed Petula and R.E. Porter, who took off his hat and bowed and then hurried after the mayor.

"Where are we heading, miss?" the man asked.

"You will see when we arrive, and in the meantime, you can ask your questions."

There was a flash of confusion on the man's face again, but it soon turned into a smile. The reporter hurried his steps to keep up with her.

Outside, the morning rain had ended, and there was just the cold wind blowing from the sea. It sent shivers down Petula's spine. She was sure there was more to it than there should be. As if someone was whispering her name. "Flesh and bone. Made from things that break," the voice seemed to add. Petula shook her head, and the voice was gone.

"Ma'am?" Mr. Porter asked. He looked bewildered, as if Petula had missed something.

"I'm sorry, Mr. Porter. Do ask me again."

"Mr. Thurston's trial has stirred necromancers to protest against the Council. What do you think of that?" the reporter asked.

"I have to be honest, Mr. Porter, the situation is confusing. The Necromantic Council is doing its duty by preventing future necromantic wars. If Mr. Thurston did indeed set a flock of restless spirits free overseas, it could have been the start of a major catastrophe, not to mention an international conflict. But what people are asking, and you are asking me to answer, is about the rules and regulations and if they are too strict. Clearly, the notion resonates with most Necropolitans. So it's an important conversation we should have."

R.E. Porter tilted his head ever so slightly.

Petula had gotten better at reading people. She never imagined she would, but Dow had insisted on coaching her on what to see and think about public affairs. Suddenly, she'd learned to detect all the nuances in social situations, to play the room to her liking. She'd found silence, listening, and speaking only when she felt it necessary were confusingly powerful tools. R.E. Porter was doing just that. And not some bullshit listening people pretended to do. The real deal, allowing anyone to talk without fretting about what to say next. She could so easily let him sweep her into his slight change of posture and plough on carelessly. The trouble with Mr. Porter was that he used his power of listening against his targets. Petula knew that.

Petula collected her thoughts, dwelling in the uncomfortable silence. She'd already said plenty to be used for and against her. Petula adopted a relaxed expression—not entirely a smile, but not a resting bitch face either—[2] as Dow had taught her to do while rearranging her thoughts.

"What I'm trying to say is, I find it hard to form my opinion, as I haven't been able to hear Mr. Thurston's account of the events."

Mr. Porter's eyes sparkled. He thought he had gotten his headline. Petula watched as the man's posture changed. She could smell yesterday's alcohol on his breath. Petula thought the man had stopped drinking, or so she'd heard, but she guessed old habits died hard.

Mr. Porter tensed up and smoothed his short dark beard under her gaze.

The coach arrived, and both of them used that time to take a break from the social interaction. Dow followed them inside, sitting next to Petula. He took his notebook out and penned something into it.

"Take us to Necrology Street," Petula ordered the driver.

The coach shook as Mr. Colton got up next to the driver, and they were finally on their way.

"Are we...?" Mr. Porter started.

---

2. The wonderful accusation women got when they were just being relaxed and themselves, especially in those situations where the other person wasn't really saying anything to merit a smile. You know.

"No, we are not going to the Necromantic Council's headquarters." Petula interrupted the reporter. Before the man could demand an explanation again, Petula continued, "I have been going over Miss Stopford's proposals for Necropolis. Her previously implemented projects have done well. In particular, our reformed healthcare system and police force have shown what trust and service mean. Individuals like Mr. Cruxh and Hortensia Caster are wonderful examples of this new line of policing. I want to understand what more our former leader had to offer. I'm going to allocate more funds to the Public Resurrection Ministration she set up a few years ago, which happens to be at the Ministry of Public Works and Home Ministry opposite the Council's headquarters."

The reporter froze. All of them knew she'd just declared war. One that might get her killed. It wasn't unknown for the Council to put a bounty on the leader's head and make sure the right kind of necromancer went for it. According to Dow, Minta had been proud of the sum of her bounty, which was astronomical. In a sick way, the Council owed Petula that money; she'd defeated Minta, after all. Nevertheless, the declaration had been made, and there was no taking back her words.

The silly thing was that the whole effort on her part was a long shot. Until now, the resurrection service had been forgotten—literally left in the basement. It was where the second-rate necromancers went to enjoy a quiet existence with nothing but tea and tabloids for company. And it was worse than Petula had feared. The small, worn-out door with blue paint chipping off led to the department to revolutionize the whole city. As soon as it was opened, they were greeted with a cloud of dust. Petula held her breath as she stepped into the basement. She was engulfed in the thick smell of tobacco and the blackest of black coffee. Narrow steps led down into the darkness towards the only light in the middle of the room, where three desks had been pushed together as if to guard against only Kraken knew what lurked in the shadows. Petula could feel whatever was there, hiding and feeding on the desperation in the air. It was like that plaguing sense of worthlessness that gnawed at your insides. A demon, most likely. The three workers ignored the sensation, playing cards, reading a book, and drinking their coffee to stay awake. Petula slowly made her way down the stairs that could give in at any minute. Their wood was half rotten and had been patched in so many places, there was no telling what had been the original design.

Petula coughed. Only the young boy straight out of the university jumped up, trying to hide the deck of cards in his hands. The woman in her mid-forties barely lifted an eyebrow, and the older man, something of a legend if Petula remembered correctly, didn't react at all. He just sat with his back to the door. Once they got closer, the woman got up, and so did the older man, rather slowly. If memory served Petula right, the man once had a glorious job at the Council, but he had publicly criticized the Council and its practice of profiting by resurrecting the underclass citizens. He had been fired for it. Discreetly, of course. Not that discretion was necessary. Everyone knew he was right, but there was nothing anyone could do. The Council made sure it got your money, no matter how poor you were. If the resurrected or their family couldn't pay, they were sent to the factories, and their salaries were slashed in half to repay the cost of being brought back to life. And there were a lot of families who needed their daughters, mothers, sons, and fathers to be resurrected to make ends meet.

"Mayor." The manager bowed.

Petula stifled the laughter wanting to come out. The newly resurrected resurrection service looked like she'd brought with her the dawn of an apocalypse. The young, lanky necromancer just out of the university with hypochondriac tendencies tried not to wiggle around. The woman looked at her with a solemn expression. And the man knew exactly what was about to come. But Petula had to give her little speech to sign her death warrant. So the script went, and she couldn't take it back.

"Afternoon, everyone," Petula started. "You may sit down. We don't need to be too formal about this inspection I asked Mr. Corpsewood to arrange." Petula nodded towards the older man.

"No, ma'am," the older man agreed and ushered everyone to sit down. "The mayor has graciously promised to aid our little department." The man tested the waters.

"Yes, as we discussed with Mr. Corpsewood, the government will allocate more money to your department so new hires can be made and new services can be added. This will happen as of tomorrow. The mandate will stay the same. You are to aid those without the means for resurrection, whose families need them to come back alive to work..." Petula went on, giving a detailed account of how the department would serve the city.

The last thing said in the basement was, "That's that then," as the door shut after Petula and the rest. Money was set to arrive, changes had been promised, and new policies were on their way. No one liked change, despite how excruciating the boredom, wrongdoing, and haunting thoughts about worthlessness were. Everything had been written down, and it would all be proclaimed in today's news. Petula was sure she had heard the reporter mutter under his breath the whole time, "Are you sure?"

She was sure. She would be free from the Council one way or another, and she would do the right thing. Whatever that right thing was supposed to be. No one seemed to agree on that. Not even with things like how to fold your socks or even whether to wear them. Humans were peculiar that way.

No system functioned without black-and-white documents. They made everything spin in a serious fashion with a hint of doom, looming over you if they weren't taken seriously. But behind it all they made matters less about the thing in question and more about the proper protocol. It was like arriving to collect your package with the right identification to prove the package is yours and still leaving empty handed because the system is riddled with bugs and the right box can't be ticked. So with the right kind of documentation, the impossible could be made possible and the other way around.

Henrietta crossed one knee over the other. She concentrated all her effort to appear unfazed at being summoned into the heart of the Council. She had taken her seat in front of Wallace Crowen's office. Somewhere in the building, Otis Thurston was under lock and key. Henrietta need only stretch her powers through the wooden floors and worm her way into the walls to sniff out where the necromancer was being kept, but that would open up another can of worms, and Henrietta wasn't yet willing to go that far. She contented herself with listening to the building moan, complaining about the new residents. It still remembered the time it had been a library. Now, inside the building everything followed a set of rules, with every second monitored, and with lots and lots of memos. Meanwhile, time ground to a halt, as if the whole building was slowly sucking the life out of those stuck in its belly. Life disappeared into the cracks in the walls, into the documents, into the endless coffee cups.

Henrietta shuddered and glanced at her pocket watch. The meeting was running late—as if it was the rule of law in every institution. You could say the little chaos of life sneaked in, making the tick of the bureaucrat run late. Henrietta smiled the smile of someone who appreciated it whenever chaos made human seriousness less tangible. She smiled despite being stuck in a place which made a mockery out of existing. Henrietta couldn't understand how her witches preferred working here. Witchery was about creativity, connection, and understanding. This place churned out mindless drones, forbidding flexibility of the mind. The idea that this was what the Council imagined the whole world to look like made Henrietta want to scream. Witches weren't meant to be paper pushers; few were. But Henrietta would be lying to herself if she thought numbers didn't matter. They had taken over everything, simplifying interactions into manageable bites.

There were all sorts of witches. As the reverent Mother, she was more than aware that some loved order, numbers, and office cubicles more than they should. Sometimes she wondered why such people were the ones who had taken over the world and not the other way around. Was it the fault of those like her who devoted their lives to plants, art, and people? Bat's flight, she knew people like Lottie Letcoffin and her army of clerks made Henrietta's life easier by sorting out the gardens' financial matters. Once a month, she and Lottie drank tea long into the night and played a game of chess over the Coven's expenditures. Henrietta was never sure which one of them won; maybe the Coven as a whole. But she also knew such existence made the core of a person ever so alienated. This was why she kept her witches away from the Council. Her rebellion wasn't all about the power dynamics. She had seen what this place did to her kind. A place where factuality meant nothing, as reality could be reinterpreted with charts, forms, and numbers to bring forth whatever the Council desired. Maybe not a place as uncreative as she had initially thought.

Mr. Crowen's door opened a minute past the quarter. Sixteen minutes past the agreed-upon time. Still the perfect time. The time when people are almost ready to give up and leave, yet linger there for that last second of hope that their commitment hasn't been in vain.[3] Henrietta was sure the man had stood behind his door with a clock in his hand, not taking any chances with his mind games.

---

3. That nasty trick of the brain called sunk cost fallacy, which makes people do weird things like throwing good money after bad because... No one really understands the because part, except social psychologists, who keep their mouths shut.

"Mr. Crowen, I presume," Henrietta said before the man could make a sound. She had seen his name in the documents received from the Council but never had a face to match it. Mr. Crowen was an undead. He wore a black suit, and underneath it, a white shirt enchanted with a purple bowtie.

"Mrs. Culpepper," the undead greeted, stepping aside from the doorway and giving her room to come in.

Henrietta made no attempt to hurry. She sat there as serenely as she could, slowly getting up, giving the man a view of *the* Mother in all her glory. Henrietta had worn her black lace dress, which shaped her robust figure to impress. She would have preferred to come here dressed in her gardening clothes, but then the Council might think the Mother wasn't taking this seriously.

Politics.

"Do come in, Mrs. Culpepper." Mr. Crowen gestured.

Henrietta smiled as nicely as she could and walked in past the man. The room was spacious, with a luxurious window looking to the streets of Necropolis, where the undead and their kind shuffled on to keep the city spinning. In front of the window was an oak desk, and behind it, the wall was full of filing cabinets. Henrietta stood, taking in the room and waiting to be invited to sit down, like a vampire would before entering a house. All superstition, but some foreigners liked the idea, finding comfort in it. What good did that do? A vampire could just knock on the front door, give a wide grin, hand over a pamphlet about resurrection and eternal youth, and that was that. Nonetheless, Henrietta didn't wait for any superstitious reasons. She waited for the proper protocol to be fulfilled to keep herself out of trouble here in the house of rules.

"Do sit down," Mr. Crowen said bluntly, indicating the chair in front of the desk.

Henrietta took the seat, gathering her hem before sitting down. She arranged herself so she could sit up straight in the uncomfortable clothes.

"How can the Coven be of help, Mr. Crowen?" Henrietta asked.

The undead's dead eyes were emotionless as he took his seat. He coughed, and Henrietta saw a bug pass from one side of his mouth to the other. It was one of those beetles taxidermists in the city had bred to eat any larvae trying to devour the dead flesh. The usual maggots involved with dying had made a nasty evolutionary jump a few years ago, becoming immune to formaldehyde and other embalming fluids, and actually having started to enjoy them a great deal. Any zoolingualist would tell you that the embalming oils got the maggots high, and it was only a matter of time before they got the bright idea to take charge of said body in a quest to find a brownie to eat. The taxidermists had been battling against them ever since. Henrietta couldn't quite remember who had actually come up with the beetles. Estela something.

"I'm afraid, reverent Mother, that this is more about what the Coven hasn't done. The Council has some concerns over the legal agreements we have with you. Some of the contracts haven't been fulfilled. Do you care to comment on that?" Mr. Crowen straightened his bowtie.

Henrietta suppressed the laughter wanting to come out. "I'm afraid you need to clarify." She knew exactly what the man meant. She had expected to get a call on the matter. Not now and not this way and not personally, but nevertheless, a demand for an explanation.

"You have refused to send your yearly quota of witches to serve under the Council. What is the hold-up? We are completely baffled by the situation. I have personally checked, and it appears that the Council has followed the contract fully. The annual payments have been paid on time. We have sent representatives to the university to speak about working for the Council. We have even allowed the witches to form their union inside the Council per your request. It's their right not to form one, and it's evident that they clearly don't want one. We have done all we can to fulfill your additions to the contract. But now I hear that you have pressured witches to quit and refused our representatives entry to the Coven. We are highly concerned about the situation. Not only because of the contract we have with you but because of the damage it does to our relationship and respect for each other. The Council has battled with how to respond to said actions, and I have been advised to say that per our agreement, the Council can stop all payments to the Coven." The man went straight for the kill.

Henrietta fought the urge to cross her arms and stare the man down. She set her hands on her lap, palms up, knowing she had to play this carefully, not giving him anything more to use against her. The Council was their biggest benefactor, and if the money stopped coming in, it would put the whole Coven on the brink of bankruptcy. Teaching witches wasn't exactly free, and the heating expenses of the glasshouses took most of the budget. She'd expected them to threaten the Coven this way, but Henrietta had counted on having time to persuade Petula to give the Coven an allowance. It was just that the mayor had wiggled out of such conversations every time Henrietta had approached her.

Henrietta took a deep breath in and said, "But there's a clause in the agreement stating that if there's a reason to worry about the safety of the witches, the leader of the Coven can cease providing witches for the Council. And according to my calculations, last year alone, five witches died in Necropolis while on duty and seventeen overseas. Those are my witches, and some of the families don't even know why their children died. Neither does the Coven. It's unacceptable. We sent you twenty fresh graduates last year, and twenty-two witches in your employment died; you are losing more witches than we send. Until my witches' work safety is addressed and the number of deaths and disfigurements decreases, I can't send you a single witch." Henrietta crossed her arms.

The undead narrowed his eyes for a millisecond, but then the expressionless face came back. Mr. Crowen cleared his throat. "We will look into the numbers and get back to you. But the Council finds this situation insufferable. It's harming our day-to-day tasks, not to mention putting already existing workers at risk when they can't rely on us to send them help."

"That's your responsibility to fix. Not mine. I have to look after my witches."

"You could have contacted us."

"I did. I sent letter after letter, but all I got was the standard reply from you, that the deaths of those witches are classified. That's unacceptable. They are my witches." Henrietta readied herself to stand up and leave.

The undead shook his head. "And how about your political commentary on Mr. Thurston's trial and the Save the Otis Group's demands? Those are also against the contract the Council and the Coven have with each other. According to our mutual agreement, both parties should refrain from inflammatory statements. You are—"

"I have to cut you off there, Mr. Crowen. The Coven is part of Necropolis, and we have a right to discuss the concerns of the citizens. The Coven hasn't condemned your actions; all it has done is question the discontent Necropolitans are feeling over the possible execution of Mr. Thurston and how it affects those in the Coven. My witches are scared that they could also be hunted, arrested, and hanged just because the Council sees fit. As I said before, Mr. Crowen, I'll defend my witches and their health." Not everyone in the Coven agreed with her, but what was done was done.

"Still, I have to remind you that our relationship demands a certain respect. You could have addressed these issues with us rather than have a public discussion," the undead said in a dry voice. "You leave me no other choice than to proceed with the task I was given. I have to sanction the Coven for the breach of contract in the amount of a hundred thousand gold pieces. The sanctions and seized payments will be fulfilled at the end of this month if you don't send us your witches."

"But—"

"I'm afraid, reverent Mother, the sanctions have been set in motion. While you think you have acted for noble reasons, contract law is to be held in the greatest esteem."

"But—"

"You should have contacted us, and this could have been avoided. We will give you a month's time to repay and avoid all this unpleasantness."

"I did contact you!" Henrietta squeezed her hands hard against the chair's armrests. That was more money than she had expected. It was exactly the amount it took to upkeep the gardens for a year. She didn't have that kind of cash lying around.

"Clearly not the right department."

The chair underneath Henrietta shook. Tiny leaves were sprouting out of it.

The undead managed to raise an eyebrow, forcing Henrietta to remember where she was and what could be done if she didn't control her temper. This was absurd. The man knew it as well as she did. She and the Coven had done nothing wrong. She had looked over the fine print, and she had a right to protect her witches.

"Of course, you can take this up with the courts," the undead added.

"What good does that do? You own the courts," Henrietta let out.

If there was a smirk, it was just a tremble of the tight lips, and only a tiny one.

"The Council is a—"

"Spare me, Mr. Crowen. Clearly, you decided how to write this narrative before I even set foot in your office. The Coven won't pay you a dime." Henrietta rose.

Mr. Crowen coughed. "If you see fit not to pay, then you must do as your conscience tells you."

Henrietta slammed her hands on the table, startling the undead.

The undead shook it off quickly and harrumphed before stating, "May I remind you that any physical threat is seen as an attack against the Council. I also want to point out that when cooperation returns to normal, all the charges are going to be dropped. That said..." The man took a pause. "It has come to the Council's attention that you have been taking in unsanctioned witches. We have been told they are refugees from abroad. The Council might overlook the fact if the stipulated changes are made, along with refraining from prying into Council matters through the witches working here. Any such attempts will be seen as treason, and such persons will either be removed from their duty or sentenced for life."

Henrietta could feel her hands shaking. She asked with a tight voice, "And how long do I have until you take action?"

"The board thought a week to be sufficient for the Coven to agree on a reply."

"I'll be contacting you in a week's time. Good day, Mr. Crowen."

The man stood up, and nothing much was said after that. Wallace Crowen escorted her to the door, holding it open. As soon as Henrietta was out of the building and on her couch, she screamed into a decorative pillow. The last part about the Coven agreeing had been a direct threat to remove her from her position. She didn't have the whole Coven's approval. There were factions who were more than willing to align with the Council. The fact that she had done all this for the Coven wouldn't matter. All the freedoms she'd gained would be sold away, and the Necro Botanical Gardens would be taken back to the stone ages. Ruby Granger, Imogene's mother, would happily let the refugees be drowned, burned, and hanged and leave those with talent without education and guidance, despite knowing how dangerous raw potential could be. All the woman cared for was power. The innocent should never suffer in the hands of ignorance. For that matter, no one should. Henrietta promised as much to herself.

CHAPTER NINE

THERE'S NO HIDING UNDER THE DESK FROM THE DOOMED FUTURE

There is this pathological need for reaction with humanoids. Percy would attest to that. Percy knelt to help Alvira collect all the files and items tossed to the office floor. The vampire snorted as she shuffled the papers into the right stacks. When all was done, she headed to her desk, carrying her share. She dropped the files on the desk with a loud thud. Then she took a tobacco bag and rolled a cigarette. She lit it while she let Percy continue tidying up the office, lifting the fallen cabinets and straightening the knocked-over chairs. For a second, Percy wondered if he should use his hexes to summon imps to aid him, but he didn't. The little demons were more prone to chaos than tidying. They were easily bored, unreliable, and toothy.[1] Percy had used them in Threebeanvalley to catch Otis, but it had come with a price.

Alvira watched him work. She took a long drag, and as she exhaled, she let out a perfect circle. "Whatever you did, and I don't want to know, you'd better not do it again," she said.

Percy lifted the last files scattered behind a cabinet and carefully laid them on his handler's invoice box. The smell of tobacco brought back his

---

1. Their taste for flesh was disconcerting.

childhood. His granny used to smoke a pipe and look out to the sea on her back porch. She was a sea witch, using storms and the element of water to alter the state of the world. Percy never saw her do anything significant, just aid the kettle to heat faster. That was about it. But she watched the sea every night, rain or shine. Even on her deathbed, she'd wanted to be taken outside. Her last words had been about duty and the sea. Later, at the university, under the Coven's guidance, he'd learned it was an old superstition that had vexed his grandma. Like other witches, she was tied to her specialty, but they weren't guardians against anything. Nature knew how to look after itself, unlike those who wielded the power.

"It's about the Coven business."

The vampire snarled. "You better not see them again."

"I was instructed not to." Percy dragged a chair under him and sat down.

Alvira narrowed her eyes and took another long drag, then she let out, "Kraken shit, Percy. It would be best if you had never come back. You are one of the best hunters I have seen in a long time, but you are hurting yourself by being such a stickler for rules. You'll get us both killed. I think it's better if you use up all your unspent holiday. Or better yet, retire."

"I can't—"

"Of course you can. You will get yourself killed if you don't. They will never forget that you know the truth about the machine, and no, as I said before, I don't want to hear the truth. If you want to survive after the trial, get some powerful friends and go public..." Alvira locked eyes with him and shook her head when she didn't get the confirmation she was looking for. "Percy, I say this because I like you. The next words you are going to say can't be, 'I can't.' That invitation I gave you yesterday. I suggest you use it."

"And you?"

"Don't worry about me. My sister invited me to come with her to the new country, Threebeanvalley, and I think it's high time I say yes to the offer."

"The Council—" Percy began.

"Will be happy to see me gone... So why did you come to see me?"

Percy leaned against his knees and squeezed them. Alvira followed his discomfort with her gaze. He sat upright again and cleared his throat. "I saw the board."

Alvira's hand trembled as she stubbed out the cigarette against the desk. "Shit, Percy."

"They told me not to go to the Coven, and as a hexer..." He couldn't finish the sentence.

Alvira picked up the tobacco bag again and rolled a new cigarette, but she didn't light it. She put it behind her ear.

Percy waited for her to comment, but Alvira sucked her teeth and reached for another tobacco paper.

"What—" Percy said.

"I already said what you should do, and now I think you better leave. It was a pleasure working with you. I'll leave a list of your past jobs for your next handler, but we are done. Good luck, and try not to get yourself killed."

Percy looked at her, confused, but when she didn't take her statement back, he said, "Thank you for all that you have done." Percy got up. He bowed and exited the room as the vampire wanted him to. In the hallway, Percy leaned against the wall. His head was spinning. He could sense all the curses needing to come out. He cited the rules the Coven had taught him. No curse let out in anger. No curse sung when happy. No curse when intentions are unclear. Reason over emotions. Curse only when necessary. Before he could recite the litany, through, a small goblin-looking man seemed to materialize out of nowhere and step in front of him.

"Mr. Allread?" the man asked.

Percy looked down and saw a balding man clutching a folder.

"Yes," Percy stuttered.

"I'm Elmer Spooner, and I was wondering if you had time to answer some of my questions?" Elmer asked.

Percy stared at the man, who smelled of mothballs and forgotten papers. The man held his gaze silently, waiting for Percy to acknowledge the words said.

"Sir, what's this all about?" Percy pushed himself off the wall and stood to his full height, which was massive compared to the other man. Mr. Spooner barely came up to Percy's chest.

"I'm an internal affairs investigator, and I'm to assess the actions and protocols the Council took when arresting and imprisoning Mr. Thurston. I was wondering if you had time to discuss the initial arrest." Elmer glanced around, then returned his attention to Percy when he'd made sure the corridor was empty. Percy's hexes located at least seven handlers in their rooms, most likely with their ears pressed against the walls. And Alvira was standing just next to the door, trying not to be heard. He could hear her repressed breathing.

"If this is official, then I have no other choice," Percy said. He was sure Alvira would be sucking her teeth and shaking her head.

"Yes, this is official. I have the Council's full authority to investigate any wrongdoings. I want to clarify that I have no reason to suspect you have done anything wrong. Your arrest reports seem to be by the book, but I would like to ask some questions. Would you mind following me to my office? Or if you need to be somewhere, we can schedule a meeting later."

"Now is fine, sir," Percy said, despite the ledgers. He followed the man. Percy sensed people were watching them and sharing hushed words. Percy amplified his hexes to pick up the spoken and unspoken words about Elmer. They seemed to state relentless and literal. Percy could live with that.

Elmer let him into his office. "Sit down." The man gestured at the chair nearest the door. He circled to take his seat behind a desk buried under papers.

Percy followed the command and took his seat, then glanced around the room. There were no windows as such. Only a small one over the desk, which barely let in light. But that wasn't what caused him to feel uncomfortable. There was something odd about the place, and it took him a while to understand what. It was the absence of smells. The place was scrubbed clean. So was the man. The mothballs and forgotten papers had been just that: the papers he clutched.

"Now, Mr. Allread, as I said, I have read your report of the arrest and your journey back to Necropolis. You have made extensive notes, and I'm thankful for them. But it seems like a few pages are missing, and some of the words have been blacked out. I was wondering if you had any idea what was said in the missing places?" Elmer handed Percy his report back.

He glanced over the twenty-page summary he had written, finding the last two pages missing, along with the fourth and fifth pages. Here and there, paragraphs had been inked black. Percy frowned.

"Is something wrong, Mr. Allread?"

"You are correct. Some of the information is missing." He handed back the summary. A glance told him all the notes concerning the machine and Otis's initial arrest at Levi Perri's alchemy shop were gone. Also, a few remarks about the friends Otis had made on the journey back home. At first, Percy had kept Otis under lock and key on the ship, only taking him out to get fresh air thrice a day. But the voyage had been a long one, and Percy found the harsh isolation to be unnecessary torture and gave the necromancers more freedom than was advisable considering the situation the Council was now facing.

"Could you recount what was written on those pages?"

Percy was about to reply, but then he stopped himself.

"I remind you, Mr. Allread, all you say here is confidential..."

"It's not that, sir. It's just that I'm not sure if I have the right to disclose the information to you. If the pages are missing, then the Council must have considered them dangerous for the public to know."

"Mr. Allread, I remind you that I have the legal right to those documents, and I work for the Council."

"You do, and I'm sure you are privy to the information, but I have been forbidden to describe what happened there. If you want to know more, I advise requesting the uncensored information from the board. I'm sorry I can't be of further help to you, sir."

"Were you aware that Mr. Thurston was denied a lawyer for the first two weeks he was in custody?"

"No, sir. I'm sorry to hear that, sir."

"I have come to believe Mr. Thurston only got his due process after his arrest went public and his notes from the voyage were published in every newspaper. Maybe notes sent under your care."

"What are you insinuating?"

"I'm not trying to insinuate anything. I'm trying to collect the facts. The missing pages and the information you are withholding are preventing me from doing my job. Mr. Allread, you have to understand, this situation might lead to an innocent man losing his life."

"Mr. Thurston?" Percy asked.

"Yes, Mr. Allread."

"He's not innocent. He took part in killing people to acquire souls for his machine. When he got caught, he let a group of spirits loose. Such actions are forbidden by the Necromantic Council and the laws of Necropolis. He's guilty of the crime of which he's accused."

"I see, and this gives the Council permission to deny his rights for lawful imprisonment and trial?"

"Of course not, sir."

"Then you agree, Mr. Allread. My duty is to ensure that the laws and rules are followed, and I think you understand better than anyone else in this building how important it is to follow the rules. They prevent us from slipping into anarchy. And don't you think they should be upheld without exceptions?" The lines around the goblin's eyes drew tight.

"I agree with you, sir. That's why I can't disclose the contents of those pages without the board's approval." Percy stood up. "I'll be more than happy to answer your questions when you present documents stating you are privileged to hear what I disclosed on those pages."

"What about Mr. Thurston's rights?"

"They should be handled according to the rules."

That was it. Both of them recognized they'd arrived at an impasse. Before Percy could leave behind an annoyed internal affairs investigator in good faith, the door to the office burst open. Elmer jumped up, and Percy prepared to cast hexes, but he stopped himself. It was one of his former classmates, Laura, who worked for the Council's internal police. She had the feared capotain hat to prove it. Behind her followed a witch and a necromancer—you could recognize a soul caster from anywhere; it was the eyes.

"Mr. Spooner, you are coming with us," Laura stated as the necromancer and the other witch pushed into the room.

Elmer turned gray and looked ready to throw up.

Percy stepped to block their entry. "What's this about?"

"Stand aside, Percy. This doesn't concern you." Laura nodded to the others to seize Mr. Spooner.

"I'm afraid this has a lot to do with me. So state your business or—" Percy said.

"Always so chivalrous. But you are in the wrong here." She produced a paper from her pocket and handed it to Percy. It was a warrant for Elmer's arrest, stating the man had stolen documents from the Council.

Percy glanced at the man, whose posture had collapsed.

"Is this true?" Percy asked, amazed at the small goblin man being able to sneak into the classified Archives protected by so many hexes that trying to decipher them would render any person insane.

Elmer managed to stutter, but no one in the room could piece together what the man was trying to say.

"It states you stole documents," Percy clarified.

Elmer shook his head. "It's untrue," he shrieked.

"That will be determined by the Council. Step aside," Laura warned Percy.

Percy looked at her and then back at Elmer. The man was still shaking his head. The remaining color was entirely gone. "I had to," the man kept repeating. "It's the truth. It's his right."

Percy stepped aside, letting Laura pass.

"You made the right choice." She smirked. "Though, you could make my day better and give me an excuse to arrest you too."

Percy said nothing. With people like Laura, there was no point. No word would make them think differently. Laura hated him because she had chosen to do so ever since their time at the university. Percy wanted nothing more than for the warrant to be illegitimate, without the managerial signatures and stamps. Then he could have wiped that smirk off her face. But he had no other choice than to obey. The necromancer and the other witch seized the trembling investigator. The internal security guards half carried him out of the room. The tips of his feet scraped the floor.

Laura forced Percy to leave as well. She sealed the room by drawing hexes on the door. Everyone knew any unauthorized attempts to go in would not only alert her but also cause some unfortunate side effects—only the hexer would know what. Knowing Laura, it was some sort of disfigurement.

Percy was forced to return to his desk to go over the ledgers, feeling restless. There was nothing he could do and no one to go to. He pushed past the feeling and added one number after another. He marked the expenditures and sums with precise, beautiful cursive. When he was done, he shut the books and took them with him. Percy headed to his manager's office and handed them over to the woman. She was dozing off at her desk, startled by his entry.

"Percy," the woman snarled.

"The books are up to date." He just stood there, waiting for her to react.

She snapped open her pocket watch and said, "You finished early."

"Yes, ma'am."

"And what do you expect? Going home early?"

"No, ma'am. I was wondering if you had another ledger that needs my attention."

He earned a snort from the woman. "Go home, Mr. Allread. And leave those on my desk. I'll go over them." She narrowed her eyes.

"Yes, ma'am." Percy did as told and left the books behind. Then he headed to his desk and collected his overcoat. A nagging thought insisted that maybe he should have done something. Maybe the man had been right about Otis. Maybe he should be spared and taken into police custody. The necromancer deserved a fair trial. Percy wondered if such a thing would be denied to Mr. Spooner as well.

He shut the office door behind him.

It was almost impossible to take back the things said and done. It was like this universal need to tally up the score, and the scores always had to be settled or something rotten snuck in. How they should be tallied was solely dependent on the person doing the tallying. Sometimes words were enough, other times only a beheading sufficed. But if you were clever enough, you could make people forget the whole thing with well-placed lies, lots and lots of irrelevant noise, or by forcing them to concentrate all their mental efforts on counting pennies for a carrot or two. Soon the newspapers would print what Petula had done. They would come at her. She could lie and distract them, but she had long ago refused to play the game of hide the facts. She would have to state over and over again how the resurrection service was for the city, and it was up to others to judge the truth of her statement. Petula watched out of the coach window, hurrying through the city back to the Town Hall. Petula sighed.

The city was ever so beautiful. But she was not in the city. She couldn't go out there and wander the bazaars in search of new strange ingredients for her necromancy. She couldn't smell the exotic spices they brought in from all over the world. Or drink the new brews of tea with a dash of milk and sweetness and a handful of those spices. Yes, she could get them all delivered to her, and she had. It wasn't the same. She was once, twice, thrice removed from the world. Yet what any commoner glancing at the coach with her crest on would think was that she had it all, she could grasp it all. She didn't want to. Not just because it felt wrong, no. It was the emptiness of such action. Only a fool would want things for free or cheat to get them without any effort.

She watched as a woman clutched a pot with a tall White Snakeroot plant in it. Burning the plant's leaves would coax spirits out of hiding. The smoke was said to awaken the unconscious. Petula had tested the flower and come to the understanding that it was the smell of the smoke that irked the spirit out rather than some extraordinary powers of the plant. The funny thing was, it shouldn't work that way. Spirits had no olfactory organs. Maybe it was how the smoke made the air vibrate. Yet that didn't fully explain it, nor why the unconscious found it vexing. There had to be... That was as far as she got. Dow coughed next to her. He'd stayed silent, letting her collect her thoughts as soon as they'd dropped Mr. Porter at his newspaper. They had to have the conversation finally, and she had been putting it off thus far.

"It's a sound proposal," Petula said. "One—"

"Minta drew up," Dow interrupted her, which was unlike him. He'd taught her never to cut someone short. It told the other you didn't respect them and their opinion.

"Yes," Petula said. Everything she'd planned to say to Dow was gone. Not that telling him about anything was necessary. Undoubtedly he already saw why she'd done what she'd done. Both of them knew the Public Resurrection Ministration would neutralize some of the Necromantic Council's power over the everyday life of the Necropolitans. It might even force the Council to go back to its original idea: leading the necromancers and setting guidelines for all to follow, not making money hand over fist from undead workers, factory owners, necromancers, and monsters hunted overseas. It was too much power for one entity to have.

"And she was right about all of it. The Ministration just needs more money, publicity, and power to make it a viable option. We can't have the poor selling their family members to factories as undead automata to pay their rent and feed their children. What kind of message does that send to the public and the rest of the world about how the Town Hall values its citizens?" She shook her head. "This is monstrous, Dow. The Ministration is just the first step. We can do more to correct the imbalance between the citizens."

Petula took a breath in. It was just that she hadn't quite figured out how to distribute the wealth equally. She couldn't make head or tail of all the economic and political theories telling her how to build a functional society. All of them seemed to have so many flaws and blind spots, making her wonder why anyone was willing to believe in them as the ultimate truths. All of them got one or more aspects of the human experience wrong. To arrange governance according to such a rocky foundation invited calamity. Maybe disaster wouldn't strike straight away, but in the future, the flaws would start to stack up. People would either turn into mindless slaves with no mouths, eyes, or ears or their minds would shatter because of the meaninglessness of their existence. Once that happened, the foundation would crumble and people would revolt. Not that any of those policies, theories, or beliefs that danced between those two extremes were without flaws. They all haggled with the uncertain future—the true emperor of everything and nothing—to try and prevent a catastrophe from sinking the boat.

"Economics," Petula snorted. She was pretty sure she wasn't even meant to try to control it. It was like trying to catch a jellyfish. But everyone around her acted as if she should take the stings and stay the course.

Dow had been watching her, and she felt herself blush for the first time in ages.

"How am I supposed to rule if I'm unable to make sense of anything? I'm forced to listen to the anguish of the people with no way to fix their cries. Dow, you have to let me have this one." Petula could feel her heartburn getting worse. It came and went, but it had been there ever since she took over office from Minta. The woman should never have left. She clearly had a better vision for Necropolis. Petula's only vision had been to escape.

"There's nothing wrong with the plan. I just wish you had told me before declaring war with the Council. You didn't give me enough time to protect you," Dow sighed.

"Someone had to do something." Petula instinctively fiddled with the pendant around her neck with the seal she used for her letters. Back at home, in Leporidae Lop, her family crest had included a sheep. But apparently a sheep wasn't a fitting symbol for Necropolis. So she'd decided a hare's skull kept something of home while being appropriate for Necropolis. Leporidae Lop was made of luck, and there was no creature luckier than a hare. She needed that luck now, beneath the watchful eye of Kraken, but luck had stepped out. Maybe the rule of Kraken was about to change. She had heard rumors of the cult of Old Man Death being resurrected; she saw his symbol everywhere. The one with the little coffins.

And symbols mattered. They were like little tales telling everyone how things should be.

"That might be, but that someone didn't have to be you. We have easier targets. The Town Hall is full of them," Dow said.

"No, it has to be me." There was no escaping the fact that someone had already signed her name on a dotted line, commanding her fate. Otherwise, she wouldn't be running around like a headless chicken. She didn't mean the Council or the bankers or the assassins they'd sent after her. She meant fate, even though she didn't believe in destiny.

"As you wish."

Nothing else was said. The coach took them back to the Town Hall, where Petula went back to answering the never-ending letters always stacked on her desk. The office sometimes felt like a cocoon that trapped her inside. A place she commanded behind the enormous desk left behind by Minta. She hadn't done anything to change the place. It still had the sofa under the window, the lighter-colored spot where Minta's spear had been, and the coat rack that looked like an eight-armed monster.

Petula postponed a meeting with Helaine Peabody from the historical society, again. The woman had tenaciously pestered Petula for months, demanding money for the city's statue repairs. She wasn't asking for pennies; she was asking for daylight robbery. No wonder, as the city was full of statues of the megalomaniacs who had donated them ever so selflessly. What she concentrated on was considering all the possible ways in which the Council might respond to her little newspaper article. She didn't get too far before the world came to collect. She heard the distinctive clap of heels against the painted wooden floors accompanied by a persistent murmur coming from the hallway.

Petula grimaced. She didn't like what she was about to do, but she didn't have the nerve for what would follow if she didn't. She dropped to her knees and crawled under the desk, hugging the papers she had been clutching.

No one could truly blame her. They would do the same. She was sure of it.

The shuffle stopped at her doorway.

There was a groan, and then they moved on.

She could always send Mrs. Maybury to the Council on her behalf. Petula was pretty sure the woman would be running the place in no time. Maybe she already did. Undead ruling the necromancers. Petula smiled. She lingered under the table just a little longer, long enough for the tabby to come around the table and jump on the empty chair to eye her. The cat looked at her with contempt, and she couldn't blame it. Petula continued sitting under the table, writing little notes about what to do and say to the Council, knowing any definite plan would be doomed from the get-go. She wasn't the master of the universe, no matter how much she wanted to be. The tabby was. And most likely, Mrs. Maybury was. The woman had probably already set up a committee to fund such plans.

There came a distinctive cough from the other side of the table.

Petula crawled out to face her secretary. She knew a line about dropping a pen wouldn't work with Dow. The man had superhuman hearing, and she was sure he could sense the change in the room through smell. Sometimes she caught him sniffing the air.

Cruxh, Mrs. Maybury's husband, a ghoul, and the finest police officer in the city, had one night in the wee hours when Petula had dined with him and Mrs. Maybury,[2] stated that the ghouls thought Dow to be some sort of werewolf. Petula wasn't sure what to make of such a confession. Especially when Cruxh never gave away secrets. Petula was sure the ghoul had said it out of concern for her future. But they all knew Dow wouldn't hurt her. He always did everything in his power to guard her. Neither she nor anyone else could deny that he had plans for her. Still, Petula was sure the ghoul was wrong. Dow couldn't be a werewolf. He didn't have the right mannerisms.

---

2. A ghoul, undead, and a necromancer walked into a bar...

Yet he had their senses. And more.

"Sometimes, you just have to," Petula said, lifting the cat onto the desk and sitting back in her chair. She watched the man and his yellow eyes.

"If you say so, ma'am."

"Did Mr. Porter already publish his article?" The city heralds published thrice a day. Usually, Mr. Porter took his time to write his editorial features, but she had given him too good a headline to miss the midday edition.

Dow nodded.

"And?"

"And he was very clear that you are taking action. Very clear."

"And the Council?"

"I cannot say. But they have agreed for you to meet Mr. Thurston and, afterward, their representative to discuss the whole situation. Three o'clock works for them. They prefer to meet before—"

"The late evening news," Petula finished Dow's sentence. Her hands were shaking.

"Shall I schedule your meeting at three o'clock?"

"Five would be better," Petula said and scratched the cat behind its ear.

Dow left her alone in the office to prepare. She stared after him at the open doorway, falling deep into her thoughts. She could just get up, walk away, and disappear for good. This wasn't her problem to solve. She owed nothing to Necropolis and its people. But she couldn't. Not only because Dow would hunt her down, and so would the Council, dragging her back kicking and screaming, but because somehow she had started to care, and the public loved her for that.[3] Anyone who knew her in the past would laugh at the idea that she cared for anything other than the science of necromancy, let alone for something living. Not her sister, though. Larissa

---

3. Not that they didn't criticize her for every move she made. Just the opposite; but it was their right. She was their leader, after all.

always said that deep down she had a kind, loving heart. That one day, she would let it shine.

"Ha," Petula let out. She would prove her kid sister wrong, meaning she had to come out alive after marching into the den of the dead.

Petula reached for a stack of blank paper on the desk along with an ink bottle and pen. She petted the cat while she drew wards on the sheets. When she was satisfied all the markings were perfect and no line was out of place, she pushed the papers inside her black vest over the white shirt she had worn today. She took more sheets and began drawing more symbols. Of course, she had her tattoos to protect her, but since those tattoos were public knowledge after the battle with Minta, she wasn't taking any chances. Also, a maid or someone else might have copied her tattoos and sold them to the Council. She wanted to trust her servants, but the Council had its ways. That was Necropolis for you. The constant competition meant she couldn't let anyone near her. Not Henrietta. Not Agatha.

Petula undid the button of her shirt collar, trying to ease her breathing. She didn't want to think about what had happened with Agatha. Petula had done just what her sister Larissa had asked her to—open up—and that had gotten Petula burned. She pushed the embarrassment, the hurt, and the rejection away and continued drawing more symbols. There wasn't enough ink to cover all the new, nasty traps necromancers and witches came up with every single day. She covered the basics: spirit infestations, demonic possessions, and curses to render her a babbling shell. Lastly, Petula kissed Her on its head and gently lifted the cat off her lap to a small basket next to her desk. She would take the cat with her.

She lifted the basket and saw Dow lurking at the door. "All set?" she asked.

"Yes." Dow didn't sound happy. It was no wonder; she wasn't pleased either.

As she walked to the doorway, she was sure Valkyries were riding out, singing their arias with an extra helping of doom. Petula couldn't blame them. If there were such divine beings, they were just hedging their bets.

Her purred in its basket, unaware of anything. Happy to be carried around and taken on whatever adventures Petula was going on. Saving Her was the only good thing Petula had done in her life. She'd rescued the cat from being maimed by a spirit let loose from its trap. Or Her had saved Petula from being killed or, worse, being possessed. Petula hadn't yet decided who had done the rescuing.

The cat's loud purring made it clear Dow was unusually silent. Thus far, the man had done everything in his power to ensure Petula always had the upper hand in any given situation. Now, he chose to say nothing.

"Dow," Petula started. She didn't know how she should finish the sentence.

"You'll be fine. Mr. Colton will accompany you everywhere. And make sure he does. Even in the cell," Dow said.

"You are not coming?" Petula hated how feeble her voice sounded.

"I have fires to put out."

"Yes, of course. I was..." She decided not to pretend to have a reasonable explanation. There wasn't one. She would be okay with Mr. Colton. The weasel-looking man was adept at handling physical threats and more. She only had to hope that would be the worst the Council would throw at her. No, she was being silly. This was a mayoral duty; they couldn't off her just like that. Not now. They could make her lose her mind, but kill her? Never.

Or at least not yet.

Outside, the sky was pale gray, and the air was just cold enough to chill your bones. Just your normal weather in Necropolis, giving Petula a perfect reason to stack layers over layers and wear cardigans. She loved all of it, favoring the gloom over the always warm weather in Leporidae Lop. Of course, it occasionally rained there when the luck system secured abundant crops for the farmers and citizens. But it wasn't as easy anymore, or so

Petula's sister had written. The luck was dwindling, and people had to work harder to obtain what they had gotten used to. It seemed like Harriet Stowe, Leporidae Lop's prime minister, was letting it all happen. She'd exchanged letters with the prime minister, but not to discuss the changing politics. Just about trade matters. Petula had realized a long time ago she would never see the shores of her motherland again. So she would have to be content with the cold rain of this doomed land rather than the pleasant showers over the green fields from her childhood.

Mr. Colton opened the door to the coach. The man looked so harmless, but she had seen him in action. There was nothing innocuous about him. Petula had learned to recognize when he was carrying extra weapons.

"Miss Upwood." The man tipped his hat to her and offered his hand to help her into the coach. He insisted on doing so despite Petula always refusing to engage.

"Mr. Colton," Dow signaled.

"Just my duty, sir. For that matter, I don't think our friend likes me that much."

Petula was sure Johnny Colton was the only creature in town who could speak to Dow that way and get away with it.

"Dow," Petula said before the door closed.

"Yes?"

"Make sure Mr. Porter knows that I'm meeting the Council now. Make sure he's there waiting for me at the headquarters," Petula said.

"Yes, ma'am," Dow said, and his eyes seemed to sparkle. He closed the door. The coach soon pulled off.

Petula leaned back. The papers under her vest rustled as they pressed against her ribs. Instead of fixing them, she flipped the basket open and petted the sleeping cat.

CHAPTER TEN

IGNORANCE ISN'T AN OPTION

T he wicked had to be punished. Otherwise, all that would be left was an empty void where nothing matters. Otis just disagreed with the Council and everyone else that he was somehow wicked. The word was antiquated and restrictive. His brilliance should be celebrated. Otis leaned over the small wooden desk in his prison cell. He tried to pen into his notebook who he had been and what he had done. Everything felt meaningless. The inspector's visit yesterday had given him hope. But he hadn't heard from anyone since then.

He restlessly drummed the pen against the notebook. Otis looked at the code he'd used to write down everything, including everything he knew about making the Bufonite. Here and there he had included details about his life, like growing up with an absent father and a mother who was unwilling to leave her laboratory. His grandmother had raised him, and while the woman did her duty, there had been no warmth between the two of them. But mostly, he wrote about the formulas, the necromantic commands he'd used to mold the spirits to Levi's specific needs. Still, there were holes in his descriptions. He wasn't sure what Levi had put in his chemical cocktails to interact with the spirits or how the cocktails made the mechanics move in perpetuity.

Otis scratched behind his ear and leaned away from the desk.

Now that Levi was dead and the schematics burned with the shop, there wouldn't be another machine. Not from him, at least. He had no desire to make one. Even back in Threebeanvalley, Otis had doubted whether he should participate, knowing well he would never sleep a peaceful night again. But there had been something about Levi that had made it hard to say no. Otis knew there was always the possibility that someone clever enough with a knowledge of mechanics and souls could piece things together from what he had written and the Bufonite would live again. He'd accepted that the clever bugger might work for the Council. But he still continued writing everything down. He needed there to be a record of who Otis Thurston had been, especially if they were going to make him disappear. A fate that had become ever so clear now.

Otis dipped the fountain pen into the inkwell, ready to write. He was interrupted by a knock on the door, followed by the locks and latches being opened. Otis quickly lowered the pen onto the desk and shut his diary, burying it under his other books. Then he turned around to face the door, his hands on his lap.

The day-shift witches came in, inspecting the room. They looked tenser than usual. Also, never before had they looked under his bed or lifted his mattress.

"Is the queen coming?" Otis laughed.

All he got was a glare.

"Random inspection, then?" Otis tried. "I promise I haven't been stuffing the gods' awful food you give me under my mattress to breed a rat population that could, under my guidance, gnaw me out of here."

This time he got a head shake. Clearly, he wasn't hitting their funny bones. However, he highly doubted they had any. Otis had become more than sure that "dull, aggressive, and paranoid soul" was in the Council's job requirement.

When the witches were satisfied and they'd confiscated all his pens and other sharp objects, they stepped out of the way as a youngish woman with white hair cut to her chin entered the cell. Her dark black eyes with a slight sparkle of their former blue peered into his soul. It was the necromancer effect. The full treatment of the body fearing and the mind enduring. He never reacted that way to the raging spirits and the schooling necromancers went through, but he had grown up in Necropolis under his mother's rule, and she was never devoid of the dead. The only un-necromantic feature of the woman was the basket she held on to. Behind the woman was a tall, slim man with sharp features and a rodent-like appearance. His eyes gleamed as well, but in a different way, like someone who sees everything as a joke. Otis already liked the man.

"Stand up, you fool," one of the witches snapped.

Otis was about to protest.

"He really doesn't have to." The woman spoke with a soft, controlled voice.

The way she spoke made the hairs on Otis's back rise and made him pop up from his chair and bow. "Your mayorship," he said. Holy corpse worms, how had he missed that? But that voice; it had to be her. They said she could command the spirits with just one word. Otis had never seen a picture of her. He had already been in Threebeanvalley when she rose to power.

"Call me Petula. I insist," Petula said. She was the only one who looked pleased by the request, leaving even Otis at a loss for words. She continued, "Do you mind if I sit?" She gestured at the bed.

"Take the chair." Otis stepped aside. He wanted to kick himself for being so stiff and losing the charm he knew he had with the ladies. He tried a smile. It only earned him a raised eyebrow. Nevertheless, she accepted his offer and sat down while Otis moved onto the bed. The rodent-looking man who hadn't offered his name leaned against the wall next to the table, staying near the mayor.

"Now, do you mind if we start? We are pressed for time," Petula said and lowered the basket next to her feet.

"Of course," Otis said, regaining control. Otis smirked. "I'm sorry, I don't have any beverages to offer, nor cake to serve, but I'm sure if we ask my pals there"—he nodded towards the witches—"they can arrange something for us."

"I'm fine." Petula kept her deadpan expression for show, or he hadn't amused her at all. Otis wasn't sure.

"How can I help?" Otis continued smiling.

"It's the other way around, but first a few details are in need of clarification. You could start with how you arranged your death and left Necropolis," Petula said. That soft tone from earlier was gone, replaced with a more immediate and demanding note.

"Aren't you a straight shooter?" Otis laughed.

Again, he was met with a raised eyebrow. Otis found it more cute than intimidating. He was the only one in the world. Okay, Dow found it amusing, but he would never say that to Petula's face.

"Fine, be that way, Miss Mayor." He waited to see a reaction. There was none. He straightened his pose. "I used poison to slow down my heartbeat and breathing to the bare minimum and used ice to cool my body temperature. With makeup and help from a friend, we established my death—"

Petula interrupted him. "Am I correct that you let yourself be buried?"

"Yes; there's enough oxygen to last you a while if you don't panic. My friend dug me up before it was too late."

"Your friend being Mr. Perri, the alchemist?"

"Yes. Then I had fake papers made and boarded a ship to Threebeanvalley. Ridiculously easy, if you ask me. I read my medical report, and it said I died of exhaustion, which might have held true if I had kept working insane hours making the glowing skulls. There seems to be no end to their use. Mark my words: one day, everyone will have one in their living room, and I can't even imagine what that might entail. But at least there would be a network for communication and we could conduct our finances from home. Or why not overseas..." Otis was about to continue, but then he remembered where he was. Yet the last statement made Otis wonder why he had ever left the whole business. He was pretty good with the glowing skulls. In a year or two, he could have been running the whole division. Then, later on, he could have sold them all over the world if the Council let him. There was that, then.

"There's a thought," Petula said.

"Huh?" Otis asked.

"Do continue with what happened next."

Otis went on to tell her about his time in Threebeanvalley. How, with trial and error, they made the Bufonite work. How residual spirits couldn't do it; that they found those who were more attuned with the universe and strengthened the connection to what Levi called quintessence. Then when he was about to tell her the formulas he used to guide the spirits into the system and make them cooperative, he woke up from the trance the mayor had clearly put him in. Otis blinked and looked at Petula.

She had just sat there quietly, letting him talk. Only filling in his pauses with an encouraging smile or a nod.

"I think that's enough." Otis frowned.

"It is. Thank you for your honesty. And you didn't work under duress or any obligation to this Levi Perri?" Petula asked. Her tone was soft again, and he made a note of it.

Otis shook his head.

"All this came to an end when Mr. Allread found out what you were doing?"

"Pretty much." Otis swallowed. For some reason, he was willing to say more.

"Causing you to counter his attempt to arrest you by invoking those spirits that gravitate towards you?"

"Somewhat."

"Mr. Thurston, I understand you feel that you cannot share what happened. But if we are to decide how to proceed here and what I can do to help, not to mention what I'm supposed to do as the leader of Necropolis and a fellow necromancer, I require the whole picture. So I beg you, please continue."

"What do you want me to tell you?"

"For example, how did they find you?"

Otis burst out laughing. "If I didn't know better, I would think you are trying to find out how to get away from the Council."

Petula's expression said more than he'd expected. There was a slight tremble around her eyes, but that was it. Still, he was sure he had hit the mark. Maybe the mayor understood better than anyone else—and of course, she did—what it was like to be a necromancer, to wield such a great power over the dead, and never get to do anything about it other than resurrecting on demand or working as a spirit removal operator. Necromancers were meant to rule the underworld and rule the living with it. She should be doing just that. She was the Kraken be damned leader of Necropolis. The wealthiest and most influential country in the known universe. She had the power to send fleets of undead to take over every continent. Otis took a deep breath in, and he saw it. She couldn't. Not when the Council lurked over her shoulder. He wanted to laugh. As a young boy, he, like the others, had dreamed of becoming the mayor. To be the beast of the beasts. And now here he was, looking at this shackled creature face to face, and he pitied her.

"Only a joke," Otis offered and winked.

And the tension was gone.

Petula shifted on her chair. "Jokes aside, I'm sure I don't have to recount our profession's macabre history. All I want is honesty between colleagues and cooperation to figure out what to do with you. What you have done or what you were attempting to do with the Bufonite is beyond what anyone could hope necromancy would stretch to. You can clearly see past the box. So what do you hope will happen now?"

"You and I—"

"I'll stop you there. There will be no sunset to ride into, or any you and I in any sense. It's you and the city and our profession. What will the future hold now we know that mechanizing necromancy is possible?"

"You—"

"Can't read your mind, but you have tried to charm me at every chance. So I calculated all the possibilities, which made the most sense when it came to you, Mr. Thurston. Your reputation precedes you."

In the background, the rodent-looking man's smirk widened. The witches held their laughter as well.

"Better to have a reputation of any sort than not to exist at all."

"If you think so. Would you like to continue working with the Bufonite? Or is it a dead-end, as they say in the newspapers?"

"Aren't you a blunt one?" Otis thought he would get a rise out of Petula, but he didn't. So he added, "You are the first one to ask me that..." And then he wasn't sure how to continue. Working for the mayor would be a better option than for the Council, but... He wasn't sure what the but was. The Bufonite was never his dream. It was always Levi's. His was to see the world and live from moment to moment. Constructing puzzles was fun, and he got lost in the jungle of problems to be solved, but what he desired was a beach and for all his worries to disappear. Maybe to own a boat. If he attempted to make the Bufonite again, he could never do that, not even if he was the richest man in the world. Levi had never seen what constraints came with owning the machine and dedicating one's life to something. Burdens and headaches and demands.

"What can I say? I want to stay alive." Otis gave a wide grin.

"Ah, I see." The mayor looked disappointed. Or Otis thought she did.

There was no pleasing everyone. But he had to, if he wanted her to get him out of here. "If lending a hand to the government to build their own Bufonite gets me a good life and betters the city, who am I to say no? Of course, it all depends on the Council."

"Hmm, thank you, Mr. Thurston. You have been more than helpful. Now I have another meeting to attend. But before I go, is there someone I can contact on your behalf?" Petula stood up.

Otis only managed to stutter no, unable to form a coherent thought. He watched the mayor leave, listening to the locks slide into place, and all he could do was keep sitting on the bed, staring at the spot where the mayor had been. He should have given her the notebook. There were so many moving parts at work that he wasn't sure what color his underpants were, let alone what to think, say, or do about anything anymore. Again, if he had only listened to the whispers written on the walls, he might have turned into a hero who would survive despite being as clueless as a newborn baby at the dawn of an apocalypse.

Policies. That was how they got you. If the current ones were unhelpful, then new ones could be made and lines could be blurred. The Council knew how to stretch the lines. Henrietta had expected them to retaliate, but not by bankrupting them. She'd expected to be assassinated. She'd prepared to be. Henrietta hurried to her office. She needed to summon the whole Coven to come together if they wanted to survive. The easiest thing would be to hide and play innocent, but truth had a habit of popping up when you least wanted it. Truth was kind of an asshole in other respects as well. It was often spoken with a great disregard for feelings and the illusions one had for oneself, life, and the universe. And Henrietta couldn't keep something this big from the other witches, who, by nature, were a suspicious bunch. It was just that those who happily aligned with the Council would be there too, and she would have to convince them that she had done this for the Coven. She would happily step down and take the blame if it meant they didn't need to succumb to the Council.

Before she got to her office, Eurof seized her by her arm. She'd missed him lingering there in the foyer.

"Henrietta," he said ever so softly. The man looked pale and sickly. In Amanita, there were always laugh lines around his mouth, and his dashing black hair shone in the soft, warm sun. Now his hair had turned as gray as the stones fencing in the gardens, and it had been such a long time since Henrietta had seen him smile.

"Eurof," Henrietta let out.

He drew his hand away and smoothed his short hair, meeting her eyes. He looked guilty. "Been somewhere?" he stated, examining her from head to toe.

"I had a meeting with the Council. Can we talk in my office?"

Already a group of younger witches had gathered in the foyer, waiting for the lessons to start. On the more relaxed days, Henrietta liked to teach the courses, especially ecology. It was the environment that made a witch.

The students tried hard not to look at them, but they couldn't help themselves.

Eurof let her lead them into her office. As the door closed behind them, some of the girls giggled. They wouldn't if they had any idea what it took to make a marriage work. Henrietta had always thought she would be one of those old spinsters, and happily so. Then she had met Eurof, and now here they were. Past the euphoria, maintaining love.

The door closing sounded like a coffin being nailed shut.

Henrietta loosened the upper buttons of her dress collar and turned to face her husband to take in what he needed from her. But he only had eyes and ears for her. It was how he stood, how he looked at her, how he was. She hated that she consumed their relationship, that she'd become the center of everything and Eurof had stepped aside, becoming a supporting fixture. A shadow.

"I..." Henrietta began. There was no time for personal. There never was. She shook her head. "The Council is threatening to pull funding from the Coven and add a hefty fine if I don't do its bidding. This could mean the end of everything. I need Petula to give the Coven a loan or funding, but she has evaded me thus far."

"Is this because of the needlepoint group?" Eurof asked. He'd never asked about the needlepoint group before, but he wasn't stupid.

Henrietta turned her back on him and walked to her lizard's terrarium, taking Nestor out. He instantly nestled on her hand as she stroked his tiny head. The lizard made her feel more in tune with the world around her. Outside nature, everything was just a giant, complicated mess.

"Yes," she said, looking out of the window.

"Is it worth it?" Eurof took a seat on the corner of her desk. She could hear the wood creaking underneath him. She gathered the courage to face those eyes of his. He waited patiently. When she turned around, he watched her, all his attention fully on her.

Henrietta felt nauseated, towering over their relationship. They weren't them. She was an institution, where biology, thoughts, and hearts and souls had to give way, or else they would crumble. He reached for her hand to beg her to come closer, to let go of the Mother. She took a step in but lingered there, just out of reach of the full embrace.

"Yes, it's worth it. But it also means we might lose all this and all my work will have been for nothing. What I need to do with Petula is..." Henrietta looked past Eurof at the bookcases around the room with the specimens she'd collected around the world. Some she'd rescued from extinction and cultivated here in the gardens. She had written books about the seeds, the deadliest mushrooms, about nature, about witchery to ensure all of it would remain. And if nature remained, so would the witches. They were more than tea leaf readers, soap makers, healers, and the Council's guard dogs.

Eurof's chest rose high, and then it collapsed as he breathed out. "Would it be so bad? We could go back home." He knew he'd said the wrong thing.

Henrietta swallowed the words wanting to leap out. Instead, she detached from Eurof and lowered Nestor back onto a small driftwood log in the terrarium. Then she went back to Eurof. She let him pull her close this time. Henrietta let out a long sigh she hadn't noticed she was holding. Her entire body relaxed, swept away by a soft, still moment. Henrietta wasn't sure why she'd stopped being near him.

"I have to stay. I have to see this through," she whispered.

"I just wish it didn't have to be you." He leaned backward, leaving room between them to stare into her eyes. "I know what you do is important, but it has buried my Henrietta somewhere deep. You don't smile any longer. Haven't for a long time."

She looked away, her chest feeling tight.

Henrietta stepped back. He tried to hold on to her, but then he let go of her.

"It's my duty," she said.

"No, it isn't. It's what Wesley wanted. Not what you desired. We were meant to see the world and then settle back home, in Amanita."

"Not now," she warned him, not having meant to do so.

"Silly me. I thought you wanted us to discuss this." Eurof stood up. "Find me when you do." He walked out, and she let him.

When he shut the door behind him, she collapsed against the desk, leaning heavily on it. The only witness to her undignified moment was Nestor. The lizard curled into a ball and shut its eyes. What did the lizard care about human perplexities?

Henrietta watched the door, hoping it would somehow morph into the jungle back in Amanita with its ancient mother trees. Those that fed their kin, the other trees in the forest, the mushrooms, the undergrowth, everything, where they were the center of the ecosystem, keeping the forest alive. Like she was meant to be as the Mother of the witches, connecting them to each other despite their deadly nature.

"Grow," she said. Instantly, branches pushed out from the door, at first bare, and then the buds changed into full-blown oak leaves. Eurof was right. Everything had been perfect back in Amanita. She had never meant to stay this long. She had meant to find someone to replace her. She'd stopped laughing. Henrietta closed her eyes, letting Amanita come alive in her, immersing herself in the vivid image. She could smell the jungle and hear the crickets and the bird calls. Feel the branches growing. Behind the nature, there was a sense that someone had violated her sanctuary. She couldn't quite get a reading on who and why. They had been here, searching her desk, peeking into her safe boxes with her diaries. There was a sense of familiarity she couldn't quite place. Then there was a noise accompanying it, masked breathing, and before that, footsteps, ever so distinct—a pattern imprinted in the wood. Someone familiar indeed. It smelled like death and fear.

A knock on her door awakened Henrietta from her trance. She jerked back into reality, away from the jungle, the wood's fibers, and back into her body. Transitioning from tree's xylem cells to human cells wasn't as tricky as one might think. The same principle of water and dissolved ions applied. It was the perspective that needed adjusting. The signals pulsing through the humans were more alarming, invasive, and plaguing, isolated even when they weren't. In the past, she'd transported herself into trees to read their sensations and their memories, to understand. Now... Henrietta snorted.

"Come in," she said and pushed herself up to her full height, like the statues towering above the Necropolis landscape, feeling a lot better.

Imogene stepped in apologetically. She had a new apron on, this one dark brown. It was already covered in patches of soil. Henrietta had to look away, and then she faced the young woman again.

"Yes?" she asked, strained.

"I came to see if you need anything." Imogene gave an ever-so-innocent smile and glanced at the branch sticking out of the door.

"Everything is fine," Henrietta said. The young witch wasn't here to ask if Henrietta needed cookies and tea. She was after information, as every witch should be. It was what kept them alive. There was no point in hiding the situation from Imogene. Not even when her mother would be the one doing everything in her power to force Henrietta to step down from her position. It would come out eventually. And thus far Imogene had shown loyalty towards Henrietta.

"The Council has made a request that will affect the whole Coven. We need to summon everyone to decide how to proceed," Henrietta said. "Can you do that?"

"Of course, Mother. When?"

"Tomorrow at midnight, as is customary."

"It will be done. Do you need anything else? Can I fetch you tea? Judika made—"

"I'm fine. How are the gardens?"

"A few snails got in, and we have been eradicating them, but it's hard, as you forbid the use of pesticide." Imogene clutched her apron, stopping herself from saying more.

"It's the fungi we have to consider. We don't want them to die, as their symbiosis with the plants keeps everything blooming." Henrietta sighed and added, "I'm sorry, Imogene. You know this. It has been a long day. Maybe you should fetch me that tea after all. Make it the good kind."

"Do you want the orange cookies Judika made an hour ago?" Imogene let go of her apron.

"Cookies are fine. Is there anything else I should know?" Henrietta noticed Imogene's labored breathing and flickering eyes. She was unusually nervous. Not that it was so different from any other day. Imogene, despite being a blessing to Henrietta's sanity, could be anxious past the necessary point. She catastrophized everything, even the minor things like serving breakfast at just the right time. Henrietta had frequently commanded the young girl to relax, but it had made matters worse. She felt helpless around Imogene when the trembling got worse than usual.

"A shipment of soil arrived today, but it's all sorted out now."

"Good, thank you, Imogene. I couldn't do this without you." Such words had done the trick in the past.

"I'll fetch you that tea now, Mother." Imogene curtsied and hurried out.

When the younger witch was gone, Henrietta sat behind her desk and tried to catch the smell and sensation she had gotten earlier. It was gone. She drew her letter writing kit closer. She needed Petula to comply this time. The Town Hall's money could prevent her from selling the freedoms she'd secured for her witches. And if Petula didn't agree, she knew about the mayor's transgressions with Agatha. She didn't like to do such things, but sometimes the end justified the means. Her past naïve self would be laughing at her. Nevertheless, she wrote the letter, folded it into an envelope, and got up.

In the meantime, she knew what would get her mind off things. That meant she had to get out of the corset, skirt, petticoat, and frock and slip into her woolen trousers and a flannel shirt.

They were where she had left them, except they were cleaned and neatly folded.

Imogene, Henrietta thought.

It took painfully long to get out of the corset, frock, and the rest. She let them fall on the floor. Before she was fully dressed, Imogene was there in the doorway with the tea and cookies. She was smiling as if she'd caught Henrietta red-handed.

Imogene handed her the saucer and plate and said, "The snails are in the north gardens, where the rhododendrons are."

Henrietta took the saucer and plate. They rattled slightly. "You know me too well," she said.

"I do my best, Mother."

"Imogene, I'll say this only once. You don't have to try so hard. Find who you are and pursue that rather than getting stuck with me here in the Coven. There's an amazing world out there."

"Thank you, Mother," the young witch said automatically.

"I mean it, Imogene. Find yourself."

"But Mother, I think I have."

"Good, that's all I ask." Henrietta pushed the cookies into her pocket and drank the tea as she made her way down the stairs. Imogene trailed after her, ready to take the teacup. She already held the plate, having taken it from Henrietta without saying a word. She took Petula's letter, too, without Henrietta having to explain. All automatic. All that slipped from Henrietta's attention as she thought about the games the Council played and the smell of decay in the wood she'd sensed earlier. She should never have answered the call to come back. In Amanita, she had been happy. Ignorance was bliss. But she was a witch, and ignorance wasn't an option.

CHAPTER ELEVEN

ALL I NEED IS A FRIEND

B oredom, that was what Petula had seen. Not greed. Not malice. Just boredom and the action which followed it. Still, it made Petula sick to her stomach. She clutched the basket and tried to keep her steps steady, following the Council's witches out of Mr. Thurston's prison cell. It was beyond cruel how Otis had made the machine. The man had played around her, hinting and retracting his statements, but Petula was sure Otis had ground the souls into their bare essence to power the machine, obliterating the person. Petula tried to control her need to gag. Despite her curiosity, she had never been willing to step over the line and hurt another being. But the university didn't forbid it. And Otis hadn't broken any laws by doing so. Maybe the naive moral laws of some, but not a true Necropolitan. He was a hero who had been able to break the barrier between the mechanical and spiritual. The possibilities for his discovery were endless.

Yet Petula felt sick, despite knowing she might be able to duplicate the marvelous device, which, in the right hands, could ease the societal pressure of scarce resources. But the thing was, the right hands were the necessary part. History had shown that there were no right hands. Petula wouldn't trust even herself to do the right thing with the machine. A cornucopia couldn't fix what was already broken. It was the mind. It was boredom. It was greed. It was jealousy. It was all of it. And nothing had fixed those things thus far. All sorts of drugs had already been tested, and still, the world produced dysfunction. Petula was pretty sure that there was something broken about the world or, more so, about society. Especially here in Necropolis, where money and power were pursued at all costs. Otis had just repeated what had been taught. In the name of money, people were stripped down to their bare essence in their jobs, and when they were finally spewed out of the industrial machine, they shattered, dying from pure exhaustion, and the only thing left behind was the question: was it a life worth living?

"Miss Upwood?" Mr. Colton woke her from her thoughts. "May I carry the basket for you?" Without permission, the man reached for her arm and held it until she stopped trembling.

"Thank you, Mr. Colton. That would be most helpful." Petula let the man take the basket.

"It's my honor."

"This way," one of the guarding witches said, leading them to meet the representative of the Council. "Mr. Crowen waits for you in his office."

"Yes, lead the way," Mr. Colton said on Petula's behalf. She was thankful. The sickening part wasn't only what Otis had done. No, the man had to live with it. What made her want to crumble down was that she would have to use him against the Council in the name of the general good and maybe free him in the process. The Council was right to keep Otis under lock and key. There was no doubt about that. Yet she couldn't back down now; nor could she let the Council have Otis. Everything depended on her getting this right: the needlepoint group, Henrietta, the witches, and the other necromancers, not to mention civic peace. She would have to work out what was right before she walked up the flight of stairs to Mr. Crowen's office. She needed Dow.

The sorry thing was that she couldn't wave this off with a we-are-sorry-it-won't-happen-again statement. The making of the machine was progress, like the glowing skulls had been. Who was she to withhold it from the citizens? Not when the voice inside her head insisted the devices had a potential to aid the greater good. In all honesty, she wanted that machine as much as everyone else in the world. And not many would object to the cost. Souls, bodies, minds were a commodity. That was what Necropolis taught. Her mother's words echoed inside her. "No policy can account for all, and no politician can control everything." But she had to. Or else, the worst would happen.

She would have to be better than every other being inside this building. All the witches, necromancers, vampires, werewolves, ghouls, goblins, undead, and humans here begging for salvation from the Council. No form could liberate them, but still, they had to believe in the institution or else there would be no society. They glanced at her like she was their worst enemy or some divine being. They made her wish that with science, knowledge, and methodological decision-making you could achieve near perfection. That she could find that salvation for them. But sitting in her office all these years had made Petula realize there was no perfect solution, unlike in academia, where you had an answer to everything, if you ignored the real world and how messy it was. Here and now, there were too many variables she couldn't control. The only variable she could truly control was herself. And her studies hadn't prepared her to solve the biggest mystery of the known civilizations: how to make people work together and stop the empires from collapsing.

"Mayor." A thin, rasping voice brought Petula back to the moment. An undead in a plain suit stood beside a common-looking office door, gesturing for her and Mr. Colton to enter.

The undead offered Petula a smile. Or Petula thought it was a smile. It was more like a sneer, but with undeads, she had come to believe if they weren't shambling towards you trying to eat your brain, then most likely they were trying to be friendly.

"Mr..." Petula began before taking her seat.

"Mr. Crowen. I'm the Council's head administrator." The undead bowed his head deep and glanced over Petula at Mr. Colton, who was probably grinning.

The man couldn't help himself.

Petula cleared her throat and said, "Mr. Crowen, there's no need for that. We are equals here."

The undead straightened his back slowly to make a point that Petula was kidding herself. He was right. They weren't equal. Petula took her seat and glanced around the tidy office, where every paper and pen was in its proper place.

The undead took his seat as well. Mr. Colton stayed near the door, holding the basket and eying both of them.

Petula took a deep breath in and began, "We at the Town Hall appreciate you letting us see Mr. Thurston. We understand it's not customary, but still, you made an exception for us. This gives us both a chance to work together to understand the restlessness the Necropolitans are feeling."

The undead attempted to give another smile, and while the muscles took their time to do what was needed, he achieved the effect. A row of pearly whites gleamed between the thin blue lips. Petula would be astonished if she hadn't read about teeth transplants. Still, it was magic what the city's taxidermists could do with dead flesh and loose parts.

"It was our duty. The matter of timing was more of an issue. We had to make sure all the proper steps were taken so your safety could be ensured." The undead leaned forward, placing his elbows on the desk.

Petula crossed her legs, letting her walking skirt drape over her knees. "Mr. Crowen, the situation is unbearable. The Necropolitans consider arresting Mr. Thurston an overreaction. They want justice, and—" Game, set, match.

Almost. "If I may ask you, what do you think?" Mr. Crowen interrupted her ever so casually.

She hadn't expected the question and almost hurried to answer with her first response. Her second thoughts warned her not to. "*Take a breath,*" they said. The thoughts after that argued back and forth about why she should take a breath, but she silenced the confrontational part of her.

"I'm not sure what to think, Mr. Crowen. I would love to be one of those people who can form an opinion instantly and know it to be the correct one, but I have to piece together the conversation I had with Mr. Thurston before I can give you an informed answer."

Mr. Crowen smiled again. This time around the expression came more readily. "Then how do you think we should proceed?"

He loved this. Petula was sure of it. Either he'd guessed what Otis would say and what her reaction to it would be, or he was fishing. "The trial is coming soon, or so I have heard…" She let the last bit hang there, giving the man an opening to answer.

Mr. Crowen took it. "The date has been set, yes."

"Will you open it to the public?"

"Ah, I see. The Council's trials have never been a secret."

Petula did her best not to reply, "*Oh, really.*" Not that the man was lying. They were open, but the Council made it impossible to know when and where the trials were held. Such information was buried in their memos, which, of course, were public. But who could read over a thousand pages of procedural details in search of that one point they were looking for?

"I see. That's a good thing then. When and where exactly is it?" Petula asked.

"It's Tuesday at ten o'clock. Most likely, it will be held in the East Chamber, which is on the lower floors." Mr. Crowen shifted nervously in his seat, partly because Mr. Colton was hovering behind the mayor and had kept that grin of his fixed on his face, waiting for one false move.

"I'll be sure to spread the word. It might lessen some of the discontent the public is feeling over the issue. But only might. I would like to hear how the Council plans to ease the hearts and minds of those who are concerned for Otis's life and his rights to a legal trial and even freedom."

"We at the Council see…" the man began carefully, searching for the right words to answer in the least harmful way. Petula wondered about the man's status and position. Yes, definitely some sort of head administrator. She was just unsure if he was the kind the Council was willing to sacrifice if everything went to Kraken shit or not.

Petula nodded for the man to continue.

"That once the trial is held and the extent of Otis's crimes is widely known, all this will pass. The legality of the situation will show itself." The man seemed pleased with himself.

Petula had to admit that he had successfully avoided incriminating anyone or giving a clear policy.

"I hope you are right. I feel that some of our necromancers have reached the point where they find themselves stuck and unable to choose for themselves. It sounds to me like they are looking for leniency. As their mayor, I wish you at the Council would consider hearing their concerns and maybe addressing them…"

"New policies?" the undead offered.

"If necessary. I'm sure the Town Hall is willing to aid you as best we can and facilitate negotiations between all parties. If it comes to that, of course." Petula went along with it. The man was cleverer than a scapegoat should be. She liked him.

"I will pass on your concerns." The man corrected his bow tie. "We considered it important for you to meet Mr. Thurston. The Town Hall must know the situation and when and where the trial is held, as you stated. Maybe there should be a press release from the Town Hall, stating that you have visited us and discussed Otis's imprisonment and trial. I was informed that there's a reporter camping out on our steps. A perfect opportunity. What do you say?"

"I'm more than happy to do so. It's best for the public if we can reach an understanding..." Petula paused, thanking herself for having requested the reporter to be there as her hail Kraken. Also, she took her time to consider whether to mention the resurrection service or not.

"...About reassessing the Public Resurrection Ministration's funding and services. Minta Stopford drafted a decent proposal, and I have been going over it and making a few alterations. I have come to see that it might ease the Council's workload, especially with the families of those undead who can't afford resurrection. Of course, the funding will be discussed in the next annual budget meeting, but for now, I have been able to move money around so five new necromancers can be hired." There, now she'd done it, sealed her own death warrant. It felt good.

The undead fixed his bowtie again, and when he noticed Petula watching, he let his hands fall on his lap. Petula's last remark would return the man six feet under in no time. He cleared his throat. It sounded like wind passing through a corroded water pipe.

"Thank you for letting us know. I'm sure the Town Hall has to consider the needs of the public and their ability to provide for themselves. We will happily look into the matter of how we can ease the burden of low-income families and their right to resurrection."

"That's all I ask for." Petula kept her relaxed smile up, as Dow had taught her to. "I'll keep you informed, as I'm sure you will us too. We wouldn't want our joint projects to overlap and cancel each other out. Now, let's not keep the reporter waiting." Petula stood up and retrieved her basket from Mr. Colton. The basket shook slightly as the cat licked itself.

Mr. Porter waited on the steps with his photographer. Behind them, the Save the Otis Group roared their demand to free the necromancer. They shouted even more when Petula and the undead stepped outside. The camera obscura was set up so that the Council's name hung above their heads as Petula and Mr. Crowen stopped to pose. The undead administrator didn't seem happy about being immortalized this way, not in front of everyone, but he said nothing. They both gave a short statement about Petula's meeting with Mr. Thurston. The witches who guarded the headquarters were tense as the interview stretched on and the crowd became more agitated.

"Should Mr. Thurston be cleared of all charges?" Mr. Porter shouted over the people.

Nasty little creature, Petula thought. "That's for the courts to decide. Justice and politics shouldn't mix."

"Can I quote you on that?" Mr. Porter jabbed back.

"If you must. But now I have to be on my way." Petula left, and so did the undead, leaving Mr. Porter and his photographer to collect their things. Petula took a long glance at the Save the Otis Group and climbed into the coach in front of the barricade keeping the masses at bay. She could already picture the headlines.

"Mr. Colton," Petula said before the man closed the door behind her.

"Yes, Miss Upwood?"

"Take me to the Necro Botanical Gardens."

"Yes, ma'am."

As soon as the door closed, Petula drew out the wards she'd pushed under her vest. Some of them were burned. They had tried to dig into her thoughts, maybe with a light spirit possession, or maybe there had been suggestive whispers to influence her. A parasitic spirit-like creature at the back of her head was not what she would call a swell time. It was bad enough that she had to endure her own toxic thoughts there. Petula took the remaining wards out and folded them next to her. Lastly, she let Her out of its basket. Petula petted the cat, slouching into the chair. Stupid games.

The lingering sense of doom lurked behind a broken system. Often enough, it went hand in hand with the feeling of utter helplessness, and the only thing one could do was curl up under the desk and wish the world would go away. But Percy didn't feel like curling up under his desk. He meant to go home, but his feet decided otherwise. They knew that he couldn't let what he'd witnessed lie, or else the doom would catch him. Thinking about Elmer's arrest made his heart beat faster.

Percy glanced over his shoulder at the towering old library, lifting his gaze to the uppermost window, where the Council sat. He felt shivers going down his spine. Something no monster had managed in ages. Percy left the wretched headquarters behind him and headed into the town. He walked the narrow pathways, ever surer that the wolf he'd sensed upon meeting Mother was following him again. This time it was up on the roofs, keeping its yellow eyes on him. There was no need to question if it was of the common variety. It wasn't.[1] He let the wolf follow him despite having several opportunities to lose it. What was the point? It was either sent by the board or someone else, keeping tabs on him. Clearly, it was the way of things now.

Percy stepped aside, letting a group of Kraken followers pass him by. Their little tentacle symbols were woven into their clothes, and their sinister air gave him no doubt who they were. While Percy believed in Kraken wholeheartedly, he had no interest in organized religion. It didn't sit well with him. Most people would assume otherwise, insisting that he was made for rules, and it would make sense that he would follow them even in his faith. But it wasn't so. He'd considered joining the Church long and hard,

---

1. It was the whole up-on-the-roof thing. A coyote could do such a thing and had been reported to do so. They even had a habit of waltzing into bakeries and taking residence there, but wolves weren't like that. They kept their feet on solid ground and made sure the forest had an ecosystem.

but he'd reasoned in the end that rules were set by humans and not by Kraken.

Percy followed his gaze as the followers disappeared around the corner. He let his hexes loose, and they came back empty. Yet there was the soft absence of voices all around him. If he didn't know better, he would think the city was holding its breath for him. Percy continued walking. He passed the usual vampire joint, where the willing donated their blood in exchange for favors. There was a whole underground market where vampires' I-owe-yous were the best currency to have. Percy had heard the city was trying to eradicate the notes, trying to force the vampires to use Necropolis Kraken Heads, but the vampires refused to obey. Just as well.

Percy stopped outside a clairvoyance shop not too far from the blood parlor. He carefully opened the front door to his twin sister's shop. The bell over the door chimed as he stepped past the beaded shade, which clung to his shoulders. Beyond them, there was no one in the small room that held a table covered with a rich, velvety greenish-brown tablecloth. On top of it was a giant crystal ball and a deck of cards. The place smelled of sweet tea mixed with incense. Behind him, a glowing ghostly light flickered on the window, inviting the pedestrians to have their fortunes told. Percy watched as the necromantic light flashed against the wallpaper with its vines and little colorful birds painted dark green and gold against the greenish canvas. Margot had made the place just as people imagined a medium parlor to be. She knew how to cater to the tourists pouring into the city from all over the world. Percy disapproved of all the glamour, but at least his sister was the real deal.

"Margot?" Percy asked.

"Don't just stand there," his sister said from the small door leading into the backroom, her hands folded. She was wearing a long silky robe embroidered with little ornaments. She had a beaded headdress on, which enchanted her heart-shaped face. Even Percy knew that her beauty was beyond the usual. Her bluish eyes drew people in. They reminded him of all the small jokes she'd played on him when they were children. They had been thick as thieves before they had been separated. Now, he barely knew her. There was this odd wall between them despite their uncanny resemblance.

She didn't seem surprised that he was there. "I have set a plate for you," she let out.

"You shouldn't leave the door open like that," Percy retorted.

"That's not a way to greet your sister. Come here and give me a hug." Margot opened her arms to invite him in.

"Anyone could waltz in," he insisted as he let her embrace him.

"And you don't think I know when someone comes with bad intentions?" She laughed and hugged him tighter.

Percy groaned.

"You still have that stick in your bum. Let her words go. Mother wasn't well, and she was a bit too neurotic when it came to you," she sighed as she let Percy take a step back.

"So, I gather this is not a social call. How can I help?" Margot watched him solemnly.

"Everything is wrong. The C—"

Margot lifted her hand to silence him. "No, don't go there. It's better if we don't speak. You know some of the bigwigs from the Council are my clients. I can't know what you are about to say. But Percy, I have seen it. I have been dreaming about you for months now. You need to watch your back and choose your friends more carefully. All I can say is that you should follow your heart, and it will lead you straight. You are a good person, Percy. Don't ever think otherwise. When our mother said you would amount to nothing but evil, she was wrong."

Margaret took hold of his jacket's collar, straightening it and patting it against his chest. "Now, if you want to see the twins, you are welcome to stay and eat. We were just starting dinner, and your plate is waiting."

"That would be nice."

Like nature, the ecosystem of a city was hard to balance. Any person thinking that it could be cultivated by picking off snails was delusional, though that didn't mean they didn't try. With a wide control over the systems, specialized guidelines, and proper persons embedded here and there, it could almost be achieved. But time, erosion, and corruption had a habit of catching on, and even the best laid plans fell short. Henrietta had to try, and meanwhile, she had been busying herself eradicating the snails in the garden. Imogene had delivered the news that the witches had been summoned and the letter was delivered. Henrietta sank her hands into the soil and squeezed it hard to draw strength from it. At the back of her mind, the familiar smell of decay lingered, reminding her that not all was well in the gardens.

"Mother?" a trembling girl's voice asked behind her.

Henrietta expected to see Imogene, but when she glanced over her shoulder, she saw Molly clutching her apron nervously. The girl had just graduated. Henrietta had hired her to work in the gardens. She was excellent with herbs. The older witches were trying to weed out her nervous tendencies. Henrietta had heard it wasn't going so well. Which was too bad; they needed someone who could guide the visitors and give them lessons on gardening and plants. Molly's otherwise amicable nature was perfect for that. When Molly smiled that sweet, bashful smile of hers, she got everyone on her side. If she only learned to wield that to her advantage, she would make a great head matron of the gardens.

"Yes?" Henrietta asked.

"There's a visitor for you. They are waiting for you at the door." Molly bit her lip.

"Then get them here." She said it more harshly than she'd meant to; she saw it in the younger witch's eyes.

"They say it's better if you two talk in private. I think they are someone from the government. Not sure, but I have seen her face somewhere." Molly slumped down.

Henrietta did her best not to correct the girl's demeanor. There was a time and place for it, and she had given that task to others. It was better if she didn't step on their toes. Henrietta got up and stretched her stiff back. She had been on the ground longer than was good for her.

"Thank you, Molly," she said.

Henrietta found Petula quietly leaning against the tall oak tree in the garden. She was clutching onto a basket, and there was a tall, willowy man with her. Henrietta wanted to laugh at Molly's comment about someone from the government.

"Miss Upwood," she said instead.

"Can we talk?"

"Sure thing, pet..."

Petula raised an eyebrow but said nothing about the slip.

Henrietta untangled her apron and corrected herself. "We better go to my office."

"Show me the way," Petula said.

Henrietta glanced at the man who was clearly coming with them, but as the mayor said nothing about it, she didn't remark that maybe it was better if they talked alone. That the letter's contents weren't for everyone.

The silence was excruciating as they walked to the main building. All the unsaid words hung there as reminders of the insecurities, failures, and possible dooms.

Imogene welcomed them at the Coven's front door, hovering around, trying not to appear to be observing them. Henrietta wondered if she should take her as a witness. There had to be a reason why Petula didn't send her goon away as she usually did. But better not. Imogene had been restless for a couple of days now. Always there as soon as Henrietta woke up and even at night before she went to bed. Even Eurof had commented on it.

"Imogene," she said before the young witch could say anything. "Will you go and put the kettle on and bring whatever cake Judika has baked today?"

Imogene lingered there a tad longer than expected, but then she curtsied and hurried to fulfill Henrietta's order.

"I'm not sure if you have ever met Judika, but she's behind all the cooking I have offered," Henrietta said, trying to lighten the mood. Petula had never been inside the Coven. The necromancer had always stayed in the garden. Now both of them paused as the young girl stepped over the threshold. Something broke, and it couldn't be taken back.

The mayor seemed restless as well. Her usual composure was gone, and Henrietta feared that more than a barrier between necromancers and witches was at stake. Henrietta couldn't tell if it was the letter or something else. She was definitely off as well.

"Mhm..." the mayor let out.

"She's wonderful. I know many ignore a witch in the kitchen, thinking their powers are wasted, but I'm sure if Judika had a chance, she could bring peace and contentment to the whole world just with her sweet cakes. It's like returning to your mother's bosom and feeling the utter hope, trust, and love we seem to lose as we grow up." Henrietta found herself blushing. She hadn't meant to say any of that. It was just Judika's food gave her enough solace to last a lifetime, especially when she was alone in her office when everyone else had gone to bed, and there was only the late-night owl hooting just behind the werewolves' howls and the stack of Coven papers in front of her.

Petula cleared her throat.

Henrietta remembered the way the mayor ate as if it was an alien concept to her, only taking in the necessary amount and not a single crumb more. But with tea, she drank the whole pot all by herself if given an opportunity. Henrietta had always found such people bizarre. Good food was celestial and could transcend a person.

Henrietta let them into her office. The branch she'd accidentally grown on the door still stuck out in full bloom. Henrietta cursed at not having done anything to it. Again, the mayor raised her eyebrow but said nothing.

"Mr. Colton, you can wait outside with Her," Petula stated before stepping into the office. She offered the basket to the man. As she said that, a cat's head popped out of the basket. It was a beautiful tabby with green eyes. It had orange fur with a white belly. Henrietta had heard about the cat but had never seen it firsthand. There was something about the way the green eyes gazed over its surroundings that made her think of the old tale of familiars. While some of her kind knew how to converse with nature, actual familiars were a myth. Yes, witches kept cats, dogs, lizards, birds, you name it, but the concept of them being helpers was just folklore.[2] Yet here the mayor's cat was, and there was something of the old tales in it. It leaped out of the basket and trotted to Henrietta's desk, jumping on it.

"I guess Her stays," Mr. Colton said and stepped out of the office, closing the door behind him.

"I'm sorry about barging in like this," Petula said.

"Don't be. I did send you the letter." Henrietta watched as the woman made her way behind her desk, scooping the cat onto her lap and sitting on the low windowsill. The terrarium was next to her, and the cat locked eyes with Nestor. The gecko ignored the huge cat and continued napping under a log.

---

2. Free will and all. The animals' freedom of choice maintained.

"What letter?" Petula tilted her head and peered at her silvery eyes with a hint of blue in them.

"Oh, I thought you came here because of what I wrote..." Henrietta let her words fall away. "The Coven sees—"

"Don't be so formal. I thought we were past that." Petula cut her short.

Henrietta stared at the mayor, bewildered. The girl just kept scratching the cat while trying to hold it, not letting it get too close to the terrarium. This wasn't the first time Petula had been rude. The mayor always danced around the fine line of honesty and hostility. But this was the first time she'd cut Henrietta off.

"I'm sorry. That came out wrong," Petula said, facing Henrietta. "I have had a long day, and that's why I came to you. I saw Mr. Thurston. But before that, I had a meeting with a reporter about my plan to reinstate the Public Resurrection Ministration, giving a perfect reason for the Council to paint a big target on my back... But you spoke about a letter?"

"Forget about it. Burn it before reading, I beg of you." Henrietta let her posture slump. She only noticed afterward when the mayor lifted her eyebrow as she every so often did.

"If that's what you think is best." Petula made her words sound like a question without being a question.

"Tell me about the meeting." Henrietta dragged a chair out from under the desk and took her seat.

Petula observed her silently. When they were face to face, the girl said, "I can't in good conscience let Mr. Thurston walk free, but that seems to be our only path out of this, if we are to go against the Council." Petula waited for Henrietta to react, and when she didn't give more than a nod, the mayor continued, "What he did was beyond what any necromancer should do, disregarding the souls utterly and reducing them to nothingness. It's monstrous even by necromancers' standards. He should stay under lock and key. But we can't let the Council have him either, or anyone else for that matter. Yet if we free him, everyone in the known world will do everything in their power to possess the man. Who knows what kind of offers the Council has already had? I have already been informed that other nations have been sniffing around. Our city is full of spies..."

Henrietta nodded.

"...Otis and his machines will tear the continents apart. The Bufonite is a curse on him, us, and Necropolis. The most merciful thing would be to press on the Council to hang him. But if we do that, the necromancers will revolt. Or worse yet, it will ensure the Council's ultimate power over Necropolis." Petula's eyes were dead and her body stiff.

"What do you want me to say?" Henrietta managed to answer.

"I'm not sure. I thought about the matter over and over again as I rode here, and there won't be a good outcome whatever I do. Not when, most likely, the Council will make him disappear so they can force him to construct the machine for them or for the highest bidder. We don't want that either. Whoever possesses it will own everything—"

"And if we release him?" Henrietta asked, more to think aloud than anything else.

"The Council reacts. I'm not sure if the Town Hall has the necessary means to protect, guard, and defend Mr. Thurston when the world comes to collect. Not even building our own machine will release us."

"Are you sure he hasn't already given in?"

"Of course not, but I got the feeling he hasn't. That's just my intuition speaking, and it shouldn't be trusted." Petula lowered the cat to the floor, where it instantly tried to get to the terrarium. The girl blocked its entry by lifting a leg in front of the cat. In return she received a dirty look and an invitation to a staring competition with a clear winner. Then the cat began to lick its paw nonchalantly, eying both Petula and the terrarium. Nestor ignored their antics, not even batting an eyelid. Either it trusted that Henrietta would keep any dangers at bay, or it knew which one of them was the dangerous one.

"Hmm," Henrietta muttered, watching the mayor and the cat interact.

"My thoughts exactly."

"That's not all..." Henrietta began.

Petula turned her attention from the cat to her. "Yes?" her eyes seemed to say.

Henrietta looked away. "Agatha..." she said, then shook her head. "Never mind about that. What I meant to say was that I had a meeting with the Council as well. They are threatening me and the Coven with legal action and cutting off our funding. We need their money." Henrietta waited for the woman to react. The usual things, like gasping for air or widening her eyes or something. She wasn't sure why she expected something like that when the mayor's past reactions had shown otherwise.

The only thing she got was, "I see."

Henrietta added in the rest.

"Something you would expect from the Council. Still, I'm sorry that they would go for the refugees. That's callous even by their standards," Petula sighed. "It seems like they are covering all their bases. How about the others? Have you heard of them?"

Henrietta shook her head. She had been too wrapped up in her worries to consider what the Council was doing to the others. Clearly, they were well aware of the needlepoint group meetings.

Before either of them could continue the conversation, there was a knock on the door, and without waiting for a response, Imogene stepped in with a tray resting on her right arm.

"Let me help you with those." Henrietta untangled her unknowingly entangled arms, got up, and stepped towards the younger witch.

"Mother, I can manage." Imogene tiptoed around her, lowering the tray with a teapot, two cups, and two slices of chocolate orange cake onto the desk. When she was done pouring the cups and adding the necessary milk and honey, she stood there.

"Thank you, Imogene. You may go now."

"Are you sure, Mother?" The younger witch glanced at the open door. Petula's guard was leaning nonchalantly against the staircase with his back and right foot, his knee bent, swinging the basket in his arms.

"Quite sure, Imogene. We can take it from here."

The younger witch left—reluctantly, Henrietta might add. Until now, she'd thought she knew where Imogene's loyalties lay. If anyone knew what was going on inside this house, it was her. Imogene couldn't be so foolish as to sell information for pennies and promises.

"We can't afford sentiment," Petula said.

Henrietta spun around to face the necromancer, sure her mouth was hanging slightly open.

"You are the second person today to think I can read minds, but I honestly can't. Just probabilities." Petula crossed her legs and leaned forward, looking hungrily at the tea.

"I don't know how you do it," Henrietta said, walking to the tray and handing Petula's cup to her.

"With great pain," Petula said and took a sip. The rigidity of her face melted away, and she looked almost soft and friendly.

"You don't trust easily, do you?"

Petula took another sip before answering. "Never learned to."

"Such a shame."

"Yes, so I have understood."

Henrietta sighed and took her cup and cake plate with her, sitting on the other side of the terrarium on the windowsill.

"So, what now?" Henrietta stated after taking a bite of the rich chocolate cake with just the right amount of bitterness.

"Honestly, I don't know."

They continued in silence, Henrietta eating the cake and Petula drinking her tea. The cat had stopped trying to get to the terrarium and had curled up on the sill, where the pale Necropolitan sun shone. In Amanita, the sun was always warm and ready to scorch you to death if you weren't careful.

"Let them try. We can deal with whatever the Council throws at us. But we better call the others and have a meeting."

"Meeting it is then." Petula lowered the teacup to her saucer and stood up.

Henrietta nodded. She watched as the mayor scooped a slice of cake onto a napkin and walked out. Outside, she handed the cake to her guard, and then they were gone. The cat jumped up and hurried after them.

"Hmm," Henrietta said. At the back of her mind, something or someone insisted that she hadn't done everything she could. That she had somehow missed the small opening Petula had given. Yet other parts of her insisted that this was the start of a beautiful friendship in a time of war. That the war to come was going to be brutal.

CHAPTER TWELVE

FOOL'S ALLY

People weren't made for passivity. At least, Percy wasn't. He stood outside of his sister's parlor. It had started to rain, the usual cold rain of December. It went straight into the bones and wouldn't leave without a good banishing spell. His sister's words hung there as a reminder of what he was and what his mother expected him to become. Percy glanced in the direction of the university's towers. The statues of the former masters were visible on the city skyline. They got their fair share of rain. Percy's home was under those towers. He could head there and ignore everything: the Coven, the Council, Mr. Spooner's arrest, and the Cunninghams' attempt to befriend him. He wasn't a friend-making sort of person. Never had been. Then there was his conscience and what it let him do. Percy muttered his hexes as he walked away from his sister's parlor, carrying with him her family's laughter. He had never fitted in with them. While the children looked at him with awe, they knew he didn't belong; that he was somehow not right. That was the curse of a hexer. Something everyone wanted to be but no one wanted to get close to.

Percy lifted his jacket's collar up and was glad his fedora kept the worst of the rain away. He ignored the other pedestrians as they did him: the university students, the late-night pickpockets, the always hungry vampires, the ghouls minding their own business, and the desperate in search of liberation. He made sure the hexes cloaked him from everyone, especially from the wolf who had hung over the parlor all this time. He could smell its wet fur. He let the hexes go forth in search of all the dangers lurking in front of him. His hexes spotted a beggar or two, who hurried out of his way despite having gotten used to living on the Necropolis streets, where you couldn't be strangers to the utter hopelessness that lingered at every corner. Percy felt a twinge of pain. Not sure why. But there was guilt involved just from existing and having dry socks on.

In Necropolis, you learned that everyone was out to get you from the second you were pulled out screaming and unwilling, taking your first breath, whatever shape and size you came in. Even the werewolves howled at their fate. The world wasn't all that it was cracked up to be. It was all the uncertainty.[1] The hexes seeped into every wall he passed. They sensed everything: curses, the beating hearts, the stories. If there were any threats, they slipped past him. A murderer chose another target.

Percy pushed his hexes past the threats to search for that one beating heart that deserved all that Necropolis had to offer. That was Laura, the internal policewoman with the capotain hat to prove it. The curses found her at the nearby cafeteria in the Council's headquarters. She was surrounded by her lackeys. Percy let his hexes move on, not letting them linger long enough for her to notice. He made them track her movements, sensing the slightest change on a molecular level. The indivisible ultimate state of existence, pushing and pulling everything. If Percy could get his hexes to work on that level, they would be undetectable. But he wasn't that good.

Percy followed the hexes to the Council's headquarters. He waited outside for the front door to be opened, letting him slip in past the witches guarding the building from the Save the Otis Group. He saw an undead lawyer shamble out with his shoulders slumped. Percy slipped around the

---

1. And other people. You know.

man, puffing his chest out with an air of belonging to calm the witches' senses. They didn't care. They had gone numb a long time ago. That was Necropolis for you.[2]

Percy glanced at the wall where all the fallen Council operatives were marked with coffins and sighed. It welcomed in anyone daring to enter the headquarters as a reminder of what the place was made of. Percy wanted every single coffin to be removed.

He found the path Laura had taken. His hexes automatically flickered between Laura and all those he passed. The clock was already turning way past midnight, but the building was full. The other witches and necromancers were too busy fulfilling their tasks to look past his hexes. Laura's tracks took him to the underground levels. He could sense the heightened level of security guarding the place. There were not only hexes but ghosts as well, and who knew what else Percy was unable to detect. If he wanted to move forward, he couldn't keep hiding anymore. It was too dangerous. He stepped out of the shadows and took his monster hunter badge out and pinned it on his jacket. He straightened his back and readied himself to stare down anyone who wanted to stop him. Here Laura's residual trail merged with Mr. Spooner's. Percy switched tracks to follow the man, walking through the narrowing corridors with gas lamps lighting his way. The stone walls around him were cold and damp, and the floor was made of gravel that crunched underneath his soles. There was no one here, but Percy didn't trust his senses.

The labyrinth-like paths spread from every junction he took and disappeared from view behind another corner. Percy had to track all the turns

---

2. However, the city would disagree. Once, it had been a place of terror, home of the great big hunt, but then the bureaucrats had snuck in, and the hunting was replaced with small print, and terror changed into utter hopelessness. It wasn't your body they wanted; it was your mind they were after.

he took, making them into stories, noticing a dent here or there on the stone, and so forth. It was a memory game he had been taught during his first year on the force. This place was made to trick you. Percy had thus far counted twenty turns. Eventually, the outline of Mr. Spooner slowed down and came to a halt in front of a door where an ugly-looking man with enough muscle to share with the next fellow sat on a stool. He glowered at Percy when he stepped into sight.

"I'm here to collect Mr. Spooner," Percy said.

"Yeah?!" the man groaned.

"Miss Devlin sent me." Percy used Laura's name.

"Did she?" The man stood up, and Percy did everything in his power not to step back. The man was several feet taller than he was, his arms wider than Percy's legs, and Percy wasn't a small man.

"I'm here on the Monster Hunter Force's behalf, and Miss Devlin has agreed to hand over the goblin to us." Percy widened his stance. He readied himself to send his hexes forward. Maybe a blinding curse, then confusion.

"Miss Devlin..." the man growled the name out, "...said not to let anyone in. Especially not a man with a pretty face and long black hair and a pain-in-the-ass attitude. You fit the bill. So one of you is lying, and Miss Devlin and I go back a long way..." The man stormed towards Percy.

Percy stepped aside, letting the curses wash over the giant.

The only thing he got back was a laugh. "You think your little curses affect me, witch?"

Kraken shit, Percy thought. He spun around to face the man, who'd already collected his momentum and was launching his huge, mallet-like fist towards him. Percy dodged. The man thudded past him. Percy hit the man in his ribs, but there was no effect. The man turned around, and Percy knew he should run. He couldn't. He faced the monstrous man warded against hexes. If the man was a witch or a necromancer, Percy would have sensed it. He was just an ordinary mortal. The man came at him again, and Percy kicked him in his stomach. Anyone normal enough would have the wind knocked out of them. The man barely noticed it. He stood his ground. He grabbed Percy by his ankle and yanked, sending Percy flying onto his back. The next thing Percy noticed was the man trying to twist his ankle out of place. Percy let out a cry of curses, unleashing his imps. The tiny creatures with claws and needle-sharp teeth ran along Percy's body. They jumped at the man, biting into his flesh. The man let go of Percy's leg, staggering backward, trying to defend against the dozen imps swarming all over him. He swung his arms, but the imps held on, drawing blood and tearing flesh away. Percy had to look away.

"A key," he whispered.

Soon enough, an imp jumped up next to him, handing him a bundle of keys. The creature stuck its tongue out when Percy reached for them. The imps hated him. Percy didn't blame them. They were independent harbingers of chaos, and he enslaved them for his amusement.

"You are coming with me," he said and grasped the creature by its neck.

The imp kept sticking its tongue out and hissing and trying to claw Percy as he lowered it onto his shoulder. The imp's oversized head kept bobbing as Percy limped to the cell door. Percy pushed the key in and drew the door open. In the corner of the bleak, cold dungeon, Mr. Spooner was huddled, hugging his legs to his chest and shivering.

"Mr. Spooner," Percy said.

The investigator lifted his head, looking at Percy with his bloodied eyes. There was a nasty cut on his forehead.

"You are coming with me," Percy said.

The man hesitated, and Percy half expected Mr. Spooner to refuse by saying he was being rightfully held by the Council. But the man stood up and limped towards Percy. His trousers were torn at the knees, and Percy saw Laura's handiwork: burned curse marks on the man's skin.

Percy helped the man to stand, letting him lean against him. The weight

made Percy wince from pain. His right ankle was shattered. Percy reinforced the limb with a hex, leaving behind soreness and a limp. Percy
dragged Mr. Spooner out of the cell and commanded the imps to escort
the giant inside the prison. He locked the door afterwards. Then he made
the imps draw near him. He couldn't send them away. Not yet.

"Mr. Allread..." Elmer Spooner started.

"I know. This is bad, but—"

"I just wanted to say thank you."

"You can thank me later if we get out alive and you make it to safety."
Percy wasn't sure where that safety was. Who he could trust and who was
powerful enough to keep them hidden from the Council. But that was for
later; now, they needed to get out. He could already hear footsteps running
towards them. He must have triggered something.

Percy turned around and dragged Mr. Spooner in the other direction,
hoping that they didn't run into anything else the Council hid in their
dungeons.

Sometimes you get a small victory, but you're not quite sure what it is, or
even if it really is a victory at all or a nightmare in sheep's clothing. Raul
groaned. He was sure that another shoe was going to drop. Yet another one
of his co-workers came to congratulate him on his interview with the mayor
and the follow-up with her and the Council. Everyone thought the articles
had been the golden Kraken tentacle they were all hoping for. The paper's
circulation had tripled, and Sandy was giving him grim looks. Raul now
led the office pool not only for the most notorious piece written but also
the most pieces published. None of it made him happy. He was past that.
Sandy clearly wasn't.

He hated his own words being reflected back on him as if they were the truth. They weren't the truth. His piece was a story—a photo-op for the powerful—that the mayor and the Council wanted him to tell. And he had done just that. And the public didn't care. They were happy to repeat the mantra he had written. All he had ever wanted as a reporter was to share the truth, make people think, be critical of all they saw and heard, and what he got was the opposite.

The printing presses underneath him made the whole building shake. It roared so loud that Raul had to read his coworkers' lips to know what they were saying. The machines printed his story over and over again, as the paper boys were running out of news to sell. He watched as Maximilian popped the champagne cork. His co-workers passed the filled glasses from one hand to another. One reached him as well. Raul's editor lifted his flute up and gave a speech. Raul didn't bother to read his lips. Like everyone else, the man didn't want the truth. He wanted money and fame and circulation. Raul desperately needed the truth. It was like this ache inside him. If he was wiser, he wouldn't follow that ache. But no one could accuse him of being wise. His past girlfriends had said as much.

The true truth he needed was hidden somewhere in that old library, where policies were made behind secret doors and where no action had consequences. The Council made sure of that. They'd reassured him that the Council agreed with Miss Upwood about the discontent Necropolitans were feeling about Mr. Thurston's arrest and what it meant. They had even hinted about making it easier to get a license to work abroad, tax cuts for necromancers, and lower prices for resurrection. It had been there between the lines, and he'd reported as much. And the mayor, she had just smiled, as her stunt to reallocate funds to her little Public Resurrection Ministration had gotten the Council to dance to her tune for once.

But all this was just a distraction from the real thing. Raul had to find a way into the Council's headquarters and speak to Mr. Thurston. There was the truth, and the necromancer held the entire city's future in his hands.

He restlessly watched the newspaper staff drink their drinks and, one by one, circle around him in the hope that some of his good luck rubbed off on them. They wanted their opportunity to be the talk of the town. There was another thing that was wrong. When the reporter became the news, something was wrong. There were exceptions. But here and now, he shouldn't be the story.

Raul had to get into that building.

He jumped up from his seat, snatching his jacket and hat, and rushed past his colleagues, who shouted after him to come with them to the local pub just down the road. He ignored them, needing air. Outside the building, the loud thumping of the printing press was still ever so present. Sometimes, when the days at the office got to him, he heard the thumping even in his sleep. But now he was sure he heard a quiet cough before his legs disappeared from underneath him. Raul tried to struggle up, but there was a boot pinning him down. There came a loud crack from his spine, as if someone was forcing their full weight down on his back. Raul was pretty sure that whoever that someone was was leaning in to say something, but they never managed. A low growl came from the alleyway not far from where Raul lay.

Raul lifted himself up only to see a flash of tattered fur, something green and yellow leaping over him. Then, there came a loud scream. The pressure was lifted, and he lay there, unsure if he should move or play dead, his cheek pressed to the cold, wet cobblestones, waiting for a sign from the universe. It never came. There was just the printing press and the absence of other noises, as if the city and anyone careless enough to be up and about was waiting to see if they should play dead as well. Raul carefully got up, feeling every move in his lower back. There was pain, but it was pain he could live with, and it was the least of his worries. The woman who had been following him around for days lay dead next to him. Her throat was ripped open, and her wine-colored dress was soaked with her own blood.

The creature who had dashed over him was nowhere to be seen.

Raul lifted his gaze to see if anyone had seen what he had seen. His eyes met Sandy's, who was standing in the newspaper office door, staring at him with wide eyes. Those eyes turned from wide to narrow, accompanied by a smirk.

Sandy screamed bloody murder.

Raul ran. He hadn't meant to, but his feet took over.

The shouting over the printing press grew louder. Sandy screamed his name like he was the reaper, and not in a good way. Raul turned into the next alley, running as fast as he could. Every step he took came with a sharp pain in his lower back, but he didn't stop. He kept going. He kept bumping into people who didn't look kindly on him, but they didn't stop him either. Raul kept pushing deeper into the city, reaching the Moorland Market, where he tried to blend into the crowd. A place which people from all over the world visited to buy all their hearts desired and more, from future readings to body parts, and fancy new fashions to give the middle finger to all those stuck at home.

Raul glanced over his shoulder and saw two officers approaching the crowd. To his luck, neither of them were ghouls or the other specials they had been hiring lately. Just two dumb humans. Raul kept his head down and hoped they wouldn't call a werewolf to track him. He stepped into the first palm reader shop he found and sat down, letting the man read his fortune, handing him his palm. The man followed the lines on his skin and then looked up at Raul funnily. Then he let go of his palm and insisted on getting his money first before opening his mouth. Raul handed him a coin.

"I wouldn't go home, mate," the man said.

"I—"

"You better leave, mate. I want no trouble." The fortune teller pointed at the door, forcing Raul to leave the incense-infested tent. Raul got up and did as he was told. Outside, the incense smell was replaced with the aroma of grease and spices. The officers were gone.

Raul stood there, his feet as clueless as he was about where to go next. Not home. Necropolis's fortune tellers knew their stuff. He could always waltz into the police station and beg for leniency, but that was too sensible. There was only one place he could go—the Council's headquarters. Only a fool would go there. And he was a fool. The biggest of them.

Chapter Thirteen

THE MOTHER OF ALL STORMS

C ollecting enemies is easy, especially if you have that one thing that makes you shine. With Petula, that thing was her title, which gave others permission to paint a target on her back. She would prefer if it was her talents. Petula turned Henrietta's envelope around in her hand. It had been in her inbox when she'd arrived at the Town Hall. The witch had asked her to burn it. Petula scratched Her's head; the cat had taken residence on the desk.

"What shall we do?" she asked aloud. "Burn or read it? Or just leave. There's no reason to torment myself this way. Necropolis was never meant to be my home. I was meant to return to Leporidae Lop after my studies."

The cat yawned, then stretched its whole body and curled up on the paper stack full of demands to put out more fires kindling in the city.

"If you are trying to tell me something, that's not helping. Truly not." Petula could still feel the burned wards, see Otis in his prison cell, and hear Henrietta's words. All her problems would be solved if she just left. All the awkwardness she felt around everyone would be forgotten. She wouldn't have to think about demands, intentions, and being used like a tool, as Henrietta had clearly planned to do. She could just open the letter and confirm her suspicions.

"It's just the two of us. The others are Kraken only knows where. We

could walk to the harbor, buy a ticket, and sail home. As simple as that."
Petula looked at the cat, who ignored the whole conversation. The cat had
never been the answering kind. That had become apparent as soon as they
had met. Still, she continued, "Why do they even think I can solve these
kinds of riddles? Yes, I have always been good with puzzles. Any kind,
really, but none of this has anything to do with logic and rationality. People
are kidding themselves if they think human affairs are composed of such
things. Or that they can be reduced to models carrying such labels. Chaos
and anomalies always sneak in. Science is rational. They should have let me
stay there and perfect the necromantic profession rather than be caught in
the middle of politics."

Her poked its head up, twitching its ears and then moving on to licking
its paw. Graceful motions in a perfect design. Nothing like Petula.

"You are right. It's what it is, and there's no going back and altering
anything. I have my responsibilities, but just to be sure, let's keep the boat
as a viable option."

"What boat is that, dear?" came from the door, and without having
to turn, Petula knew Mrs. Maybury stood in the doorway. She'd let the
undead sneak up on her. Something no Necropolitan would ever do.

Petula spun around, her walking skirt fanning out in an almost complete
circle before stopping. Dramatic effects, that was what Necropolis was
made of, and now even she'd joined in.

"Mrs. Maybury," Petula greeted and tucked the letter under the cat.

"I came to see how you are, now that you are no longer hiding under
your table."

Petula felt herself blush. What a marvelous creature Mrs. Maybury was.
There was no one else like her. No one with such great power to render a
person naked and vulnerable with one seemingly small observation.

"Perfectly well, Mrs. Maybury," Petula replied, hoping the blushing
wasn't too obvious.

"You don't seem or sound perfectly well. I have told you before, and it seems I have to repeat it, but I'm here for you, *girl*," Mrs. Maybury said.

The girl part meant Petula was to obey. Of course, every aspect of her wanted to disobey. But there was no point in an unfruitful rebellion. She might as well tell her, because in a very twisted way, Mrs. Maybury was there for her. She didn't lie about that. The trouble began when there was an action to be taken. Then the arguments and pouting were imminent.

"Do come in, Mrs. Maybury," Petula said.

Mrs. Maybury shut the door behind her and shambled to the couch, not letting her gaze leave Petula for a second, as if to prevent Petula from backing down. She wasn't going to. It was just that starting the conversation was the difficult part; starting anything was. Whatever words you were going to say, whatever action you were going to take, it wouldn't be perfect, it wouldn't be what you wanted. Petula took her time, letting silence linger there between her and Mrs. Maybury, expecting the undead to jump in. But Mrs. Maybury wasn't a simple-minded creature as so many expected her to be. If she wanted, she could be subtle, but only if she was in the mood, and only if it advantaged her somehow. Here, silence served her better than the chatter people seemed to create to cut through the awkwardness.

"I visited Mr. Thurston today," Petula began, pausing to think what to say next.

"The necromancer," Mrs. Maybury offered.

"The same fellow, yes... While I want nothing more than to stick it to the Council and align with the public view that the treatment of Mr. Thurston is unacceptable, I can't. What the man has done is wrong on so many levels, it makes me sick. So I'm damned if I demand him to be released and damned if I don't." Petula crossed her arms.

"And you think you can influence the Council?" Mrs. Maybury asked. There was a hint of amusement in her voice. Still, it was a genuine question.

"There's a way, I'm sure of it. The travel and working ban is upsetting the necromancers, and they are now willing to voice it, along with some other stricter rules. Also, by reallocating money to the Public Resurrection Ministration, we give both citizens and necromancers the option to choose their resurrector and employer. The Council knows this. It's leverage. But I don't want Mr. Thurston freed. I want him to serve his time. Better yet, he should be hanged. Even though I don't believe in capital punishment. The Council will surely hide him and torture him until he gives them the formulae for the Bufonite. If the Council gets it, there's no holding them back."

She'd said all this so many times that the litany came out like a rehearsed testimonial. She found herself clutching her arms tightly. Petula forced herself to uncross her arms, letting them drop by her sides like dead weight. How could such a simple move mean so much? Petula could still hear her teacher drilling her on all the social gestures people made and what they meant.

"I see." Mrs. Maybury crossed her legs one over the other using her hands. "I don't see a problem or the ultimatum you are so *fixated* on. Everything is a trade-off in politics, or it's about partnering up with some-one or someones. What I have gathered is that the Council needs a partner right now. The people of Necropolis don't actually want Mr. Thurston freed. They want to free themselves. So make that exchange you are already planning."

"What about—"

"The Bufonite? You are clever. Use that brain of yours. Can such a machine even exist? I don't think so."

Petula just stared at the undead. With her irritating manner, she was so easy to dismiss as an—Petula didn't even want to come up with the derogatory term, not after how much Mrs. Maybury had helped her. Mrs. Maybury had survived thus far in Necropolis and not only survived, she'd been a key player. Because of her, undeads could now own their own businesses. She was brilliant. In her own way, Petula might add.

"Yes, you are right. Still, it leaves me compro—"

"Didn't I just say compromising is the way of politics? Ideologies have to be put aside if people don't violently demand them." The undead sucked her teeth. There were more of them than the last time.

"Do you want to come—" Petula didn't get farther than that.

"To your little needlepoint group?" There was scorn in the undead's voice.

"Yes," Petula said.

"Mind if I do." And that was that. There was hurt behind the undead's eyes. It would never be mentioned out in the open. Kraken forbid, if Petula ever brought it up, there would never be an end to it.

"We meet in two hours, and we can go together in my coach," Petula offered. Before the woman could answer, she added, "Now I have a report to write to the Town Hall."

"Let one of your pets do it." Mrs. Maybury narrowed her eyes when Petula was about to protest. Mrs. Maybury spoke over her. "It really isn't that hard. It should state the mayor had a meeting with the Council to discuss Mr. Thurston's arrest and imprisonment. That's already public knowledge, yes? Then add that the mayor met with the prisoner in question and saw him in good health. Further discussions will be had between the Town Hall and the Council before Mr. Thurston's trial. There! Easy."

Petula was sure her mouth was hanging open. It would have taken her hours to come up with those words, and Mrs. Maybury just flung them out without blinking an eye. Actually without blinking an eye.

"Write that down, girl, and stop gawking." When it wasn't enough to make Petula move, Mrs. Maybury added, "I used to be a press secretary for old Susie Dent. You know, the agriculture minister. That's how my political career got started. Clean, honest job."

"I didn't know." Petula grabbed her official paper and a pen to write down exactly what Mrs. Maybury had said.

"Not many do, so keep it that way. What's forgotten should stay forgotten. Not that I'm not proud of what I did; I am. But you know how things are."

Petula knew how things were, and whatever you put out there, no matter how positive, people found a reason to tear it down. She nodded.

"Now, before I forget, I came to tell you that the university's sociology department, along with the school of economics, hasn't heard from you. I checked..." The woman gave Petula time to argue back.

She didn't. It was a trap.

"So I set up a committee on your behalf..." Again, Mrs. Maybury waited for Petula to argue back. This time there was a good reason to do so. But if someone did the work for her, saving Petula from having to interact with other people, she wasn't going to say no even when it undermined her power.

"Excellent," Petula said. "They know where to start?"

"I told them to figure out what it will mean if the machines come here."

Vague and big, Petula thought, but instead said, "Then everything is set. And the funding?"

"They were more than happy to jump on it. Silly buggers had nothing to do, as I made clear."

Petula held back a laugh.

Nothing else had to be said or done. Mrs. Maybury let Petula finish the statement, get it to her staff, eat and clean herself up, and fetch her needlepoint basket, and all this while the woman, in an almost meditative state stared at the cat, who was napping on the desk after having received its meal. If there was a battle of wills going on, Petula was sure the undead would win, meaning Petula was on the losing end of who bowed to whom. Oh well.

Petula glanced at the letter Henrietta had sent her and then at Mrs.

Maybury in fear that she could read her mind. The undead woman seemed disinterested. Petula threw the thing into the little furnace in the corner. Again, the undead said nothing. The only thing that jolted Mrs. Maybury awake was Petula shrugging on her overcoat. She didn't take the cat with her this time. She left it to mind its own business in the Town Hall, where everyone knew Her belonged to Petula, and there would be consequences if a hair was out of place.

As they rode to the Necro Botanical Gardens together, Petula hoped she hadn't made a mistake by bringing the undead—who was getting visibly restless—with her. Why Mrs. Maybury was nervous, Petula had no clue. Of course, she could ask, but most probably, she would get some sort of answer. An elaborate one. It was just that the questions weren't usually the issue. It was the answers that got you screwed.

Justice was a funny notion to have in a universe that didn't seem to function that way. It was like asking for gods to care. But people had to pretend justice existed or there wouldn't be empires or huge monuments to remember the past by. Just immediacy and all that followed from that.

"I did steal the documents," a wretched voice rang out in the labyrinth-like maze.

Percy dragged the sniveling man through the corridors in hope of finding an escape. He heard running footsteps behind them. The imps next to Percy were sticking their ears out, some grinning widely with all their teeth showing in neat little needle-sharp rows, meaning human flesh, chaos, and a whole lot of conflict was to come.

"What?" Percy spat out between breathing heavily and trying to ignore the pain in his ankle and concentrating his hexes behind them. He wasn't willing to send the imps against whoever was coming at them. There was a possibility they weren't here for them, and if the imps went, they would surely drag something back into that nothing with them.

"If you were thinking, was this merited or not? It was. I did more. I gave the documents to Otis's lawyer. I did it all." Elmer trembled next to him.

"Why are you telling me this?" Percy groaned and readied his hexes simultaneously to see if there was someone at the next junction.

"So you can leave me behind and save yourself. I deserve this. I knew the consequences before I did anything, and I accepted them." Elmer squeezed Percy's arm to make him stop.

"No," was all Percy managed to say.

"No?"

"Not now, Mr. Spooner. Not here. This is not what you deserve, but we can discuss semantics later. Now the witch who arrested you is heading for us, and she's not alone." Percy pressed them against the wall. He had almost missed Laura's hex web looming in front of them. She'd tried to hide it, herself, and the four others who were with her, but the gas lamp had made the web flicker against the stones. She'd made a mistake. But he couldn't underestimate her. Laura came equipped with nasty, brutal tricks.

"Mr. Allread," came Laura's sing-song voice after a while. "We know you are there." Percy was sure she meant, "*I have been waiting for this ever since school.*" Percy had gathered, despite how socially thick he was, that Laura resented that he had been accepted into the Monster Hunter Force and she hadn't. And she couldn't understand why, so he had to be the problem. But even Percy knew what loyalty and camaraderie meant. Percy had always been willing to sacrifice his life for the cause, for his mates. Laura wouldn't, and she had always been a second-grade hexer. She could have been the best, but she'd kept herself back. It was her unwillingness to admit she didn't know something or that she needed help, or, worse still, that she was wrong. You couldn't become the best with such a mentality. Only a victim of mediocrity.

Percy glanced back at the tunnels they had come from. He had seen other corridors, and some of them might loop behind Laura and her men or the web. But there were no outrunning curses, and Laura was a hexer. The nasty sort. He already felt her attempts to reach them. Easy ones to ward off. A test. The next ones would be harder to defend, especially as Mr. Spooner wouldn't be immune to them.

Percy could let the imps attack Laura and her men to give them time to disappear into the tunnels.

"There's really no place to go, Mr. Allread. So surrender yourself, and we can go the amicable route," Laura said as she sent another wave of curses meant to make Percy lose his mind.

He blocked them easily. It meant nothing. She wouldn't let him walk away from here alive. That much was sure.

"Murder and torture aren't amicable," Percy said.

"There you are. I knew it was you," Laura countered. "And what's a little stabbing and torture but a friendly reminder that you are still alive and valuable?"

Percy heard one of Laura's men whisper something. He didn't actually hear it, but the imps did. One of the imps climbed up his trouser leg and happily passed on the message. "Just fry him out already," it stated.

Yes, indeed, Percy thought. He put his curses forward to map out what he was dealing with. In addition to Laura, there were two other hexers. No wonder; a witch with a tendency towards premonitions and lucid dreaming wasn't precisely combat material. Not when the future was ever-changing, with the habit of falling victim even to the slightest flutters. Then there was one elemental one. Percy could be wrong. But he rarely was. There was a slight feeling of wet electricity in the tunnels. The last one was a necromancer. Spirits, that was all he needed in this situation. Only Kraken could save them now.

"I'm sorry," Percy whispered to Elmer.

"No, it's me who should be apologizing to you. I should have never gotten you involved." Elmer let go of his arm and pushed himself away from the wall. "I'll go to them, and you can find the tunnel that leads out of here."

"What tunnel?"

"There's one that leads to the shoreline. I read about it in the library's history. It should be somewhere nearby."

"Why didn't you say that straight away?"

"It's not like we can—"

"Yes, we can... Rise." He said the latter not to Elmer but to his imps. The dozen imps he had already manifested turned into a hundred, and he unleashed them all on the corridor where Laura and the others were. They were instantly met with screams.

"Let's go." Percy didn't wait for the man to reply. He dragged Elmer past the hex web, going first, feeling them burn his skin. "Show me the way," he commanded, ignoring the unnerving feeling of sacrificing the imps. He knew they would resurrect back in whatever dimension they came from, yet he hated unnecessary bloodbaths. This was just that. Lives lost for silly games. And the next time he summoned the imps, they would be pissed off, and he would have to do everything in his power to keep them from ripping him apart.

"The-the-there wasn't a picture, just a blackened mention, but I cross-referenced with my granny's book, and there it was..." Elmer stuttered.

Percy had almost forgotten what the man was on about. "Okay," he said as his jacket's hem fluttered. The necromancer was invoking the spirit wind. The imps were working hard, from the sound of their screeches.

"I'll use my curses," Percy said. He muttered a simple location-finding spell with a hint of malice, sending it forward. It ricocheted from wall to wall, showing dead ends and open passages, creating a clearer picture of where they were. He took a better hold of Elmer and dragged him faster towards the left tunnel. The investigator moaned but didn't complain even though it was clear his legs were hurting. Both of them knew there would be a lot more hurt when Laura got to them.

The imps were already dying out. They let out little screeches here and there, yet they kept fighting. They didn't care if they died or if they lived. All they wanted was to follow the command given and tear into the flesh as deeply as they could. Even the most peaceful of the imps chirped in pleasure at the cries humans made. What they didn't like was the nasty spirits ruining their fun and picking them off one by one. They were running out of time.

Some of Laura's curses were gaining on them. Every distraction Percy left behind was countered, and they followed Percy and Elmer relentlessly. Keeping up the location hexes and the protective wards and the imps was getting harder. Percy's hands were shaking.

The tunnels got narrower and damper. There was a slight scent and feel of sea air to the place. For a moment, Percy felt a glimmer of hope that they might escape. But Laura and her men had been gaining ground. Almost all the imps were dead. Only one survived, and when it reached Percy, it made a rude gesture and dematerialized back to the realm it had come from. No more imps then. Not without a significant personal sacrifice.

"You go ahead and find a reporter or someone to guard you. Maybe the police. I'll stall them." Percy let go of Elmer.

"They will—"

"Kill me? We both die if they get to us. This way, at least one of us lives. Now go."

Elmer shook his head, but he shuffled onward, leaving Percy behind. Percy widened his stance and waited for Laura to appear. She did, her men still with her. Blood and tears covered their faces, and their clothes were torn to pieces. Percy never felt good about letting the imps do that to another human being. Yet he had done so, and he would live with the consequences.

"Percy." Laura spat out blood.

There was nothing he could do. Just face the punishment. Then again, he had his *hex*. The one big one he had been toying with ever since the university. One that every hexer dreamed of letting out. It was risky, and he was sure his life wasn't worth the possible cost of letting it loose into the universe. There was no telling what it would do once he was dead. So, Percy stood there, letting Laura do her worst. She didn't disappoint.

The woman knocked the air out of him by sending her hexes forth. His intestines felt like they were on fire. Like they were putrefied. He dropped to his knees and curled into a ball, wishing for a quick death. Laura pressed her boot into his face so hard that the gravel pierced his skin. His right hand was twisted underneath him, and the skin scarred from the burns stretched tight, sending out electric pain.

Laura barked at her henchmen to go after Elmer, leaving only the necromancer with her.

Percy pushed past the pain eating his innards. He screamed out an immobility hex to give Mr. Spooner more time to hide, to flee. It would take their hexer only a moment to unravel, but that moment might be crucial. One of them had to survive, and it clearly wasn't going to be him.

As if on cue, Laura said, "You can decide how it ends. A curse driving you mad or me crushing your skull." She took some of the pressure off his head and removed the hexes putrefying his innards to give him a moment to breathe.

Percy gasped in a lungful of air as the pain subsided.

"Does it really matter what I answer?" Percy spat blood out of his mouth.

"It could," Laura snorted.

The necromancer, who had stayed behind with her, shook his head and looked away. But Laura didn't notice, or if she did, she didn't care.

"Do what you must," Percy said, looking Laura in her eyes.

She flinched. But she twisted her face into an angry pout and pushed her boot down. That was as far as she got. A scream echoed farther in the tunnels. From the sound of it, it was Laura's men rather than Mr. Spooner. Or if Mr. Spooner had joined in, it was hard to tell.

"Get him up," Laura snapped at the necromancer as she took her foot off Percy.

Percy felt the spirits lift him up. The tiny ghostly hands dragged him across the ground behind Laura and the necromancer, towards the screams. They didn't have to walk far, as Laura halted suddenly. Percy blinked several times, trying to adjust to the low light of the darkened tunnel. Then he saw what made Laura hold her breath. The tunnel was full of ghouls. Not only on the ground; dozens of them hung from the walls and the ceiling. From their midst came the always correct tone of Mr. Spooner. The three witches who had gone after the investigator were pinned to the ground, kneeling. Next to them, Mr. Spooner explained himself to a ghoul dressed in a blue walking skirt and a white blouse.

Ever since the police force had been reinforced with ghouls, the ghouls altogether had taken it upon themselves to dress as any citizen would. The rags made out of discarded hemp sacks were gone. Percy had never come to terms with what to think about the ghouls. He had nothing against them, but the sudden change was sudden, and he had been overseas most of the time as it had happened. Good for them, was the only coherent thought he managed to form.

The spirits keeping him upright wavered, and the necromancer found it challenging to concentrate both on them and the situation. The necromancer's face was damp, and his hands were trembling. It was no wonder. Spirits disliked ghouls. The ghouls were known to devour souls. Not that Percy had heard of such events happening in the current era. Something to do with high morals and the respect ghouls had for sentient beings. Of course, in general, it wasn't frowned upon to use spirits as labor. No necromancer could function if it was, but destroying a soul completely was a murky area that you didn't enter. Not at least in public, and if you got caught, you better have a very good reason. Something to do with life and death. The ghouls crawled on the ceiling just above them, and some lowered themselves as well, keeping the spirits on their toes.

"What the Kraken shit is this?" Laura growled.

The ghoul with the blue skirt stepped closer to Laura, and Percy had to give it to the hexer. She didn't flinch. If there was a scariest beast in the world, it was ghouls. Their intelligence and deadly bodies were highly effective. If they weren't so docile and happy to keep to themselves, Percy was sure they could take over the world. But such matters didn't seem to interest them. Yes, they had become political, but only to secure their rights and the survival of the underground city. A place many Necropolitans wanted to visit after it had become public knowledge, but if the ghouls took anyone there, they did it for the few and selected.

"A-rrre you thei-rrr maste-rrrr?" the ghoul lisped.

"I'm their commander, if that's what you ask, and this is Council territory. So you better release my men and hand Mr. Spooner to me." Laura didn't budge.

Percy collapsed on the ground as the spirits holding him fled the scene. The necromancer was breathing laboriously. Percy lay there, unable to move.

"An-d you a-rrre?" the ghoul asked.

"I'm Laura Devlin, with the internal police of the Council, and I have the juridical right in these tunnels." Laura widened her stance.

"It iss..." the ghoul seemed to taste the words. "Is nice to meet you. You can call me Sirixh. But I'm afraid this part of the tunnels is ours. I can send one of my team to fetch a document signed by Miss Upwood."

Laura snorted. "Still—"

Sirixh didn't let her finish. "And Mr. Spooner there has requested asylum for him and the man behind you." This time the ghoul looked straight at Percy. There was kindness in the dead black eyes. He was more than willing to go with her, but he looked in Laura's direction. She was snarling. Percy was sure this was going to end badly.

He was wrong. Laura stepped out of the way, letting Sirixh walk to Percy and help him towards Mr. Spooner.

"I want my men released," Laura demanded. Before she'd finished the sentence, the ghouls holding the witches down let go of them.

"Thank you," Percy muttered to Sirixh.

"Just doing our duty," the ghoul said.

Percy smiled, but then he winced as his ankle sent a sharp pain up his leg.

"Don't think it's over, Mr. Allread. The Council will be in touch." Laura turned around. The men with her weren't as comfortable. They withdrew from the situation, keeping their attention on the ghouls. When they vanished around the corner, Percy heard running footsteps. He couldn't blame them.

"What now?" Mr. Spooner asked.

"We take you to our city and send word to the Town Hall and the Council." Sirixh smiled. It was the smile of a person who knew that what would follow was the mother of all storms, and despite it, she was willing to do what her morals dictated. The right thing, one might say.

The ghoul barked something in her language. Two ghouls hurried to Percy, lifting him up, and one to Mr. Spooner. They were carried out through a crack in the wall not too far from where they had been. Percy glanced behind him as he passed through to see some of the ghouls remaining to seal the opening as if it had never been there.

Just a few clicks away from him, Mr. Spooner chatted away with the ghoul carrying him, asking about the old library and the tunnels they were in.

"I'm pretty sure the library's history didn't have these tunnels documented. Are these sanctioned..." Percy tuned out. More so out of the pain his whole body was in. While the curses Laura had used were gone, his innards still felt as if they were half melted. He gave himself a few hours to live at most.

Chapter Fourteen

EMBRACING LIFE WITHOUT THE FEAR OF SLIPPING AWAY

Hunted or hunter? On the plains that was an easy choice to make, but here in the jungle made of tall stone buildings with their gargoyles and the rain gutters, the choice got a lot murkier. Even with no signs of pursuit, Raul still couldn't relax. Every shadow, every passer-by, reminded him that someone might be out to get him. And the honest truth was that someone probably was. Maybe not the someone he thought, but someone nevertheless.

Raul lifted his jacket's collar up, trying to pass as any other creature outside at this godforsaken hour in the rain. The only thing that would make him more believable was to have murder, hunger, or madness in his eyes. His was too normal for that. Though, no one on the streets would have thought so. His obsession was starting to leak out. Not that the Necropolitans minded a little obsession. It kept the soul going and made the cold, dark nights a little more cheerful.

Despite how calm he fancied himself, he jerked at every noise, every too loud step behind him. He was happy to notice a half-rotten undead trying to mug him or a vampire gliding out of its den to lure him into donating his blood. The poor sods. Necropolis's dreams were too much sometimes. Being nothing was devastating. Everyone wanted to be something. Not that Raul had ever understood the desire to be that something. Then again, that was the talk of those who were someones. Raul would argue that he never had the intention in the beginning. That the truth mattered. Everyone knew that was just crazy talk. That underneath it all, he, like everyone else, wanted to be loved and cared for, and somehow he and the others had confused love with admiration and status. Nonetheless, Raul ignored the poor sods and moved on after leaving a tip for the undead and a suck for the vampire.

Raul faced the old library. It rose behind the gaggle of Save the Otis Group members camping outside its steps. The guards dominating the main doorway were alert despite the group losing some of its enthusiasm as the days went by. There was no way he could just march in. He needed a back door. It was just that the Council was famous for not having one. At least, not one that would be easy to spot without extraordinary talents. He waited there for an hour, getting a snack and coffee from a vendor not too far from the crowd. He kept observing the constant stream of people going in and out of the headquarters. Some were workers, others were cleaners, and then there were the customers with their grieving hunches, having lost their mothers and fathers. All were checked out by the gargoyles on the roof and the witches by the doors. None got past without good reason. There were twice as many guards as there had been that morning, and it wasn't because it was nighttime. Not when mornings were just as scary as any pitch-black corner. It was the mornings that brought the burdens of chores, duties, and the inevitable rut that was everyday life. Compared to that, a swamp monster with a penchant for tiny toes and tender flesh was a picnic. Even a ghost with an ax to grind was more welcoming than the dawn of a new day.

The only explanation was that there was something going on. But Raul had already decided he was going in, and there was no backing down once he set his goal. The only way in that Raul could think of was to cause some major scene with the Save the Otis Group, who were cold, hungry, and ready to take the coco out and sing songs about camaraderie and social injustice to make them feel like all this protesting was doing some good.

The witches were eying the group, waiting for that tipping point to happen so they finally had an excuse to fry them up. Raul didn't like the odds of that. There had to be another way in. He didn't get the chance to try out his plans or even think of another suitable one. He saw the same tattered green-and-yellow mane he'd seen outside the newspaper. The thing's yellow eyes stared down at him from the Council's headquarters roof instead of the gargoyles that had been there a moment ago. The creature made sure Raul followed its gaze to the rope ladder hanging beside the building. Raul shook his head. It was too risky and too foolhardy. He was just a drunken fool, and there was no way he could climb the ladder. But there was no other way in.

He cursed his luck and then looked around to see if anyone was paying attention to him or the ladder. No one was. He'd become a permanent fixture, and the ladder was like that spot-the-mistake puzzle, where you stare at the obvious flaw without seeing it. Raul circled the crowd, and when he was sure no one was looking, he took hold of the ladder. He knew this would get him killed, especially as the creature had already killed. But it had killed for him. And that made a big difference in Necropolis. Then there was the fact that while being convinced that this was a good idea on an intellectual level, on a practical level, he was having second and third thoughts. Getting up the ladder was harder than he expected. The rope swung uncontrollably and shook when he put his full weight on it. Raul's stomach lurched, and his spine cracked in several places. He got off and put all his weight back on the cobblestones. Jolts of pain shot up his back. But he took a better hold on the ladder and got back on. He clutched the ladder harder as he dragged himself up one rung at a time. Before reaching even the midpoint, he was already sweaty, shaking, and gripping on for dear life.

If he survived this, he would have to get back into shape and get rid of all the jiggly bits that seemed to make the climbing impossible.

Raul let out a laborious sigh and moved his shaking hand higher. His legs were ready to give up as he neared the edge of the roof. The image of dropping down and getting his head cracked open flashed in front of his eyes as he took hold of the roof and hauled himself over the edge, causing the painful blisters on his hands to burst.

Raul let out a long wail and gripped harder, unable to let go. His whole body convulsed, scraping against the roof tiles. He couldn't let go, but he couldn't get up either. His hands were permanently frozen. Raul gasped for air as he lay there until he was sure he wouldn't drop to his death just from passing out. Raul got to his knees and crawled along the narrow path to a window. The roof made a pyramid shape over him with the usual Gothic-style tiles the city was so fond of. It towered over the Save the Otis Group, who were all stirred up. Raul heard their shouts, but he couldn't care less what they were shouting for. All he wanted was for his heart to stop beating so fast and to be done with this all. He'd arrived at that point that he was even willing to fall to his death to make it stop.

The roof's tiles scraped against his knees. He imagined them holding on to him. He moved one knee at a time, edging towards the small window in the roof where the creature had been. The thing was already gone, but there was a hatch left open. Raul reasoned that it had to be where the head of security came to chat with the gargoyles. Raul moved as slowly as his nerves dared him towards the hatch. He stepped over the ledge to the opening, feeling the open space underneath him. He closed his eyes as he tumbled into the building.

Raul collapsed on the floor of the indoor attic. Once again, his heart was contemplating calling it quits and moving to more relaxing pastures. His readiness to succumb to death was interrupted by a low growl at the door. Raul lifted his gaze, waiting to see the beast, but the creature he'd followed in wasn't there. The sound was coming from the hallway past the door. Raul got up. His legs shook. They weighed at least a hundred pounds. Nevertheless, he made it to the door despite the ache. The creature wasn't in the hallway either. But there were narrow stairs, curving down. He took a step and paused.

He was being stupid. He was going to get caught.

Raul glanced at the attic door. There was no way he was going to go back to the roof and climb down.

Again, the low growl commanded him to follow.

He did.

Would it be a gift or a curse to know someone else's mind? It was already hard to keep track of one's own, let alone be responsible for the values and morals it held. And if you knew what they were thinking, accountability would follow, and there was no escaping that once it took hold of you. Petula gave Mrs. Maybury her time. They stood outside the Necro Botanical Gardens' gate and watched in silence as the mist rose behind the glass buildings, hiding the main building from sight. The rain had stopped. Now the streets were moody and mysterious.

Petula restrained herself from guessing why Mrs. Maybury hesitated to enter the grounds. She had never witnessed the woman hesitate. She always went for the kill. And now something kept her stuck.

The path between the glasshouses and the opened gates stood there, waiting for them to go in. But the undead couldn't. She glanced at Petula and then shook her head as if offering an answer to a hidden conversation. Time ticked by, following the laws of gravity, especially around the persuasive mass of Mrs. Maybury, and the undead stepped into the gardens.[1]

Petula sighed and followed the undead in. She had an unnerving feeling that this wasn't going to be pleasant at all. That Mrs. Maybury had an agenda. But she couldn't send her away now. Petula trailed after the undead, who clearly knew exactly where they were going and which glasshouse to pick. Their steps echoed in the almost empty gardens. If they had squinted, they would see witches watching them. For now, they preferred to stay out of sight.

The others had already arrived. Petula could see their shapes in the middle of the trees and plants through the door leading in.

"Petula," Mrs. Maybury started. "Before we go in, I just want you to know, I have always liked you. You remind me of my younger self."

The undead looked straight into Petula's eyes. Petula wanted to recoil. Instead, she said, "Thank you," unsure whether to take the statement as an honor. The mere thought of being like the woman sounded nightmarish. Petula knew she was being unkind towards the older woman, who had been nothing but supportive and was no fool. It was just the bitterness and cynicism that came with Mrs. Maybury was discomforting. And Petula realized that if she examined herself, she was heading down that same path. She could already feel her disappointment in reality wreaking havoc in her mind. She could try to control it as Mrs. Maybury was trying to do, or accept that the only thing she could ever control was her own reactions. Thus far, she had always let her disinterest and annoyance over others do all the talking. She rationalized that everyone else was morons, and she was already busy pursuing what she valued the most: to understand and master

---

1. The great philosophers and pretty much anyone proclaiming to know a thing or two about the nature of being might debate whether she did it out of her own free will, but Mrs. Maybury would show them what free will looked like and how the inanimate could become animate again.

the universe, necromancy, and creation. Maybe that had been the case with the older woman as well. Maybe she'd had hopes for herself and others, and reality was nothing like she'd wished for. Mrs. Maybury had become Mrs. Maybury, feared by all, loved by none, and with the constant desire to be right and dominate the situation. Petula shuddered and looked at the glasshouse door.

"I don't know what I have done to deserve your guidance," Petula finished.

"Maybe you have not deserved it yet, but you will," Mrs. Maybury said more to herself than Petula, sounding somewhat disappointed.

Petula had offended her by not embracing the statement with open arms, but... but who wanted to be like Mrs. Maybury? Again, Petula felt a twinge of guilt mixed with sorrow. Why wouldn't people want to be like her? The undead had done everything to advance the causes she believed in. She was relentless. She knew her mind and wasn't afraid to let it be known. It was just the style in which she delivered it, but maybe there was a reason for it. And had she or anyone ever tried to figure out what it was and why?

"I wouldn't have gotten this far without you. You have backed me up more than once, and every time I have asked you a question, you have answered with me in mind and not your political aspirations. I don't say this enough, but I'm truly thankful for what you and your husband, Cruxh, have done for me."

The undead woman's solemn face melted away. She reached for the door, holding it open to let Petula go in first.

Petula stepped in.

As she'd surmised, the others had already arrived. They sat on their seats, and there was no extra one for Mrs. Maybury. Petula cleared her throat to get the others' attention. The only one who'd noticed their arrival had been Henrietta. As Petula had walked in with the undead shuffling behind her, she'd observed the wide range of emotions passing over the witch's face.

She couldn't blame the woman. Not for a second.

She coughed again, and the others turned their attention to her. There was no missing their astonishment.

"Good evening," Petula began. "I'm happy to see all of you could make it despite the short notice." Petula let her gaze move from Lattice Burton, the HR manager, who sat close to the aisle, to Ida Mortician, the banker, and then to Annabella Sepulcher, the former lawyer and reborn Church of Kraken devotee—a fact which made Petula uneasy, unsure how much the woman reported to Madam Sabine, the head priestess of the Church—who sat next to Henrietta. Lastly, she let her attention stay on Henrietta, who still fought for control of her face.

"I asked Mrs. Maybury to join us, and she graciously accepted. If one of you has an extra frame, needle, and string to spare, it would be appreciated. And Mrs. Maybury, you can take my seat." Petula gestured towards the only available chair.

The undead woman didn't hesitate. She sat down and looked around the group members.

"So this is the group the whole city is whispering about?! How does this work? You discuss what to do and jointly shape Necropolis to your liking?"

Petula clenched her right leg so as not to laugh. She couldn't help but marvel at the woman and her bluntness. But it was also clear that she would have to change a lot so she did not end up like the woman. Not that she didn't appreciate Mrs. Maybury's candor and the fact that everyone, including Henrietta, was staring at the undead with their mouths hanging open. Whether astonished or appalled, any reaction was better than no reaction at all.

"Not quite like that, dear Mrs. Maybury. We do needlework and discuss current events and share our opinions about them, and hope for an amicable solution. But yes, we do our best to lend a helping hand when help is needed," Annabella jumped in.

If Petula remembered correctly, Annabella and Mrs. Maybury had known each other when they had been alive in the more usual sense. Though here in Necropolis, you truly came alive once you could shed your own mortality and embrace life without fear of slipping away in the dead of night.

"I see," Mrs. Maybury said, sounding somewhat venomous. Most likely about being called dear. "Yet, as I have gathered, you are trying to take down the Council. You have your work cut out for you, especially as I recall Miss Lattice Burton being the Council's administrator before taking her position at the newspaper. And I wonder how many of you are in deep trouble already? Skeletons and all that."

Petula squeezed the handle of her needlepoint basket. So this was why the undead woman had come. And that was why she'd warned her at the front door. Not out of sentiment, but because she was going to make everyone pay for not being included.[2]

---

2. But that was a callous way to put it. People and undead alike did funny things when they thought they were protecting someone they cared for, with or without being asked.

CHAPTER FIFTEEN

WHAT IS THE PRESENT BUT A PRELUDE FOR THE FUTURE?

K illed by the system. There was a thought. But it did happen. Sometimes people fell through the cracks between the forms and they slowly starved to death without sustenance for their bodies and minds. At least Percy wouldn't die because form three-b told him to. Or okay, in a sense he did, but that would stay on Laura's conscience and not in his. He would die because he'd followed *his* conscience. Percy just had to endure a little longer. Just so he could see the ghoul city. He fought hard to stay awake while he was carried by the ghouls. It wouldn't be too long before his body gave in to the curses Laura had unleashed on him. He could feel the full hatred in them. It was no wonder. They had his name fully twisted in them with the tense emotions of bitterness, jealousy, hatred, disgust, distaste, and so much anger. He glanced at Mr. Spooner, who leaned against a ghoul. The man would make it all worth it. He had done the right thing, and that was all that mattered.

Percy shut his eyes just for a moment, letting out a cough. That made the ghouls hasten their steps in the tunnels they'd built. Percy tried to keep his eyes closed, but every jerk made him open them and watch the bare walls turn into murals and reliefs with intricate depictions of life the closer they got to the ghoul city. In the murals, ghouls leaned on each other, built things, and celebrated their own. Every now and then, among the ghouls were humans, but not too many. Their faces had been painted and carved ever so delicately, illuminated by the glowing mushrooms that were everywhere. Percy wondered how the mushrooms got their light, as no sun shone here to supply their spores with luminescence. It had to be some other mechanism, which he couldn't think of.

If he died, at least he had seen what everyone in Necropolis wanted to see. There were so many rumors floating around about the ghoul city. They spoke about immense wealth, treasures, and adventures to be had. All here for Percy to see and grasp, but none of it could be stolen or sold. Their wealth didn't come from the gemstones embedded in the murals; it came from how the ghouls came together. They seemed to embrace each other. To support each other. And they'd saved him and Mr. Spooner without hesitation. It had been the right thing to do.

Percy had read in the newspapers that people were reading the books and thoughts of the great ghouls, and their insights into what it means to exist, what the universe is composed of, and the nature of perception. Their views were not even close to the nihilism and hedonism of those that plagued the Necropolitans. Their beliefs were founded in the relationship between the one and the many and the cosmos. It was borderline mystical, and annoying as Kraken, as the Church said. It was no wonder Madam Sabine had warned about the false prophets and the new age of mumbo jumbo. Percy had read that some of the devotees had turned to the ghouls, following their words as closely as they could, seeing them as divine. A religion, they said.

Percy would have his salvation too, at least. Though in a more concrete way.

Percy fought to keep his eyes open so he could have that glimpse of the city. Then maybe, his life wouldn't be a complete waste. They spoke about a diamond illuminating the city, and he wanted to see that. Not because of value, but how could a lifeless rock, pressed hard by ages, give light where there was only darkness? And what if he saw that light? Would it make it easier to let go, to accept that he had seen enough for a lifetime?

The tunnel ahead glowed more brightly, a pale bluish-green. Percy tensed his muscles. He gasped as they came to an enormous ledge overlooking the city. The rumors had been right. The place was magnificent. But instead of a diamond, there was a colossal glass construction with mushrooms growing inside it. It was not as bright as the sun, but it didn't matter. It cast this dreamy, haunting glow over the marble houses down in the cave, spreading wide and far. Amongst them were statues to amplify the effect of the glow. The ghouls themselves glowed too, moving in the narrow pathways.

Percy sighed and closed his eyes. He had done his part.

"Mr. Allread," he heard Elmer scream. Then came the feeling as if he was flying in the air, but that was all there was. Percy's body convulsed. He let go.

Violence seemed to follow humankind. It was the systems that were meant to prevent it, but what if they had it all wrong and there was violence in the system keeping those down who shouldn't be kept down? Henrietta held Ida Mortician, the banker, away from Lattice. The HR manager shivered in her chair as Ida screamed at the woman. Behind all of this, Mrs. Maybury sat silently observing as her revelation unfolded. Whether she was pleased or not, it was hard to tell by her expression.

"How dare you sit there?" Ida shouted at Lattice and struggled against Henrietta. The banker could shake her off easily, but clearly, some part of her didn't want to do the unspeakable thing the other part was ever so willing to do.

Henrietta pleaded, "Please, Miss Mortician. Not like this."

"Then how?" she growled in response. Her words echoed in the glasshouse, taking up the whole space as human will often did.

"We have to know why and what." Henrietta relaxed her grip on the banker.

"You want to know what? What you want to know is that suddenly half of the necromancers closed their accounts with my bank, along with a few manufacturing firms. Who do you think is behind that? And they won't have any trouble making the remaining clients walk away." Ida shook Henrietta off.

Henrietta let her go. "I didn't know," she said, hearing the defeat in her voice. Of course, the Council had done its worst to the others too. Henrietta glanced around the room, meeting everyone's eyes. There it was. They had been attacked as well. Henrietta let her gaze fall back to Ida.

"They'll ruin me, and I can't even complain about it." Ida drew her painted lips into a pout and crossed her arms. Her black lace sleeves draped down beautifully by her sides, full of drama. Sometimes Henrietta wished she was like Ida, who was comfortable with being showy. There was no denying it had an effect.

"I'm sorry," Lattice kept muttering to herself and rocking back and forth on her chair. Some might think her a fool for not trying to run away, but where could you hide from a necromancer, witch, lawyer, and banker? They could haunt you with small print even in your afterlife.

"Sorry won't cut it," Ida spat out.

Petula walked past them and knelt in front of the manager. "Tell us," she said and took hold of Lattice's hands.

The older woman recoiled from the touch, but Petula kept the woman's hands in hers. Henrietta noticed the touch was soft and comforting, yet the rest of her body was stiff and uncomfortable. She just hoped Lattice didn't see past the act. Not that Henrietta doubted for a second the mayor wasn't making a genuine effort. She was. It was clear to everyone.

"They gave me protection over your spirits," Lattice stuttered. She was clutching her handkerchief, trying to fiddle it between her fingers. Petula let go of the woman's hands. The necromancer glanced at Henrietta and nodded.

Petula faced Lattice again and said, "That's nice of them."

"You can't harm me." Lattice sounded unsure and confused.

"We won't harm you. We just want to understand."

"Yes, Miss Upwood is right," Henrietta added. "All we want is to understand." The only one who disagreed was Ida, who snarled next to Henrietta but didn't say a thing. If she was already in deep trouble with the Council, she would be in deeper waters if she went against the mayor and Henrietta too.

"And we can help you," Annabella said. The lawyer sent a nasty glance at Mrs. Maybury, who chuckled.

"Are you sure?" Lattice stopped rocking back and forth and finally lifted her gaze from the handkerchief. But then she shook her head and said, "You can't. They'll kill me, and not only me, but my family as well. You don't know them as I do."

Henrietta couldn't help but think some of it was stretching the truth thin. While the Council's notorious methods were widely known, and she wouldn't entirely rule out the possibility of them having killed her former mentor, Wesley, they weren't stupid. Lattice's death would be bad publicity, especially now. She had probably lost her value already, and even if the rest of the needlepoint group went public, no one would care. Spying and extortion were just Necropolis for you, and the Council had a way of spinning stories to fit their narrative. They had the whole newspaper industry behind them, as was clear now.

"No one will be killed on my watch," Petula stated. She wound her hands around Lattice's again and directed the woman's attention to her.

"None of us will let that happen to you. You just have to tell us what is going on and how we can help you."

"You wouldn't understand." Lattice pulled away.

"Try us," Petula said.

Henrietta knelt down next to Petula and looked at Lattice. "We are not here to judge you. You did it for your own reasons."

"Of course I did," Lattice snapped. "Mrs. Maybury is wrong. I wasn't in it from the beginning. I truly wanted to make a difference, and I wanted the news to be free and not handpicked by the Council. I truly did. I was ready to convince others to unionize. It could have worked. You have to believe me." Lattice leaned towards Petula and Henrietta. "I never wanted to hurt you. Especially you, Petula. You are strong, just like Minta. You too, Henrietta. Wesley would be so proud of what you have made of the gardens. Both of you, all of you, can make this city be more. But..." Lattice shook her head. "The Council just wanted me to tell them what was said here, and at first, it was harmless, but then... then you started speaking about action, and they pressed me, and I couldn't lie. Not to them. You don't lie to the Council. They have ways to get the truth out of you, and you don't even notice it."

"Why?" Henrietta asked.

"I can't." Lattice pulled away again.

"Money or blackmail?" Ida snorted.

Lattice looked away from all of them towards the door.

"Please," Petula said.

"Or both?" Ida continued pressing.

Lattice looked back, and her eyes were wide, and some of the color in her face had drained away.

"Both it is then," Ida said and laughed. "You fool," she added.

Henrietta glanced at the banker to silence her. Ida refused to look back, going with the only bulletproof way to make the world exactly as she wanted it: avoidance. It was a pretty effective tactic in any situation. Okay, maybe not the most useful or one that, in the end, got you what you wanted, but at least it was a way to "win", especially when combined with the martyr's silence.

Henrietta let the banker be. At least she'd stopped talking.

"I'm not a fool. You know nothing about what it is like to be me. All of you are much better off than I am. I can barely live with my salary in Necropolis. Rent has gone up, and so have the other expenses. If I want to keep up and feed and clothe my daughters, we need money. Their university expenses are building up. It's easy for you," Lattice let out.

None of them could deny this truth. Everything had become a lot more expensive after the banks had been bailed out. Salaries couldn't keep up with the utility bills: gas, coal, rent, and food. Henrietta battled with the bills every day to keep the gardens afloat. Luckily, they grew some of their own food, taking some of the pressure off. And they had patrons. Witches who had been or had become wealthy, and other people with enough money to throw away on the curiosity of the paranormal. Without donations, private parties, and shows, the garden would have gone bankrupt a long time ago, even with the Council's money. Necropolis was too expensive, especially as you couldn't hide from utility bills. They had an almost magical ability to find you even in the deepest jungle and suck you dry until you became a sobbing ball.

"You could have told us," Annabella said.

"And you would have done what? Paid my invoices? Got my daughters into the university as the Council promised?" No one could miss the scorn in her voice. "I didn't think so," Lattice added.

"And the blackmail?" Ida asked.

"I don't have to tell you anything." Lattice stood up, forcing Petula and Henrietta to scramble away from the woman.

"No, you don't, but it might help your case," Annabella said before Ida could spit out a threat she was clearly forming.

"And let you use it against me? No, I'm leaving," Lattice said.

"You are not—" Ida began.

"Let her go. She has made her choice, and there's nothing we can do to change that," Petula interrupted.

"You bet you can't." They watched Lattice gather her basket and strings and storm out.

Henrietta was sure she'd heard the glasshouse's door open and close one more time, but she filed it under paranoia. "Was it wise to let her leave?" she asked.

"Better than detaining her. She has done nothing wrong, not in the eyes of the law," Petula said.

"Well," Annabella began.

"Not truly," Petula countered.

"No, not in a sense, but you can always argue—" Annabella continued.

"We won't," Petula stated.

"You should," Mrs. Maybury said. Henrietta had forgotten the undead was there. She had been sitting silent, content to watch the show.

"Why so?" Petula asked.

"To make an example out of her. Let everyone know there are consequences if you work for the Council. If it's indeed your aim to bring the Council's rule down?"

"She makes a great point," Ida agreed.

"And then what? They fulfill their threats against us?" Henrietta asked.

"If you let a bully—" Ida said.

"Spare me." Henrietta lifted her hand. "They are a powerful bully, and they have some of us on a shorter leash than others."

"What do they have on you then?" Ida's voice was tight, and she wasn't done arguing.

Henrietta looked at Petula. She nodded but made sure Henrietta knew it was her choice to disclose her situation. Henrietta wasn't sure if she wanted them to know. It would open another can of worms Henrietta might not want to deal with. But her silence only made their imaginations run wild, and it might jeopardize more than she was willing to pay, especially as the Coven was to convene after this.

"They are pulling their funding and forcing me to pay a fine for breaking a contract. It's enough to bankrupt the Coven. Or I can play along. Either way, there's no telling if I'll be running the Coven in a month's time."

Everyone in the room looked at Petula, waiting for her to react. Petula seemed to be staring at Mrs. Maybury. Henrietta didn't know what was going on between those two. There were rumors in the city that it was actually Mrs. Maybury who was ruling through the girl. This was absurd, yet clearly, there was a special bond. Henrietta knew for a fact that Petula lunched with the undead and her ghoul husband once every two weeks. What was discussed there was the talk of the town. Something no journalist or other prying eyes had yet figured out. Or she might be thinking along the lines, as Henrietta was, that all this was out of the undead's pettiness. That she'd just said all this to spite them for not inviting her in the first place. But Henrietta couldn't be further from the truth. Petula knew that Mrs. Maybury was petty as Kraken, but not on these matters. And Mrs. Maybury had long ago refused to act on the petty whispers that seemed to plague her. They'd ruined too much for her and left her alone and bitter. Her grandkids only visited her once in a blue moon when the money ran out. It was too bad that no one had actually noticed that Alice Maybury had changed. That she had finally found inner peace and tamed the monsters inside her. That she had a purpose, making the past and the present okay. No one had asked. And she wasn't willing to tell.

"I think the Council has achieved just what it wanted: the group turning on each other. You have no choice. You should yield. This is not a battle we can win. It's not worth it to see our life's work go up in flames," Annabella said.

"You want us to yield when it has already cost me more than any of you?" Ida asked.

"You can—" the lawyer started.

"Don't say beg for it back. I won't bend over and give them my ass," Ida snapped, and Henrietta couldn't blame her. "What have they done to you then?" Ida added.

"Nothing. They have nothing to hold against me." Annabella slumped down. "Sorry," she said when Ida looked like she was ready to blow a gasket.

"The Church?" Petula asked.

"Yes, it's my protection against everything," Annabella said. "Also, I have run a clean practice even when going head-to-head with the Council. It isn't that hard. They give you all I need to use against them, and I don't have the resources to bribe the judges as they do," Annabella said. "Not that I have ever won. Maybe that's why they have left me alone." She sighed.

"So, Miss Upwood, what do they have on you?" Ida ignored the lawyer's last statement, sounding highly annoyed.

Henrietta found herself holding her breath.

Petula dragged Lattice's chair closer and sat down. She crossed her legs, taking her time as the others stared at her. She arranged the hem of her skirt and then said, "Nothing as dramatic as with any of you. It's more about my conscience. I'm afraid I can no longer condone setting Mr. Thurston free. As the Council claims, he did break the necromantic rules, and not only that, but he went against the basic rights of the soul."

Ida snorted. "What does that have to do with anything? This is not some moral dilemma. This is about politics and letting the Council walk all over your citizens. If you let them get away with this, you are enslaving yourself and all of us. I'm sure they have broken more souls than Mr. Thurston ever could, even if he continued doing whatever he supposedly did from here to eternity."

Henrietta let out a long breath and took a seat as well. No one was getting out of here anytime soon.

"You all are fools," Mrs. Maybury stated. Henrietta, with the others, turned her full attention to her. The undead took it in with pride. "You think that this is over because of what? What's the present but a prelude to the future? Your true work can begin when you have gotten rid of the Council's influence. I hope you didn't expect the Council to go down without a fight. Those are some high favors they are asking, to make necromancers jump ship and abandon Miss Mortician's bank. Costly favors, I would say. And big threats with you, Mrs. Culpepper. You have them, and if you back down, you will lose your opportunity. Stop concentrating on Mr. Thurston. It's you who matter. All of you."

"Especially Miss Mayor," Ida said spitefully. "Mrs. Maybury is right. We can't back down now. We only have to use Miss Upwood's mayoral power to take control of the Council. Use their own Monster Hunter Force against them. You can do that. I know my laws. You are their rightful leader and not the Council as everyone thinks, and you let them. I bet there are a lot of employees in their stolen little army who are willing to work for you and turn against their unlawful masters. With the right incentive, you can buy them back," Ida said.

Good Kraken, Henrietta thought. The banker wasn't wrong.

No one had time to answer. There was a loud knock on the glass door, and soon after, Imogene burst in.

"Ma'am," she said, not getting any further. Behind her came ghouls dressed in blue police uniforms led by none other than the famous Cruxh.

The moment you wake up and your dreams dissolve, reality has the potential to be whatever you want it to be. That is, before who you are and who you are meant to be catches up. One could live for those disappearing seconds before the call of the morning birds.

Percy woke up to the sound of people talking. He wasn't sure where he was or what had happened, or if he was happy that he was alive. He had a sense that he had given himself permission to die, and a good death was such a pity to waste. But he was alive, that much was sure. His bones pressed against something soft, and the pain... the pain was not there. Percy kept his eyes shut and listened to the voices, rewinding back to that moment when his life had made sense. The only coherent image he could muster was as a child, when he had pushed his bare feet into the wet sand in search of fossils with his grandmother. He had a nauseating feeling that he would never be that content or curious again. Never discover anything as wonderful as the signs of past eras sealed in between rocks. All that was left was a miserable creature who, if he recalled correctly, had just blown up his career and life on a whim.

"Will he be alright?" Elmer's voice asked in the background, pulling him away from the shores and the little apartment he had called home between the killing and the accounting.

"I think I got most of the curses out. But there might be some internal damage. I tried to correct the nasty tricks hidden in them, but we will see if I succeeded once Mr. Allread wakes up," came another voice. It was a soft, strong voice Percy could listen to all day. A voice like his sister's. It almost made it feel okay to lie there as a ruined man.

"Thank you, Miss Lace," said another voice. It had an almost metallic and broken tone to it. A ghoulish tone.

"Mr. Spooner," Percy coughed as he opened his eyes in search of the smallish goblin man. Laura, the ghouls, the city, the illuminated mushrooms, and his childhood faded away as Elmer's face came into focus an inch from his, peering at him with concern in his eyes.

"You are alive!" the man let out and squeezed him.

"Of course I am," Percy wheezed. He looked over Mr. Spooner's shoulder at an impressive-looking woman and two ghouls standing next to the bed. The room was spinning a little. It might be due to the fact that Mr. Spooner was squeezing him tightly.

He blinked and gasped for air.

The woman took a step closer and laid her hand on Elmer's back. "I think that's enough, Mr. Spooner. I think we should give Mr. Allread some space to breathe."

"Yes, of course." Mr. Spooner withdrew awkwardly, unable to look Percy in his eyes.

"May I?" the woman asked.

Percy nodded.

The woman sat next to him on the bed. Her long dark curls shifted on her face. Her amber eyes were soft and friendly as she looked at him. "I'm Philomena Lace, and I'm a witch doctor. I took out all the curses I could find. If you could..."

"Yes," Percy said, shutting his eyes. He sent his own hexes into him, searching for any residue. "Nothing," he said and opened his eyes again, looking at her. She shifted her gaze to his stomach, and he nodded. The woman took his shirt off, revealing bandages smelling strongly of seaweed, peppermint, and a fruity scent Percy couldn't quite place. She took the bandages off. The white had turned a dark, moldy black.

"I think you will be fine, Mr. Allread. You were lucky that I was here. I will give you an ointment for the bruising on your ankle, but otherwise, everything should heal in days. However, you need to take it slow for the next couple of weeks. The patch-ups I needed to make are delicate, and the damage done to your insides might revert back."

"Thank you, Mistress Lace."

She closed his shirt, buttoning it. He seized her hand in his, and she was startled.

"I can do it," he said apologetically.

She got up, giving him room. She was one of those women you couldn't pin down. One moment, she looked short and bulky, and now, as she stood up, she looked tall and nimble. It was like she was toying with his perceptions. Who knew if she was? Doctors in the city were weird. They mixed ancient herbal knowledge with the new science of cutting open bodies and testing them with stuff. What the stuff was, Percy wasn't sure.

"Now we'd better leave them alone," Philomena Lace ordered. The two ghouls followed her out, leaving Mr. Spooner behind. The goblin-looking man sat down on a bed next to Percy's. The room was smallish, yet the white walls and the illumination coming from the mushroom tubes on the ceiling made it look like the space stretched into eternity.

"What happened?" he asked.

"The doctor—"

"Not here. In the tunnels."

"Oh, I'm not sure, but I think the ghouls heard my wailing. Suddenly the cave wall burst open, and the hexers tried to run, dragging me with them, but..." The man didn't have to finish the sentence. No one could outrun ghouls. No humans, at least. Werewolves, maybe. And if there had ever been such a race, it was never spoken of. At least not to humans.

"Aren't we lucky then?" Percy remarked.

"Indeed," Elmer Spooner let out with the same confusion.

"So what does this mean? And how long was I out?" It was hard to picture what would happen next. While ghouls weren't these mysterious creatures—you could see them everywhere in Necropolis, minding their own business—their inner life was a puzzle no scholar was privy to. There were rumors that the mayor was friends with the ghouls, but in Percy's books there was no trusting the gossip floating around in the city full of vipers. Yet one thing was agreed upon: as long as Percy remembered, ghouls had been portrayed as beasts with matching souls. None of that was present here. Not in the reliefs he had seen on the cave walls nor in the ghoul city with its breathtaking mushroom chandelier. There was no wonder that, throughout Necropolis, whispers about poetry and art were suddenly associated with the coarse-speaking, corpse-eating creatures. Even more so as here in the inner sanctuary, there was no sense of death. The air didn't stink of corpses or decay and mold. It felt fresh and clean. Not full of smoke that seeped indoors like Necropolis. No wonder people so desperately sought entrance here, and no wonder Mr. Spooner's wails had been heard. The ghouls must have increased their patrols and rearranged their tunnels to hide this place from adventurers after their riches.

"You have slept through the night. I think it's midday up on the surface, but I'm not entirely sure." Elmer crossed his hands on his lap. He had been bandaged as well. Percy could see them bulging under the man's shirt and trouser legs.

"Are you okay?" Percy asked.

"Mistress Lace gave me her ointments, and I feel wonderful." The man's eyes gleamed.

"Good." He knew there were better responses, longer ones. But he found unnecessary words unnecessary. People always thought him to be slow because of it. At the university, his classmates chose him as an easy target in the mock-up witch battles because he didn't have quick, snarky remarks for comebacks. He'd let them. Who was he to stop someone from making a mistake? If they saw witty remarks and walls of banter as intelligence, it was their doom and not his. He wasn't that keen on insulting someone, even in good humor, as the others insisted on doing. Spite was spite whatever form it came in, and it had never inspired him to perform better. Maybe others functioned differently. He was sure they did. Percy had come to realize the wittiness and banter associated with the social realm was alien to him. With rules and proper conduct, he could live with them, but the rest made his stomach turn. Here with Elmer, there didn't seem to be a need for all the chatter.

"Good," Elmer repeated, not to mock him but as a recognition of something. Percy wasn't entirely certain of what, but clearly Elmer wasn't used to all the social interactions either.

The investigator gave an awkward smile as Percy looked at him. "I wanted to thank you for coming to get me. If you hadn't, the Council would have..."

"Why would they do this to you?" Percy asked. The Council should know better. Torture was never the solution. It was like suddenly the institution that had been formed on reason had lost just that and now ran like a headless chicken towards the unknown. If the Council had wanted to silence its investigator, there were more effective ways. A memo would have sufficed, or better yet, a promotion. Promotions were fantastic tools. They worked well with obstinate workers who couldn't be fired. Create a useless position in the basement, forget them there, and add in a hefty raise, and they won't complain. The silly thing is that most won't figure out that they have been replaced, especially if you keep sending them impressive-looking papers. And the ones smart enough to figure out how absurd their tasks have become also realize it's the perfect opportunity to pursue their creative projects on the company's time. A win-win.

"I found out more than the papers I showed you. I know the Bufonite is real. That it was created, and something happened to it. Also, I know they sent an expedition to Threebeanvalley to retrieve the machine, the remains, and the notes of Mr. Perri, the Alchemist, and other possible tools they can use here on Necropolis soil..." Elmer went on.

Percy let him speak, despite wanting nothing more than to silence the man. The more he knew, the more it became real that there was no return to his former life.

"...They have already prepared how the trial will go. The judge is bought and paid for. She will read her lines, and Mr. Thurston will be sentenced to death by hanging. Then they will obliterate his soul, but that will be just a charade for the public. They will keep him trapped in this realm and make his spirit work for them. I was this close to getting the department in charge of detainees to sign a transfer for Mr. Thurston to another prison while I could process all this information." Elmer held his thumb and forefinger slightly apart.

"How—?" Percy propped himself against the wall.

"The board think they can bury their decisions in their thousand-page-long memos, but... but I can read fast. Books and documents speak to me. I might not be a witch or a necromancer, but there's magic in the written word, especially in official documents. I only have to look at them, and I see the meaning as clear as day. You are the first one I have ever told this to." Elmer looked at him with his innocent, honest eyes, waiting to get his approval.

Percy nodded. "Then you really didn't need to get me involved." Percy let his thoughts slip out.

"No, not in the sense of needing information. But I needed a witness in order to convince others that the accusations in the documents I stole are real. I'm sorry I got you hurt." Elmer made the bed creak as he shifted his weight.

"I was already in trouble with or without you. It seems no one can escape the chaos around Mr. Thurston once they have met him. Rose should have let him perish in the fire with Mr. Perri and the whole building. I should never have disclosed the fact the machine didn't go down in flames. Anyway, I would hate to be the one who has to decide what will happen with any of this."

Elmer moaned.

"You share the sentiment with me?" Percy asked, looking at the investigator.

"I have no opinion about the past or the future. All I can say is whether something is done according to the rules. Wishing one thing or another is a waste of—"

"Time." Percy smiled. It was weird being on the receiving end of his own antics. He wondered if he sounded as clueless and offensive as Elmer did.

There came a knock on the door. Before either of them could reply, Sirixh entered. The ghoul looked bashful for being so forceful.

"I'm sorry to barge in. It was noted that Mr. Allread is awake and doing well." She said it not quite as a question. So Percy didn't answer.

"I would like to give you time to rest as Lace requested, but time is somewhat of an issue here. Not in the grand scheme of things, but here and now, within this phase of our existence." Again, the ghoul looked bashful. How she, possessing claws, mauling teeth, pitch-black eyes, and grayish skin, managed to do that was an impossibility. She continued after the small embarrassment, "But the Necromantic Council have already contacted us, and they want you returned and arrested. And..."

"You want to give us away?" Percy finished.

"No, Mr. Allread. We want to do the right thing. So we have contacted your police department and sent a letter to the Town Hall. Cruxh will be here in a few hours. We will proceed from there. Meanwhile, if you need anything, just ask the ghouls outside your doors. They will fetch you food, fresh water, anything you need, within reason." The slight lisp from earlier was gone, and Percy noticed she stood taller, pushing her hunched back straight.

"Thank you, Mrs. Si-ri-xh," Percy said, finding it hard to repeat the name as she had given it to them.

"It's my pleasure, Mr. Allread." She took her leave.

Chapter Sixteen

THE INVASIVE SPECIES

J ustice was just another story. A great one with morals, laws, and responsibilities attached to it. Not that skeptics would agree with any
of that. There was no proof about any of this justice business. It was not
written into the fabric of the cosmos. It just suddenly appeared when
humans did, and now there was no getting rid of it. And the biggest pain
was that cities needed it to exist. It didn't matter whose justice or what it
looked like. The important part was that it existed, that there was a great
book written about it, and you could use it to smack anyone who disagreed
with you. Here in the huge silence under the Necro Botanical Gardens'
glasshouse, justice was a poignant reminder that whoever sat at the top
could write the script for how others should act. Petula observed all the
people around her.

The second of silence stretched into eternity. Ida Mortician's hands
were still up in the air after having been interrupted mid-sentence arguing
how and why Petula should use the Monster Hunter Force against the
Council. Petula was happy that conversation had been cut short. It was a
disturbingly functional proposal. Henrietta sat stiffly next to her. Petula
could hear her heartbeat. It was loud and fast. Annabella leaned backward
on her chair, her teeth bared. Then there was Henrietta's secretary, Imogene, who appeared ready to have a panic attack. Before Petula addressed

the intrusion, she glanced at Mrs. Maybury. The undead was as surprised as everyone else at her husband having barged in. At least that part was not planned.

Cruxh and his officers stood in their places. Cruxh avoided gazing at Mrs. Maybury.

"Mr. Cruxh, to what do we owe the honor?" Petula stood up, and time started moving again. She positioned herself between the needlepoint group and the police officers.

The ghoul cleared his throat, and the spell was broken: Ida let her hands fall down, Henrietta breathed out, Annabella leaned in, her teeth still bared, Imogene panicked, and Mrs. Maybury squinted her eyes.

Cruxh tugged his suit and said, "Your mayorship," concentrating on Petula. He had never used such an honorary title before. Petula knew she wasn't going to like what was to follow. Petula drew her lips tight. Cruxh kept his poise and shifted his weight from one foot to the other, as if unable to deliver the message. "You are expected to arrive at the Town Hall immediately," the ghoul said.

"And you needed a police convoy to get me?" Petula asked.

The ghoul shook his head. "No, ma'am. I'm not here for you. That was just..." Him giving her a heads-up. Meaning everything had gone Kraken shit, and a storm was coming. *This is it,* Petula thought. More so as Mr. Colton lurked behind the officers, restless. Something he never was.

"Ma'am." Cruxh paused and locked his eyes with hers. "The Necromantic Council has accused Mrs. Culpepper of slander, persecution, and violating her contract with them. They have pressed charges against her and the rest of the needlepoint group for insubordination and incitement to violence. Accordingly, I have a warrant for their arrest, signed and sealed." The ghoul took the document out of his vest pocket and handed it to Petula.

Annabella intercepted Cruxh. "Let me." She took the paper from the ghoul. Cruxh and his officers graciously waited for Annabella to read it.

Petula didn't. "And me?"

"No mention, ma'am," Cruxh harrumphed.

"Everything seems to be in order," Annabella said and handed the paper back to Cruxh.

"Good. Henrietta Culpepper, Annabella Sepulcher, and Ida Mortician, I'm arresting you on suspicion of inciting a riot and spreading false rumors. All that you say might be used against you in the court of law. You have a right to your attorney and the right to remain silent until one is found or presented. Mrs. Sepulcher, do you want me to contact a lawyer for you?" Cruxh looked towards Annabella.

"Yes," Annabella said and glanced at Henrietta, who nodded. "We want the Coven's witches to represent us."

"Now, if you could." Cruxh gestured for all of them to turn around and put their hands behind their backs to be cuffed.

Petula watched as the needlepoint group let themselves be shackled. Mrs. Maybury had shuffled next to her, and she muttered, "They are taking this too far. Something else must be afoot."

"Yes, but what?"

"We'll know soon."

Petula kept looking at Henrietta, who held her head high. Petula was sure she saw the woman's hands shaking. Also, she was sure Cruxh and Mrs. Maybury didn't even exchange a glance the whole time. Cruxh was a stickler for the rules, meaning this was bad. But there was a chance the ghoul wouldn't let this go too far. The arrest had to be made. There was no doubt about that.

The police officers escorted the needlepoint group past the witches, who kept pouring into the gardens. There were more witches than Petula had seen before. It was as if they had been summoned here to witness this. Her first instinct was that the Council was sending a message, but this went too far even by their standards. This was the Coven's business.

The witches parted, letting the officers escort Henrietta, Ida, and Annabella out. Henrietta stopped next to Imogene, who clutched her apron.

"Get Lottie Letcoffin, the accountant. She will sort out the Coven while I'm gone. Also, get me fresh clothes and whatever else you think I might need and bring them to the station. And tell Eurof what has happened and tell him not to get too worried. And get Mag to represent us."

Imogene nodded. The young witch looked like she was ready to faint. Her whole body trembled as she kept bobbing her head up and down.

Henrietta lifted her gaze to meet the other witches'. "Letcoffin will be the next Mother if anything happens to me. I promise I will be back and fight these preposterous claims."

Finally, Henrietta looked towards Petula and said, "See to it."

Then the needlepoint group was taken away, and Petula and Mrs. Maybury were left behind with the confused and angry witches. Mr. Colton hurried to her, putting himself between Petula and everyone else.

"I think it's better if we leave."

Petula frowned. "You are right. Get me to the Town Hall and then find Dow."

"Yes, miss," Mr. Colton said and began pushing his way out of the glasshouse. The witches' eyes landed upon them. Whispers spread, none of them kind. They accused her of bringing down the Coven. They whispered how Henrietta should never have let a necromancer into the gardens.

Mrs. Maybury trailed after Petula. No witch dared to address the undead.

When they got into the coach and it pulled off, Petula could breathe. She clutched her hands into fists and thought about war. Either she or the Council had to yield; either way, Necropolis would be forever altered. She would make sure the suffocating, saturated, stagnant state the city was in wouldn't slowly burn her and others alive. The deterioration caused by the Council's greed would end. If it meant she had to become a martyr to shake the city free from the corrupted, old-fashioned institution that held every citizen at gunpoint, then so be it. She was ready. But there would be casualties. Not only the guilty would pay. Innocent grannies would get trampled, but there were no cookie-baking grannies in Necropolis. They all had bodies in their closets. And they would fight along with her if given the right ammunition.

"Breathe," Mrs. Maybury said. "It will be a shit storm anyway. So make it yours."

You could sniff out the core function of an institution just by stepping in. It was how the tiles were arranged, how the walls were painted, and how one's voice echoed inside the building. The walls of the Necromantic Council whispered all around Raul. They spoke of numbers, papers, forms, and secrets with a disjointed chatter about the things done and left undone. All Raul had to do was stay put and write everything down, and he would have all he needed to slander the Council, but he wanted more. He had to follow the pre-laid plan set by the creature. It was clearly taking him somewhere. Raul had always taken the difficult road, never letting anyone tell him what to do. Now he let the strange creature guide him past all the witches and necromancers, and he blindly trusted it to keep him safe. All his past lovers would laugh that he would rather trust a monster than them.

The creature warned him of any upcoming dangers with a slight change in its growl, never leading him astray. But it always remained just out of sight. There was a story there, which Raul couldn't get too obsessed with. The present was already too much to handle, and the Council came first.

They had already gotten past the first two upper floors with ease. The building was growing ever more restless the farther down they went. There was an extra sense of security. Yet, somehow, he slipped past the witches, the hexes, the necromancers, and the undead alike. The creature was doing more than warning him. That was for sure. Raul pressed his back against the wall when the creature growled. The air vibrated around him, full of hexes. They sniffed him out, moving on, deeming him irrelevant. Raul was sure that it wasn't because of the protection stitched into his jacket's lining. Something every Necropolitan carried with them.

There came a growl.

"Where are you taking me?" Raul asked louder than he liked.

There came only dead silence and then a growl to warn him of the upcoming witches. Raul had gotten good at reading the slight change of tone. He ducked through an open door just before a group of witches ran past him. He stood there despite the growl urging him to follow. He waited for the nauseating feeling to pass. The room smelled like someone had smoked there non-stop, cigarette after cigarette. Raul observed all the filing cabinets left open, and the chair behind the small wooden desk knocked down. The seat had worn-out cushioning with little flowers on it. The seating was indented after all the hours put in. A carved metallic plaque stood on the desk with Alvira Calhoun's name on it. The name glistened in the low light from the open door.

It was the office of Percy Allread's handler. Raul had interviewed the woman, or tried to. From the look of things, she'd left in a hurry, or had been dragged out to Kraken knew where. There was a half-finished cigarette on the ashtray. The vampire wouldn't have left it behind willingly. Raul remembered she was one of those who had sworn off blood. He'd made a note of that. Staying away from blood wasn't an easy thing to do. She was killing herself gradually. Nicotine couldn't replace the hunger. Yet some vampires saw it as a merciful way to exit; not be a victim of their urges. Hogwash, if you asked Raul. They were what they were.

Raul glanced around the doorway. The hallway was empty again. He saw a glimpse of a tail going in the opposite direction to where the witches had run. They had gone towards the main entrance. Part of him wanted to stay and investigate Alvira's room, but he followed the creature into the corridor. There was another set of staircases leading farther down into the building. The air got thicker, and it rippled as he moved down the steps. There weren't only curses hidden in the walls; Raul could sense spirits sniffing him out. Yet nothing stuck. No alarm was sounded. He'd made a strong friend. Raul didn't like it one bit. There were no free favors in the city of the dead. There was always a price to pay. Every action came with a cost. Not in any karmic sense, no. Just your body wearing out and decay catching up with you. Raul had always thought you could tell when it was your time to go. It was in the steps, the eyes, the speech, and the shaking of the hands. Somehow Old Man Death warned you before his deliverance. Raul didn't care for the old god, who had re-emerged a year ago. Necromancers had started to openly affirm their devotion to the forgotten, forbidden god. Madam Sabine had given a public speech about the corrupting power of death. She declared that Necropolis had always been about the macabre way of celebrating life rather than embracing the void beyond.

Game of souls, Raul thought. All the god stuff was above his pay grade. All that mattered here was that there were no signs of Old Man Death lurking in the corner of his eyes. No shortness of breath. No black aura around him. Just the usual pain of existing.

Raul followed the stairs as far as they went. They led to a basement level with a thick metal door marked with bold letters: Archives. The door was partly ajar. Raul reached for it. His hands trembled. This was why the creature had gotten him into the building. This was all anyone could hope for. The Council documented everything, and Raul meant everything. Everyone knew that the Council had a vault for the secrets of the universe and all the relics that came with it. The Archives were the promised land for reporters, relic hunters, for anyone hoping to know how everything ticked, and here they were, hidden in the basement guarded by only Kraken knew who.

Raul tugged the sleeves of his jacket up instinctively and glanced behind him, half expecting the Council's goons to appear. There was only a small space under the staircase, and it was empty except for a few ghosts, but they were not in any hurry to shake him up. They didn't give a shit about Raul or what happened at the Council. They were taking a break in the only quiet space in the building where they could have a smoke and complain about incompetent workmates.

Raul slipped in through the door and searched for something to pinpoint where he was meant to go. Farther away from the door, there was a front desk, which was empty. There was a steaming coffee cup on the desk and papers and folders scattered about, as if someone was sorting them out, but no person to whom they belonged.

Raul took a step forward and froze when he heard a scream. It was coming from the back of someone's throat somewhere in the Archives. Raul could hear why. The huge metallic shelves crammed with brown acid-free cardboard boxes which filled the room from top to bottom like a vast ocean were shaking. The boxes kept tumbling down, making a cacophony of sounds.

"Who the Kraken shit let their ghosts loose?" someone kept repeating in a desperate voice.

Raul dragged the door shut behind him as quietly as he could, wondering what the point was, but somehow it seemed like the right thing to do. The Archives were bigger than he had ever imagined. The rows of shelves seemed to stretch into eternity, and they were neatly arranged into easily cataloged rows with signs. Raul looked at the labels. None of the letters and numbers made any sense. It was like a hidden code with no chronology involved. Raul searched for a map or an index card system, but there was none to be found.[1]

Raul crept past the first shelves and glanced around the corridor. The gas lights flickered above him, giving him a headache. Raul cursed under his breath, well aware that letting curses out here wasn't wise, yet he couldn't help himself. He searched for a tail and listened for a growl. Nothing. He again searched for the indexing system. There had to be one. There wasn't. He had come this far, and now... If there was one true god, the great spirit in the sky, who had made all of this, then they had to be a bureaucrat at heart to play a joke like this.

He headed towards the screaming. The Archivist would know where Otis's files were kept, along with a few other items Raul wanted to get his hands on. He would have to lie his way out of this one. Something he'd done many times before. He was sure he already had a fake inspector license for the city's Archives. He could use it. As soon as he took a step towards the corridor where the Archivist was, the gas lamps overhead started to flicker faster. He frowned and continued. The flickering was getting more hectic. He glanced up and saw that only some of them were illuminated. He let his gaze follow the clear path they seemed to form. Nasty tricks.

He turned around and hurried his steps away from the fading screaming. The shelves had stopped shaking, and the wails had turned into snivels.

The gas lamps led him to a huge door with locks from top to bottom.

---

1. In fact, the whole system was stored in the Archivist's head with all the tiny details only an insane person would remember. All of which could be wiped out just like that if the Archivist got killed. But that would never happen. Nor would the man retire. No employee ever retired. They either died or changed jobs inside the institute, and the dying part was the most usual method of exiting the employment roster. But that wasn't the reason the Archivist and the contents of his head couldn't be lost. It was the Archivist himself. He was the personification of the Archive—a form composed of all the dead energy floating around combined with knowledge absorbed into the papers. A perfect guardian who hated giving out any documents and only cost the Council a daily pot of coffee. Good coffee, to be fair.

A tiny note was attached to it, declaring Authorized Access Only. Raul glanced over his shoulder. The creature wasn't there, but neither was anyone else. Raul looked at the locks. There were bound to be curses on them. Raul closed his eyes and took hold of the door handle and twisted it. There was a clicking sound. Raul let out a long breath and opened his eyes to check if he was still in the same shape as when he had come in. He was. He carefully pulled the door open. The creature had clearly rendered the locks useless, or they were there just for the show.[2]

Raul left the door ajar, not wanting to get stuck inside if the locks somehow started working again.

The room wasn't much bigger than his apartment, yet there was enough space to hold all the secrets of the universe known to man.[3] The shelves that framed the room stretched to the ceiling and bent under the sheer volume of boxes. Raul stared at the old artifacts, the wooden boxes, the golden cups, the carved stone figures, the specimens of weird creatures inside glass jars that spell out ancient gods, and held his breath. He only had to reach out and he could be whatever he wanted to be; only a drop of blood had to be sacrificed. But he didn't want to have some ultimate power or to be anyone else, least of all the messenger for the impending doom coming from the skies, which would wipe out the whole of existence one day. None of it. What he searched for was the truth. A truth that needed to be spoken now.

Raul drew the first box from the shelf nearest to him and peeked inside,

---

2. Actually, neither was the case. The door had been reached and broken not so long ago by a small goblin man, Elmer Spooner. His tactics had rendered the curses and the locks obsolete, not to mention the Archivist, who was having the worst day of his existence. He let Elmer get past him, thinking the scrupulous man was made of the same stuff as him and perhaps they could be friends, only to end up letting the man leave with secret documents that should never leave the ridiculously untouched Archives. And now the poltergeist.

3. Not that the Council had any of those hidden inside its walls. And if they did, they were hidden in the left corner on the bottom shelf box marked Accounts from the Great Beyond.

forgetting everything around him. This was his chance to discover the truth about what the Council was and what it actually did, and if indeed Petula Upwood was their puppet. Okay, the last part was too far-fetched, but he might as well look for the evidence—for the people.

CHAPTER SEVENTEEN

MISHAPS AFTER AN INJURY

T he coach to the Town Hall rattled over the cobblestones. The quieting trot of the horses made the ride calming amongst the chaos humanity birthed. Petula sometimes wondered whether it was the fault of man that everything seemed to fall apart, or was it the basic function written into the laws of physics that demanded erosion exist even in human affairs. Or was she focusing on the wrong things? An octopus sacrificed herself for the survival of her offspring. A mother otter taught all her tricks to her cubs to ensure their survival. Yet here she was, watching as, again, humans fell short in their cooperation. Either there were too many of them, or there was indeed faulty logic behind the making of a man. Petula had started to lean more towards the faulty logic, especially as the odds were stacked against a person.

Petula glanced at the undead sitting next to her. The woman looked calm. The Council arresting the needlepoint group didn't seem to have affected her in any way.[1] Petula herself felt oddly calm too. Not that she had ever been capable of the great emotions the poets wrote about. That had always been reserved for others. But undoubtedly, the Council had stepped

---

1. Okay, she was wrong about that, but it was too easy to assume the contents of the interior based on the exterior.

out of line, and she would have to follow this with action. Another thing that seemed to always lurk behind everything: action. It was like a bad curse no one could escape. Sometimes Petula wondered if she stayed really still and quiet, would she disappear, or would the world slip past her. But that didn't seem right. Wasn't this all about figuring out the whole existing thing before time caught up with you rather than letting it sail by? Okay, maybe that wasn't it. Neither was it about personal growth. Mostly, it seemed to be about survival, composed of reaction after reaction in situations where no one knew what all the moving parts did.

The needlepoint group had done just that. Reacted and reacted. They had been nice about it, following the rules that were meant to maintain social cohesion. But it was clearly time to stop playing nice.

Petula snorted.

"So, you finally grew some balls?" Mrs. Maybury asked.

"You cannot say such a thing."

"I can say anything I want."

"That you do. Was it necessary, what you did to Mrs. Burton?"

"You knew?"

"Of course I did. She meant no harm by it, and only a fool would think the Council didn't know what was said and done there. And I liked Mrs. Burton."

"Oh," Mrs. Maybury said. "How? I thought—"

"That I kept Dow out of it. I have. He has nothing to do with the needlepoint group, and he hates that I even attend it. But he did ask me to network and make friends. I did just that. So what if we talked about taking the Council down in the midst of drinking our tea? It's a perfectly reasonable way to stretch one's mind. It's not good to let things get too dusty up there."

Mrs. Maybury narrowed her eyes.

"It was obvious from day one that there was a possibility she couldn't cut her ties with her past. I gave her several chances to do so, but her pride got in her way. And yes, I do my own research too. I can't keep putting my life in Dow's hands. That's too much power for one person to have over another. You know that as well as I do. That's why you keep hanging around me and protecting me, if I haven't misjudged you."

"Don't think too highly of yourself, girl." This time it was Mrs. Maybury who snorted. The woman turned to look out of the window.

Petula did as well. The city seemed more anxious than usual. As if it could sense the unrest to come. That feeling wouldn't stay dormant, waiting to be ignited. It was already worming its way into the lives of anyone who took residence in the city of the undead, wreaking havoc, making everyone snap at each other just because, and that just because led to hating themselves and others, and most importantly making them numb. Everyone the coach passed knew that if only they acted and said something, maybe it would all be better. But they couldn't. There was no room for mistakes, no room to speak, no room to demand, and no room to exist in any other way than pre-stated.

"I wouldn't dare," Petula said, turning her gaze away from the city behind them consumed by greed and selfishness sustained by apathy.

"Good."

"So, how are you going to get them out? I gather you would rather not see Henrietta hanged." Mrs. Maybury faced her once again. Her eyes seemed to accuse her prematurely of all she would do.

"I wish I knew."

The coach stopped. Mr. Colton let them out, offering his hand to Petula. Petula took it and squeezed it. The man winked at her but said nothing. Instead, he situated himself between Petula and the reporters, whose flashes commanded the space as soon as Petula stepped out. They were worse than vampires, sniffing out an open wound. They had clearly been tipped off about what had happened at the Necro Botanical Gardens. If the Council thought this would intimidate her, they were wrong. She had no plan to let the reporters crucify her with their red eyes.

Petula searched for R.E. Porter in the crowd. She only found the man's trusted photographer. Then she shifted her gaze around, looking for Dow. The man was absent, as he had been all day.

Petula pushed past Mr. Colton, refusing to get caught up in fear. The Council wouldn't dare to assassinate her here, nor anyone else for that matter. Though such a play would cater to the dramatic side of Necropolis, and the crowds would love it. Such was the crude hunger of a dying empire that lost its grip on the world with every second that ticked by. Petula wasn't too sorry to witness Necropolis finally coming to its knees. She was a Leporidae Lop first and had seen what Necropolis control had done to her country. It was time this inherited country of hers stopped making money out of the misery of others and instead cooperated with them. But that battle was yet to come. Now she had to live through this one to guide Necropolis out of the darkness that would follow.

Petula positioned herself on the Town Hall steps and lifted her hand. The reporters fell silent and looked at her with their hungry, wide eyes. Yes, there was that hunger again. It was like the city was insatiable. Petula let her gaze glide over the reporters, letting their eyes peer into her. She even withstood the stares of the werewolf reporters.[2] Their ears poked up in the air, making the situation somehow more calming. This was Necropolis. This was not Leporidae Lop. Here she was the top necromancer—for now.

"Some of you have already heard that the head of the Coven has been arrested for treason, and I was present when that happened. My association with her rebellious group can't be denied. I was part of her inner circle of

---

2. The werewolves had set up their own publication last year, even daring to come out in public half-morphed. You could see that not everyone was pleased about it. There was a vast open space around the half-man and half-wolf. Birthed to be a beast and judged as such.

friends who discussed our beloved city while doing needlepoint…" Petula could hear the city's shop owners filling their shelves with needlework packs and flowery embroidery patterns, pushing all the other handcraft items out of their window displays and drawing special offers on their signs.

"…The legality of the actions taken by the group is for the courts to decide. So is the fate of Mr. Thurston. As of today, the Council will have two days to deliver Mr. Thurston in front of the Town Hall's committee and explain why Mr. Thurston should be in their custody instead of the government's. That's all."

Petula turned around, giving no time for questions, doing the thing she hated most: putting on a show to force her political decisions upon others. She had actually planned to follow her statement and not just toy with the public's perception. Still, politics had become nothing more than optics.

The reporters shouted after her with their questions. She headed inside despite hearing a couple of good ones. She was greeted with a pair of scolding eyes.

"Good evening, Elvira." She nodded at the receptionist.

The harbinger of doom turned up her nose at Petula and said with distaste, "Evening."

It would be all too easy to think the woman hated her, yet both of them knew that Elvira favored Petula over anyone else in the Town Hall. So much so that once a day, she scolded Dow for how he restricted Petula's independence. But the scolding could never stop. There was no giving in to friendliness, not as a harbinger of doom. Petula let the play unfold on its own, liking the situation more than those moments where everyone bobbed their heads in agreement with her then talked behind her back.[3]

Petula left the receptionist alone and headed to her office, Mrs. Maybury trailing after her. Mr. Colton slipped away without a word. Petula knew he would head to report to Dow. That was what the man did.

The undead's gentle shuffle behind her reminded Petula how bizarre this world was, especially as she could feel all the dead energy around, searching for a way in and asking the mayor of Necropolis to hear their pleas. Once a month, she held a seance, giving resolution to those she could. A few murders had been solved since she had made it a habit, and a lot of forgiveness had been made. A very cathartic way to serve the community, Petula had found out. It almost made her happy. But only almost.

She took her letter kit out and began composing a letter to the Council. Oh, of course, they knew her demands already. But optics again. She had to do this the right way, or they would hang her by her balls, as Mrs. Maybury would say. Next, she composed a note to her lawyers, instructing them to go to the police station to examine the charges against Henrietta and the rest. The whole time she was busy composing her letters, Mrs. Maybury sat on the lounge chair, silently observing her. The tabby cat curled up next to the undead. Heat was heat wherever it came from. Which in Mrs. Maybury's case should be impossible. But who knew what modern taxidermy could do?

If you are going to rebel, make it count. There's no half-assing it, or you find

---

3. And Elvira was having a blast. Finally, there was enough chaos in the city to make bad things happen. She was sure someone would die. She could smell it in the air. But damn her soul if she was going to show that to the dumb human child. Elvira had been around long enough to know that people came and went, and she stayed. There was no reason to get overly attached to mortals.

yourself in a noose or some prison on the other side of the border, where torture serves as a reminder of your failure. Henrietta didn't find herself in a noose, but she was in a cell with the rest of the needlepoint group. There was no torture yet, but that might come if the Council claimed them. So the situation was somewhat amicable for now. In the good old days, there would have been no question, just an instant execution or heavy torture and then a public beheading. And all they had done was state their political opinion. But there was no room for that any longer.

Annabella had been in and out of the cell, sorting out the lawyer situation. Technically she could represent them, but she'd explained it wasn't ideal. So they waited for the Coven's lawyers. Henrietta observed Annabella through the bars. The undead woman sat with Mr. Cruxh at the ghoul's desk, a helpless expression in her dead eyes. The retired Kraken follower had never seemed so small. She could save herself and walk out of here—she was an undead, after all—but she'd stayed. It was the most civilized thing to do despite laws and systems being abused all around them.

Henrietta couldn't hear what was said, but she'd figured out that this would take a long time and she wasn't getting home any time soon. She crossed her legs and leaned against the wall, trying to familiarize herself with her new environment. There were other detainees in the cell with them, but they kept their distance. She could see them eying her and Ida, who sulked next to Henrietta. Most of them were drunks who had been hauled here to sober up. Then there were the officers, who strolled by the cell to get a glimpse of the mighty who'd fallen. They looped past the bars and then back to Cruxh and around Annabella before they settled to their tasks. Henrietta could imagine all the rumors already floating around the city. She hoped the words "overthrowing the Council" were among them, but most likely they would be about corruption, secret societies, and grannies knitting. She could hear the whispers in the pubs: "*Thank the Kraken good lads of ours caught them before they got their panties all twisted and went and stabbed someone with their knitting needles.*"

Henrietta couldn't help but smile. Revolution by a needle. There was a thought.

"What?" Ida asked.

"Nothing. Just a passing thought," Henrietta said, and her smile died. The worst thing would be that there was no news. No report. No discussion:

"Don't hold back now. It's not like I have anywhere else to go." Ida uncrossed her legs and leaned on her elbows. Somehow this imprisonment thing was working for the banker. She seemed more at peace, as if she was this highly dangerous criminal. She even glanced under her eyebrows at anyone who dared to look at her, and she was instantly obeyed.

"I was thinking about the headlines of our arrest: *a needlepoint group arrested for instigating a riot in the city.*"

Ida scoffed. "I wouldn't give them any new funny ideas to add to our charges."

Henrietta took a deep breath in and shut her eyes, trying her best not to snap at Ida. There was no other option than to take this lightly. If she got caught up in her emotions, rationality would fly out the window, and she would make a mess. Of course, she could argue with Ida about the old saying that if you can't beat it, join it, or better yet, accept it and make the best out of the situation.

Henrietta could, of course, change it. She could make the wood around the bars bloom and bend to her will and walk out of here as the wooden floor seized the officers and pinned them down. Nature was the mightiest force there was. Humans were fools to forget such a thing and consider themselves the masters of the universe. But that would be another mistake, forcing the Coven to obey the Council and condemn her. It was strictly forbidden for a witch to use her full power. Not in here. Not out there. Only under guidance and supervision.

The thing was, she had more power than anyone truly knew. She'd dedicated her early years, her stay in Amanita, to actualizing her full potential. She could make nature do her bidding. She didn't want that. She'd realized that the same nature would pay the price and not her. So, instead of making a public spectacle, she did as she taught others: respect the situation and the elements they worked with. And partly, she hid her talents for self-preservation. The Council would have done everything in its power to remove her. So would Ruby Granger, Imogene's mother, who had doubtless had a hand in Wesley's death and all of this. Henrietta slightly opened her eyelids and saw Ida had followed her example and decided to rest.

Soon enough, Annabella came to the cell. She shook her head. "I'm sorry, I can't get any of us out. They will hold us for questioning and then transfer us to state prison to wait for the investigation and trial if it comes to that."

"It's alright. We expected something like this." She had, at least.

"No, it isn't. This is no way to treat someone of your or—" Annabella started.

"Don't finish that sentence. I have to insist. Isn't that the same line of logic we are trying to fight against? We are no different from the Council if we force the laws to bend in our favor because of our stature. Things have changed a lot, and it seems we won't be tried by the Council. Otherwise, we wouldn't be here," Henrietta said. "Cruxh will come through. I'm sure he will." What she left out was that she was doubtful if the Coven would. She had a bad feeling about the fact they hadn't already sent their lawyers here.

"I'm not so sure. There's merit to the Council's claims, especially if Lattice is willing to testify. We have conspired behind the Council's back, and we have aided the Save the Otis Group, and they have made some inflammatory statements." Annabella took her seat between Henrietta and Ida.

"We are screwed," Ida said.

"Not necessarily. Something feels off. The Council wouldn't do anything like this if there weren't something amiss," Henrietta reasoned. That was another thing she had been thinking about for a while. The Council never used the police for their dirty work.

"I'll say," Ida sighed. "But what can we do?"

"We play for time and wait for our lawyers to communicate with the Council and the outside world on our behalf."

"You mean with the mayor?" Ida asked.

"Her too."

The undead woman smiled, and the hump on her back straightened and her eyes became sharper. Annabella was about to say something, but Cruxh interrupted them. The ghoul coughed. He stood behind the bars with keys in his hands and a few other officers next to him.

"Mrs. Sepulcher, Mrs. Culpepper, and Miss Mortician, stand up. We need to process you and escort you to your overnight cells," Cruxh stated and motioned for a ghoul and a scrawny-looking monster Henrietta didn't recognize to head inside the cell as he opened the door for them.

Annabella was about to protest, but the ghoul was faster. Cruxh said, "And no, we will not question anyone without their lawyer present and having had a good night's sleep per your request."

"Good."

Annabella got up, and Ida and Henrietta followed suit. They put their hands behind their backs and let them be cuffed for the second time. They were escorted to the police station's backrooms, where there were overnight cells. Each room had a bed with a passable mattress, a washing bowl, and a bucket to do their business in. But what was most luxurious was the window on Henrietta's wall. She could look at the stars, twinkling behind the thick gray clouds against the pitch-black sky after the rain. Behind her, the door clicked shut, and Henrietta was left alone. She heard Ida curse and protest about the separation, but Annabella silenced her.

Henrietta went to the bed and lay down. She peered out of the window at a tall oak spreading against the black sky not too far from the station's backyard. Henrietta could make the tree shoot its roots against the station's wall to break her free. She didn't. Instead, she made the dry tree search for water deeper underground, guiding more fungal growth into it and into the city. As a first-year student, she'd dreamed of making Necropolis into a green city, but that had been a foolish dream. The citizens preferred cobblestones and high buildings with gargoyles over any greenery.

Before Henrietta could fall asleep, there came a knock on the cell door. She swung her legs down and sat waiting until the locks were opened. Eurof came in with an officer and Cruxh behind him.

The ghoul stated, "We are making an exception this time. But one of my officers, Petty Officer Lawrence, will be listening in." Cruxh gestured towards the huge unknown monster. There was something ghoulish about him, but he was a lot taller and bigger than your average ghoul, and less rotten.

The officer saluted and slipped inside the room. Then it was like he wasn't there. Despite his blue uniform and somewhat grotesque goblin features mixed into his ghoulish ancestral line, the creature melted into the background. But all that was just background noise as Eurof rushed towards her and knelt on the floor, holding her hand.

"I'll get you out of here," he said.

"No, you won't. Don't do anything rash. The process will prevail." Henrietta had to believe in that, especially as the petty officer was watching.

"This is serious, Henrietta. You can't take this lightly. The Coven..." Eurof shook his head and squeezed her hands harder.

"The Coven what?"

"They are talking about replacing you and not sending their lawyers. It looks bad, Henrietta."

She squeezed his hands hard. "They can't do that."

"They have. You need to be careful. You need to let me help you."

"I can't let you get involved."

"I am already involved. I'm your husband, and you should have let me help you a lot earlier. Not kept me in the dark." Eurof got up, still keeping his hands on hers. He sat next to her and drew her nearer.

"I should have, but—"

"There's no but, Henrietta. There's only what you want me to do now."

Henrietta held her breath. Eurof looked into her eyes, ready to get hurt again. Ready for her to push him away. She wasn't ready to let him leave, even if there was an empty space where their relationship had once been. A space she would weave back together.

"I need you to be my eyes and ears at the Coven. Don't let them push you away from the meetings, and see who's doing what and why. It's important. I need to set this right before we can sail into the sunset." She nodded at the tickets in his chest pocket. She loved him to bits, but he was daft if he thought he could break her free after marching in here with tickets for a sea voyage leaving tomorrow. She couldn't blame him for trying. He had to try. That was evident.

Eurof gulped. She wanted to laugh and embrace him, but he got there first. He took her into his embrace and whispered in her ear, "Maybe you are right. But I'll hold on to these. I'll change them to an open date. When you get out, we are leaving. And I won't accept any other answer."

"I agree; we are going home to Amanita. The Coven will survive without me. It survived before me and has for centuries. I'm not irreplaceable." The last part was said more for her than him.

He clutched her harder, and Henrietta could feel his little sobs.

"We'll be fine. I'll be fine." Part of her was dying with those words. She wanted nothing more than for them to be true. That she would walk out of this ordeal as a free woman, and they could go home. But the part of her who had loved running the Coven and making the gardens prosper, who flourished when the other witches came to her and sought her expertise, who would do anything to make the Coven stand on its own feet and not be a lackey to the Council, didn't want to go. She knew she would have to give all that up if she wanted to live a more balanced life and make Eurof happy again, and herself too.

She hadn't been happy for a long time. Not only because of this divide between her and her husband, but because the responsibilities and compromises had gradually consumed her. The only way she could leave was if someone who had the same goals for the Coven in their heart would step up. Imogene wasn't the one. She thought pesticide was the way to go, that fungi should be eradicated, and so on. She knew nothing of the balance nature needed. Imogene should venture out into the world as Henrietta insisted. Imogene needed to grow up and step out of her mother's shadow. Until then, the girl would lead only over her dead body. Henrietta pushed the thoughts away as an unnecessary distraction from hugging Eurof. She did it as softly and warmly as she could, as if giving him an apology for everything she'd done and had become.

The sobbing stopped, and she let go. "Be my eyes and ears until we get out. It's the only way for me to survive and for us to leave. I need a successor."

"If that's what you need," Eurof said.

Not much else could be said. Their time was up. The huge ghoulish creature stepped out of the shadows, opened the door for Eurof, and locked Henrietta back in. She lay down on the bed and felt her body begin to shake. She stopped herself from tearing up, holding it in like a reasonable adult should, and tossed and turned on the bed, unable to sleep. There was only one thing she could do to stop her head from spinning. She reached out for that tree outside her window and made its roots and all the fungi connected to it travel to the Coven. Henrietta felt her fists clench, but it was just ghostly action in the distance. All her focus was on the fact that Imogene stood in front of the whole Coven, declaring Lottie Letcoffin to be unfit to be the temporary Mother and demanding a replacement. Herself, to be precise. Behind the secretary, her mother lurked, highly aware that the Coven wouldn't let her lead, but Imogene was a different matter entirely. Everyone knew her, and everyone liked Imogene. Everyone felt sorry for her for having Ruby as a mother. Yet they didn't hold it against her. Henrietta had done that.

The house shook a little as Henrietta pushed the roots under the Coven. But the witches didn't react. They just stood there, dazed by the debate. Imogene insisted that Lottie knew nothing about leading the place; that she had already been doing just that for Henrietta for a long time. She kept on saying that Henrietta would want it this way. That it had been a mistake for Henrietta to name Lottie instead of her.

"Mother was distressed... You all know me. You know that I can keep this place running until she comes back," Imogene stated.

Ruby kept her expression blank behind her daughter. Even a slight smirk would offend the witches. Some already were. Judika cleared her throat. The kitchen witch said, "This is pointless. We already have a leader, and instead of bickering here, we should be out there freeing her."

Henrietta watched Ruby snap her fingers, and Imogene flinched. Henrietta had always feared that Imogene couldn't set herself free from her mother. Here was the proof. Henrietta wasn't sorry for all the hours she'd put into teaching the young girl. Imogene had so much potential, and if even a part of Henrietta's words stayed with her, it was more than she could have hoped for. But this wouldn't happen. The Coven would be doomed if Ruby got her hands on it in this state. Ruby was vindictive, petty, proud, and small-minded, and worst of all, she had always advocated for the Council. Her only way to power. Stupid woman.

"But you don't have to solely believe in my words. You can trust our bylaws," Imogene began. "Clause eighty-six in the appendix was made for these kinds of situations. We collectively put it there after Reverent Epith died. Mother endorsed it as well. Don't get me wrong, Lottie Letcoffin is a brilliant woman whose cunning with the bookkeeping and financial matters has kept us secure. But even she has to admit that running the Coven takes a toll, and she has her health problems. We need someone who knows how day-to-day business is run, who knows the gardens by heart, and who served under Mother tirelessly…"

Henrietta wanted to jump in and cut off the words and say, "*The appendix is for when there's no successor named.*" But she didn't have to. Instead, Judika, the Coven's cook, did the speaking for her.

"But Mother wanted Lottie to replace her. Such is her will." Judika had her hands on her hips, and the always sunny woman looked strained. The meeting had been going on ever since the arrest happened.

"Yes, she did—" Imogene began.

Judika interrupted her. "And she did it with a sound mind. She hasn't lost her mind to the cackle. That was another reason why the clause was added to the appendix. Lottie was her choice. She has a right to the title until the matter with the courts has been settled and the outcome is clear. Then we can reconsider. Now we need to concentrate on liberating Mother rather than bickering amongst ourselves about who gets to run the place in her absence."

Kraken bless the woman who ties us together with her divine food, which cures any ache of the soul.

Ruby snarled and reached for her dolls as her daughter swayed in the face of the cook's conviction. An electrified wave hit the crowd, making Henrietta wince.

"Of course we do," Imogene said. "Correcting the injustice done to Mother is the first thing we need to do, but we also need to keep the Coven running. We must not lose our base of power and influence. The Council has threatened to pull our funding and give us a hefty fine..." Imogene continued, but Henrietta didn't hear the rest. Everything got murkier. Something tugged her fingers and yanked at her legs. The call to come back was too strong, and Henrietta had to release the connection, or her mind might shatter. Henrietta freed her hold and let the mycelium guide her back to the police station.

Henrietta opened her eyes and saw Cruxh standing beside her bed with a witch close by. A hexer, from the sense of it.

Cruxh coughed. "I have to ask you to—"

"I won't do it again," Henrietta said and sat up, knowing well that the walls would be sealed after the hexer was done.

"That would be very kind of you. I would hate to put it on my report."

Henrietta nodded. "Thank you." Both of them knew the public wouldn't like it if she used her powers this way. And both of them understood that Cruxh would take this as a miscommunication and leave it out of his report if she went to bed nicely without making trouble.

Cruxh and the witch left her there after the little hexes were put in place. Henrietta lay on the bed, trying to fall sleep. But sleep felt ever so elusive tonight. Not even the sympathetic nod from the witch had made a difference. Henrietta stared at the super-moon taking up half of the sky and wondered if there was any surviving this. If she could keep her promise to Eurof and sail back to Amanita once this was finished.

Chapter Eighteen

THE LAST FLOATING RIB

The question of whether one should be imprisoned was never a question for the one. It was the many who had in their shared intelligence decided the one's fate. The thing was that there was not always a great deal of intelligence involved. Sometimes it was a lynch mob who couldn't see past their reactions. There needed to be a system, a process, and professionals involved without emotions attached. But even the system could get things wrong, especially when the trust was gone and the gap between the judged and judges was incomprehensibly wide.

The question of whether Otis would ever get that intelligent sentencing was still up for debate. He found a dark wool coat, trousers, and a white shirt thrust into his hands, along with underwear. The witch who had brought them didn't look happy about it. She was a tall specimen and had a regal look about her. Otis didn't doubt for a second that she hailed from an aristocratic line. Not only because of the way she looked down her nose at Otis but because she had grown so tall and robust in Necropolis, where food was seen as a secondary part of scraping by. Not to mention the toxic fumes from the factories, which took half the city down. Behind her, another witch, a man in his thirties who was shorter and stockier than the woman, lowered a washing bowl and a pitcher with rags and a bar of soap onto the writing desk.

"Get clean and ready," the man growled.

Otis just sat there on the bed, staring at the two witches.

"Get moving; they want to see you," the man growled again.

Otis wasn't sure who they were, but from the disdain in the witch's voice, he could guess. So, Otis took the clothes and laid them on the bed. The witches did not move to leave.

"Are you going to watch?" he asked.

"Yes, and don't for a second think we are enjoying this," the woman said, staring him down.

"Of course not. Watching a fallen necromancer get dressed wouldn't fulfil any fantasies," Otis laughed.

The look on the witches' faces said everything.

Otis took his prison trousers off under the woman's watchful gaze. She didn't look away, but she wasn't exactly staring either, which was somehow worse. It was like his flesh and bones were just a thing. He quickly pulled off the rest of the clothes and hobbled to the desk, where they'd lowered the washing bowl and pitcher. He kept his eyes on the ground, only glancing at his notebooks, wondering if he was ever coming back or if this was it.

Otis sighed and poured the water into the bowl. He dipped his head in, holding his breath a little longer just to pretend he was elsewhere; that he could change himself into a fish and swim away. Every bone in his body ached; he had not morphed himself into anything else for an eternity, or so it felt. He tested whether he could slightly alter his appearance to make his grin slightly wider, but the hexes carved into the walls of his cell prevented him. He lifted his head from the bowl and gasped for air.

"Stop playing around," the witch commanded.

Otis glanced over his shoulder.

The woman narrowed her eyes.

He returned his attention to the washer, taking the soap and rubbing it against his skin, using the cloths to finish his bath. Otis returned to the clothes and hurried to get dressed. He once again glanced at the desk where his notes were. There was no way he could get away with smuggling them out. He wondered if he should stall, but most probably, he would get his head bitten off and sewn back together. The woman wasn't going to disappoint her supervisors. She was just that sort of witch. Brainwashed into obedience. She should have taken his offer of a fallen necromancer; maybe then something would have shaken her free enough to possess a thought of her own.

When he was done, the witch stepped next to him and barked, "Get up and spread your legs!"

"Not going to happen until you tell me where I'm going," Otis said.

"You get to see the Council. Lucky you." The woman grinned. "But I'm happy to leave you here if you don't spread your legs and hands so I can make an inspection."

Otis did as told. The woman patted his hands and chest and squatted down to pat his legs. Otis was too preoccupied to smirk, knowing his fate would be decided now and not in the courts. His only hope was trying to escape from the witches.

But that really wasn't in the cards. There was a loud click. The woman had cuffed his legs. Without having to check, Otis knew they were carved with hexes to make him compliant. He could feel the slight electric current against his skin from hexes lying dormant under the surface. They needed to be used. They wanted to wreak havoc; the malicious wish was ready to rip you apart. They needed to be used and not just be stuck in line for a Ferris wheel, never getting on, but never getting off either.

"Thank you," Otis said, shaking his legs. "They go well with the new suit."

He heard the man snicker.

As a response, the witch zapped Otis with hexes, making him let out a squeal. Otis tried to keep his mouth shut for the rest of the inspection as the woman scanned his body with her powers. It was for show and for the little acceptable torture for which no one would condemn her. She was displeased when she deemed him harmless.

Hexers were like echo-locating bats, letting their little nasty thoughts bounce back from surfaces as they navigated the strange world of Necropolis. *Bloodsuckers*, Otis thought. But that was a rude thing to say about vampires, who were quite lovely fellows when you got to know them. The whole blood-drinking thing was like drinking tea, just through your neck. Otis had donated once, and he had gotten a cookie and orange juice out of it. The rest of the day, he had felt lightly sleepy, but that was about it. No need for all the moral outrage.

"Look after him," the woman snapped at the other witch. The short, stocky man took hold of Otis's arm, standing there with his legs apart, trying to appear tough. Otis was a lot taller than the man, and if the shackles didn't cut off his talents, Otis was sure he could take him down both physically and mentally.

The other witch took all Otis's notebooks and letters with her. Then she gestured to the door. Otis shambled after her as requested, sandwiched between her and the man. They took him through the darkened halls of the Council. Otis realized that he had been summoned in the dead of night. Something was amiss. More so as there seemed to be extra guards everywhere.

"What's going on?" Otis asked.

"You are being escorted to see the Council."

Otis tried to get an answer a few more times, but all he got was a grunt. So he kept his mouth shut and followed the witch. Every time he made an erratic movement, he got zapped with a hex. It made the woman smile and pissed him off. Otis made it to the upper floors without too many burn marks on his skin. But there were a few, which had started to itch. He was about to test the witches again, tired of walking, but he was interrupted by a small undead man in a bowtie and pinstripe suit, reminding him that he should have demanded his lawyer to be present.

"Mr. Thurston," the undead greeted in a very tight, posh voice.

"That's my name. Can't seem to shake it off no matter how hard I try. So, what can I do for you? Do you like my new accessories?" Otis nodded at the shackles and then at his escorts.

"They seem to suit you." The undead stared at him without moving a muscle.

Otis let go and looked away.

"I will accompany you to meet the Council. You may call me Sir Wallace Crowen," the undead said.

"All that? Oh well, it's going to be a mouthful. And yes, do indeed join the fun. I have always said the more, the merrier. But how about taking these shackles off and we go to a pub instead?"

The undead laughed. It started quiet like a whistle but then turned into a full-blown roar. "I like you, Mr. Thurston, and I do hope they find you a better sentence than death."

Otis tightened the muscles around his jaw to mask any emotion. What a clever undead indeed.

"Shall we head in, or do you want to add more?" the undead asked, taking the notebooks and letters offered to him by the witch.

Otis watched as the undead dropped his whole life into a black leather briefcase and snapped it shut. The noise echoed in his mind.

"Before we go in, Mr. Crowen, I have to demand my lawyer, Mr. Pod, be present," Otis said.

"Wouldn't we all like to demand a lot of things? We can wait for him to be fetched if you absolutely insist. But I fear that the Council gets easily restless and hungry and thirsty, and the time seems to tick away, and you know what they say about judges, lunches, and sentencing on a hungry stomach. So, the decision is all yours, Mr. Thurston. I'm sure you are adept at speaking for yourself. You seem to possess a golden tongue."

Otis was about to protest, but the undead cut him short. "And we can always help you make the decision." The man nodded at the witch.

The woman punched Otis in his ribcage, making him wail.

"What do you think?" the undead asked.

"By the feel of things, that's my ribcage, the lower half, to be precise," Otis breathed out.

There was another jab.

"Yes, that's the one. Unfortunately, I do not possess the anatomical knowledge to name the specific location, but do try another one, as we have already established these ones exist." Otis grimaced, trying not to sound too winded.

"They would be your false ribs, the eighth, ninth, and tenth. Underneath them are your floating ribs. Very annoying when dislocated. Healing takes time, and if you move or breathe, it will hurt you," the woman said. Otis couldn't mistake the pleasure in her voice. She at least had found the right kind of employment to let her talents really shine. Still, all was fair in Necropolis. The Necromantic Council and the witches had every right to beat him senseless; there was no actual law against it. And she clearly thought working for the Council was a good way to earn a living.

"Ladies and gentlemen, we have a clear winner this lovely night. She's the champion of champions. The one and only jokester!" A fist pressed harder against his ribs, and Otis swallowed the rest of his words. Something was amiss big time if they were going this far. Either the mayor had pulled some strings to obtain him for the machine, or the pitiful man, Mr. Spooner, had worked his magic.

"I didn't like Mr. Pod anyways, and I do possess a golden tongue," Otis said under his breath.

The woman let go of him. Otis straightened up and was greeted with pain on his right side. He bit his lip and didn't moan.

"I'm glad we agree, Mr. Thurston. And I do hope a solution can be found so that you don't have to hang. It's all up to you," the undead said and, without further ado, went to the double doors and pulled them open. The witch nudged Otis to move. He obeyed. He stepped into the boardroom and was swallowed by the darkness.

There's a huge difference between following a function and knowing why you follow it. It's like that morning ritual, which calms all the senses before the day can start pulling you under with its uncertainty. But if you forget the reason why you put your socks on before your trousers or drink a glass of water before the tea, it becomes just another task to obsess over, and the freedom of choice is gone.[1] Percy used to have a strict morning regime. First, he stretched, then he did his combat training, and only then, when he was all washed and ready, would he drink his coffee and eat his oatmeal. But here and now, in the ghoul city, he slowly got his feet out of bed under the watchful eye of Mr. Spooner. The investigator twitched every time Percy groaned, every time his movement looked labored, but to Percy's gratitude, the man didn't rush to his aid. Percy tested his feet against the floor. The smoothed stone felt warm against the soles of his feet, making Percy wonder if the warmth came from the bedrock or if there was some heating system in place. Whatever the reason was, it was done for the humans. Ghouls' dead bodies had no use for the warmth.

Percy grabbed for the side of the bed, squeezing his hands hard against the stone structure. He took a deep breath in and stood up as he pushed all

---

1. Okay, the whole freedom thing might be a scam thought up by free radicals. Or it might be just the opposite, and the philosophers and the physicists are getting it all wrong, and there's no need to press their buttons when the light flickers on.

the air out of his lungs. For a moment, everything went black. He swayed on the spot, unsure if he would fall back down or not. The smallish hands of Mr. Spooner seized him by his waist, steadying him.

"Mr. Allread?" the man asked.

"Call me Percy."

"Percy, will you be all right?"

"In a second, Elmer," Percy said, tasting the man's name in his mouth. It felt so odd to call him so. It had to be done if they were stuck here together for the unknowable future.

"You may let go of me now."

The small goblin man stepped aside.

"I will head to the washing bowl," Percy declared, taking a few steps to test his balance. His eyes stayed focused on the dresser on the other side of the room, where the pitcher and the washing bowl were. He took the remaining steps, leaning heavily against the wooden construction. Elmer followed him with his gaze but left him alone. Percy took the pitcher and poured the cold, fresh water into the blue-and-white bowl. He took the small soap from next to the washing bowl and immersed it in the water between his hands. Then he put the soap back on its tray and washed his face with his soaped hands. Percy lowered his head down to splash the soap off with the fresh water, letting the surreal moment seep in.

Time seemed to slow down, and there was nothing but the water and his skin. Percy couldn't remember a moment when he wasn't rushing to work, perfecting his curses, or being tormented by the accounts he'd left unfinished. He was pretty sure he should feel highly worried about the Council and how things had gone, but after Sirixh had left the room, a sense of calm and acceptance had washed over him. His destiny was out of his hands. But it wasn't in the Council's hands either.

Everything now depended on the ghouls. Ghouls who had clearly taken other humans here as refugees. Why else would there be heated floors and washing bowls? Now, as he thought about it, the ghouls were the perfect antidote for Necropolis and necromancers and all the tricks of the city above. Corpse eaters. Ghost eaters. He and Elmer being here was like a divine intervention. Kraken's wish.

Percy searched for a cloth to dry his face on against the dresser. Soon a towel materialized, handed to him by Elmer.

"Thank you," Percy said as he straightened himself to his full height.

He walked more steadily back to the bed, where clean clothes had been set out, most likely by the ghouls. Percy unbuttoned his shirt, seeing the bandages wrapped around his torso. They smelled bitter, sharp, and refreshing. Whatever the witch had put on them emanated warmth, and if Percy was at his best, he would notice that they seemed to calm him down. But he wasn't.

Percy glanced at Elmer, who looked at his feet, away from the undressing Percy. Percy reached for the clothes at the end of his bed. The fabric felt soft and strong between his fingers. He slid his fingers over the stitching, which was fine and precise, like magic. Percy had never seen anything like it before. They were ghoul-made. They were the best-fitted clothes he had ever worn. Simple black garments, tailored to perfection and made for him. Nothing had been made with him in mind before. He had always done the serving. Even as a child, he'd done everything in his power to please his mother. When she died, he'd served his grandmother, who'd devoted her life to the sea and Kraken. Then, he had given his life to the Council. Now...

"You know, Elmer, it's a miracle we are here and alive. That has to count for something." Percy was unsure what it all meant, but there was an odd feeling inside him stemming from not having a script to follow or a task to complete.

The goblin man nodded but said nothing. He let Percy dress fully. Percy staggered up and flexed his whole body to feel the tightness of the bandages and his bruised body. It would heal. He could already sense some of his strength coming back.

Elmer followed him out of the door.

Outside the bedroom, there was a small parlor with a desk set out for them. On it lay an abundant breakfast with fruit, vegetables, freshly squeezed juice, meats of all sorts, bread, eggs, and porridge. The food could have fed a whole battalion. Percy didn't complain, and neither did Elmer, who was the first to dig in. Percy took his coffee, fruit, and vegetables and stayed away from the meats. He had never been a keen carnivore, and neither had his grandmother.

All that was missing was a porch and a view of the sea. But the sip of coffee was enough to make him feel more like himself.

They ate in silence. Occasionally, Elmer looked like he was about to say something, but then he changed his mind. Percy didn't encourage the man to speak. He needed this moment of peace. His nose itched, meaning there was a storm to come. But for now they got to enjoy the calm before the pressure got too much. Percy closed his eyes and drifted out to the sea he always carried within him. His grandmother sat on a little boat there, fishing and smoking her pipe. She had her yellow rain cap on, and she turned her gaze to him and winked, startling Percy, who spilled his coffee. Elmer frowned as Percy wiped his clothes and table with a cloth.

The door opened in the middle of the process, bringing in Sirixh along with a small ghoul in a tailored suit. Percy stopped drying himself, letting his full attention fall on the ghouls. He knew the man by his reputation. Cruxh had been the talk of the town a few years ago when the new mayor had appointed the ghouls as fully fledged members of the police force. Cruxh was the first one to join. His name mattered. He had a reputation for being honest, hardworking, and always getting the guy. Crime rates had plummeted when he and the other ghouls had pledged to serve Necropolis, so much so that the internal corruption had emigrated out of the city.

Percy stood up and bowed his head. Elmer followed his example. The only thing they got in return was discomfort.

"Do sit down," Cruxh said.

They complied.

"I was called to meet you here. I'm Cruxh, a police detective for the City of Necropolis Police Force. My ID number is eight-nine-two-seven. Now, my sister, Sirixh, has related last night's events and your plea for asylum. As a police officer of Necropolis, I can't comment on that. That's between you and the ghouls. I have been told a meeting has been set for you after I leave. I'm here in an official capacity, asked by the ghouls and the Council. The ghouls have notified the authorities of your attack in the caves and contacted the Council about the matter. The Council has requested you to be arrested, as you have violated the laws of the city by escaping imprisonment and breaking and entering into private property. Also, they state that you have stolen important documents and assaulted their workers. They also divulged that further charges might come forth with further internal investigation. The Council requests you to be handed to them and to be tried. Now, I have heard their side of events. I would love to hear how you see things from your perspective." Cruxh took a seat at the table and drew a coffee cup in front of him.

Percy had never seen a ghoul eat human food, and he watched in fascinated horror as the constable drank the coffee and popped in a piece of fruit or two. If it was meant to reassure him, it wasn't working. Lines were being crossed, manners broken, and reality thrown out, making Percy feel highly unlike himself.

Cruxh took another sip of coffee and opened his notebook. There was something about the way the ghoul moved that made Percy think he'd had a Kraken shit night; that he hadn't slept a wink. Not that Percy thought he could read a ghoul or that they needed sleep at all. But there had to be some sort of rest period to allow the body and mind to recuperate from having to run around and interact with other sentient beings.

"So, Mr. Allread and Mr. Spooner, what do you say to the charges the Council has laid against you?" Cruxh put the cup down.

Percy felt panic rise. He hadn't prepared. He'd let the moment catch him, and now he wasn't going to make it. His eyes met the ghoul's, and the officer seemed to agree with him. The ghoul pushed his pen so hard against the notebook that the tip of it broke.

"Excuse me." The ghoul got up. "I have to fetch a new one from my nervous colleagues outside." The ghoul gave a smile and took his exit. As soon as the door closed, Percy faced Elmer. The man was sweating. His skin was moist and clammy, and his eyes were wide as plates.

"If there's stress, there's calm." Percy repeated what his grandmother used to say to him when he was feeling as anxious as Elmer. Instantly, the goblin man's breathing got longer and slower. Percy observed as the hex he had tied into the words worked its way inside Elmer. He made sure that it didn't turn nasty, as hexes had a habit of doing. Percy felt guilty for resorting to a curse, but it had helped. And Elmer needed to be calmer about what he was about to propose. They'd done just what the Council had said they had done. Denying the reality wouldn't get them far. They would have to confess and rely on the mercy of the Council or the pity of the ghouls. Either way, he wasn't going to lie.

"Mr. Spooner," he began.

"I agree," the man wheezed.

"But I haven't—"

"You want us to confess and agree and, most of all, tell the truth. Am I correct?"

Percy nodded.

"I agree."

They waited for the ghoul to return in silence, each seeking that calm that stress opposed. The instability stayed dormant, undecided on which way to slip. One more mishap and calmness would succumb. Such was the way of the last straw. It could take down even an ox.

Percy pressed his right leg hard against the floor to remind him where he was and what he was supposed to say when Cruxh took his notebook out again and faced them once more.

"We accept the charges. I broke in to release Mr. Spooner after he stole documents from the Council and was jailed for it. I also assaulted the guard stationed outside his door by unleashing imps on him. The imps also attacked the witches and necromancers alerted by the broken curses at Mr. Spooner's cell door. I would have been killed and Mr. Spooner detained if the ghouls hadn't intervened and Mr. Spooner hadn't asked for asylum. All that happened, we don't deny it. But we ask for sanctuary because our opinions will kill us if we are handed back to the Council. We are willing to disclose the information Mr. Spooner stole to the relevant authorities on the surface and face the consequences, but not in the hands of the Council," Percy finished.

The ghoul smiled and closed the notebook. "You need not disclose anything here. When things move on, I might need to hear it, but for now, I have all I need. I will pass the message to the Council, write a report, and contact the Town Hall. However, you might have to disclose the information to the ghouls for them to decide. Are you prepared to do so?"

"We are willing."

"Thank you, gentlemen. This is all we can do for now. I won't be arresting you today, but if the ghouls don't accept your plea for asylum, I have to arrest you as soon as you surface on Necropolis's soil. Are we in agreement?" Cruxh asked.

Percy nodded.

"I will be contacting you again." Cruxh stood up.

"Thank you, Mr. Cruxh," Elmer said, pronouncing the name in perfect Ghoul.

"Only doing my duty, sir."

The ghoul left, and Elmer and Percy were left alone once again. Sirixh hobbled after her brother, stating she would be back soon.

"So it went," Percy let out. More to himself than to Elmer.

"Yes," Elmer murmured. The man fell deep into his thoughts, and if they were anything like Percy's, they were gloomy. He wasn't sure if he wanted to stay the rest of his life here in the ghoul city.

They ate in silence, and Percy drank the bitter coffee until he couldn't drink any more. It took a long time for Sirixh to come back, but when she did, her cheerful manner was gone, and she was like most ghouls, her expression inscrutable.

"My mother and the ghouls will see you now," Sirixh said.

"They are sending us away, aren't they?" Elmer asked.

Sirixh stared at the investigator without saying anything for a while, which made everything a lot worse. Finally, she scratched her head and then shook it.

"I'm afraid not all want you to stay, but you have your chance to plead your case. I hope you are prepared."

CHAPTER NINETEEN

THIS IS GOING TO BE ONE OF THOSE LONG DAYS

All of it was in the documents. It was how rational systems worked. Those established with bureaucracy to lead and evade corruption; or so it was meant to be, but it never took into account human creativity. It was mind-boggling what could be conjured up, altered, and shifted with the right kind of documentation. Worlds could be shifted, forests uprooted, and humans exterminated, and the writer wouldn't have to do anything more than pen their name on the dotted line. There would be no blame, no emotion, no attachment, no connection, just a desire to alter the state of being according to one's wishes. That's all. No objective fact, no for the general good, no calculations, just a desire rationalized through documents. Okay, that might be too harsh, as sometimes there was a spark of joy, hope, and common decency. Some bureaucrats actually aimed to improve the lives of those whom the matter concerned, but that was a fluke at best.

A low growl made Raul look up, startling him. Raul had been immersed in the Council's documents. So much so that he hadn't noticed the time passing. His notebook was filled with little comments so he wouldn't forget anything. He wanted to steal the papers, but he knew that would raise an alarm. Undoubtedly the Council had the same system as the newspaper had. Any documents removed from the perimeter would alert the hexer who'd cursed them, who would unleash all their talents against the intruder. There was always a hexer hanging around the office.

Raul put the files back where he'd found them. He shuddered as he put the last box in its place. He paused and reached back for the box. He knew he was going to make a mistake, but he did it anyway. He stuffed as many folders as he could underneath his vest and hurried out of the door. They had the proof he needed in black and white to bring the Council to its knees. Raul would be the most hunted man in Necropolis, even more so than Mr. Thurston. His mouth was dry and his hands clammy. He'd gotten more than he could have dreamed—possibly more than he could handle.

The Archives were peaceful. There was no sign of the creature or the Archivist. He glanced up at the lights. They were flickering again, showing him a path to take. They weren't as obvious as they had been when he'd entered. They were taking him out of another door. Raul Kraken shit hoped the creature knew what it was doing. He clutched his chest, squeezing the notebook and the folders pulsing inside his vest. The secrets didn't want to be stolen. Raul muttered the little curses he'd been taught to calm the words. The vibration became less obvious. It was still there.

Raul sped up, glancing behind him to the Archivist's desk. He was sure he'd heard a chair being pushed back and someone sniffing the air. There came a loud screech as the Archivist screamed, "Thief." The word took over the whole Archive, echoing from shelf to shelf and to the walls and back to him.

"At B seventy-eight, aisle nineteen!" came another screech.

Raul saw the same letters glowing in the upper left corner of the bookshelf he was passing.

"Corpse worm," Raul muttered and started running. Behind him, a wind was starting to form, flapping against his back. The air was full of electric charge and something else, making the pressure more tangible. It was the feeling you get before the first summer storm. It makes all the hairs on your arms stick out and your skin crawl like it wants to escape what is to come. Raul felt it, and it made his stomach lurch. He ran, holding the files so they didn't slip out of his jacket. His steps thundered against the floor. He almost got away, but then the Archivist screeched behind him. The sound made his blood run cold, and his feet stuck in place. He knew he wasn't going to make it. The Archivist would kill him. Raul kept holding on to the files as the wind pushed against his back. He couldn't move.

There came a growl, and the creature that had evaded his view thus far appeared in front of him. Its tattered mane was ruffled by the wind. Its skin was green, yellow, and reddish brown. It was the size of a jackal with bright yellow eyes and claws that could take down an even bigger beast. Raul had never seen anything like it in Necropolis. It looked like it belonged in the jungles, where it would be worshiped with human sacrifices, bones, blood, and hot cocoa.[1] Raul glanced over his shoulder to see the Archivist floating in the air, his hands spread wide as words squirmed from his fingers towards Raul. The man's eyes were milk white, and his face was twisted into a demonic mask. Raul knew what words could do and what such a face wanted.

There came another growl, a longer one with the suggestion of words attached to it, and Raul found his feet unstuck.

"Old Man Death, don't take my soul," Raul shouted and ran towards the creature.

The thing looked at him and then past him at the Archivist and bared its teeth. It rushed past Raul, and there came a noise Raul wanted to forget immediately. It sounded like bones being crushed, and there came a loud whimper. Raul continued running to the open door leading into a narrow

---

1. Raul wasn't sure where that came from or what hot cocoa was, but it had to be something nasty if it helped to tame the beast.

corridor. He made it to the door, refusing to look back. The screams and the agony weren't over, and it sounded like someone was losing all their dreams along with their sanity, flesh, and bones. The sound anyone would make when hurt, but usually stifled in adulthood. Raul needed to see, but he knew that nothing good came of looking over one's shoulder. Just the spooky past following close behind, ready to take down an overly worried glancer.

Raul left the door open behind him and kept running up the metallic stairs, spiraling all the way to the upper floors. Raul yanked open the first door he found, tumbling into the lobby. It was filled with people, and not just any people. Somehow the Save the Otis Group had pushed through the doors, and they'd taken over the space with all the coffins pinned to the walls. Raul could see some of his reporter colleagues amongst the group. Arlo was there too. The man was his personal photographer.

Raul motioned to Arlo, and he waved back, begging Raul to come to him. Raul pushed his way through the crowd, who shoved him aside, everyone trying to keep their space and all worried about having entered the sacrum of the beast.

"What's going on?" Raul let out a long breath, taking hold of the photographer's hand and dragging himself closer to the man.

"The better question is what are you doing here?" Arlo let out and shook his head, holding Raul close, not letting the reporter be swept away by the crowd. He kept his camera obscura even closer. "Actually, don't answer," the man said, glancing at the witches, who were trying to keep the group from entering any farther. "Just leave and run. Sandy said you murdered some poor sod. The police are looking for you. They took all your possessions from the office. Max is livid... You need to leave and hide."

Raul had forgotten the whole murder part already. It had happened to a person who wasn't there any longer, who wasn't carrying the Council's most valued documents with him.

"Don't worry about that. It was—" Raul tried but couldn't get any further.

"I don't believe them for a second. But still, you'd better go. Sandy is out for blood. I'll try to fish out what really happened. But go."

"Thanks, mate," Raul said. "And here?"

"Someone let them in and tipped us. There's also a shitstorm at the Town Hall. But that's not important. Nor is why you are here." The photographer made his box flash just as a witch was coming at them, blinding the witch and everyone around him. "Leave," the photographer commanded.

Raul did, staggering through the door that was packed full of reporters trying to get in and the more cautious protesters holding their signs. They struggled against Raul, forming a wave. He followed the little holes in their defense, greeting the damp, clammy Necropolis air, which hit his skin and the back of his throat. The somewhat rotten smell mixed with coal and formaldehyde fumes smelled divine—like liberation. It was better than the forgotten odor of dry books and potatoes in the Archive. Raul was ready to dance in the toxic fumes or even kiss the cobblestones, but that felt like a step too far. Instead, Raul did the more sensible thing and ran. Not sure where. He ran where the streets looked almost empty, with no officers in sight. The soles of his feet made a cacophony as they hit the stones, the noise bouncing around him like a heartbeat.

The sound roared inside Raul's head as a reminder that he was alive, but only barely so. He couldn't help but glance over his shoulder to see how much attention he was drawing. The crowd of people gravitating towards the Council's headquarters averted their gazes. Of course, people did notice. That wasn't the issue. It was more that they just didn't care. Most of them thought, "poor sod, better him than me," and in a few seconds they forgot all about him. They would barely remember him later when asked to describe the scene to the police. Just fantasies of a man in an overcoat with burning red eyes and a malicious grin on his face.

But that wasn't Raul's concern. He had long ago forgone worrying about his self-image and the accuracy of it. Such a thing was for fools. Anguishing over what others thought about you was an endless swamp. You would only end up drowning in it. It was a fact of life that there was always someone who thought ill of you, someone who wanted to put you down to make themselves feel better no matter how good you were, and especially then. Shame and envy were the friends you never asked for and were hard to get rid of.

Raul kept running. He didn't get too far. A massive hand that could be used to demolish houses grabbed him by his collar and yanked him into the alley he was just passing. Raul came face to face with the man. The man had a wide face, thick eyebrows, and a yaw that could crack nuts without even flinching. Next to him was a much shorter man, but he made up for it with his wide shoulders and muscles that would make even a rhino jealous. The man looked solemnly at Raul.

"Master says you better come with us," the shorter man said. "For your own safety, master says," the man added when Raul didn't look convinced.

"Who the Kraken shit do you think you are, and what the corpse worm are you talking about?" Raul snapped.

"Master said to say thank you for helping him around. He also said to protect you," the shorter man said and nodded down the street. There was a huge wolf there, which was in the process of morphing into an even bigger one with all the weres attached to it.

The short man cracked his knuckles while the taller man maintained his grip on Raul's collar. He didn't look in any hurry to release him or in any way startled by the wolf blocking their exit.

"So are you coming with us or...?" the shorter man asked and nodded towards the werewolf. When Raul didn't answer straight away, the shorter man added, "The ghouls will be here soon too." The man said it with a just-so-you-know tone, irking Raul. But there was no time to get into the semantics of pressuring someone to go somewhere against their will. The wolf meant business. It had shifted into its full werewolf form and stood on its hind legs, flexing its claws. Its teeth glowed in the dark, if that was even possible. It was the lack of a clear light source forcing one to question the laws of physics, but here in Necropolis dramatics surpassed any need for matter to function as matter was supposed to. Theatrics came first.

And the wolf wasn't going to roll on the floor and beg for stomach scratches. Raul nodded. The shorter man walked slowly past Raul as the bigger fellow held on to Raul's collar. The werewolf launched itself at the man. The short man didn't budge. He stood his ground, and Raul closed his eyes instinctively, not wanting to see the man's innards sprayed on the street. He opened them again to the sound of a pitiful howl. The werewolf lay on the ground instead, whimpering loudly as the short man stood over the wolf, massaging his fist.

"They don't need to know you found him," the short man offered.

The wolf narrowed its eyes.

The short man shook his head.

The werewolf tried to get up but halted the effort as the short man squeezed his fists tight. The wolf let out a low whimper.

"Go to your pack," the short man let out. "They might let you live."

The wolf let out a low growl.

"I mean it. Or we can do this the other way, and they will know exactly how you found him and failed, and no pack will save you."

The wolf bared its teeth but nodded nevertheless.

The shorter man stepped away, giving the wolf room to get back up. The wolf glanced at him, unsure if it should try again, but the shorter man just stared at it, unfazed. The werewolf ran away, changing into just a normal wolf.

The short man turned around and said, "Now, Mister Porter. You can call me Rugus Angerstein, and the fellow next to you is Monty, Monty Emerson. We better get you out of here before the ghouls come. They might not be as easy to reason with as our old friend Wolf there."

Raul nodded, still smelling the somewhat bitter odor of the wolf. He swallowed, trying to get some control back. He was sure his heart was ready to give in. Then again, his mind was saying that he was already in deep shit and he'd survived it. Going with a man that could take a werewolf down in one hit wasn't going to change his chances of survival. Actually, his brain was insisting that it might increase the chances of him keeping his head attached to his body. Though it was highly clear that he was doomed whatever he chose. And it wasn't like he had a plan before the two men had interrupted his flight. Also, he was kind of hoping the creature who'd gotten him in and out of the Council's headquarters would come and rescue him if things got too sticky, given that the beast had survived the Archivist and it wasn't part of whatever this was.

Then again, Raul knew not to put too much trust in hope. It was never there when you were in dire need of it, and when you really shouldn't have hope, it was there shouting that everything was going to be fine and you should jump. But all you managed to do was tumble down head first through all the rocks and branches, hitting every one of them. Hope was a bastard of a god to rely on. Yet he had no other god left on his side. So Raul went with the two men, letting them lead him out of the alley into a coach parked not too far from the Council's headquarters. His notes and the folders were still pulsing inside his jacket. Truth wanting to get out.

So did the knowledge that was stolen under Raul and the Archivist's noses, but Raul didn't know about any of that. He didn't have a clue that he might be a pivotal part of setting something dark and powerful loose in Necropolis.

That desire for liberation, for an escape from the mundane and the now, pestering the subconsciousness like a plague, was the dream of those who were trapped in the absurdity of existence. In other words, every inhabitant of the city. Henrietta woke up as the door creaked open. She'd just fallen asleep, almost achieving the perfect bliss of just existing. You know, the state where everything is possible and all the burdens of reality are absent. But the world doesn't work that way. It doesn't let you stay in perfect bliss or anything close to it. It's all the movement and entropy that trickles in. So as the rules dictated, Henrietta was yanked from her dream of diving under the waves and swimming amongst the fish in the vanishing rays of the sun. For a moment there, she'd been completely weightless and calm, and now—now, there were thoughts. Thoughts that were always there, pestering one's mind about the state of being and the future of oneself. There was something fishy going on there. A parasite, maybe.

Henrietta's mind seemed to ask why. And not in a good way.

There was no answer. Just the silent torment of existing.

Petty Officer Lawrence, who'd crept in, let Henrietta wash herself and change into the clothes Eurof had brought with him last night. The clothes she wore when she needed comfort but still needed to appear presentable. Henrietta wanted to freeze herself in this moment. Facing the fact that she had been arrested for treason was beyond absurd and would probably get her killed if the Council wished it so. She gave the officer permission to escort her out of her cell.

Ida and Annabella were already waiting for her in the hallway, two ghouls close by. Her comrades had dark circles under their eyes that weren't there before. At least, Ida did. The undead woman's eyes just looked unusually dulled even for an undead.

"Morning," Henrietta said.

All she got was a groan from Ida.

Annabella just tilted her head ever so slightly.

The ghouls led them from the cells into the police station's common room. They were welcomed with flashes, as the press had found a way to sneak in. Henrietta kept blinking as the ghouls drove away the reporters and their photographers. Afterwards, Henrietta and the others were processed and booked to be transferred to the prison where they would stay during the investigation and trial.

Henrietta had a bad feeling she would never be free again. She watched and listened to the procedure between Annabella and Mr. Cruxh. Papers changing hands. Her name reduced to a number. Henrietta wondered how the innocent could find their way out from the enormity of the organization with black-and-white rules. All she or anyone else could do was trust the process. She glanced at the ghouls around her. There might be a process to be trusted. But the Council could drag this on for an eternity and force them to live in limbo, where life happened to others, floating past her, not seeing her.

"Ladies," Cruxh began.

Ida groaned loudly, making it known she didn't appreciate the ghoul's choice of words. The banker had been in a foul mood as soon as she'd emerged from her private cell. She'd sighed and moaned and groaned as Annabella and Cruxh had gone over the papers.

Cruxh continued despite Ida's protest, somehow managing to look apologetic for a ghoul.

"I have arranged that you will be taken to Necropolis' Reformatory for the Criminally Insane and Other Offenders." Cruxh smiled, or actually didn't smile, but there was some sort of softness in his expression, letting them know he'd acted out of kindness to send them to the only decent prison in Necropolis.

"Thank you, Mr. Cruxh," Henrietta said before Ida could start a war between her and the pacifist ghoul. They needed all the help they could get. And Henrietta was sure Cruxh would be their savior somehow. That without him there was no getting back to the gardens before Ruby and Imogene turned the Coven into the Council's vassal. The thought of not knowing what was happening at the Coven made Henrietta's stomach turn. The older witches would support Lottie Letcoffin, but others would see Imogene as more fitting to take the lead, as she was Wesley Epith's illegitimate daughter.

"I have to cuff you now." Cruxh took the cuffs from his belt, looking at her under his eyebrows or something similar. The other officers with him followed his example.

Henrietta got up and offered her hands to the ghoul, listening to the clicks as the metal was secured around her wrists. There came a flash from somewhere. The officer that had escorted Henrietta out of her cell warped next to a smallish man, an undead from the look of it, and took him by his collar. The undead handed over his homemade camera obscura, which was a lot smaller than a lady's handbag. The bugbear, as Petty Officer Lawrence seemed to be, let go of the man. The man shuffled off, leaving behind his camera and picture, which would have made him a rich man.

Ida and Annabella followed Henrietta's example after the incident and let themselves be cuffed. No one else tried to immortalize their humiliation, to Ida's annoyance; unlike Henrietta, she understood the power of notoriety.

They were escorted through the police station. There was an awkward silence as the whole police department came to watch. A tall, lanky girl Henrietta knew to be the chief leaned against the staircase to the upper floors. She nodded at Cruxh as they passed. Cruxh reciprocated.

Outside, a prison transport waited for them. Henrietta half expected there to be more reporters, but there were just more undeads and their like in blue uniforms guarding the street. The prison transport was a hasty construction, reminding Henrietta of a garden shed on wheels. What made it more than just a shaky hovel was the words Metropolitan Police's Prison

Transport and the Kraken head painted on its sides. Henrietta had always been baffled by how words could change matter. It was obvious that fantasies powered societies. Henrietta ducked her head as she was guided in with the others. The doors closed behind them, and the carriage shook when the ghouls climbed onto it. Then the horses pulled off.

"This is absurd," Ida let out. "We should have been out by now."

"They are doing this by the book," Annabella answered. "But—"

"How can you be so calm about this?! You should know by now that by the book doesn't matter when it comes to the Council." Ida shook her head. She looked paler than she'd ever been.

Annabella slumped against the wall. "There's no point trying to argue. You are right. Mr. Cruxh told me they have had difficulty contacting anyone to advocate for us. But he'll try the Coven and others again."

"And you are telling us this now?" Ida shouted.

"He'll come through. I'm sure of it." Annabella nodded her head as if she had some inner conversation going on.

Ida was about to protest, but Henrietta silenced her with a head shake. Even though the banker's objections were merited, this wasn't the time or place for them, and none of them were in the state to have the discussion. Annabella looked defeated. She needed time to recuperate.

They rode the rest of the way in silence.

But the truth was that the Coven should have sent their lawyers regardless of anything going on with Imogene and her mother. It was in their bylaws. But Ruby knew her way around the system. It had to be her, keeping the lawyers away. Henrietta should have never let Imogene into her inner circle, as the other witches had warned her.

Yet Henrietta was sure the girl's adoration towards her hadn't been just for show. Imogene had more than willingly helped Henrietta to take care of Nestor and all her unique plants while helping to run the Coven and soaking up everything Henrietta taught her. There had been long nights with the girl delivering cakes, tea, and everything else Henrietta needed while she tried to figure out the Coven's finances, curriculum, and supply orders. That was above and beyond. But Imogene... Henrietta stopped her mind running too far with that thought. Letting any sort of paranoia in would result in a doomed ride to an early grave. She knew that. She'd seen plants dying from stressors in the environment.

The carriage came to a halt. Outside the prison transport, a thin man with a mustache and short haircut welcomed them to his prison. He stood, waiting for them by the prison gates. He seemed nervous as he stuttered, "Mother," and bowed as soon as Henrietta got out. Henrietta's first response was to reproach the man. She wasn't in the mood for the whole Mother business. But she didn't, understanding well that respect was a currency she couldn't afford to decline.

She knew who the man was. Henrietta had often seen James Hardrick's name and picture in the newspapers, always accompanied by slander. Other prison wardens didn't like Mr. Hardrick and his so-called modern conventions of punishment. The man blatantly ignored the profit mantra and ran his prison with minimal return. Prisons in Necropolis were privately owned, getting municipal funding for every head inside their walls. What tipped the other wardens over the edge were the rumors about prisoners learning a trade and getting to see a shrink. Despite the outrage, Mr. Hardrick refused to change his ways or even increase his prison population. A fool, as the so-called high society said. But Henrietta had a report somewhere on her desk that the man was thinking of expanding. That he had been sniffing around the lesser prisons and poorhouses.

"Due to your circumstances, we have arranged private cells and..." James Hardrick started.

Cruxh left them there in the hands of Mr. Hardrick and the other correctional officers. Again, there was a perfect opening to escape. Henrietta sensed all the trees on the prison's grounds. Their roots ran underneath them. One word and they could push through the stones and seize the guards. Henrietta continued to listen to the man giving a speech about the prison and how their stay would be handled from now on.

"...I have a presentation for you in my office." The warden finished his little speech. They were taken through the prison's wing for female offenders. All the way to his office, Mr. Hardrick explained how the wing was run, the day-to-day routines, and the rules, not leaving out any small detail. The rhythm of their feet and the gentle, almost apologetic speech made Henrietta's head swim, reminding her that she'd slept only a wink and had been yanked even from that.

Henrietta drew in a deep breath to keep her head clear. The smell of the prison and its tobacco-infused walls only made her head swim more. She focused her gaze on Annabella, who was scratching a balding spot where the remnants of her living hair had been. The woman had dislocated her arm to manage that with handcuffs, but that didn't seem to bother the undead. Before her, Ida made little jerking motions to keep the fear from sneaking in.

The warden and his guards were highly agitated. The funny thing was that they were the only nervous creatures in the prison. It became more evident as they reached the lower levels, where the other prisoners were nonchalantly eating their breakfast. Henrietta heard chatter and laughter. The pale petrol-colored wooden paneling everywhere and the smiling guards made this place feel almost homey. Even the prison cells they passed had soft mattresses to take a long, comfortable sleep. Henrietta glanced at Mr. Hardrick. It was obvious the man knew some serious juju.

"Here at the Necropolis Reformatory for the Criminally Insane and Other Offenders, we see sleep as the foundation of good health and an intact person. The lights will go out at eight. Along with sleep, I see exercise and healthy eating habits as the..." Mr. Hardrick said.

Henrietta looked at the unlocked doors they passed. The newspapers hadn't exaggerated at all when it came to Mr. Hardrick and his prison. They'd left the most outlandish features out because no one in Necropolis would believe what unfolded before her eyes. The food alone would make most Necropolitans do anything to become a ward of the prison.

Mr. Hardrick pushed a door open, which carried his name. "Do take a seat." Mr. Hardrick motioned at the benches in front of the back wall. Each seat held a rag, a washing bowl, and inside it, a small bar of soap and a comb. Instead of soap and a comb, Annabella got a small bottle of formaldehyde and a needle and thread.

Henrietta scooped hers up and laid them on her lap as she sat down and looked around the room. It was a bare office. There was a desk with a high stack of papers on it. The morning sun shone through the ceiling window, where spiders had made their home. Henrietta counted three who'd webbed the window. Underneath them and behind the desk stood colossal wooden filing cabinets. Over them was a black-and-white picture of Mr. Hardrick looking jovial, and beside him was a woman who was sneering at best.

Henrietta focused back on the warden, who spoke. "They are yours to keep during your stay. Soap and other hygiene items will be distributed at the end of every month, and you are to make do until then. But let me introduce Mr. Philpot, Silas." He gestured towards the grave man who had been following the convoy all the way through the prison. He wore a white coat, had a highly serious expression with bushy eyebrows, and a narrow mouth drawn tightly shut. "He will give you a more thorough lecture about our health and hygiene requirements. He's the prison doctor and will assist you with anything you need. I—"

"This is all Kraken shit," Ida interrupted. She threw her washing bowl on the ground. The nearest guard was ready to come at her, but Mr. Hardrick lifted his hand to stop the man.

"Miss Mortician, I assure you—"

"You assure nothing. I demand to see my lawyer and be freed immediately!"

"Do forgive me, Miss Mortician. I was under the impression that your lawyer had been informed of your arrival. We will let you know as soon as they arrive and secure you a meeting room for such an occasion. In the meantime, I do ask you to cooperate, so we can make this process as amicable as we can. Mr. Philpot has prepared—" Mr. Hardrick looked pleadingly at Ida, having to occasionally glance away, as Ida kept her eyes locked on him, and not in a friendly manner.

"All lies!" the woman declared. "I want to see our lawyer straight away. We will not succumb to this witch hunt just because of who we are and because you pocket money from the Council. We have our rights, and they should be respected. So, Mr. Philpot can be whatever he likes to be, and can, for all I care, jump out of that window..." Ida's rant made Mr. Hardrick glance at the window and the spiders and then pleadingly back at Ida.

Ida disregarded any such emotions and continued, "I will stand here until we see our lawyer." To make her point, Ida kicked the bowl on the floor, making it rattle.

The sound made Henrietta's ears ring. This was going to be a long day, Henrietta thought. She wasn't sure if she would survive it with the amount of sleep she'd had.

"Please," she began.

Chapter Twenty

A SHOW OF HANDS

T he unspoken rules and laws that governed human interaction were perplexing. Sometimes Petula wondered if they were there because of all the emotions thundering inside a person. But then she came face to face with someone incapable of feeling emotions, and all the decision making went haywire. Then there was the frightening thought that what if someone void of emotions sat on the throne? Petula sighed. More than anything, she wished she didn't have emotions. Even stifled and managed, they still seemed to make things uncomfortable, yet they were needed.

Petula sighed again and watched as the city's lawyers squirmed under her gaze. They shuffled their feet while Petula tried to keep a somewhat amicable expression on her face. She tried not to let her sarcasm get in the way of dealing with the matter, but all the words she tried in her head had that snarky tone her mother said would end up making her a spinster. Petula had always had a hard time seeing the downside of such a fate. Her mother had insisted her life would be as miserable as Aunt Essie's without a husband. And she'd told her that she didn't need another human being to babysit and that there was nothing wrong with Aunt Essie's life; that she was rather looking forward to it. Yet somehow here she was, babysitting the entire nation.

"You are telling me that you got a note from the Lawyers' Association informing you that representing Mrs. Culpepper and the others would get you disbarred?" Petula stated. She aimed to sound neutral, but even she would admit there was nothing neutral in her tone. Again, Petula couldn't help but think of those unspoken rules and laws, the good ones that made communities tick, keeping them a step away from madness and tyranny.

"Yes, but—"

"If I remember correctly, doesn't our law state that everyone has a right to representation? But you are telling me that treason is somehow an exception?" Petula crossed her legs and laid her hands on her lap. The two men looked sheepish as she changed her posture.

"Yes, but—"

"I see. And the Mr. Thurston matter?"

"We would recommend retracting your call for Mr. Thurston to be under the city's custody. We see it as a highly volatile situation and fear that the city doesn't have the necessary means to detain Mr. Thurston with his necromantic abilities and shapeshifting curse," the braver of the lawyers offered, ready to recant his words if necessary.

Petula drummed her fingers against her knee. "I'm afraid that won't be an option. Make me an ironclad order which will get Mr. Thurston sitting in front of me in this very room tomorrow morning. If you don't manage to do that, then I suggest, you start looking for employment overseas." Petula stood up, making the lawyers back away.

"Yes, ma'am." They fled from the room.

"See, that wasn't so hard," Mrs. Maybury said, lifting her head from the lounge chair she had been lying in. Petula had forgotten the undead was still in the room with her. The primal part of her, which recognized a predator, wanted a weapon of some sort to pierce the undead, but the civilized part[1] of her just snarled, "No, not hard at all."

---

1. The one that remembered that undeads were people too.

Petula had always left the heavy lifting to Dow, and now she wondered why. There was something highly satisfying about bossing people around and seeing the fear in their eyes. However, all that meant was involvement and engagement and abandoning her twisted pacifistic views of participating in other human beings' lives. Until now, she had been happy if all parties avoided each other. There would be fewer conflicts, less hassle, less heartburn, and fewer wars to go around. And Petula would insist on more freedom and equality. But humans were weird. They came with urges to connect, cooperate, and copulate and thus create conflicts. So leaving all this for Dow was better than the short high she got from commanding two lawyers, who by no means were going to do what she asked. Their fear for her was lesser than their fear of what the Council might do. No wonder tyrants liked to dish out punishment. Institutions had a way of making the world do their bidding. Not only through the disgruntled employees who decided the fates of god-fearing folk, but also through the sheer gravitas of their existence.

"You should head to bed. You are going to have a long day tomorrow," Mrs. Maybury ordered.

"I can't. Those two idiots won't do anything. It's up to me to get Otis here. Where's Dow, anyway?" Petula asked.

"How should I know? He's your pet." Mrs. Maybury crossed her arms.

Petula held her breath. She wondered if the undead would ever acquire any social manners.

She left her office to look for Dow, annoyed by the undead shuffling behind her everywhere she went. Maybe this was the woman's way of seeing that Petula didn't get hurt, which was a highly accurate guess on her part. She didn't have an actual clue what she should do next to force the Council to obey. She doubted that words were enough, but she would be surprised how far one could get with a good story, confidence, and coins and threats to silence anyone willing to disagree.

Dow wasn't in his office or anywhere in the Town Hall. Petula even asked Elvira if the secretary had seen Dow go out. The woman shook her head. She would have asked Mr. Colton, but even her guard was missing. Again, a paranoid person would think that Mr. Colton and Dow had sold her out. Petula wasn't willing to go down that road. She silenced her inner doomsayer, to Elvira's annoyance. The secretary would love nothing more than for the leader of the land of the dead to go insane.

"I'm sure they didn't mean to exclude you," Elvira offered.

Petula shot a glance at the secretary and squinted her eyes. The woman returned her gaze with a steely stare.

"Wouldn't even have thought of that," Petula said. "But I guess you are right. No excluding was done. Now, it seems I have to get back to work. Would you, Elvira, be so kind as to bring me the Rules and Laws of Necropolis? You know, the thick book that holds up the table in the employees' lounge."

"I wouldn't bother with it, but if you insist," Elvira responded, still keeping that steely stare of hers on Petula.

Petula kept her own stare in place. Something nasty might sneak in if she looked away. Petula was right. Elvira was willing to let in a little more calamity, having lost some faith in the smallish human leader's ability to seek it on her own. She could smell the doubt from the necromancer, and doubt was never a good thing.

Though some might disagree. Doubt was there for a reason: to ask the awkward question of whether the action was good or bad. But then again, that would lead to a metaphysical debate of the reality of action. Further down that road lay the question of ethics, and whether action can ever be defined with such archaic terms as good and bad. Or for that matter what the Kraken shit good and bad even meant.

But the three women didn't share a philosophical bone among them. All of them were highly practical, dealing with the present and what needed to be done. Even Petula would detest the whole mentality that came with the so-called philosophical thinkers. While she was fascinated with the science of necromancy and all, she wasn't willing to mess with reality and state that it was an illusion dreamed up by a demon. Elvira would disagree; she was pretty sure she'd dreamed up the world to entertain her. And Mrs. Maybury knew that the whole reality was in itself a demon. Why else would life be such a miserable experience only to be stolen in the end by Old Man Death? Life was not all it was cracked up to be. Death was another thing entirely. It allowed the inner shadow to roam free and say no to anything it wanted to.

"I insist," Petula said.

The banshee sucked her teeth and got up, reluctantly removing her gaze from Petula.

Petula's posture collapsed ever so slightly. She listened as the banshee glided across the wooden floor to the backrooms, hissing as she moved. All the time she stood there in silence, Petula could feel Mrs. Maybury's eyes on the back of her head. Other people were hell. There was no escaping that fact. But other women and their judging eyes were next-level torture even a demon dreaming up existence couldn't come up with.

When the banshee returned, Petula took the thick book and opened it on the secretary's desk, stealing the woman's chair. She heard a gasp behind her, but Petula ignored it. She let her gaze glide down the index, looking for keywords that would unravel everything. Petula had no illusion that she was better at finding loopholes than the lawyers, who were trained in the trickery of small print, but she had to try. She knew what she was good at. That was necromancy. And there were plenty of ghosts hanging around who hated the Council as much as she did. Okay, that was too harsh a statement. Petula didn't hate the Council. They had an important function. But they didn't need to be jerks about it.

Petula let out an incantation invoking the spirits always hanging around her. Even being mayor didn't shield her from the dead, who sought to be heard. Actually, it increased the ghostly mass around her manyfold. It was all about the misconception of stature and wisdom combined. However, Petula was pretty sure the spirits gravitated towards her looking for revenge rather than a soothing trip to the netherworld.

As she spoke the words, there was an odd sensation inside her. As if her innards shifted the wrong way and something clutched onto her tighter. She pushed the sensation away, concentrating on the group of lawyers, who had been instantly drawn to her invitation.

The pages in the book in front of her flipped as the ghostly hands tore into them. Petula watched as the immaterial ghosts took the shapes of their former bodies. Their hollow eyes in their sagging faces burrowed deeper into the legal text. They pointed their fingers, letting their darkened nails highlight fragments of sentences. Petula followed their fingers as the ghosts jumped from page to page.

She started to laugh. It was all hidden in the legal text—how the Council had stolen power from her and the mayors before her, from the witches, and the citizens. They hadn't. They just acted as if they had, and people let them. The power was still hers and the Necropolitans' to keep. She was the head of the Council. Any action they took should go by her.

"How?" Petula asked.

One of the ghosts roared and disappeared for a flickering second, only to come back with another tome. The ghost dropped it onto the desk. The history of Necropolis opened to the page showing the face of Oliver the Great.

She should have known that. Only a mad and greedy man would sell out his country for money, fame, and power. He'd let the Council do whatever they liked. Write more laws. Introduce more unofficial rules. And people obeyed.

"And Minta?" she asked.

The ghost wailed.

"She fought against it?"

There was another wail.

"She did. And Dow knows?"

Yes, again.

"I see."

There came another wail.

"What am I missing?"

The ghost slammed its finger at the picture of Oliver the Great. Petula frowned. She looked at the illustration on the page. Oliver the Great stood in front of his court. Petula squinted her eyes. She didn't get it. Their former leader was in the coronation room of the old, abandoned castle now housing the Necropolis Reformatory for the Criminally Insane and Other Offenders. That wasn't it. She searched the crowd and saw it. She shifted her gaze between the picture and the ghost.

The ghost wailed.

"That can't be?" Petula said, jumping up from the chair, almost knocking it over.

"What?" Mrs. Maybury asked. There was no way she or the banshee had seen the full interaction. The dead were for the necromancers to keep.

"I need to find Dow, and now!"

The simple things were easy. They shouldn't be ignored. The big, messy things would line up after you got all the little things right. Then again, the whole right and wrong parts were easy to misunderstand. You always had to ask whose right it was. Sometimes the so-called right thing was just a ruse to get you to do things for others at great personal sacrifice.

"We d-on't have tim-e for thiss. They are waiting for yourrrr," Sirixh insisted.

"There's always time." Here Percy was right. There was always time in a poetic sense. Thinking there was no time was a common mistake people made. Something to do with great expectations and doing the right thing. A very good way to get your mind screwed up and be a slave to circumstances. Truthfully, not doing a thing was sometimes the best course of action. Not here, though, but still, there was always time to wash the dishes.

"Mr. Allread," Elmer begged.

"No," Percy said. He knew he was being foolish, but he couldn't help himself. He insisted on washing the plates and getting the excess food to those who needed it.

Elmer kept repeating his apologies to the ghoul, hobbling after Percy as he took the necessary steps to wrap the food and put it in small crates to be delivered to the human community just outside of the ghouls' lair. Percy felt good about it. Someone had to do it. It was his duty.

When it was all done, Percy found himself outside the ghouls' Town Hall, staring at the stony steps leading into the colossal building with magnificent reliefs and two weird-looking bunny statues guarding the door. Sirixh took them into a big auditorium-like room, which was a mix of the ghouls' aesthetics and what the humans were used to. There were chairs, but none of the ghouls sat on them. Instead, they seemed to prefer to sit on the floor cross-legged. On the walls were regal portraits, mimicking human ones but depicting ghouls with big ruffs around their necks. Percy wasn't sure what to make of any of this. The ghouls kept screeching and clicking their tongues, making the room into a cacophony of noises impossible to keep track of.

"I'm sorry about this. They are usually not this loud," Sirixh whispered next to him, meaning the usually mild-mannered ghouls were agitated because of Percy and Elmer.

"I'm the one who should be sorry," Percy stated. He thought he'd whispered it, but his words echoed in the room.

An older-looking ghoul with slightly lighter gray skin and black fingernails and lips stood up.

The ghouls fell silent and stared at them.

Elmer let out a quiet yelp.

Sirixh whispered, "My mother, the revered leader of the ghouls, Gwerrusxh. You should…" She didn't get to finish her sentence, as Percy assumed he was meant to bow.

"Your reverence," Percy began, still keeping his head low. "We are honored by your presence and the hospitality you have shown. We are in your debt."

"Hu-ma-n foolish-ness-h. Get-h up boy," Gwerrusxh growled.

Percy stood up and looked bewildered.

"I'm no reverendhhh like my daughterrrr saysss. She picksss up these thingsss from you lot." The ghoul leered at Sirixh.

"W-eee are eee-qual here, and while I may decide the final vote when there'sss a difference and help with disagreementsss, I'm no more in charge than anyone in the city. This lot here…" she swung her hand around the ghouls on the floor, "…are just shirking their other duties and putting entirely too much weight on the importance of their opinions about this matter. Now both of you take a seat." Gwerrusxh's tone shifted as she got used to speaking the human tongue.

Percy looked at the empty chairs, then at Gwerrusxh, then to Sirixh, then to Elmer, and finally decided to sit down on the floor.

Gwerrusxh laughed. "Now we can begin," she said. "To recap what you missed while you were washing the dishes…" She paused for Percy to react.

Percy didn't.

The ghoul continued, "…Some of us see it as our moral duty to help you in your hour of need. But some of us feel bringing more humans in and granting asylum will change our den into something it was never meant to be. Some see all this," she pointed at the chairs and the decor, "...as the start of our degeneration into humanity. All of us agree that if we grant you asylum, there will be no peace."

Percy cleared his throat. Elmer shot a horrified glance towards him. Clearly, the investigator was braver and more adept when it came to papers than actual contact with living things. Percy felt an odd sensation composed of confusion and a bizarre out-of-body and -self experience. Rose Pettyshare would laugh at the comparison between Percy and Elmer and probably say, "*I'll be damned.*[2]"

"Thank you, Gwerru-s-xh." Percy knew he'd almost got it. "We are thankful for all that you have done for us. Without you, I would be dead, and Mr. Spooner would be languishing inside a prison cell. You have given us extra time to consider the right thing to do and how to act." Percy looked around at the ghouls. Their black eyes were disconcerting to gaze at, especially when they gave him their fullest attention. With humans, there was always a tiny voice at the back of their minds going: "*me, me, me...*" But with the ghouls, there was just the moment.

"Do go on, Mr. Allread." Gwerrusxh exhaled.

"Yes, as I stated before. We will do our part. We will work hard for you in every way you deem necessary if you grant us asylum. But to decide what to do with us, you need the full facts. The truth is that the Council has in its custody a man who can build a machine that can produce wheat and gold out of thin air. I have seen this machine, and I was the one who arrested Mr. Thurston for violating necromantic rules. I'm to give a statement of the man's actions in the courts, and he will be sentenced according to my account... most likely to die.

"Mr. Spooner is the one who investigated any misconduct from the

---

2. Though it was good to remember that all creatures in Necropolis were damned.

Council while arresting and detaining Mr. Thurston. He found incrim-inating evidence and wrongly stole documents to prove that. Thus he was imprisoned by the Council. I broke into his cell, harming a guard, several witches, and more than a dozen imps in the process. We are not some innocent victims here, and you should know that before you decide. You should also know that if the machine is ever built, it will reshape the world up there—for the worse, from what I have seen.

"I have doubts that Mr. Thurston will ever see a noose. The Council will most likely fake his death and hide him in their cellars to make the machine for them. That's all I have to say..." Percy took a deep breath in. "...Also, you don't have to decide our fates jointly. Mr. Spooner is a whistleblower and acted in accordance with his morals. I, on the other hand, caused bodily harm and destroyed property and should face consequences for my actions."

"Thank you for your candor," Gwerrusxh said.

"If you want us to leave while you decide, we are more than happy to give you time to deliberate," Percy added before the ghouls could start their debate.

"There's no need for that. Everything is done out in the open." Gwer-rusxh leaned forward. Outside the room, more ghouls had gathered. Not only there. Several ghouls were hanging from the wooden window frames, trying to get a better look at what was going on. Percy saw Philomena amongst them. She smiled as their eyes met.

"And Mr. Spooner, do you agree with the statement?" Gwerrusxh asked.

"I do. Not fu-fu-fully, though. Without Mr. All-all-allread and his tac-tics, I wouldn't be alive. The Council used unnecessary force against me while I was detained and while they tried to question me to find out how I got the do-do-documents, where I hid them, and who else I had talked to. I would like to add-add-add that while our actions were un-un-unlawful, they were done in the spirit of wha-wha-what was right," Elmer stammered.

"Thank you, Mr. Spooner. Do either of you have anything else to add?" Gwerrusxh asked.

Elmer shook his head. So did Percy.

"Then we will decide. Now, with a show of hands, will we grant asylum for Mr. Spooner and Mr. Allread?" Gwerrusxh asked.

Percy watched in confusion as the ghouls raised their hands. Not one left them down, inside or outside. Philomena had her hand raised as well. Percy waited for the ghouls to say that it was a joke, or that the show of hands meant the opposite, but nothing of the sort occurred.

"It seems like we keep bringing in stray puppies," Gwerrusxh sighed. "So be it then. We will contact the Council and the Town Hall and state that you'll be staying with us. The Council still has a chance to plead their case, but we will not accept any bodily harm, nor will we hand you over to any other prison. While you are here, you'll be assigned a liaison to ease your transition into our routines and living underground. We insist. While you might now consider yourself to be calm, we have come to realize that in a week, you will get highly stressed and anxious. The reality of having tons of stone above you sneaks in gradually. Your tutors will help you with that, along with finding you an occupation based on your skill set. Will that suit you?"

Both of them agreed.

"You are free to move around the city. However, we wouldn't recommend venturing into the tunnels; they can be tricky to master, and we are not the only inhabitants."

Percy knew from the monster hunter manual that several monsters kept dens inside tunnels, from giant spiders to bullheaded creatures, but none of them dared to live here. In reality, the tunnel's only resident was a melancholic dinosaur, who'd lost all its mates and had been driven out of the world by apes who thought they were some sort of blessing, with intelligence like no other. Gwerrusxh didn't see the point of warning them. The dinosaur wasn't the eating sort. It was more of the I'll-trap-you-in-my-existential-angst sort. The only escape was thinking of rainbows, kitties, and ice cream and trying really, really hard to ignore its sad eyes and the lulling tone. But it left the ghouls and the humans alone. It rather liked sulking in the basement.

"Thank you. This was more than we could ask for," Percy said.

"Don't thank us yet. Sirixh!" Gwerrusxh snapped.

The ghoul seemed to materialize from thin air next to her mother. "Yes," she said.

"You found them. You keep them."

"Yes, Mother." Sirixh bowed.

"No more of that nonsense," Gwerrusxh snarled.

"No, Mother." With those words, Percy and Elmer were escorted out of the room. The ghouls who had been hanging around gave them space and seemed to eat them with their eyes. Not in the hungry-for-your-flesh sense, but more I'm going to figure out what your dreams are, what you have seen, done, and experienced, and what you have to say.

Percy shuddered.

Philomena caught them on the way out and said, "Hey!"

She received only a half-assed response from both him and Elmer. Percy's head was swimming. The enormity of the events and the rock above him had only now started to hit him. Yesterday his life had been carefully planned out, and he only had to ride the weirdness until Otis was tried, but now the future was unknown.[3]

"When you have time, find me. I'll be happy to help you get settled in,"

---

3. Actually, nothing had changed. The future was always unknown. And by accepting that, life got some of its zest back.

she said.

"Thank you," Percy responded, barely registering what the woman said.

"Also, nicely done. Mr. Spooner, what you said about the spirit of right sealed your fate. If you want to survive here, you have to know ghouls are highly moral creatures, and they accept no foolery." Philomena tried smiling to get their attention.

"You didn't do so badly yourself either." Philomena looked Percy in his eyes.

"Thank you," he muttered, now seeing her and the sweet smile she was giving.

The witch glanced away but then met his eyes again.

Percy always forgot what an effect his brooding attractiveness—as his sister called it—had on others. But he found himself wishing there was more than his handsomeness having an effect.

"Not a thank you matter, just stating the obvious. It was really touch and go there initially, especially based on the chatter I heard earlier. But now, all that has passed. Just wanted to say I'm happy to aid you to settle in and show you all the best spots when you want to be alone or feel more like a human." Philomena offered a smile.

Percy looked away.

"We better get going," Sirixh said, interrupting them. She indicated all the curious ghouls nearing them.

Philomena nodded and followed them towards the house Percy and Elmer had been living in so far. Philomena chatted peacefully about how to conduct yourself with the ghouls. Her advice was simple. "Be polite and don't lie, answer their questions, and if you can't, then say so. They'll help you with anything you need, just tell them why."

"If I may ask, in the spirit of the ghouls' openness, why are you here?" Percy asked. He was blushing and wasn't sure why.

"That's too long of a story to tell you now, but I promise I will later.

There's nothing as notorious as with you two." Philomena laughed. Her voice was music to his ears, making him feel more human than he'd felt in a long time. She was relaxed and happy, or seemed to be. She wasn't carrying the usual darkness the Necropolitans did, and there was no false happiness as there had been in Threebeanvalley. Instead, she was genuinely contented, and Percy let himself think for a fleeting second that maybe he could be as well. Perhaps he hadn't been cursed after all.

Sirixh let them into the house, and Philomena bid her farewells. "I'll be back later to check your wounds. Now you better get settled in and rest. You two look like something dragged you out of the bottom of the ocean."

Sirixh left them too with instructions on where they could find bread, jam, and fresh cider. Percy closed the door behind them, thinking that Otis should have invented a machine that would pause time to enjoy stillness, suspending time without new mornings following the end of each day and without the next moment ever materializing. He needed to pause everything to catch a breath and catch himself. But it seemed life wasn't made to be stationary. And as far as Percy knew, Otis was the sort of fellow who didn't know how to stay still. Neither did the world.

Chapter Twenty-One

CLARITY OF THE FALLEN

And events had to happen. That was existence for you. The blackness of the room sucked Otis in. If he was being highly accurate, he was being pushed in, and there was no way he could escape into the hallway and out of the building. Otis could smell the witch's foul breath as she kept herself close to him. She pushed him down into a seat and left the room with the other witch by her side, closing the doors behind them and taking away the only light there was. The last thing Otis saw was the silhouette of the undead man standing inside the room next to the doors.

"Mr. Thurston," came a voice.

"That would be me, but it's up for discussion if necessary. I have always fancied a stronger name, like Warrick. Warrick could be someone who never got himself in trouble. He could be someone who just worked himself dead at accounting or as a manager of some petty office no one cares a corpse worm about," he offered.

Someone coughed.

No wonder, Otis thought. The room smelled of old flesh and mothballs.

"No takers, I assume," Otis said. "So, what do you want to discuss?"

There was another cough, but he heard a chuckle as well.

"Let's not prolong this with nonsense. Some of us were already sleeping when the call came," the earlier voice said to Otis's left.

"I'm all ears. Don't let me detain you from getting back to your pajamas." Otis turned his head to meet the voice.

There was that chuckle again.

Otis relaxed a bit. He hadn't noticed all the tension he was carrying. However, he was highly aware of the bruises forming on his sides thanks to the not-so-friendly witch.

"I won't have this—" the voice began.

"Leave it, and let's get to the point," a woman's voice warned.

There came a murmur, but the first voice didn't say anything else.

"Now, Mr. Thurston, as has been established to be your name," the woman continued. "Your existence has caused a stir, and we have to figure out what to do with you. It seems like we don't get to decide this at your hearing. So let's figure it out now so all of us can go back to bed. As I have gathered, you have broken all the rules we have set to guard against all the past nonsense. But here you are, stirring up those rules. No wars have yet come about, but it's just a matter of time. Out there, beyond these walls, nations are already gearing up to take ownership of you. They don't care if the machine is real or not. They want you and it. We could pretend your imprisonment is about the ghosts you unleashed and what could have followed or about the fact you left the city without approval and practiced necromancy overseas. If asked, the Council condemns those acts to their full extent and will pursue punishment over them, meaning either lifelong imprisonment or death by necromancy if you do not cooperate, as you already know. That's all trivial and we all know it. I won't insult your intelligence by pretending otherwise."

"Thanks, I guess," Otis stuttered, not sure if there had been a threat there or not.

"Yes, thanks are in order. We have protected you and kept you alive thus far, Mr. Thurston. It hasn't been easy. In exchange, you have given us what? Grievance for your imprisonment and your silence over the machine we taught you to build," she persisted.

"I thought the university..." He stopped himself there and said instead, "If this is going to be my trial—"

"No, Mr. Thurston. This is not a trial. This is your opportunity to cooperate. You'll die tonight, but you can decide if it's on your terms or on ours."

"You can't just kill me." Otis jumped off his chair, knocking it down, the clatter reverberating around the room.

"Do sit down!" the woman barked.

Otis continued standing, feeling his knuckles go white from squeezing his fists so tight.

"I have to insist you sit down. As I said, death is inevitable, but there's a chance for rebirth, Mr. Thurston, or should I say Warrick," the woman said.

The undead who had escorted him here touched his arm and dragged him back into the chair, which the man had set upright again.

"Oh," Otis let out.

"Yes, oh, Mr. Thurston. You need to die a good, believable public death tonight. There's no other choice. But if Warrick wants to live, he'll have to give the machine to the Council and work to build it, or there won't be a Warrick. Only a quick death by the ever-so-ready mob downstairs. I have been told they are making their way upstairs as we speak. And while they want your freedom, or so they think, there are always lunatics who see violence as the solution. Do you understand me?"

Otis just stared at the blackness of the room. No one spoke. No one dared to breathe too loudly either. There was just the rasping of his breathing filling the space.

"I do," Otis half whispered.

"I didn't quite hear you, Mr. Thurston. Do you agree that Warrick should live or not?"

"What does that mean exactly?" Otis asked.

"We provide all the materials you need, and you work for us."

"Where?" His question was met with silence. They clearly hadn't thought it through.

"That's not the point—"

"It is for me. If you are going to stuff me into some old potato cellar and forget me there, then I'd prefer to die, thank you very much," Otis dared to interrupt the woman.

The woman stuttered, or Otis was sure she did. He was sure he'd shocked her; she had that expression that always came when he said or did the wrong thing. He wasn't backing down. They needed him.[1]

"Mr. Thurston, you are not in any position to negotiate. This is not a question of what you want. This is a question of whether you want to live or not," the woman continued. She was starting to get a headache, which was the usual side effect when dealing with Otis.

"Yes, boy. You are not coming out of this as the winner. So stop fooling around," a male voice said.

Otis heard a chorus of sighs around the room. If he was familiar with the board, he would know daft old Mr. Cummings had spoken and that the man was nutty as a fruit cake. He was only kept around because he could be bought and commanded. Also, it was good to have someone dafter than you around to get that extra superiority boost. Nevertheless, he was right, and Otis was starting to realize it. The way the woman's voice hung in the air told him they meant every threat they'd said. He would die tonight.

"Miss—?" Otis tried.

"I mean it, boy, no more funny business," daft old Mr. Cummings said.

---

1. There Otis was wrong. No one actually needed him. He was wanted. There's a great difference between want and need. The Council didn't need the machine. They already had plenty of power.

"Just trying to give the proper respect."

"Then give us the machine and do as you are told," Mr. Cummings retorted.

The woman who'd spoken coughed. "That's truly unnecessary, but I'm afraid, highly accurate. There's no room for negotiations. It's this or death, Mr. Thurston. So what are you going to decide?"

Otis had waited for this moment ever since his imprisonment. He'd toyed with all the possibilities, especially with saying no, but there was something highly disturbing about death and dying, even for a necromancer.

"I—"

The doors to the darkened room burst open, letting in the unholy light from the hallway. There, in the middle of the doorway, stood a woman in a wool coat, her white hair cropped short, her walking skirt doing an impressive pirouette around her legs. She was flanked by serious-looking guards. Some clearly belonged to her, and others not so much.

"Mr. Thurston, you are to come with me," Petula Upwood said.

"Who do you think you are?!" daft old Mr. Cummings shouted.

"I'm the leader of Necropolis and thus the rightful dictator of the Council. Here," she said and slammed a document into the undead man's chest. "Read this, and when you are done, contact me. But now Mr. Thurston is coming with us. Mr. Thurston, get up," Petula ordered. The officers around her widened their stance. They clearly knew they were in a sticky spot of history, and there was no way of telling who would come out of this the winner.

Otis scrambled to his feet as fast as he could. He let the guards seize him. He took a last look around the room, but the board members were hooded and doing their best to avoid the light. The only one showing his face was the undead, Wallace Crowen, the manager. He had that snarl of someone who wasn't happy at all about what had happened and would get his revenge after finding an appropriate comeback.

Otis was dragged away. He heard Petula say, "We will be seeing you around." Then she turned around and headed after Otis so fast it made her skirt rustle.

Free will, responsibility, and all that other icky stuff made action a whole lot more complicated. Raul found himself contemplating his life choices while sandwiched between two huge men inside a small coach with no cushioning or curtains to speak of.

He had followed motion after motion for the past couple of hours, never stopping to think if he should do what was laid in front of him. Was he responsible for any of it, he wondered? Pre-determination and all that. It was just that a sneaking feeling inside him told him that he really couldn't blame the beast or anyone else for ending up here, watching the blackened windows. He had this trigger inside him that made him obsessively pursue answers, and here he was, his feet pressed against the floor where blood had been spilled more than once.

Raul fidgeted, trying to breathe. The two men didn't budge, keeping their mouths shut when Raul asked where they were heading. He was starting to think that this wasn't going to end well. That he would find himself at the bottom of an unmarked grave. Not an optimal result, but then again, he had had a good run, and to be honest, things had been looking dodgy for a while. He'd moved from one story to another, each worse than the last. The big successes he'd had as a writer were way back when people were interested in the news rather than the stories of the bold and the beautiful.

He shook off the bad memory of how things used to be. The world had changed. It had to, or else. Raul wasn't sure what the or else meant, but he was sure evolving had to happen whether you wanted it or not. But he had an opportunity for redemption. It was just he wasn't sure what good it would do to reveal who ran the Council. It wouldn't matter. There would be thousands of reporters like Sandy who would spin things in favor of the Council. No soul, backbone, or morality. Just pursuing a paycheck and the high life, snorting down formaldehyde and dancing with the skeletons all night, drenched in the blood of the little people. That was Sandy.

The bigger of the men coughed. Monty, if Raul remembered correctly. "It's time," the man said. As if on command, the coach stopped.

The two men stood up in unison, taking Raul up with the same movement. He followed the shorter of the men outside as the bigger one breathed down his neck. There was something highly uncomfortable about being stuck in the middle of two men who smelled like they hadn't showered in weeks. They reached what looked like your neighborhood's abandoned haunted house. The two-story building in the middle of nowhere with its iron fence overrun by vines and rose bushes stood there like a colossal reminder not to go with strangers.

The iron creaked as Monty pushed the gates open and closed the gates behind them again. This wasn't the way Raul thought he would die, but then again, there were a lot worse deaths out there waiting to happen. He'd never fancied slipping away in his sleep. The idea of Old Man Death lurking around the corner and creeping over his bed made his whole body go into goosebumps. He would take a good old stabbing or choking anytime.

Rugus, the shorter of the huge men, dug around in his jacket pocket and finally produced an old iron key. The man unlocked the wooden door with the painted glass window. Raul looked around the foyer full of family oil paintings and chandeliers. Someone really loved Gothic architecture. Raul would bet his month's wages that there was a ritual altar in the basement. There was, but not at all for the reasons Raul expected. The family that had lived here had prayed for a giant fluffy bunny, and not for carrots, and not very successfully. But Raul wasn't there for the decor. The men pushed him into the parlor and sat him in front of a machine that reminded him of the typewriter he used at the office, but this was more advanced. It was smaller, slimmer, and with that brass finish he had seen the alchemists and engineers in the city use.

Monty slammed a stack of papers into his hands and said, "Write!" That was all they said as the two men left him there to stare out a window into the back garden, where the rose bushes had gone wild.

He listened to the wood of the house moan as the two thugs moved around. The empty pages in front of him seemed to magically appear in the typewriter.[2] His fingers began to push the keys, and everything whirling inside his head came out. There was no thinking, just a flow of words that needed to be said. Not even the strong smell of coffee taking over the house roused him, and Raul desperately needed that coffee[3] to function. He wrote feverishly, the pages forming neatly into a stack next to him. He found himself reaching for a cup and took a sip of the strong coffee. He had no recollection of how it had gotten there. Yet there it was to fuel him. Raul immersed himself in the words that seemed to float out of him. It was the truth he had been looking for all these years.

---

2. Not magically. His hand had jumped the gun, knowing better than his mind what he wanted. But it has already been established that minds are jerks, making everything a whole lot more complicated, especially if out of tune with the body.

3. Clarity in a cup.

CHAPTER TWENTY-TWO

NO TIME FOR SENTIMENTALITY

It would be so much better if one could marvel at the absurdity of any given situation from the outside and not be bothered by the annoying little things like feelings, ego, and worries about this and that. Because once those three got a hold on you, rationality flew out the window and a gnawing feeling stepped in. Henrietta could feel it, in her and in Ida: the inescapable fate of not having a choice.

"Please," Henrietta repeated when Ida continued to make her stand. The horrified stillness in the warden's office was all-consuming, but Ida wasn't ready to let go. She contemplated reaching for the enamel washing bowl she'd thrown on the floor and bashing the warden and the doctor with it. Henrietta was all up for aggression. It was a perfectly reasonable option in the face of uncertainty—a perfect emotion for self-preservation when knowing one's value is necessary. The trouble was more with the application than the emotion itself. Bashing the warden's head with the bowl and sticking the bar of soap into the doctor's mouth—which had even crossed Henrietta's mind—and escaping through the roof window wouldn't get them any closer to freedom. Quite the opposite. All sorts of creatures would be sent after them, meaning Cruxh, and Henrietta was pretty sure the always helpful ghoul wouldn't bring them back here a second time. Some lost dungeon would have their name written on it, where paranoid delirium and catatonia waited for their prey.

"Clearly," Henrietta said, when her previous word had no effect, "Mr. Hardrick is doing the best he can to aid us, but because of the extraordinary situation, we are stuck here without a lawyer. Yet Annabella and Ida are right. It's imperative we speak to one. So, if it's possible for you to contact the Coven on our behalf again and ask them to send their lawyers to meet us as soon as possible?" It was a long shot. But at least it would be official then, and they could make a complaint.

The warden nodded. "It will be done straight away," he said without taking his eyes off Ida. The warden commanded one of the guards to go to the Coven and deliver the message. The young boy dashed out as soon as he got his instructions.

Ida snorted but sat back down, glancing at Henrietta and then at Annabella.

Henrietta hoped Ida could read her expression and know that there might come a time when Henrietta wouldn't hold her back, but for now they had to behave. Otherwise, the Council would win. Even Cruxh and Mr. Hardrick's kindness couldn't wipe away what the Council was capable of. Their innocence wouldn't matter, not then and not now. This was political, and politics were out to get them. They needed friends, they needed a lawyer, and more so they needed Petula. Petula, Henrietta thought. There was a slight chance she'd sold them out to save herself, but Henrietta didn't want to go that far. Ida might.

Henrietta glanced at Ida. She squeezed her knees, hunched over.

"Now do go on, Mr. Philpot," Henrietta said.

The doctor looked startled.

Henrietta gave an encouraging smile, which wasn't needed. The doctor was one of those types who were highly sure about themselves. Those who just needed a perfect excuse to talk, and there was always a good excuse around the corner. Silas Philpot gave his pep talk about hygiene.

Henrietta half-listened to the man as she tried to compose a plan and a possible letter to Petula. The doctor told them that there was an in-house shrink they could see and discuss any concerns they had. "Especially about mothers.[1]" The man continued talking about bugs and germs. Henrietta paused to listen and then shook her head. Henrietta knew what germs were, but clearly, the doctor didn't. She played with them all day in the gardens. The doctor wanted to eliminate them all. No witch would. Where he saw danger, the witches saw vitality. Bugs and germs were propellers for change—the tiny deviation that altered the now. Thinking about the garden made Henrietta automatically reach for her pouch and squeeze it. She felt it pulsate between her fingers.

Follow the fungi, she thought.

"It's the same with the head. All the germs the mind produces have to be washed out. I have to insist you see the shrink and remove any nonsense about witchery, undeads, and necromancy. Those are the by-product of an overactive imagination, and an overactive imagination will make you ill," the doctor babbled on.

Everyone stared at the man in stunned silence. The doctor didn't notice. "...A model prisoner will get over their trauma and accept their past without blame and take responsibility for their own actions. They will seek out a profession and cure all the ailments in their body. Finally, they will be normal, free of that trauma. It's your salvation from the madness Necropolis breeds."

Henrietta stared at the man in stunned silence. No witch would ever be a model of anything. Witches were meant to rebel, to walk their own path so that society could let go of their ridiculous rules. They were the outsiders.

Henrietta had looked after enough traumatized witches lost in the vortex of madness to know that they were the sane ones, not pretending that

---

1. Mothers were highly important when it came to criminal elements.

normalcy was normal. In Henrietta's book, it was more insane to consider reality to be logical, as it wasn't. And she didn't mean the undeads or the gargoyles or the vampires. She meant beings using beings. She shrugged off the doctor's silly talk and let his words fade into the background. Some people couldn't be helped, and she had more serious matters on her plate than rescuing one poor soul from his own backwardness. She needed to see what was happening at the Coven. She let her powers move through her feet to the wooden floor and into the stones, traveling through all the joints and plaster and finally reaching the ground, where the fungal network took her to the Coven. She moved faster than the messenger the warden had sent.

She saw Imogene all dolled up. Her mother stood by her side, dressed more regally than her daughter. Imogene wore all black with lace and velvet, which made her look more like a tablecloth than a Mother. There was no sign of Lottie or Judika. Eurof was there, holding on to Nestor's terrarium as the two women moved into Henrietta's office. She couldn't hear what was said, but it was clear what was going on. There was no sign of Henrietta's books or her specimens. They had been replaced with dolls, skulls, and what looked like a collection of blood. Ruby, Imogene's mother, had always hungered for the powers that came with blood magic, even when she was a hexer. Yet the woman was a hack; her talents lay more in her scornful looks and slashing tongue. But there was no denying how effective her methods could be. The woman hated Henrietta from the bottom of her heart, obstructing Henrietta's leadership at every chance she got. They hadn't always been enemies. Not before Wesley had chosen to mentor Henrietta over Ruby despite everyone knowing he was intimate with the other woman.

The warden's messenger finally reached the place. She stood in front of the two witches, seeking shelter from Eurof's shadow and failing. Ruby narrowed her eyes, and Imogene shook her head. That was as far as Henrietta saw the scene unfold. She was yanked back to the prison.

The doctor stood in front of her, holding on to her pouch, having torn it off her neck. "Mrs. Culpepper, I have to insist you let go of these artifacts. They are making you sick. Your eyes just went all white."

Henrietta wanted to laugh. She glanced at Ida and Annabella. The banker raised her eyebrow in question. Henrietta shook her head, making Ida snarl and state, "She's perfectly fine, you silly man. That's hers, and you shouldn't be playing around with it. Who knows what kind of germs might leap onto you."

Henrietta winced.

The doctor's eyes widened, and he looked at the pouch like it was highly explosive. However, he didn't let go.

"Even more so, I have to insist that the prisoner won't have access to this kind of fetish. It clearly makes her ill, reinforcing her obsessive behavior and beliefs about the supernatural."

Everyone in the room turned to stare at the man again, most with their mouths hanging open.

"Don't look at me like that. I know what you Necropolitans believe about witches and necromancers and all sorts of weird undead creatures, but that is all hogwash. Modern medicine has proved it to be the fantasy of the mind manifesting itself in a physical form. As soon as you let go of your obsessive thoughts, you will be cured."

Silas crossed his arms. He left out that this was the reason he had come here. Silas had heard about the unruly place and how it insisted on running the world with its illusions about the dead. He'd sworn to teach the Necropolitans what sanity looked like and that it wasn't okay to bully the rest of the world into believing in their hallucinations. Mr. Hardrick had been the first one to listen to him, and by that time, Silas had learned to keep his mouth shut about his ideas, which had received nothing but mockery. Here he had a perfect specimen to prove himself right. If he could cure Mrs. Culpepper's delusion about being a witch and the foolish notion that it was perfectly fine to keep company with corpses—the man glanced at Annabella—then others would follow.

Henrietta tried to get a word out, well aware that the doctor was looking at her funny, but she couldn't quite figure out what to say. She wasn't the only one finding the whole situation bizarre. The awkward moment was defused as Mr. Hardrick said, "We will hold it for now. You can hand it over to me, Mr. Philpot."

The doctor was more than happy to let go of it.

"Now, I think we are done here," the warden said. "The guards will escort you to your joint cell to have breakfast." The man gave Henrietta an apologetic glance, which seemed to say, "*He's new and cheap.*"

Henrietta gave him a slight smile to let him know everything was fine. It was just that she needed the pouch back, and if she didn't get it, there would be Kraken to pay.

Silas interrupted the exchange by thrusting his finger towards Henrietta's face and saying, "Follow my finger."

Henrietta was beginning to think, for her own sanity's sake, that the man was another prisoner instead of a doctor—one of those mad scientists the city produced in such abundance. Either way, he was a quack. Anyone who didn't recognize astral projection was kidding themselves about how the mind and, better yet, the cosmos worked. Still, Henrietta did as told. Her eyes had gone all white from traveling to the Coven, but she wasn't willing to disclose that to the warden.

"You are quite new to this, aren't you?" Henrietta asked as she followed the finger gliding back and forth in front of her eyes. It was quite hypnotic and calming while the storm of what she'd witnessed waited for a perfect opportunity to come out.

"What makes you think that, Mrs. Culpepper?" the man asked.

"A hunch." Henrietta gave him a polite smile, trying to stay on good terms with the man.

Next to the baffled doctor, Ida stifled a titter and squeezed the washing bowl she'd retrieved.

"Thank you, Mr. Philpot. I'm doing a lot better now," Henrietta said before Silas had time to comment on the last remark. "Now, if you don't mind, I would love to be escorted to our cell. Sitting here on the hard bench doesn't do any good for my old bones," Henrietta said and stood up.

"Yes, of course," Silas stuttered and fled from Henrietta. "Everything seems to be quite in order. She can be escorted to her cell." Silas took some of his control back before scurrying farther away as they were escorted out.

Tit for tat. That seemed to be how it worked. Or at least how the social scientists thought it worked. But the best strategy wasn't a tit for every tat. There needed to be forgiveness, but if that forgiveness was returned with a tat, then a tit should follow. Petula was sure the Council wouldn't see it that way. She watched Mr. Thurston, who sat relaxed on the seat in front of her.

"Mr. Thurston, I need you to play nice," Petula said, bracing herself as the coach rocked away from the Necromantic Council's headquarters. It was undoubtedly a threat, but even she wasn't sure what kind. She'd risked everything to obtain the man, and now she was supposed to use him to get everything the city needed. It was just that the city clearly didn't know what it needed or deserved. Most citizens were just happy that the decisions were made by someone else—her. The necromancer shifted uncomfortably in front of her as she peered into him. Petula had seen enough people in her life to know some people weren't worth the hassle. Unfortunately, the world didn't see Mr. Thurston as she saw him.

The man was tucked between the city guards, who were nervous after having just offended the Council. The Council was like that one friend you should never cross, or else.

Otis grinned. "I always play nice, Miss Mayor."

"I wasn't flirting with you. I was stating a fact," Petula said, making the guards around them titter. She didn't care.

"Me neither," Otis retorted, making the stifled noises even louder.

"Good, then we are on the same page. There's no telling if either of us will survive this night." That made the noises die out. "Which means we need to cooperate and really figure out what to do with you."

Some of the color in the man's face drained away. Petula wondered if Otis finally realized he would forever be a marked man.

"Yes, Mr. Thurston. There needs to be a solution that will satisfy not only you. I'm highly certain you know enough tricks to flee this transport, but we both know there's no place for you to hide. Not when everyone will send their fiends after you. They will hunt you to the end of the world, if necessary. If it's any solace, only a few will want you dead. But I wouldn't put it past the Council or Madam Sabine to get their way. The Church sees you and the machine as blasphemy, and some of its members are calling for your immediate death."

"Death is irrelevant. It's always—" Otis began.

"...Good to be wanted, Mr. Thurston? I highly doubt that," Petula stated. "Nevertheless, you are right; you are wanted, Mr. Thurston. The question is by whom, and who will get you."

"I thought you got me." Otis grinned, causing the guards to snicker again.[2]

"Yes, and now it seems I have to keep you. Alive or dead, though, has yet to be decided. If it was up to me, you wouldn't exist at all. It is your lucky day: I will let the public decide what will happen to you. The trouble is, first you and I have to survive this night. And I wouldn't trust our lives

---

2. The old wonderful cause and effect, reason and consequence be damned.

solely to our tittering guards here. So I'll take off your shackles, and you will have an opportunity to show me that you have a working backbone." That silenced the whole coach. Otis was a necromancer, after all, and everyone knew what Petula's action meant.[3]

Petula leaned towards him, motioning for him to hold up his wrists. He silently offered them to Petula, his gaze meeting hers. Petula didn't look away. She commanded the nearest ghost to wiggle into the locks and burst them open. The ghost protested and complained the whole time, stating that it was impossible, yet when the locks opened, the dead soul beamed with pride. It would be so easy to think death robbed a soul of all the emotions that made life that much more miserable, but there was no way to hide from emotions, even in death. They had a funny way of finding you no matter how hard you stifled them.[4]

"Now, go away and rest in peace. It doesn't matter what your father said twenty years ago. He's long gone. So are you. Let it go," Petula said.

The ghost wavered in the air, trying to make up his mind whether to let go and guess whether Petula's words were a thank you or not. The choice was his to make. But he lingered there longer than Petula had time for. She squinted her eyes, and he was gone. Petula hoped that he took her advice and followed the tunnel wherever it led rather than staying forever in the limbo of bitterness. Petula wondered if she should start keeping a list of all the silly ways in which humans let themselves be consumed by life. Her motto was not to dwell on things.

"There," Petula said.

"Thank you, Miss Mayor," Otis said and massaged his ankles and wrists.

Petula tilted her head and then shook it. "We have a lot to do, and there's no time for sentimentality. We are heading to my manor. I would rather

---

3. That cause and effect again, playing buckaroo.

4. It wasn't rationality keeping ghosts around.

take you to the Town Hall or to a prison of some sort, but I fear my place is more secure than anything our city has to offer."

Petula couldn't help but think that when the press got wind of this, she would pay a price. She didn't have a good, reasonable explanation that would satisfy the masses despite the truth. Not that it was possible to satisfy everyone, least of all Dow. Petula could already picture him frowning for all that she'd done. He had every opportunity to be there and stop her, but he was absent. If this was him testing her, she didn't like it. Or perhaps this was his highly cruel way of showing her that she needed him. Of course she did. She was the leader of the biggest nation in the world. That was a lot for one person to handle.

"You know what you are doing," Otis said, more out of the obligation to reply than real conviction.

"Yes..." Petula let her words fall. "There will be a public hearing tomorrow at noon."

"Okay," Otis said, looking like he was ready to give in, still staring at his free hands, unable to decide what it meant. Petula didn't trust the moment of stillness. Mr. Thurston seemed to be a creature who always got back up and had the stamina of a sugar-infused child, able to cause havoc to match his mood.

Petula let him be and leaned backward, closing her eyes for a second. It had been a long night, and she desperately wanted to go to bed and sleep the day away. There was no way that the Council would let her. This was war. The mere thought made Petula sneer. When politics started referring to things in terms of battle, you knew some very important part of society had gone bust.

Petula took in the quiet moment before the storm and let go of any ideas of societies, the right thing, her duties, and most of all the machine and the necromancer in front of her with the ability to kill her on the spot. She just sat there, her eyes closed, listening to the rattle of the coach. She was sorry that the flight had to come to a halt eventually.

The guards escorted them into Petula's manor. They peered at every nook and sidewalk on their way from the coach to the old manor house situated in the middle of the city. The white stone walls with black window frames seemed so alien yet welcoming. Inside, Petula had tried to get rid of all the grand decor, but the staff kept bringing it back, insisting it was more fitting for the mayor of Necropolis than her ascetic style. She'd let them win the battle. The staff was already waiting for them, lined up in the foyer. So was Mr. Colton, who leaned on the little pillar that had magically appeared there during the day. Her bodyguard was holding Her in his lap. The cat didn't seem impressed. It looked highly annoyed but was ready to be placed on Petula's shoulder.

Mr. Colton winked at her.

Petula lifted her eyebrow, and he didn't even flinch.

"I have secured your study for you," Mr. Colton said as if in excuse for his absence.

"Is Mr. Spurgeon here?" Petula asked.

"No, ma'am. He's still out on his business. But we have made sure your wishes have been met."

Petula flinched. "Good," she said. "The study will be perfect. I need my kit."

"It's already there, ma'am," Mr. Colton said.

"You seem to know me," Petula let out and patted Her.

"One always does his best to serve." Mr. Colton gestured for them to follow him into the study situated on the first floor.

The room instantly made Petula feel better. Being surrounded by her book collections made the world seem more sensible. Petula glanced at the fireplace, which was already lit. The room was warm enough to welcome anyone in from the moist, cold December air. The square red carpet with a golden pattern made the room more homey. Petula walked to the small desk where she wrote her observations of necromancy on those rare occasions she had time for herself. Her necromantic kit was laid in the middle of the table. A small rucksack Petula had put together in case of emergency.

She lowered the cat onto the table and opened her kit. She took out her pen and papers. The papers were specially made by her for sticky situations when others had sneaky thoughts about killing her. They had intriguing patterns pre-drawn on them. She would have to fill the rest in to activate the necromantic effects. She methodically moved from one paper to the next, making the patterns work. She glanced up, following Mr. Thurston's gaze around the room. The man let his eyes glide over all the books. When he was done, he chose the divan near the fireplace and sat down.

"So I pegged you right," the man said.

"How so?"

"Reader instead of a doer." Otis flicked his hand towards the books.

"Not a great secret there," Petula said, offering the first papers to Mr. Colton, who, without the need to say anything, attached them to the only window in the room behind the desk. The cat followed the exchange nonchalantly, licking its paw.

"I guess not," Otis said and flung his legs over the divan. "But it would have been nice to be proven wrong. So do you have anything to eat while we wait for our collectors to come?"

"If they come. I'm sure my cook can muster you something," Petula said and took the little bell from her desk. She rang it, and instantly a footman arrived. Petula instructed the man to fetch something for Otis to eat and a pot of tea and a biscuit for her, then to take the staff to safety and keep them out of the way.

The man nodded and headed out of the room, leaving Petula to get back to writing her protections. Mr. Colton attached them to the walls and to the door as she wrote them. They wouldn't hold back anyone who knew what they were doing, but they would slow them down, giving Petula time to react. She just hoped the Council wouldn't be this stupid. Not that Petula had ever been shown otherwise. Petula finished the last paper just before the tea arrived. So did the food for Mr. Thurston, who happily ate the cook's spread. From the look of it, the man had gone all out with the supper. Petula was sure it had something to do with her eating habits and having a first-class chef on her staff.

"What now?" Otis asked.

"Now we wait." Petula stood up behind the desk and stretched her back. She walked to the bookshelf and took out a book about the inflictions of deadly possessions. Usually, she would head to the divan. She glanced at the desk chair and thought otherwise. She sat down in the middle of the floor on the red carpet and folded her legs. Her instantly leaped from the desk and curled into Petula's lap.

Petula opened the book and felt time slow down as she read and nibbled the biscuit. She barely noticed Otis staring at her and Mr. Colton watching every move Mr. Thurston made.

Petula was disturbed from her reading by Otis's occasional restlessness. A question here and there, and chatter about this and that. It became clear Otis expected her to be curious about him, the machine, and his imprisonment. She let the man chat away when he deemed it necessary, but Petula had already figured it out. Every detail of it. Even the Bufonite, down to the essence of it. What she hadn't figured out, she was sure he would tell her if she just stayed silent. Petula wasn't sure if she wanted to know. What if the knowledge was like a curse, pushing her to create the machine just to see if it was possible? And what then? She would be forever tied to it.

"Mr. Thurston, I have to stop you there..." That was as far as Petula got. A loud crash interrupted the conversation. It sounded like a man dropping down with full force.

Petula closed the book and stood up slowly. The cat jumped up from her lap and stretched its body. Petula made her way to the bookshelf and put the book in its rightful place.

Otis had gotten up also. He was looking bewildered.

"Mr. Colton, I think you'd better leave now," Petula said.

"Ma'am, it's better if I stay."

"No, you'll just be in my way."

"Ma'am—"

"Mr. Colton, you can stay if you sense the spirits set loose in the house. If you don't, you know what to do; the staff knows what to do."

"If you insist," Mr. Colton said and gestured at Otis.

"I'll be fine," Petula said. "And if I am not, then you will have a new master to serve. Take the cat with you."

Mr. Colton chuckled, scooped Her into his lap, and headed to the bookcase in the corner of the room, opening a secret passage between the walls.

"What about me?" Otis asked, looking after Mr. Colton.

"Now we fight, Mr. Thurston. Or you can hide. It's up to you. But I'm afraid I can't let you leave." Petula smoothed her walking skirt, rolled up her shirt sleeves, revealing her tattoos, and faced the study door.

The secret door behind her slid back into place, and Otis sighed.

"Isn't it nice, Mr. Thurston, that people are predictable? It makes things a lot easier, I would say."

"If you say so," Otis said.

Chapter Twenty-Three

THE FLICKER BETWEEN STAGES

The wise say that only the mind can build prisons, and that only the mind can set you free. Henrietta was pretty sure they were right, but not in a philosophical sense. It was the human mind which had come up with the need for cells and torture with funny things like metallic bars and needles under the nails. Ask a cat to do that and it will bite you.

The cell, as the warden had called Henrietta's new residence, was a small room with three iron beds crammed into it. At the end of one bed, there was a portable writing desk with a letter-writing kit on it. Somehow Henrietta guessed that it wasn't a normal thing to have in a prison cell. Annabella seemed to be relieved to notice it, and when the breakfast hassle had been sorted and they could finally retire back to their cell, Annabella took the papers out and began composing a letter to their lawyer. Henrietta hadn't yet told Ida and the undead what she'd seen at the Coven. That there might not be a lawyer.

"Add a letter to Petula as well," Henrietta said as she flung her legs onto the bed. Her head was still spinning, and she desperately needed to shut her eyes.

Annabella agreed, and she insisted that she would stand guard for her and Ida and that both of them should rest.

Henrietta didn't disagree. She shut her eyes. Not that any silence greeted her instantly. Instead, the invasive thoughts came first. She refused to play games with them. She navigated through them out of sheer tiredness. Then she fell asleep. If there were dreams, she wasn't privy to them. The only thing there was the heaviness of everything. She usually had something. Just a flicker would do. Whenever dreams were absent, her sleep was shoddy at best. But Henrietta was sure she had been sleeping or still was. She couldn't tell. There was only the stillness and the heaviness.

It felt wrong. Henrietta tried to open her eyes. They didn't open. All that persisted was the pitch-black darkness. There was always a bloom or a leaf. Now, with the dark, the apparent loneliness became ever more pressing, and if she let it, it would consume her. Henrietta tried to shake the sensation away. This was just her being tired. The stress of the worst coming to be. Henrietta took a deep breath in, but it got stuck in her chest, making everything ache. Once again, she forced her eyes open, but the same blackness continued.

There was her name. It came like a whisper. Then there was the reality and the situation. All true. But the truth didn't matter past a certain point. Human societies were built on mutually agreed-upon stories. If you were a great storyteller or had money enough to hire one, innocence, guilt, right and wrong, and everything associated with justice meant nothing. Henrietta knew this, and she knew that her witches could spin tales. And here in the darkness, she was willing to resort to the forbidden, ancient techniques to tell a better story to be released into the world. Hexers were small-timers compared to those who could twist the truth. They could and had in the past shaped cities, especially places like Necropolis, where making money by any and all means possible was a rule rather than a deviation. Now they kept their talents hidden and bound. Henrietta knew only of two who had told her their secret and taught her a thing or two. One worked as a fortuneteller. It came as close to creating fantasies as was permissible. The other was inside a mental health institution. He hadn't been able to let go of the stories. So he had been given a room where reality could be of his own making, courtesy of the Council.

Henrietta told a story of a bloom in the darkness. A story where the Council would be crushed. She added a light breeze to the wish. Nothing changed. There was only the whisper of her name again and the torment of not being able to breathe. Whatever was going on was spreading to her face. It was all numb, prickling with pins and needles. She reached for the missing pouch around her neck, but her arm wouldn't lift.

No, they wouldn't, she thought. She pushed to the outskirts of her mind, to the point where her senses met facts. She didn't get past the barrier. This was no dream; this was a hex. They'd trapped her inside her own mind. Judging by the shortness of her breath and the numbness of her face, she was slowly suffocating. Henrietta gasped, taking a shallow inhale in, causing her to ache all over. She tried again and again with the same results.

She shouldn't panic. It wouldn't serve her. So Henrietta concentrated on slowing things down.

"Henrietta," came again. It was as loud as if someone was shouting into her ear.

Henrietta attempted to sit up. Nothing moved. The hex didn't let her, meaning it had a spell of immobility attached to it. Easy to sneak past any wards. And she hadn't kept hers up. Her pouch being taken away was a bad excuse, but it mattered. She would laugh if she could. Here, inside the emptiness, there was only a hollow idea of laughter. Nothing actualized when the sound and motion were sealed inside her. Laughter was meant to be heard.

The Council had gone too far. This was against the rules. Or it was Ruby and Imogene. No, that didn't matter now. Her body was shaking. The tremors would take her if she didn't find the hex, but she wasn't a hexer.

There was pressure on her chest and around her mouth. They were trying to save her through conventional measures. It would be pointless.

"But thank you, Ida, for trying," she whispered.

This wasn't how Henrietta had pictured going. She'd wished she and Eurof could go back to Amanita in their final days, when the time was right. He could be the wise man who helped around the village, and she could roam the jungles and come back home when the dusk settled, and they would have their supper. Then one day, she would just stop breathing in her sleep and slip away. Her before him, because she was selfish and couldn't bear to be left alone with her grief. But before that, she would have made sure the Coven was independent and continued its work to preserve all the plants and flowers and be a safe harbor for all the persecuted souls.

Another tremor went through her.

"Henrietta."

There wasn't time. In a way, she'd lived a solid life. Not the greatest. Not the happiest. But she'd devoted it to something other than herself. It had to count for something.

No, this wasn't her talking. It had to be the hex. They were trying to subdue her and ensure that the Council would win. They wouldn't get away with her murder. A small voice inside her told her that they already had. She shouldn't fight the inevitable. This was how things were meant to go. If she just let go, everything would be better. Henrietta could already see the waves and the green jungle. It had to be waiting for her on the other side, or what was the point of existing at all? If it was going to end in nothingness, why create consciousness at all? Such a thought felt cruel. But the truth, the funny old thing, was that to some, nothingness was a blessing, finally being able to let go of oneself and the agony it brought. But how was one to measure such existence? A brief moment and then nothing, no hope, no solace. Just gone. Just like that.

Henrietta's body shook again. It heaved up and then crashed down. No, the Council couldn't win. There had to be a way. She searched for the compounds of the hex. She had been right. It was made to make her lose her mind while immobilized and while her respiratory systems failed.

Her gasps became shorter by the second, and she was starting to feel numb inside as well as out.

"Henrietta," the hex said again.

The hex had to be tied to her name. Such an elementary spell, yet there was no denying its effectiveness. The hex was made with extreme malice. Someone had put all their hate towards her inside it or borrowed hate from someone who abhorred her. There was a long list. She couldn't think of a way out of it. Not here. Not stuck inside her own mind with her spirit removed.

The pressure on her chest stopped. Ida had given up. But Henrietta was wrong. Quite the opposite, in fact. Her arm was lifted, and something was put inside her fingers. Then whatever it was, was raised over her heart.

"Fight," she heard Ida whisper into her ear.

"Don't," the hex said. "It's better if you go. Nobody needs you. You are nothing and will be nothing if you wake up. If you let go, you'll do a service to others. You won't be a burden. Now they worry. But once you are gone, all their problems, all your problems, will be solved. They, you, can be free. Think of them."

Henrietta snarled at the elementary spell. Yet it was draining all the strength out of her, and she couldn't focus. The pouch in her hand felt far away. Not hers. Ida had done the right thing, but it might be too late. She had been a lousy Mother. She'd let this happen. If she'd played things better, then maybe she wouldn't be in prison and the Coven wouldn't have been taken over by Ruby and Imogene. Maybe they would look after the witches better than she did.

Henrietta gasped for breath. No air entered her lungs.

Darkness was her friend. It would release her.

"Henrietta," the hex said.

Henrietta let go.

Sometimes the little escapes are those that make life worth living. Percy had slept the best sleep he'd had in a long time. He would have expected his broken ankle and the rest of the bruises to ache, but his body was free of any ailments. Though he was starting to notice the slight tightness in his chest, unsure why. He concentrated on watching Mr. Spooner, who snored in the next bed over, ignoring the reality wanting to catch up with him.

Percy's mind drifted to Mistress Lace and the herbs she'd used to cure him. He tried to recall all the Laces he knew. In the city, it was all about who belonged to whom. Names mattered. Allreads had been witches for eons, enduring the changing times. Percy's sister had ensured that the name would continue for another eternity. Not all Allreads were witches. The gift passed erratically along the family line. To his mother's dismay, Percy and his twin sister Margot had the blood. Their mother had wanted them to be anything else but witches, a life which had consumed their grandma and grandfather. To his mother, the gift was more of a curse than a blessing despite the fact that it kept their family name relevant in Necropolis. Not prominent, but good enough to be respected at the local shops and sought for a consult from their neighbors. Grandfather was a medium, as was Margot. There was always a need for such gifts in turbulent times.

None of which mattered here and now inside the ghoul city.

There was no point in dwelling on the past. Such an easy way to let bitterness consume you. A notion which had driven his mother to her early grave, tormented by something that couldn't be changed. That was why Percy had been sent to his grandma and Margot to his grandfather. Both lousy at raising small children. The only ones left of their so-called family were his estranged father, Margot and her children, and his grandfather, who still swindled money from his customers with positive life reviews.

And what good had he done as a witch? He had worked as a Monster
Hunter for the Council, letting them extend their control, allowing the
Council and Necropolis to dominate other nations. And here he was with
the monsters, the ghouls, who not long ago had been seen as free game for
anyone daring enough.[1]

Percy shut his eyes. He lay there waiting for something to happen while
fighting to clear his mind from the chatter it so readily produced.

Mistress Lace came to get them, waking Mr. Spooner up. Sirixh stood
outside waiting for them as well. Ready to show them around. The little
rest after the decision to let them have asylum for now had been a Kraken
send. Percy wouldn't have been able to take in the enormity of the ghoul
city without it. The city was magnificent. Not only due to its size and
architecture but due to its inhabitants. Here time ticked slower than above
ground. The ghouls took time to chat with them and casually got on with
their tasks, mending the city or looking after the little shops free for anyone's use. Sirixh and Philomena introduced them to the city's contribution
system. Everyone chipped in to the best of their abilities. It was just that
with the ghouls, the best of their abilities was beyond anything a human
could dream of.

Ghouls lived hundreds of years, meaning they had time to put their
ten thousand hours into anything without all the foolishness of getting
overly attached to ego, meaning, destiny, hierarchy, and emotions. All they
did was concentrate on pursuing understanding. Even with bookkeeping.
Percy was questioned by the senior ghouls about his knowledge when it
came to the art of tracking deeds. Ghouls had adopted these customs ever
since starting commerce with Necropolis.

Percy happily took the test to see if he could aid the ghouls in any way.
But the speed at which the ghouls could do calculus was astonishing. They

---

1. Mind you, there had been a lot of attempts, but none had been very successful.

seemed to do advanced mathematics Percy had never heard of, and when he looked at the numbers, they were out of this world, creating their own realities.[2] What Percy gathered was that the ghouls didn't like money. So the sum after every day was zero. Income and payments lined up in perfect equilibrium, a position highly sought after with any cost. The thing was that when Percy did the calculations, he always got a surplus. But that was wrong, according to the ghoul who was teaching him.

Percy had asked about what happened to the surplus.

"Mr. Allread, money goes where it should. Where it's needed, not wasted." That was the only answer he got.

"No one can be the master of it," the ghoul might add if he truly insisted.

"What about when it's in the red?"

He earned a shrug.

It never was. If there was ever a hint it might be, suddenly it wasn't, as some trader would notice that they'd overcharged the ghouls and correct their calculations. It was the most bizarre sort of magic Percy had ever seen. So he helplessly sat at the outdoor assembly's stones and tried to figure out the mathematics. The ghouls were overly patient with him while he felt like a halfwit.

Percy was happy to go with Philomena and Sirixh when they came to invite him for dinner. As they walked to Philomena's place, Percy learned Elmer had gotten an investigator's position. He was going through claims, requests, and accusations people above sent to the ghouls. Elmer reported

---

2. Which they actually did. The ghouls had discovered the power of numbers and their ability to shape the cosmos to their liking. It was all about wishing and wanting and showing to the tiny particles that governed everything that actually, according to this formula, they should be doing it like this and that. When they were shown the error of their ways, the particles corrected their behavior. Thus, there were several-ton pillars floating in the air in the ghoul city. In addition, Percy had noticed that the stones sang to the ghouls. They could make them into anything, even the impossible, as could the ghouls doing the bookkeeping.

peculiar things happening there as well. After a brief exchange of letters, everything seemed to go better for all, both the ghouls and the land
dwellers. Percy asked if there were any mathematical formulae embedded in
the letters. Elmer assured him that only the alphabet was involved, making
them both conclude that similar magic was happening with the words
ghouls used. Words that weren't even their native language.

Philomena laughed at their conversation. "My first months here made
me question everything I knew about the world, social behavior, and societies. The ghouls love their zero-impact policy. I know it's odd, but I have
kind of learned to like it. It's refreshing compared to how Necropolitans
make wealth from every part of your body, souls included."

Percy looked at the witch as she served them plates and poured wine into
small glasses.

"But it's not right. What they are doing is against the rules of mathematics. I feel ever so—"

"Helpless? Useless? I do too, but you'll learn to handle it," Philomena
said.

Percy wanted to argue that she wasn't useless. Her knowledge of all possible healing agents made her valuable. More for the humans, but ghouls
were picking things up, including the strange practice of mending their
bodies. They didn't seem to care if a finger or two was missing or if a tooth
fell out. They saw it as a normal process of time. A concept many of the
ghouls didn't believe in. They saw time as a by-product of the mind and
gravity and not an actual entity in the world.

"But—"

"Don't worry about it, Mr. Allread," Sirixh said. The ghoul had stayed
silent throughout the conversation. Percy had almost forgotten she was
there. Her words made Percy blush, seeing his tutor teaching him ever so
politely how bookkeeping was done all over again. Part of him wanted to
scream that he had been the best accountant the Council had had, that he

knew his numbers. Even more so, he wanted to scream that if the ghouls just followed the real numbers in his calculations, they could own the entire Necropolis. Still, his mentor had corrected his numbers, subtracted here and there, and the number had come to a perfect zero.

"But Sirixh, zero isn't an answer," Percy let out.

"You are right, Mr. Allread, it isn't an answer. It's a state."

Percy gave up and took his glass, washing down the bitter taste in his mouth with the perfectly rich red wine. He wished he could be in Necropolis, back where the numbers behaved. In the state he was in, he was willing to exchange his freedom and be tortured by the Council for numbers to be what they were. Flesh burning was flesh burning and not some cosmic alteration of states which tore apart reason. Yet Percy realized that burning flesh was more than a rug being pulled from under his feet. He could try to accept the alterations to reality rather than shut down just because of his preconceptions.

"But the numbers," he insisted.

"Try again, Mr. Allread. They will make sense when you see it." Sirixh offered him her napkin. "Forcing things and holding on to facts about how reality should be restricts you from seeing the flicker between stages of what is and what could be. When you let go, a new formula can arise to open up all the possibilities. You have to be patient and wait for your true composition."

Percy took the napkin and took a pencil from his pocket. He followed the numbers his teacher had shown him. When he ran through them, they made perfect sense, yet no sense at all. It was like the formulae were lying to him. There was no balance within the universe, no constant motion of gravity that pushed beings to obey.

"I give up," Percy sighed. The ghouls spoke of abstract forms. Such realizations were not for a literal mind. Percy had never been good at openness and creativity, nor at trusting his intuition.

"Don't, Mr. Allread. You will get there. I'm not trying to insult you. It's just that when you say this is possible and this is impossible, this is true and this is false, this is how everything is done, and this is how we, you, and everything is, you have already lost sight of the world in its fullest form," Sirixh said.

Sirixh didn't lie. Percy had seen that the ghouls lived as they preached. They sat for hours upon hours listening to their young ask questions. They let themselves ask silly questions, wonder aloud, and most importantly, play. Percy had seen throughout the day the ghouls jumping around, goofing with each other. The answer he had gotten from his teacher was that it was all done to free up their senses. When the mind got older, it got stuck. A normal course of events, because stability and "truths" made the world more secure, life more predictable, and interactions more accessible. It was just that. It also caused the mind to stagnate.

"I think we should let our guest rest. It has been a long day," Philomena said and stood up. She collected the plates. Percy hurried to help her.

Afterward, Philomena guided Percy and Elmer to a beach. "Seeing the stars will help you clear your mind," Philomena had insisted. Percy had been ready to call it a night, but Elmer had wanted to go. Sirixh wasn't with them. She'd received a call to see her mother.

They walked through the city towards the secluded tunnels leading out to a private beach where Philomena had promised to take them to ease the pressure several tons of rock being above you put on the mind. Around them, ghouls marked their path but made no move to interact. They went back to whatever they were doing, some creating art, others debating about everything, and the remaining cultivating the landscape by raising more stones to hover over the city where small green mushroom patches were grown.

Percy clutched his hands, ignoring his desire to ask about the route they were taking. He had to trust Philomena's navigating skills and that no melancholic dinosaurs or hungry spiders would get in their way. The witch chatted on to brighten the mood.

He hated that he'd turned from a functional Monster Hunter into a jumpy, disorganized civilian. His mantra about preparation and reality was now gone. The ghouls didn't plan. They sat patiently and waited to see what would happen and then acted, but only if necessary. What they saw as a necessity was the common good of the community and the pursuit of knowledge.

Percy counted his steps.

"The beach will clear your mind," Philomena insisted again.

"I'm sure it will," Percy agreed, more for her than him.

Elmer just followed in silence.

"It's just around the corner. I often come here to feel more human. Sometimes the ghouls are too much and their city feels suffocating, but whenever I see the sea and the stars, I understand," Philomena said.

"That sounds lovely." Percy wanted to say more, but Elmer grabbed his arm.

"Someone is coming," the man said.

They all turned around to see Sirixh hanging from the ceiling, making noise for their sake. She let go and dropped in front of them.

"Sirixh?" Philomena asked.

"You need to come back. There's news."

"What's going on?" Percy asked.

"Mother will explain." That was all they got out of the ghoul. She took them back to the ghouls' town hall. The room was full again, and another debate was taking place.

Gwerrusxh lifted her claw up to silence the crowd as they arrived.

"Mother," Percy said and bowed his head.

"Nonsense, but I'll allow it this time. We have newssss." The ghoul seemed to prolong the word. "The Council has drawn up their response.

They are willing to let the matter go if you keep silent and stay here for your remaining life, but if either of you ever surfaces, you will be executed. All stated in a highly legal way. They have attached documents for you to sign."

Percy and Elmer glanced at each other. Elmer took a step forward.

"Unfortunately," Gwerrusxh began, stopping Elmer in his tracks, "that's not all. I have a report that Mr. Thurston is in the mayor's custody. The Council headquarters have been invaded by the Save the Otis Group, and there have been reports of violence. The Mother of the Coven has been arrested, and there has been an attempt on her life. And there has been a duel at the mayor's mansion. Cruxh is there, but the results are not known."

Percy stared at the ghoul in stunned silence. "What?" Percy let out and then added with more conviction, "I have to go. This is my fault. I brought Mr. Thurston to Necropolis. He's my responsibility."

"We can't leave. The Council will kill us," Elmer protested.

"I have to. His life is my duty."

CHAPTER TWENTY-FOUR

NOTHING A GOOD CUP OF TEA CAN'T FIX

Sometimes the honesty of a good lynching made people think there was justice after all. But was it a lie to round up the kings and queens and their lackeys and string them up on the lampposts, or was it the only justice the meek could muster? Otis watched as the mayor widened her stance in her study. She stood there in the middle of the red carpet, ready to defend herself from whoever was coming. They were getting closer. Otis could sense them. There were the crashes. Otis was sure people had died, but who was an entirely different question. The constant pressure of spirits raging loose in the house was giving Otis a headache. It had been a long time since Otis was in contact with anything other than his prison walls with their illumination and wards. The real world of necromancy was too much. But he would be lying if he said he didn't find the spirits' static charge intoxicating.

The mayor's tattoos burned as the assassins sent their attacks forward, searching for Petula. Petula's fingers flickered as she held herself against the spirit tidal wave. She kept muttering incantations under her breath. They sounded like mathematical formulae. And to Otis's dismay, he could follow them. She spoke of bending the invisible world of air and tiny particles around her to push away the spirits and the malicious attacks coming with them. She spoke of numbers and subtractions and divisions and integrals, on and on.

And Otis was the monster who had used souls mechanically?

Otis watched as a ghostly sword shattered the aura the mayor was creating. It was impressive, but it came at a cost. The color was starting to drain out of the mayor's face. She looked as dead as the spirits around them.

The spirits sniffed him out too. Mostly as an afterthought. Otis got his wards up and fast. He retreated to the back of the room, behind the desk, glancing over his shoulder at the window. The wards there had burned to the ground, but still, the window made him want to scream. She had added something else there. Something preventing any necromancer from leaving the room.

Otis grimaced. He tried to decipher her spell, but it gave him a zap, making his whole body convulse from the charge. He tried again with the same result, and as he tried the third time, the door to the room burst open, and a man in a long leather coat stepped in. He had his black hair loose around his bewildered face. Entering the building hadn't come cheap. He had blood stains all over his clothing and face, as if he wore the death of the mayor's guards as proof of his excellence.

Otis ducked behind the desk, his whole right arm prickling with pins and needles. He could see the mayor and the man there, but he hoped they were paying no attention to him as he massaged his hand back to life. He needed to find another way to break through the window.

"Mr. Wicks," Petula said.

"Mayor," the man said, tilting his head with respect.

"I didn't expect you, but I have to say I'm not surprised they would choose you to kill me. How's Agatha?" the mayor asked. The air around her was on fire. She was keeping the ghosts away. One by one, sending them back to eternal damnation. Forever to be unknown to this world. A destiny waiting for all one day. Even the undeads in the city wouldn't last for eternity.

The spirits weren't leaving willingly.

Otis watched as both the necromancers used the dead, who'd lingered in this world in hopes of Kraken only knew what, for their own games. All the statistical charges with the colors only necromancers could see were beautiful. They were like the black powder, potassium nitrate, charcoal, and sulfur cocktails he had blown into the sky as a kid to amuse the other children in the neighborhood.

"She's fine," Mr. Wicks spat out.

"Ah, this isn't a social call then?" Petula asked and took a step back, wavering. She added a litany of calculations to her phrase, stopping the attack Mr. Wicks had sent forward and making the man take a step back as Petula turned his attempt against him. Another display of colors with a heavy tone of purple illuminated the room as the spirits flew at the man's wards.

Mr. Wicks groaned.

"Does Agatha know you are here? No, that's not important. So the Council thought you could lead our fine city then?" Petula asked, sounding out of breath. Her posture collapsed.

Otis had to lift his hands against his ears as the spirits screamed their death wails. He let go of his ears as deadly hands rose from the floor, trying to catch his ankles. He leapt onto the chair, away from the hands, which kept tugging on the chair, rocking it. Otis got onto the desk, meeting the eyes of Mr. Wicks.

They knew each other. Vernon Wicks was doing his doctoral dissertation when Otis studied his first year at the university. The necromancer was one of the prominent Wicks, who had founded Necropolis. And he never let anyone forget that. He, by right, should be the leader of the city of the undead. He had the arrogance to match it. He'd shown as much at the university, making Otis's existence miserable. Vernon had to be the best. He'd ensured that by dueling with everyone who showed any promise. Otis had shown some promise, and he'd paid the price for it. Luckily, while the university accepted duels, they frowned upon killing the opponent. Vernon had incapacitated Otis for a week. He had barely been able to walk. Otis's friends had carried him to the dorm, where he lay for the next day in pure agony, fighting against a spirit infestation.

Vernon grinned when he laid eyes on Otis. His eyes seemed to spell that he was glad to get rid of both of them at the same time.

The table shook as the hands kept rising against it. They'd already latched on to the mayor's legs, pulling her down. But she managed to remain upright from sheer force of will. She wouldn't last. Vernon had perfected the talent. He commanded the hands individually, meaning the mayor would have to concentrate on them individually as well while keeping her wards up.

Vernon kept the grin on his face, but it was starting to look like a deep snarl as he gasped for breath. The mayor was giving him a run for his money. The stupid man had thought she wasn't up to it. They would kill each other, and... skull fuck, Otis thought. He could do whatever he liked. He could walk away from here. The paper wards the mayor had put up were burned to charcoal. He could walk through the front door and have his freedom. Or he could stand his ground.

Otis stood up on the desk, which kept shaking. Otis waved his hand over the desk, and the shaking stopped. The hands retreated as he stepped down. He looked at the mayor and then at Vernon.

Once the written word was invented, power dynamics got flipped on their head. There was no more trusting what someone could do when they got hold of a pen and paper. They could make their thoughts multiply and spread wide and far. So the Ministry of Truths, censorship, and propaganda sneaked in, just to be on the safe side. There was no telling what the citizens might get into their small heads. If you think about how clever the species has to be to invent such institutions, you really start to question the whole cleverness bit and start to think along the lines of shades of madness. It has to be the controlling part doing all the talking. There's no telling what kind of bastard the future is.

Raul looked out the window of the haunted house. He was not sure what to think about the whole future part. He was still tangled up in the uncertainty. But he was starting to get used to it. And he had written it. His white whale, his holy grail, his word. The full article about the Council and how they organized their power.

Raul wasn't sure if he had actually written it or if it had manifested itself. Now he wasn't sure what he was supposed to do with it. Rugus and Monty, as the two men called themselves, although he doubted those were their real names,[1] were somewhere in the Gothic manor. He hesitated to place the article in their hands. Whoever got it was in the position to negotiate with the Council and bring them to their knees.

Necropolis would riot if the truth got out. Truth about the undeads, the board, the Monster Hunter Force, the mayor. The board was composed of old families unwilling to let go of their clutch on the city and using the Council as their base for power, fame, and money. And the undead... Raul bit his lip. He had stayed on the facts even when he could have used adjectives to paint a highly vivid picture of the Council to win over the minds of all. But even with the most heinous megalomaniac dictator, calling their actions a tantrum, you were stretching the truth thin. He trusted his readers to make up their own minds. That was what he wanted.

---

1. This was where he was wrong. They were the given names their parents had chosen for them, no matter how unfortunate they might be.

He wanted his word to spread wide and far.

Raul got up, making the chair underneath him creak. He paused to see if the two men had noticed the sound. There was no other noise. He slowly got out of the chair and reached for the article he'd just written. He folded it inside his jacket along with the folders he'd stolen from the Council. Raul got as far as the door when he saw the biggest of the men standing at the entrance. The man looked as if he had been woken from a night of sleep or taken away from an angry conversation. Either way, he had a somewhat constipated look on his face.

"Leaving so soon, Mr. Porter?" Monty asked.

"Wouldn't dream of it, Mr...."

"Emerson." The man smiled.

He was a dead man. "It was kind of you to rescue me from the wolf and lend me a typing machine, but I think I should be heading back to clear my name," Raul tried.

"A very important task. We are not trying to detain you here in any way. You can find your way back into the city by following the road to the south," Monty said.

"But?" Raul asked.

"There are no buts, Mr. Porter. We were asked to keep you alive. We have done that."

Raul looked at the man, astonished. This wasn't how the world worked. Guardian faeries, however big and hairy they might be, didn't just manifest out of nothingness and keep you alive. There always had to be a payment. And there actually had been, if Raul remembered correctly. He'd done something for their master, as they had said upon their meeting. Raul had almost forgotten the small yet important detail. The nature of that something was never mentioned. Raul should press on to find the truth. For the first time in his life, he wondered if he wanted to know the truth. There were truths that were better kept in darkness. Not for a second did he believe in such reasoning. He would be equally guilty whether he knew it or not. But payment had been made, and he preferred it that way. To have someone hold goodwill over him was the worst thing imaginable. Even worse than being eaten alive or stolen by Old Man Death in the dead of night.

"Thank you, I guess," Raul muttered. "What about...?" Raul asked, not sure what to say without sounding like a whiny, scared twit out of Necropolis.

"The werewolf, Mr. Porter?" Monty offered.

"That and the ghoul officers?" Raul added.

The giant shrugged. "Maybe your illegal trespassing and alleged manslaughter have been forgotten, who knows. They might be irrelevant. It's a busy news day out there," Monty said. "But if you feel like staying for a night or two, the house is at your disposal." As Monty said the last statement, something howled outside.

Dawn was already fighting its way out from the darkness. The faint light was seldom strong enough to keep the bogeymen away.

Raul shivered. "I..." he said.

"Rugus is making tea. There's enough for us all. There should be some of those little sandwiches as well. And if you don't feel hungry, upstairs, there's a bed ready." Monty gave a slight smile, which was as smug as they came.

"Tea and a bed sound nice."

Monty turned around, and Raul followed him through the house to the kitchen. He could already see the sandwiches and the steaming pot of tea. But he didn't get quite that far. Monty turned around to face him.

"Now, it would seem like a waste if your words weren't read. Might I take a look?" the man asked.

Raul sighed and handed the article to the man as the giant held his hand out. Monty kept his hand outstretched, and Raul handed him the folders and his notebook as well. Then he was escorted around the table, and Rugus pushed a plate in front of him with a hearty sandwich on it. Raul bit in and drank his tea while the giant read his words in silence.

"So?" Raul asked. He was chewing the last bite of his sandwich. The haunted house moaned around him with its forgotten ghosts and the wood that had seen good use. Raul looked at the empty plate, contemplating if he should ask for seconds from Rugus, who had made the first divine sandwich. It had been savory, salty, and fresh. Raul glanced at Rugus, who hovered beside the round table next to him and Monty. The kitchen was warm from the stove lit in the corner. There was something brewing on it, making the room smell homey.

Monty looked up from the article and reached for his second cup of tea. "So?" Monty repeated in a similar fashion.

"Was it any good?"

"I wouldn't say it was bad. Some might think it's very riveting reading..."

"Not you, then?"

"My opinion doesn't matter, Mr. Porter." Monty handed the papers back to him.

"Everyone's opinion matters," Raul said louder than he'd meant to.

All he got as a response was Monty's raised eyebrow, and then, after a long silence, "If you say so. You are more educated than I am on these matters."

"Are you messing with me?"

"Wouldn't think of that, sir." Monty got up. "But there's no time for this; we have company." As the giant said that, there was a knock on the front door.

Rugus wiped his hands on the kitchen towel he was clutching and lowered it onto the counter next to the stove. He cracked his knuckles.

"What do you want me to do?" Raul asked.

"They are here for you. So you better follow us to the door. No need to make the bad situation any worse."

Raul swallowed. "I thought..."

"It's time, Mr. Porter. We can't keep playing house here forever, and you are not in mortal danger anymore."

"How do you know that?"

"He has a sense for these things," Rugus offered.

All Monty did was shrug. The giant turned and headed out of the kitchen to the foyer with its ancestral paintings, candle chandeliers, and painted glasswork. Rugus followed the man. Neither of them forced Raul to do the same, but he did it anyway. But before he did, he hid the article and the folders in the giant's jacket, which hung from the backrest of his chair.

Monty pulled the door open when Raul arrived in the foyer. Raul held his breath and waited to see the Council's witches with their official uniform, including the feared capotain hat. Instead, he saw a smallish creature with talons reaching to the ground. The thing was wearing a blue police uniform fitted to its deformed, hunched figure.

"Good evening, gentlemen," Cruxh said and corrected his posture. "May I come in?" Behind the detective, there were more men and ghouls in blue uniforms. There was even one lanky bugbear that was bigger than Monty, yet somehow he looked scrawny.

"Mr. Cruxh," Monty said.

Rugus just grunted.

"To what do we owe the pleasure?" Monty continued, blocking the entrance.

Raul couldn't help but notice that there was a strange balance between Cruxh and the men. That somehow the ghoul knew who he was dealing with and didn't push it. But also, Rugus and Monty, knowing that Cruxh knew who they were, were taking the piss out of the situation. It was not in the words per se, but more in the way the men and the ghoul danced around each other: the posture, the tone, and the glances.

"I have a warrant for Sir Raul Emerett Porter's arrest. He's wanted for murder."

"I didn't do it," Raul let out. He never thought he would be the type who would shout such nonsense. He had always thought he would be the one who went quietly with the police and only at the station asked for his lawyer.

"Nevertheless, I need to take you in, sir," Cruxh said as politely as one could.

Raul clutched the leg of his trousers. "Yes, of course," he said after waiting for Monty or Rugus to say something. The two giants didn't make a move. But it was clear from how Rugus held himself that the man was ready to go a few rounds with the ghouls if Monty gave the signal. And somehow Raul believed that the man stood a chance of coming out of it unharmed. The two men were strange beyond anything Necropolis had ever seen. They were as normal as men came, yet normalcy was stranger here than having fur or eyes as dark as the coldest sea.

"Sir, we can forget the cuffs, if you willingly follow me to the transportation," Cruxh offered.

"I will," Raul said, again glancing at the two men, who kept their silence. He took a step forward, darting another glance at the men. They hadn't moved. "Okay, then," Raul said, the last syllable rising into a question rather than a statement.

"Okay, then," Monty repeated and stepped from the door, letting Raul leave.

"Oh," Raul said and followed the ghoul out of the old haunted mansion. He made a quick glance behind him at the door, seeing Monty close it after him. The sound made Raul flinch. Raul was sure this wasn't how it was supposed to go. He turned and faced the police transportation and let the ghoul escort him inside. Raul took the seat nearest to the head of the small wooden hovel on wheels. The plank underneath him made him feel like time had stopped, as if he had arrived in a strange dimension where numbness overwrote the present. It was all the uncertainty pouring in with the realization that he couldn't control the situation.

"Don't worry, Mr. Porter, we will sort this out. I promise you that, sir," Cruxh said.

Raul was sure the man had sighed as he said the words, as if he was as numb as Raul felt, or maybe more like disappointed at the reality of things.

"Thank you, detective," Raul said. He'd almost gone with the man's name, but that had felt wrong. Ghouls didn't have surnames, but addressing the man by his first name was out of the question. Raul squeezed his knees, trying to be more present, to switch back to being the reporter he was. The one who found everything interesting. The one who knew there was a story behind every situation. Cruxh could tell him so many things about the city and what was going on. How the ghoul had been running from one place to another, the city and his chief trusting him and him alone not to get this wrong. It was just that even if Raul tried, the man was a vault only a few were privy into. But Raul didn't try. He was starting to feel like he was running out of stories.

"Just doing my duty, sir," Cruxh answered.

"May I ask who I supposedly killed?" Raul asked.

There was a deep frown on the detective's face. The man seemed to taste his words before he opened his mouth again. "I'm not sure, sir. A woman wearing a red overcoat and walking skirt, from the sound of it, with a blue blouse and felt hat. With a petite nose and a strict gaze."

"Sandy," Raul let out.

"Sandy, sir?" Cruxh repeated.

"No, I mean... I'm not sure what I mean. What do you mean?"

The ghoul coughed. "There's no body, sir. Just an eyewitness stating that you were found standing over a dead body only a moment after you were witnessed arguing with said person. A knife was mentioned, and something about madness." The ghoul was clearly offering him more than he should. Raul wondered if this was a tactic or an involuntary betrayal.

"I... I don't understand." Raul scratched his head only to notice that he'd left his hat back at the mansion. He would miss it. It was a gift. The only good thing he had ever received in his life. Though again, some might say that was an overstatement. Once again, his mind was playing tricks with his perception of things. It was too easy to remember the bad instead of the good. Raul had had a good life compared to most Necropolitans, who worked hard for the little they owned just to live a bleak, small life. And it was Raul's own downfall if he'd pissed it all away by turning to the bottle. At the mention of booze, good Kraken, Raul needed a drink to sober up.

"We got several reports that there had been an incident. By the time our officers got to the scene, the body was missing. And yes, we checked for zombies, but there wasn't even a whiff of it," Cruxh said.

No one could turn someone into a zombie that quickly. Not that Raul had heard of. "But your officers had to have smelled something," Raul said.

The ghoul shook his head. "Nothing, sir."

"Then why am I being dragged into the station?"

"We have no doubt that a crime happened, and you were involved. We need your statement, for now, and we can't have you running around the city and getting into places you are not allowed. Not when such acts might turn the restless situation more dire."

"I see," Raul said.

"I hope you do, Mr. Porter."

CHAPTER TWENTY-FIVE

MURDER, I GUESS

And there it was, a branch pushing and growing inside the darkness, coming towards her. Henrietta made the branch grow a leaf, then more leaves, and it came fully alive. It was lilac from her childhood garden, in full bloom, with its purple flowers and strong, sweet smell Henrietta always associated with spring. Early tiny blue flowers began to grow around where the tree stood alone in the grass. She let the image take over every part of her. The roots inched into her lungs, making Henrietta's whole body heave as she got a solid breath in. The grass underneath her feet waved in the light breeze. Henrietta pushed her toes into the ground and shut her eyes. She searched for the hex. It was on the outskirts of her mind. The hex was feeble now she had her pouch in her hand.

Henrietta twisted the branches around the hex. It tried to resist her, but Henrietta knew that if she gave in, she would die. So she strengthened the tree and its roots, giving it history and care. She wove around the tree the memories of her childhood. All the gardens she'd visited. She gave it the soul of the lilac tree from her childhood home, which meant everything to her. She strengthened the sweet spring smell of the bloom. The hex finally shattered as the branches pressed harder against it. Before letting it fully go, Henrietta tore into it like an open corpse. She had been pretty sure she would find Mika's handiwork—one of Ruby Granger's followers—but there was just an empty space where a line should have been. Whoever had cast the hex was powerful enough to hide themselves. But it had come from the Coven; that much was evident in the lines drawn inside the hex. Not the Council, then. Not directly. Yet Henrietta wouldn't put it past Ruby to ask for compensation if Henrietta had died. But she hadn't. Not yet, at least. If there was another hex to come, then there was a chance. She had barely made it out alive from this one.

Henrietta lay there, feeling the prison mattress pressing against her back. She was fully awake, but she kept her eyes shut. She needed that one moment before she faced what waited for her. Henrietta dug the soles of her feet harder into the mattress and let herself breathe. There came a gentle touch on her shoulder. Henrietta kept her eyes closed but lifted her hand to the caring hand and squeezed it.

"Thank you," she wheezed.

"Thank Kraken you are alive," Ida replied, kneeling next to her, still holding her shoulder. Behind the banker, Annabella had cornered the prison doctor in the farthest corner. Silas Philpot tried to peer over the undead. Annabella did her best to block the doctor. The warden hovered at the foot of the bed, looking ghostly pale.

Henrietta glanced at the pouch in her hand. Lilac flowers poked out from it. Henrietta squeezed it tight, feeling the smooth fabric mush against the soil. *Home*, Henrietta thought. Her locus.

"You did the right thing," she said to Ida.

The banker's worried expression turned into a stoic one. "Anyone would have done the same if they had half a brain," she quickly replied and glanced at the warden.

"That may be, but it was you who did it. Thank you, Ida. I owe you my life."

"The hex clearly made your head soft. Now stop being so dramatic and get up. We still need to get out of this prison run by imbeciles." Ida withdrew from Henrietta and stood up. She crossed her hands and stared at Henrietta uncomfortably.

Henrietta pushed up to lean against the wall. Her breathing was still laborious. She was careful to keep her posture. The doctor complained about being kept away from the patient. Henrietta nodded at Annabella, who let the doctor loose.

Henrietta braced herself for what was to come.

Silas Philpot rushed to her, taking her pulse and doing what the doctor felt was a fitting cure for... that was the thing, the doctor couldn't find a rational explanation for what had happened. He did his best to ignore the pouch in Henrietta's hand and the bloom poking out of it. He moaned and sighed as he tried to piece together what had happened, spouting claims like Henrietta was letting her hallucinations run her life.

Henrietta didn't interrupt the man. She even followed the doctor's finger when he asked. But her mind wasn't in it. She listened to Ida and Annabella reason with the warden that this had been a direct attempt to murder Henrietta, and they demanded better protection and their lawyer to be present. They also wanted to make a statement to the press to let them know what had happened. The warden didn't know how to act. He squirmed under the two women's demands. Eventually, he succumbed, even agreeing to make the doctor leave Henrietta alone and leave with the warden. Silas Philpot complained, but he couldn't argue against a clear command.

When the two men had left, Annabella and Ida rushed to Henrietta's side.

"I'm fine. It's over."

"But—"

"Someone from the Coven tried to have me killed. Ruby and Imogene have taken over the Coven and..."

Annabella laid her undead hand over Henrietta's. Henrietta patted the dead hand and gave it a squeeze. "Don't worry. I won't let them get away with this and have the Coven." She would make damn sure they didn't. Henrietta let the seed of her thoughts travel through the same network she'd used in the warden's office, finding her way to the Coven. She made sure her lilac bloomed in the gardens to strengthen those witches who believed in her and who stood by her.

Death would be a lot easier if there was no question of what next. Necropolitans had found a way to circumvent such uncertainty, and funnily enough, there was a huge market for it. There would be no resurrection for Petula if she died. It was this and the great beyond. Petula heard Otis getting off the desk, but she was too busy taking down Vernon's hands. Petula's whole body shook as she tried to stand in the middle of the red carpet, not letting the hands pull her down. The pressure they were putting on her legs made resisting agonizing. The spirits she pushed against the necromancer were making a dent in the man's concentration. It was still not enough for him to let go. The tattoos on her skin were burning. She suppressed a scream. The tattoos on her legs felt like liquid steel. Petula bit her teeth together, concentrating on the next command.

Petula opened her mouth, but no voice came out. Just a gurgle. The hands underneath her tugged Petula to the ground. She collapsed on the floor. Petula elbowed herself up, but the individual hands seized her arms and legs, pinning her down. The carpet she had ever so carefully chosen was torn to tatters. What was left was shreds and the hardwood floor, which scraped her skin. Petula forced herself to watch as Otis stepped over her, unaffected by the ghostly hands.

The necromancer made sure not to glance at her.

Petula bit her lip as the hands burrowed deeper into her skin. She focused all her effort on fighting, but her thoughts were overly attached to the fact that Otis had stepped over her and was leaving. Petula didn't care for her first thought nor for the second one. Her third thought said aloud, "Critting Kraken shit." Petula slammed her fist against the floor, causing a shock wave to roll over the hands, making some of them let go of her. There were enough to keep her down, but at least she could now lift her head up. Otis hadn't escaped through the door as Petula had expected. The man was facing Vernon, and by his side was a human-like form. Otis had forced the dead around him to become a fleshy fettle. The thing had its muscles out. They looked like they were made of rancid meat oozing out of a nonfunctional skeleton. There was a distinctive smell of sulfur.

Vernon had turned the hands that weren't pinning Petula down against the fettle. The creature howled, yet moved towards the necromancer, stomping the hands. Vernon sent more to counter it, but the fettle just howled and reached closer to the necromancer.

Vernon's eyes went wide, and he looked like he was ready to throw up.

Otis stood behind the flesh fettle, moving in place as if he were the thing, the master behind the machine.

Petula snorted. That was what the man did. Make a machine out of anything and everything. There was nothing but a lever inside the creature to make it move. No will. No spirit. Just motion for motion's sake determined by what? That was the greatest question there was. But you can't prove what doesn't exist; nor can you prove something you don't know exists.

It was clear as day that Vernon had run out of juice trying to kill her. The man's posture had slumped, and he was backing away. Even the hands he was using to pin her down were getting weaker with every breath he took. Petula made Vernon's hands release their grip on her. She sent them back where they'd come from. By the time she stood up, the fettle had seized Vernon and was squeezing the life out of him. The necromancer thudded to the floor, releasing with him the spirits he'd brought into the mansion.

Petula drew them towards her, making a spiral out of the dead to surround her. They were more than willing to cooperate, having lost their master and the false promise of resurrection Vernon had given them.

Otis and the fettle turned to face her. There was no emotion in the being's eyes. It had only one will, and that was Otis's.

"Are you planning to kill me as well?" Petula asked, glancing at Agatha's brother collapsed against the bookshelf. Vernon's fall had sent the books tumbling from the shelves. They lay scattered around him.

Otis just stared at her. So did the fettle. Otis's eyes twitched, and the fettle moved onward, mimicking the nudges Otis made. The smell of the thing was getting stronger the closer it got.

Petula wanted to throw up, but she forced a smile onto her lips. "So you think you are up to being the mayor? It won't grant you that freedom you seek."

The fettle stopped. Otis stared at her and then at the thing. Silence lingered there between them. Petula didn't press on or move. What she did was draw the spirits closer to her, weaving a tighter knit for her protection. She wasn't planning to kill anyone today, but she wasn't going to die either.

"No," the necromancer finally said.

"No?"

"No." Otis glanced behind him at Vernon.

"Don't worry, you didn't kill him. I made sure of that," Petula said.

Otis let his eyes linger on the fallen necromancer. He said nothing. Just stood there, as did the fettle.

"I didn't do it for you, if you are wondering. Miss Wicks wouldn't like her brother dying," Petula said.

"You were protecting him this whole time?" Otis asked, returning his attention to her.

Petula nodded. She had. The fool had almost gotten himself killed by carelessly throwing around his spirits like that. To be honest, it hadn't been easy to keep him alive and fight him at the same time. She'd almost gotten herself killed. Petula's first thought insisted that getting herself killed just because she didn't want to look bad in the eyes of Agatha was moronic. She had every right to kill the man or, better yet, let Vernon get himself killed. He was clearly stupid enough to believe the lies the system told him about power, the Council, that he could be their good little leader without strings attached. A person like that should die.

"Shut up," Petula said, making Otis raise his eyebrow. "Not you, obviously. Yes, I protected him. I don't care for unnecessary sacrifices. If they think a necromancer like him can take me down, then they are even more out of their minds and out of touch than I thought. Now, Mr. Thurston, you could have killed me, or at least tried."

"I have never been driven to be a moron. And clearly, for wanting to rule Necropolis, the requirement is to be one."

"Ah, yes. I'm afraid so," Petula said. "Indeed, only someone completely out of their mind would think you can rule something as complex as a nation."

"No?"

"Just guidance, Mr. Thurston, and then hope for the best."

"And there I thought becoming a leader would grant every wish my little heart could desire."

"Oh, it does. Don't get me wrong. It makes things a lot easier. Others take you more seriously, but only a fool thinks they can turn everyone around them into puppets. Cooperation, Mr. Thurston, that seems to be the key."

"How unfortunate."

"I entirely agree. Now, I think I need to get Mr. Wicks a physician." As Petula said that, she made the ghosts around her surge onto her desk and explode it. Splinters flew around her, and the hem of her walking skirt pressed against her calves. "And clean up the mess," she added and felt a lot better, as the excess spirits and their ignited rage had been defused.

"And me?"

"I'll ask the servants to make you a bed. It seems the hearing will happen tomorrow. No escaping the mob." Petula turned around to take the small servant bell from the remnants of her desk. She rang it. "If you would, as we wait, you might as well make that thing... disappear." Petula glanced at the fleshy fettle.

Otis frowned.

Petula took a deep breath in. "You tried already. Didn't you?"

"Yes, that might have happened."

"And?"

"And it seems to be getting a mind of its own, and you know, when it comes to life, it seems to be all that anyone is raving about. So..."

"So it stays. Dismantling it would mean—"

"Murder, I guess." Otis finished her sentence. Not that it was what Petula would have chosen.

"Yes, that would be the word used when talking about a sentient being. I guess existence and survival need a working mind."

"It would seem so," Otis said, sighing loudly.

Mr. Colton stepped out of the bookshelf at the same moment.

"Miss?" he asked as if nothing had happened. He was still carrying Her in his lap. The cat didn't seem pleased about being in the man's arms, and it struggled free, hopping to the floor. The cat trotted next to Petula and brushed against her leg. Then it started to lick its paw as if no brushing had ever happened, occasionally stealing a glance at Otis and his flesh fettle.

"Mr. Wicks needs some medical attention, and Mr. Thurston needs a bed. Also, we have an extra guest this evening, who—" Petula lifted her gaze from the cat to the thing Otis had created.

"Mort," the fettle groaned.

Petula raised her eyebrow but continued without missing a beat. "Mort here needs some assistance as well. Not sure what kind of assistance, but I think it will become apparent soon enough."

"As you wish, ma'am," Mr. Colton said, unfazed by anything. "Shall I send for Mr. Cruxh as well? A few of the city guards have died and..."

"Yes, yes. Do that."

Mr. Colton walked through the room, past the fettle and Otis. "You two follow me," the man said.

Petula watched them leave and wondered if everything had to be named to exist. Did life, reality, and everything always form a consciousness? Was it a requirement for the form to function? And when the function ran its course, did the consciousness fade as well?

The cat eyed Petula.

"Yes, yes," she answered. "Let's get you food, but first we need to deal with him." Petula nodded towards Vernon.

The cat shifted its focus to the fallen necromancer. The cat was clearly conscious and highly sure of itself. Petula had seen it dream. The question was just what did it dream about? A big rat or some vast complex dreams about existence? Not that Petula was very sure about the whole existence part. It came with a lot of annoying moving parts—like people.

Petula walked to Vernon and lowered herself next to the man. His pulse was there, weak but going steady.

"You'll live, I'm afraid. Don't know what they will do with you now. I have heard that where they cast failed necromancers isn't such a nice place to be. But at least you didn't die by my hand."

Petula waited there for Mr. Colton to come back with the physician. What she got first was Cruxh and his officers. The ghoul had a deep frown on his face, like he was going to have the worst headache of his life any minute now, despite the fact that dead flesh didn't really get headaches or worst days.

"Miss Mayor?" Cruxh asked.

Petula raised her eyebrow. The ghoul was usually more eloquent. Oh well, she thought.

"We had an intruder who thought they could fix all the problems by killing me. I'm afraid I'm still standing, but it seems not all of my guards are. They need to be transported somewhere where their last wills can be read and resurrected accordingly after you have assessed how they came to lose their lives."

The ghoul scratched his head. "And this one?"

"Still alive, and ready to be taken to the Council after one of my physicians has a peek."

"Good."

The police couldn't charge Vernon. That was the law despite him having failed in his attempt. It was his legal right to try to assassinate Petula and claim the title of leader of Necropolis. That had not always been the case. Imprisonment and public execution had been the previous go-to for any failed attempt. But the law was now removed. Not because it was an unusually cruel punishment. No. No would-be assassin had ever survived before. No necromancer had shown mercy for their opponent before Petula, if you didn't include how Petula had gotten the position. But that was a special case, and it was all down to the fact that Minta Stopford had gotten fed up with running a nation of undeads and its necromancers.

The law was removed as an antiquated remnant of archaic methods no one cared for. No drama. Just execution. Yet to Petula, the removal had given her hope. She saw it as the first step towards Necropolitans coming to grips with a modern concept of choosing a leader: elections. Though she was starting to think she was the only one with a modern way of thinking. Necropolis liked its tyrants, as long as they played ball with their citizens. Then it was anyone's right to kill the fellow by any means necessary. In a way, you could say that the constant fear of death kept the leaders somewhat honest. But then again, the constant fear of death made making hard decisions slightly harder. But it was nothing private armed guards, extortion, and bribery couldn't fix.

Petula groaned.

"Miss?" Cruxh asked.

"Just thoughts, Mr. Cruxh. They seem to be the bane of my existence. I fear I could do without them."

"I have heard that one before, miss. The root of all evil, some would say."

"There's that too. I was thinking more along the lines of making everything unnecessarily complex."

"Aah, I see, miss." Without missing a beat, Cruxh barked in his own language for the ghouls to search the house and get the corpses. "What is the alternative?"

"Bliss, some might say. Yet I can't wholly agree."

"No, miss?"

"No, Mr. Cruxh. One has to live up to the requirements and deal with them. Changing the chemistry and the history of it all would require one of those people who call themselves shrinks, and anyone calling themselves one won't get anywhere near my head."

"Wouldn't recommend it, miss."

"So how are things in the wide world beyond these walls, Mr. Cruxh?"

The ghoul scratched the back of its head and said after a long pause, "Chaotic. I am required to be in five places simultaneously and wanted in none."

"But if you didn't..." Petula shook her head and stopped her sentence.

The ghoul shrugged. Both of them helped the fallen necromancer to the divan, which miraculously had endured the combat. Both she and the ghoul knew that her help wasn't needed, yet she wanted to be part of the process.

When the physician had come and assured them that Vernon would survive without any damage other than bruises both mentally and physically, the ghouls took the necromancer with them along with the guards. Before they left, Cruxh gave Petula one meaningful glance. She wasn't entirely sure what message the law officer wanted to convey. She didn't have time to think. Mr. Colton came to get her, having secured Mr. Thurston a room and locked the fettle into the attic. Even the usually unfazed Mr. Colton seemed to be disturbed by the thing. Petula couldn't blame him.

"Make sure Mr. Thurston doesn't slip out," Petula said.

"I will."

"Has Dow returned?"

The man shook his head.

"What is he up to?"

"Ma'am," the man said.

"I'm sure you know and he told you not to tell me."

"If you are sure," Mr. Colton replied.

"I'm too tired for these games. I'm off to bed. Wake me with enough time to prepare for Mr. Thurston's hearing."

"Of course, ma'am."

Mr. Colton escorted Petula to the kitchen first to feed the cat and then to her room. She listened to his footsteps depart only after she'd locked her door behind her. Petula headed to her bed without taking her clothes off. She curled up next to the cat, and as soon as she found a good position, she fell asleep.

Chapter Twenty-Six

BAPTIZED IN DEATH

R eality had a habit of coming back no matter how desperately one needed an escape. Sometimes it came back with enough cuteness to make up for the fact that it had to start up again. Petula woke to Her licking at her hair. She stretched her hand over her and scratched the cat's stomach as she peered out of the open window of her bedroom. The air outside was still crisp and dark. Petula let her feet touch the ground, careful not to wake up her maids or anyone stationed behind her door. This was her hour, after all. There was no telling if she would ever have another moment for herself.

Petula examined her bare legs against the floor. They bore the marks of what had happened last night. The bruises had turned a darker shade of blue where the ghostly hands had tugged her. They were visible over the tattoos that snaked around her legs. Some tattoos were gone, burned off. Others' colors had faded. They had to be redone. She had lost their protection.

She glanced up at the window again. The witching hour outside stretched thin as the nightly creatures made their way back to their homes. There was this beautiful understanding between the city and its inhabitants that everything was still and silent in this sacred hour. It was that magical hour that proposed that there was more to life than money and keeping oneself busy. No trace of doing. Only the swirl of hot tea or coffee was allowed.

Petula got up from the bed and drew her morning robe around her, which lay on a small armchair next to the window. She was sure she'd gone to bed fully dressed, having fallen asleep from exhaustion. But the only thing she had on was her undergarments. Petula found yesterday's clothes neatly folded on the chair at the foot of her bed. Someone had mended the holes torn by the ghostly hands Vernon had sent against her. Petula glanced once again out of the window at the still moment even the werewolves and the ungodly creatures were too respectful to break. Everyone held their breath for the morning to come. No one wanted commerce to take the magic of being away.

Petula tiptoed to the back wall and pushed the secret panel open, revealing a small room with her necromantic kit, shelves full of notes and books, and her burner and microscope on the makeshift wooden desk. She slid the door closed after waiting for Her to trot in. The cat yawned and hurried after her. Then it gave her side-eye to let Petula know that no hurrying had ever happened. The cat jumped onto the stool in the corner, where she always observed Petula working. Petula petted the cat's head.

"My little protector. One day, you will have to tell me if the gods sent you, or perhaps it was my Aunt Essie."

The cat wasn't impressed. Still, it closed its eyes and pressed its head hard against Petula's hand.

Petua lit two candles with the matches she'd left on the desk. The desk spread against the length of the right wall. The whole secret space was no bigger than a walk-in closet, but to Petula, it was an entire kingdom. Her kingdom. A truer leader would be preparing for what was to come outside the walls, but for now, she wanted nothing to do with that. She needed this moment to observe the meaning of everything found under the microscope.

Petula reached for the metal box on the table and opened it. She took the vial Cruxh had given her out, and once again marveled at the black liquid swirling inside it. The liquid was supposedly the essence of ghouls. So Cruxh had told her. She took a pipette full of the blackness and dropped a drop on a glass plate, then sealed it between the plates. There it was. Petula lifted the specimen and inspected it in the dim light. It carried less gravitas than it should. Out beyond this room, the only interest she might get from others was the question of whether it could be turned into money. That was what humanity boiled down to. Money, money, and money. And they seemed to have forgotten why money had been created in the first place. Clearly, dragons were real. Not the kind with scales, though. Just with two hands and legs and a head that weighed more than it should. Ghouls weren't like that. Instead, they lived solely for the questions of why and how.

Petula slid the plates onto the microscope. She dragged a candle underneath the plates, and the liquid reacted. It came to life. The initial blackness stepped aside, and the heat made tiny, shiny particles appear. They looked like fireflies, swimming in the darkest night.

Petula could forget herself here. It was the most beautiful thing she had ever seen. A substance made of a ghoul. How it had come to be and what it was composed of, she had no clue. Jeremiah Black had used it to control spirits. So it made sense that it had something to do with life force. The thing the dead hungered for. But there was more to it. The question made her mind and body sing. This was life. This was a reason to live. This made sense.[1]

---

1. Petula was right. The black liquid was indeed why everything existed, even though it would be impossible for her to grind it down and prove it. It was the quintessence Levi Perri had searched for and found, but he was as clueless as her about what it was and how it had come to be. Further, if they had looked more extensively, testing it against other creatures and the cosmos, they would have found out that it was something that was in all of them. The only thing that differed was the amount and compounds which it was tied to.

The fire didn't make the essence evaporate. This was what Petula had observed time and again. It just came alive. What it also did was emanate heat, and a lot of it. Petula could feel her forehead bead with sweat as she bent over. She stood up, putting distance between her and it, massaging her stiff neck. She had been staring at the microscope so long that she'd lost all sense of time. It was clear that what she saw was pure energy. Energy that didn't jump around, electrons that had come to rest and form something. Petula frowned. There was a thought that kept slipping away. Something to do with making everything come together. She knew that if she was given enough time to concentrate on it, she could figure it out.

But as always, politics demanded her attention. Mr. Colton slid the panel open and gently coughed.

"Is it already time?" Petula asked, stifling the candle flame.

"Mhm," Mr. Colton let out.

"And Mr. Thurston is still with us?" Petula asked as she used the pipette to collect the essence back into its bottle. She sealed the cork tightly.

"Not a hitch," Mr. Colton said.

"I guess that's a good thing then," Petula sighed. "You know, Mr. Colton, here inside this bottle is life in its simplest form, telling us what it means to be a ghoul. But instead of simplicity, it breeds the complex creatures in front of us, you and I included, who manifest these silly games and build cathedrals for them. Still, we can't even begin to fathom why we are here, if there is a point, or why such complexity has even come to be when bacteria and viruses are perfectly functional entities surviving where we cannot. Or take Her." She nodded towards the cat, who was curled on the stool. "She's the most sublime form. The grace, the determination, the chaos, and those huge eyes. Yet I don't see her having to rush out to correct the power imbalance when all parties are playing a game of who blinks first while wearing blindfolds. So I guess what I'm trying to say is, why is everything silly and why do I have to play along?"

Mr. Colton smirked. "The answer is very simple. With complexity, you never get bored. And boredom is the enemy of men. But that's not a complaint. On the contrary, I find all this highly entertaining. Though I have to admit, the key is not to be in the position where you have to do the running. It's the watching that makes a smile stay on one's lips."

"Then you are the wiser of the two of us." Petula put the vial back into the box. She scooped Her into her lap and walked to the door where Mr. Colton was leaning on the frame. "But I guess I have to do that running you mentioned now. Any ideas where I should run?"

"That's for my betters to know."

"I was afraid you would say that. So let's begin with Mr. Thurston and see where that leads us."

"If you wish so, ma'am."

"I wish nothing but to stay here with the vial and my books, but I made the mistake of opening my door several years ago, and what I want has not been taken into consideration since."

"Ma'am, did you find out anything new about the substance?" Mr. Colton changed the subject as they left the room.

"Just life being weird as crit."

"It tends to be like that, I'm afraid. But if it is any consolation at all, I have found that being a lot weirder helps."

"I'll keep that in mind." Petula glanced at Mr. Colton. He gave a slight nod and took a step back to let her drop the cat on the bed. You didn't birth and teach people like Mr. Colton. They just came to be.

Petula found the maids waiting for her, ready to bathe and dress her. Petula sighed and let them get her ready to be the leader.

Not all that could be done should be done. And there was no telling if an action is morally right. The whole moral part seems to evade the concept of truth, causing words like relativism and utilitarianism to be thrown around. No one actually knows what these words mean in the end. Not that they know what the end is either; just that interactions are complicated as Kraken shit and that people's inner lives may not be something to base everything on.

Here Percy was, pacing around the room inside the ghouls' Town Hall. Next to him, the mock-ups from the bunny statues that stood in the doors of the Town Hall smirked at him. His exit back to Necropolis hadn't been a simple request. Some of the ghouls felt betrayed. They were right. There was no denying he was putting the ghouls in great danger, but they had to understand what was at stake. He'd excused himself to leave the meeting, not allowing his emotions to get the better of him. A statement he never expected to make. Everything, especially everyone playing with the laws, was getting on Percy's nerves. Otis's trial had turned political, and as soon as it had, the rulebooks were thrown out. It wasn't right. He had to fix it. It was his responsibility. Otis was his responsibility. They would be tied together until what had to be done was done. Escaping here in the ghoul city had been a perfect fantasy. A fantasy he let himself believe for a second. But duties didn't go away with a change of scenery. Percy had always known he would die for his duties. He had just thought there would be some righteous plan to follow when he did. He didn't expect his actions to be the cause of it all.

The door to the room crept open slowly, and Philomena peered inside. "Can I come in?" she asked.

Percy grunted.

The witch stood silent for a while in the little annex room. She gathered her courage and asked, "Are you okay?" She had that concerned tone people used when everything fell apart. Percy couldn't help but observe that she was wearing a new outfit. A long checkered walking skirt and a matching vest. Her long dark hair was tied in a tight bun. She looked more composed and professional than she had a few hours ago.

"Have they decided?" Percy asked instead of laying his heart on the witch.

"I don't know. I have been to Necropolis," Philomena said.

"Why?"

"The why is not important. What's more pressing is that you were right. You are needed up there. Mother is alright. She survived the attack. She's still imprisoned, but alive. Later today, they'll decide Otis's fate. And whoever wins will have access to this machine you told us about. The ghouls ran their calculations, and if their results are right, the machine needs an endless supply of energy. If, as you say, it's powered by souls, then the ghouls see it as an abomination. We all know that down the line, someone will think it is okay to feed the machine with street kids and the fallen," Philomena stammered. She collected the hem of her skirt and found a chair to sit on. Despite the new outfit and her neat hairstyle, she looked weary.

"Then the ghouls know I need to go up, that the mayor has to hear my side of things before she decides?" Percy wasn't sure if he was asking or stating.

"They know. But that doesn't mean they can let you leave."

Percy had to look away from her. His face would show her what he was feeling, and that was too much. Percy shifted his attention to the tiny bunny statues. Their eyes mocked him. He had been told that a prominent artist, Herbert Ringworm, had made them. Every time the name was mentioned, it came out like a sigh, as if something had to be forgotten or forgiven.

"What are you thinking about?" Philomena asked.

"The statues," Percy replied truthfully, focusing on the irrelevant despite knowing whatever passed here would most likely decide his fate. It was just as well, as the current moment was the hardest thing one could face. Percy didn't care that it was the default pitfall of the human mind. What he cared about was that he didn't live up to his ideal self. The one always in control, always doing the right thing.

Percy dragged a chair out from under the table and sat next to Philomena. She instantly leaned forward, taking his hands in hers. Percy froze. He couldn't help himself. He hated to be touched. Philomena kept her hands around his.

"I know you think it's your duty to see this thing through with Mr. Thurston. I get it. You brought him here. Gods only know what other ways you could have gotten rid of the necromancer, but still, you did what was expected. But it's not on you. You followed the law. What will follow is in the hands of others." As she said the last part, she squeezed tightly. "You can live a good life here. I mean it. The feeling of strangeness will pass, and you will find your purpose here. I have. So let it go. You don't need to leave."

The woman's soft hands were suffocating. His whole upper body flinched, and there was a hurt look on Philomena's face as she let go.

"I didn't mean it." The words got stuck in Percy's mouth.

"You don't have to explain. There's no need. I stepped over a line I shouldn't have." Philomena stood up.

He had to look away from her again. He was always like this. "I'm the problem here. I'm sorry that I offended you. You were trying to help and..." Percy shook his head. "I was an ass. You are right. In a way, it's not my responsibility to see through this thing with Otis. It is madness to jeopardize my life for it, and yours, but I won't be able to live with myself if I walk away. I had many opportunities to get rid of Otis. He offered to pay me to let him disappear, promising that he wouldn't use his necromantic talents again. He only wanted to retire to some warm, sunny place where he could take it easy. I believe he was telling the truth. Yet I had to do the right thing. He had broken our laws in so many ways. He'd inflicted sorrow and terror on Threebeanvalley's soil. There was no guarantee he wouldn't do that again when the sun and relaxing got too repetitive. And who was I to decide such a thing over the laws written by far superior beings than me? I'm sorry, there's no other choice than to go through with this. It's the way I am."

"If you are sure, then you must do what your conscience says. Shall we?" Philomena gestured towards the door.

"Yes, let's go." It was clear he'd stalled long enough to hear the verdict.

They found Elmer Spooner in the hallway coming to get them. He looked gray, meaning only one thing.

"They approved me to leave?" Percy asked.

The man nodded. "I'm coming with you. So are the ghouls. We can settle everything once and for all if it must be done."

"What do you mean?" Percy asked.

"They will escort us up, protect us, and take part in the meeting. If Otis's machine is of such great importance, they will also have a say. Sirixh is already at the Town Hall, but she's there on behalf of the Differs Soul Party. The ghouls will have their own representative."

"What now?"

"We are to wait until Cruxh and his officers meet us at the entrance. The ghouls sent a message to him and to the Town Hall that we are coming."

"How?"

"It was never about if, but always about the best way to do it. The discord you heard before was only to clean the air. The ghouls told me they don't believe in holding one's tongue. Not when it's about important things like someone's freedom or security. They wanted me to tell you they are sorry they made you think otherwise. It's understandable. Human customs are odd to them. They haven't yet learned it's customary not to say certain things aloud." Elmer gestured for them both to follow him back to the audience chamber.

Percy complied. "Thank you," was the only thing he could think to say. Yet something didn't sit right with him. Percy went back to what Elmer had said, listening to the conversation more thoroughly as he replayed it inside his head. The statement about ghouls didn't baffle him. Not anymore. Clearly, they were far superior beings, capable of more flexibility than humans. That wasn't it. It was the fact that Elmer was going to come with him.

"No," Percy said, making both Philomena and Elmer stop and shoot a glance at him. "I can't allow you to go with us. Such a thing would be perilous."

"If you are going, so am I," Elmer stated.

Philomena smirked, but Percy ignored any innuendos the smile might entail. So what if Elmer was attached to Percy? Wherever he went, the man seemed to be there, bound to him. It was only natural. A survival mechanism left there by the lingering uncertainty and Percy saving him once. Nothing more. Yet he couldn't ignore the thought which pestered him, that Percy's presence might be the only thing keeping Elmer functional here, in the ghoul city. They would have to have a serious conversation before leaving. All this reminded him that he hated the old saying about being careful who you saved. Especially now, as he was seeing that every life was worth saving. It made him consider his sanctioned killing on behalf of the Council as murder. In him, the Necropolitan, who had been baptized in death, was disappointed beyond repair.

"No, you won't. They can't kill me right off the bat. I'm too visible. But no one knows about you, and they can and will use you against the ghouls and me. Too dangerous," Percy insisted.

"Don't you think it's Mr. Spooner's decision to make?" Philomena interrupted before Elmer could get a word in.

"It would be if the situation was different. But as I said, his and our safety is at risk," Percy said.

"I aghree," came a voice from farther down the hallway. Gwerrusxh stepped into view. The ghoul looked tired and irritated. Percy had gotten better at reading their emotions. Before his stay, he had thought there were none. "Mr. Allread ish righth. Mr. Spooner leavingh will put everhy one at risskh. But it'sh up to Mr. Spooner to decide. Not ourrs choice to makeh."

Chapter Twenty-Seven

OFFER ME THE WHOLE KINGDOM AND WE WILL SEE

I t was all a play, and Petula had yet to figure out why she had been cast. She'd left the sanctuary of her home and arrived at the Town Hall just in time to see the whole city flocking in. Mrs. Maybury had been the first to greet her, and now the undead was muttering something about Otis, but she didn't listen to the undead woman. Instead, she had her eyes on Dow, who had magically appeared at the Town Hall this morning without an explanation of where he had been and what he had been up to. He chatted with the Council's administrator, the undead, who had arrived at the Town Hall escorted by his witches and lawyers. They were wearing the capotain hats to command attention. All the people buzzing around, from reporters to politicians to the Church of Kraken followers, shot side glances at the Council.

Petula straightened the vest over her white shirt. Her fingers brushed against the stitching of lined coffins and a skull and bone with a top hat embroidered on the inside of the vest. It hadn't been there the last time she wore it. It had to be her servants who kept stitching them on her clothes for her protection. Petula wasn't sure why they had chosen Old Man Death to guard her. She hoped that the god extended the courtesy to the guards, Mr. Thurston, and his flesh fettle, whom she had tucked away in her office with every known necromantic spell to guard them. The flesh fettle had smelled less bad today. It had also taken a more solid form. It and the other guards wouldn't be enough, if the Council decided to play dirty. Especially because Mr. Thurston had been in a foul mood ever since he had been woken. Mr. Colton had assured Petula that the man hadn't attempted to run away. Petula gathered from the conversation she'd had with Mr. Thurston that the necromancer trusted her to deal with the situation as best she could. She didn't trust a word the man had said. Petula could do with less need for trust and a lot more action.

"Don't you get killed, girl!" Mrs. Maybury finally got to her, mostly because she reached for her arm and clutched it.

Mrs. Maybury was starting to get on her nerves. But she let her hover around her. The woman was unaware of the attempt on her life and had given Petula one of her talks... Petula wasn't sure about what. There had been a lot of words and a lot of demands, and more than enough concern.

"Wasn't planning to, but one day there will be a beheading if we let the Council win today." Petula stepped away from the undead and headed to meet the Council.

"Mr. Crowen, what a pleasure," Petula said as the crowd parted to give her space. She offered her hand to the undead, giving a slight nod. All eyes were on her. Madam Sabine's especially. Not to mention the painted eyes of all her predecessors framed on the walls haunted by only Kraken knew who or what. Petula had let the Town Hall become as spooky as it wanted, giving permission for the cellar doors to creak ominously and the spiders to make their webs where they pleased. Petula had always liked the little critters. She was sure they held knowledge beyond her imagination in their webs.

"Mayor," Mr. Crowen said and took her hand. The witches and necromancers behind him bowed. There was one woman who had her face torn by talons. She averted her gaze as Petula glanced towards her.

Dow circled the Council's convoy and arrived beside Petula. Petula stole a glance towards her secretary, who leaned on his right leg.

Mr. Crowen glanced at the secretary and then at Mrs. Maybury, who'd followed Petula. Then the undead man began, "I think we should have a private audience before—"

"Yes, of course, then we better not waste the little time we have by standing here and bobbing up and down like marionettes," Petula interrupted him.

Dow harrumphed next to her.

"Yes, I mean no, of course, ma'am," the undead man said.

"You'd better follow me then." Petula turned around on her heels, facing Mrs. Maybury. She gave the woman a wink, startling both of them.

"You better come along as a witness, along with Madam Sabine," Petula stated aloud, making the room gasp. Petula ignored the murmurs from the crowd and the tension from Dow and Mr. Colton, who'd stepped out of the shadows, looking highly displeased. Petula walked through the crowd to the audience chamber's entrance connected to the foyer. It was hidden behind the wall full of paintings. She nodded at her predecessors. Their eyes darted away to stare at the frames. Petula pushed the panel open. Dow materialized next to her, trying to create room between her and everyone else, who had been stalled by Mr. Colton.

"Miss Upwood," the man started.

"Yes, I'm playing with fire, and no, I will not change my plans. Plans I made when you left me to fend for myself." Petula kept her steps long and fast, letting her walking skirt rustle against her legs as she searched for her usual place in the chamber. For the first time, Petula noticed Dow struggling to keep up with her. His left foot limped slightly with every step he took.

"Is there something I need to know?" Petula asked.

"No, ma'am." Dow seemed to swallow the rest of his words.

Petula didn't press on. She turned to face the Council and its drones along with Madam Sabine and Mrs. Maybury. Mr. Colton was fighting hard to keep the rest of those who'd gathered in the foyer out of the chamber.

"The floor is yours, Mr. Crowen," Petula stated, letting her gaze linger behind the man on the afternoon sun shining through the weeping willows and the city landscape visible through the huge windows at the back of the chamber. The faint light had driven the gargoyles, werewolves, and other nightly creatures to crawl back to their resting places. Petula could stand there forever, observing as the city shifted from one mode to another. But instead, she turned her attention back to the room, waiting for Mr. Crowen to start.

"Ma'am, I'd rather we talked about this in private. Both of us know this is a highly flammable situation that needs cooperation from all of us. I appreciate you calling on Mrs. Maybury and Madam Sabine to bear witness, but this is a judicial matter and not a public matter. Mr. Thurston has broken several laws critical to the safety of our city and the balance between necromancers. The Necromantic Council is responsible for maintaining that safety. Our efforts are most adequate to keep Mr. Thurston imprisoned until a trial can be held," Mr. Crowen stated, doing his best not to glance at the two women.

"I do agree, Mr. Crowen, but we slightly differ. I see this as a public matter and think it should stay so. So whatever you want us to discuss before the hearing, you can do it now," Petula said, trying to keep the slight amusement out of her tone as she watched Mrs. Maybury and Madam Sabine hold their tongues.

The dead flesh around the man's mouth went into wrinkles as he bit down on his words.

"But I can't deny that some matters are better discussed in the privacy of my office. We have a lot to discuss about the changes happening in our city. You can secure an appointment from Elvira at the door. I'm sure that I have some free time on my calendar for today."

After a prolonged silence, there came a roar. Madam Sabine couldn't help it. She gave a full belly laugh, which took over the entire audience chamber. The witches and lawyers flanking Mr. Crowen didn't welcome it kindly. They narrowed their gazes and tightened their mouths. Petula hoped that the head priestess had her guard up against any hexes, or she might find herself crushed by horses today when heading home.

"Young girl, this is not how we do things in the city," Mr. Crowen finally let out.

Petula composed herself to prevent her emotions from getting the better of her. She took a second. One that seemed to stretch into eternity. Then she released everyone.

"No, it seems we don't, but it's high time we start to follow the laws and rules in the good book of ours that founded the city. If you want to discuss any changes to the laws written in our constitution, then that's definitely a public matter. And now, as the lawful *head* of the *Necromantic Council*, I have shifted the venue where Mr. Thurston's hearing will be held. It will be held here and now, where everyone has a right to argue for and against sentencing Mr. Thurston. After I hear from all parties, I will make a ruling on what happens to Mr. Thurston. Now, if you will excuse me, I have to prepare for said hearing. It will start in two hours. You may produce the necessary witnesses, such as Mr. Allread."

"Ma'am," came a voice from the door, interrupting everyone trying to argue back at the same time.

A nervous clerk stood there, aware that he had all eyes on him, having shouted over the roar. Mr. Colton stood next to the poor thing, who looked ready to throw up. The bodyguard was grinning.

"Yes?" Petula asked, raising her voice and eying Mr. Colton, who had clearly encouraged the clerk to speak up. The clerk had a written message in his hand, which shook so much that Petula could see it from the other side of the audience chamber.

"I... I..." The man swallowed and looked at the paper and then up and then back at the paper. He cleared his throat and said, "I was told to tell you that there has been an attempt on the reverent Mother's life, but Mrs. Culpepper survived the attempt and is being looked after by the prison's doctor."

"Thank you, Mr. Vagy. You may go," Petula said to the nervous clerk. The man bolted right away. By the look of it, he would lock himself in the staff lunchroom and rock in the pantry until the trembling passed. And he wouldn't be happy at all about Petula knowing his name. Leaders didn't do that. Mr. Vagy had one goal in life, and that was to be as anonymous and replaceable as possible.[1]

"This meeting is over," Petula said. She kept her composure as she added, "We will convene in two hours. Until then, if you want to discuss anything with me, you can make an appointment with Elvira."

Petula hurried out of the room before she exploded. Dow hobbled behind her as fast and as subtly as his clearly broken leg would let him. Mr. Colton wasn't too far behind. Petula half expected Mrs. Maybury to try to follow, but she didn't. Mostly out of common decency and partly because she'd struck up a conversation with the head priestess.

Petula at first headed to her own office, but then she remembered that she'd secured Mr. Thurston there. She spun around and walked past the ogling crowd to the steps leading to the basement, where Dow's office was. She almost ran down the stairs, getting her breath back only at the office door when she put all her weight on it. Petula gasped and drew the door open.

Dow followed her in. So did Mr. Colton. They both let her have the only chair in the room behind a small wooden desk that was as dreary as they came. The room, like the desk, was dismal. It had no windows to call its own. It had nothing but the desk and the chair and a stuffy, suffocating atmosphere.

"Fools. Why would I think they wouldn't try to kill her as well?" Petula rambled, mostly to herself. She knew she had just shown the Council that they could get to her through Henrietta and the others. Petula cursed under her breath. "Fool."

Petula lifted her head to meet Dow and Mr. Colton's inquisitive eyes.

"Don't look at me like that," she said. Before the two men could comment on anything, she said, "Send someone to protect Henrietta and the others at the prison. And get those foolish lawyers of mine there ASAP."

"Ma'am—" Dow began.

"No, get it done and now," Petula insisted.

"I know someone who can help," Mr. Colton offered.

"Good, make sure that someone knows a trick or two."

"They do," Mr. Colton said. "Shall I?" He lifted his eyebrow.

"Yes, go." Petula waved her hand.

Her bodyguard glanced at Dow. The secretary gave a nod, and the man was gone.

Petula squinted her eyes but said nothing. Her head was spinning. The adrenaline from the earlier encounter hadn't worn off. Dow looking at her in a funny way, leaning on his good leg. It didn't make her feel any better.

"Where were you?" she blurted out.

"Making sure you stayed alive."

Petula snorted. "Then you missed the main event."

"You can handle any necromancer they send at you. You know that there are more entities in the city than the Council who want to get you killed. The Worthwrites haven't forgotten what you did to them. Nor are Madam Sabine and her priests ready to give you the power to decide over

Mr. Thurston's soul and his machine. You pulling him from the Council's custody has made you everyone's prime target."

"Is that so?" Petula retorted, biting her lip so as not to snarl at the man. Her secretary was right. This thing with the Council had left her open for attacks, and with bankers like the Worthwrites who smelled an opportunity to profit from your weakness, even a slight crack in your defense could be fatal. Yet Dow had offered her easy bait. The truth was something else.

Dow was about to open his mouth, but Petula stopped him. "What is with you? You have been odd for a couple of days now." Petula crossed her arms.

"You wished for independence." Dow shifted slightly. There was clearly something he had done, and he wasn't ready to disclose it. He observed her differently, as if he was waiting to see... see what? Petula hadn't quite figured out what that "what" was.

"That's all?" Petula asked.

"That's all." Dow sighed.

"It must be lonely to be you. And I don't mean this as an attack. I'm saying this as a friend... or as something close to one," Petula said.

There it was. A tiny horror in the man's eyes that he would have to disclose something personal. He knew as well as she that if he didn't, something significant would break between the two of them. And if she survived this, they most likely still had years of working together ahead of them.

"Never mind. Let's just concentrate on the hearing to come," Petula said.

"Mr. Colton seems to do as you want," Dow said out of the blue. "I would even go as far as saying he has taken a shine to you. Somewhat obsessed with your safety, I must say," Dow stated.

"Oh," Petula said. "I guess I make it exciting for him."

"It would appear so, ma'am."

"I thought we got rid of that word."

"Which one?"

"All, but in this case, ma'am."

"It's a fine word, ma'am."

Petula ignored his last remark. "I better catch you up on what has happened in the past couple of days."

"I would appreciate that..." The man hesitated.

"You can say it."

"Ma'am." The man's tight posture collapsed ever so slightly.

Petula told Dow why and how she had gotten Mr. Thurston out, about the arrest of the needlepoint group, and of the events at the manor. As she spoke, she was sure there were odd whispers around her, as if everything was more alive. She sensed movement in the corner of her eyes. She searched for the dead spirits that were usually there; there were none, yet the whispers stayed. She shook her head and continued explaining that Mr. Crowen had ruled the Council for decades, that he was behind the board somehow, and in truth, he ran Necropolis.

Dow said nothing.

Once again, it was the change that was hard to wrap her mind around. Henrietta wondered if she should feel betrayed or just accept this was how it was and had always been in Necropolis. In Amanita, there was betrayal, but it had consequences. Here in Necropolis, it was like a person's morals withered away and what was left was an empty vessel, devoid of connections and meaning. Henrietta rested on the prison bed, still feeling woozy from the attack. She stared at the ceiling, trying to figure out how she could keep her morals intact in this land. She had gotten extra rations from the prison's kitchen without having to venture out. Annabella and

Ida had been out and about, attending the orientation. From the sound of it, they kind of liked prison life.

Henrietta glanced at the towering woman who had taken residence at the entrance to the cell, sent by Petula. While Henrietta was a tall, robust woman with enough mass to go a few rounds with anyone, the other woman wouldn't have to; the sight of her would make any would-be aggressor happily walk away. She was probably a professional wrestler.[2] The woman had come with a message attached. She was to stand guard and escort them everywhere until a trial was held. Karin Rotbell had arrived a few hours after the attack. The woman hadn't said much, and every time one of them had tried to chat with her, they hadn't received more than two-word answers.

Henrietta moved her gaze from Karin to Annabella, who was on the other side of the room, immersed in the legal documents. She would defend them. There hadn't been any word from the Coven's lawyers. Ida was somewhere out there; only the gods knew what she was up to. Karin Rotbell hadn't been happy about the banker leaving the room, but Ida had explained that her life meant nothing to anyone, and thus she was safe to do as she wished.

Ida was on her way to making herself the queen of the prison. Even in the short time they had been there, Ida had seized control and was undoubtedly throwing out the sensible orders the warden had established. Henrietta hoped they got out before the banker could build her empire inside the prison. Henrietta liked the soft-hearted warden, who was always readily available, yet somehow managed to keep control. A weird balance

---

2. She was. A werewolf wrestler. But unlike most in her trade, who trusted agility and cunning when it came to their canine instincts, she trusted brute force. She had learned to use what nature had given her, and that was mass. This wasn't about the feather and cannonball dropping from a tower. This was the other kind of physics.

to master. He had even tried to give her hope, offering to let her run the prison gardening program. Henrietta swung her legs down from the bed. Instantly, both Karin's and Annabella's eyes moved to her. They followed her unsteady wobble to the prison door. She wasn't sure why she was heading there. It just felt like she should. The cold stones against her bare feet made her joints ache. Yet she stayed at the door, waiting for something to happen.

Ida soon rushed to the door, the warden, James Hardrick, by her side. "Our lawyers have arrived," Ida blurted out before the warden could.

"Yes, Miss Mortician is right. We have secured you a room to talk with your lawyers if you feel up to it, Mother." The warden fought for the remnants of control. The man's disheveled appearance and tired eyes made it feel like an eternity had passed since Henrietta and the rest of them had arrived at the prison. It was almost easy to forget that they had only been here since the morning.

"I'm feeling a lot better, and there's no need for the whole Mother business. Call me Henrietta."

Horror flashed in the warden's eyes.

"Or Mrs. Culpepper," Henrietta offered.

"Mrs. Culpepper, I'm glad to hear you are doing better." The warden jumped at the opportunity. "This shouldn't have happened. I'm sorry. I'll do my best to keep you safe." The warden glanced uncomfortably towards Karin Rotbell. The woman was a prisoner, or so she had been told. But all of them knew she could do as she pleased and leave anytime she wanted. A truth that went against all common sense. But the thing was that widely shared truths didn't have to have anything to do with reality. What mattered was the appearance of things. For example, let's say that everyone believed it was okay to pay billions of bucks of taxpayer money to the bankers to bail them out of the catastrophe caused by their irresponsible money lending and false bookkeeping. But... when you looked at where all the money went afterwards, it turned out the bankers all got nice bonuses and not a thing changed. Meanwhile, the world went on as if none of that had happened. As if nobody remembered that in the eyes of the law, the bankers should have headed straight to jail.[3] Funny old reality. So Karin Rotbell did what she pleased, and everyone looked away, even the always upright warden.

"It's not your fault, Mr. Hardrick," Henrietta said, shaking away the haunting sensation that there was a shift in existence that shouldn't be there.

"It is. I should have known that something like this could happen. We have the normal guards up for the usual hexes, but this was—"

"Let me stop you there, Mr. Hardrick. We all know that this is not a normal circumstance we find ourselves in. You are not the culprit, and that's all that matters."

"But the safety—"

"Of course, it is. But I think we have our lawyers waiting for us."

"Yes, yes, sorry." The warden stepped out of the way as Karin Rotbell escorted Henrietta and the others through the prison. The warden tried to keep up with them, shouting directions. As they walked, Ida got slight nods from the other prisoners. She even made a few tremble.

As promised, the warden had secured them a private room to meet the lawyers. Two gentlemen in smart frocks waited for them in the bluish-green interview room. They stood stiffly on the other side of the wide wooden desk and hurried to bow as Henrietta entered.

"Mother," they said in unison, glancing at Karin Rotbell as they deepened their bows. Both looked like they had seen a ghost.

"Gentlemen," Henrietta started. "You are not from the Coven."

"No, Mother. We are here on behalf of the Town Hall," one of them

---

3. If the crime was big enough, you could get away with anything.

answered.

"Ah, I see. And Martha and Mag from the Coven are detained, I would presume?" Henrietta asked, just needing to hear it aloud.

"No, Mother," the man stuttered. "The... the... the thing is that there's a danger of disbarment for those who take your case."

"Bastards!" Ida let out.

"Yes, bastards," one of the lawyers repeated laconically.

"And you are brave enough to go against such a threat?" Henrietta asked, taking one of the chairs available.

"It's everyone's right to be defended. Such is our law, Mother."

Henrietta frowned and said, "Glad to hear that there's some decency left. And your retainer?" Henrietta crossed her legs and leaned on the chair's backrest. She felt woozy again, smelling the scent of lilac. Annabella sat down next to her in the only free chair, glancing worriedly towards Henrietta.

Henrietta signaled she was okay, that there was no need for any fuss that might follow.

"Our retainer has been paid," one of the lawyers replied.

The other one added, "We have sent a demand to dismiss your charges based on clauses six b and seven hundred and eighty-four."

"False persecution?" Annabella asked.

"Yes, we think this falls under such a category. You have a right to assemble and discuss any political matter and, as private persons, support any group you see fit. We presume you supported the Save the Otis Group as private persons?"

"And you think that will get us out?" Annabella asked.

"It's the first step," one of the lawyers said, looking more comfortable now, as talk had turned to simple things like toying around with black-and-white clauses.

"And the second step?"

"To countersue."

"So you are going with trickery then?"

The two lawyers looked confused. Not so much by the word trickery, more so at the tone used, as if there was something wrong with using the law to get what one wants.

"Just using the law as it was intended," one of them offered.

"But—" Annabella started.

"Let them," Ida said. She was leaning against the wall next to the door. "There's nothing pure about the way this has been handled. So let them be as dirty as they please."

There was that confusion again. "Ma'am—"

"Miss," Ida corrected.

The lawyer coughed. "Miss, we are acting according to the law."

"But not the spirit of it." Annabella couldn't help herself.

"Yes, yes," one of the lawyers said, dismissing Annabella.

"Before we proceed with legal matters, may we ask that only the necessary parties be present?" One of the lawyers changed the subject. He glanced at the bodyguard and the warden.

"Of course, yes. Do forgive me," the warden said instantly, hurrying to open the door. "Miss Rotbell?" he added.

"It will be fine, Karin," Henrietta said.

The woman frowned but followed the warden out.

"What was that all about?" Henrietta asked.

"This is a private matter, Mother, and should be treated as such for your defense," one of the lawyers offered.

"We have this too," the other one added, reaching for a letter in his pocket. He handed it to Henrietta.

Henrietta expected to see Petula's handwriting, but what she saw was nothing close to it. Instead, it was a letter from the Council offering to drop their charges and reinstate their positions and wealth if they sold out Petula, naming her as the master agitator. They even went as far as promising Henrietta additional funds for the Coven and more spots for witches to be educated.

Henrietta clutched the letter.

"What is it?" Ida demanded.

Henrietta gave the handwritten note to the banker. It was as much hers as it was Henrietta's. There was an offer for Ida to handle the Council's banking.

"I thought..." Henrietta started.

"The Town Hall sent us," the lawyer hurried to say. "But the press is waiting for you outside the prison steps, eager to hear your version of events. I'm also told that the attempt on your life was made by Miss and Mrs. Granger. There are even rumors that they are behind sending you to prison with a false testimony. All that will be handled if you agree to the terms."

Henrietta glanced at Ida and then at Annabella, who was reading the letter now. The Council had gone above and beyond with the offer to the undead. They had proposed free necromantic and taxidermy services along with a chance to run the legal department at the Council for life.

"This is..." the undead began.

"It is," Ida sighed.

"So we agree?" Henrietta asked.

"I think we do," Ida said.

Chapter Twenty-Eight

FOR THE COURTS TO DECIDE

Generally, everything was about being stuck. Stuck in the situation, stuck on the path taken, stuck being you, stuck in the system, where one had no say about anything. And just stuck. Otis found himself stuck between a huge man and an even huger one. They'd arrived an hour ago, driving away the other guards, but not the flesh fettle, who was examining everything it could get its hands on. Otis was ready to make a joke about dumb and dumber and the conversion between brainpower and body mass. He expected to get a reminder of his mortality with a severe head bashing. He thought better of it. Still, he would be more distraught to find out that he would end up having a philosophical conversation about intelligence and how it might be tied to one's appearance, but more so to family lineage or environmental factors like having teachers who believed in you. Again, it was all about the question of the chicken and the egg. So, it was better that Otis didn't make the joke despite it wanting to escape his lips ever so badly.

Otis had been locked in the mayor's office long enough for him to get bored. The flesh fettle was irking him as well, refusing to budge or cease to exist.

"Whatever you say, boss," Otis said, answering Petula's warning that it would soon be time to face the music.

In addition to the two men, the flesh fettle, and Petula, Petula's personal bodyguard was there. He lingered close to the mayor, leaning against the wall with one knee bent. Otis recognized the aloofness of the man, yet he seemed to care about the mayor, watching every move around Petula, occasionally glancing at the fettle.

Then there was the fourth man.

"So, what shall I call you?" Otis glanced at the small man, who looked like some evil megalomaniac hiding in plain sight in the most unremarkable body there was, sitting in front of him and reading the papers scattered on the small coffee table.

The man drew his lips closed in a way that made Otis regret asking.

"You may call me Mr. Spurgeon." The man opened his mouth, using the prolonged silence from earlier to his advantage.

Otis swallowed. Of course he was there. The man had been the former mayor's secretary; why would that change? Otis had heard rumors about the man. They said that he was the monster of all monsters and was the one who truly ran the city. Not that anyone dared to say that aloud or call the current mayor or the previous one a puppet. Dow would rip your throat out for that.

"Mr. Spurgeon, do forgive me for not recognizing you."

"Why should you?"

"For no reason." Otis leaned away from the man.

"And?" Otis glanced at the two men who'd sandwiched him onto the couch.

"Aah, Monty Emerson is my secretary." Dow nodded towards the taller of the men. "And Rugus Angerstein is his junior assistant."

Otis wondered where the senior was, not actually wanting to know the answer.

"Sure thing," Otis said, falling silent after that. He drummed his fingers against his leg, then moved on to tapping his feet. That earned him an angered glance from Rugus. Otis continued for a while. But when Rugus silently begged permission from Dow and got it and was about to open his mouth, Otis stopped.

"So, what are you?" Otis asked Dow, who had gone back to reading the papers he'd gotten from Petula. They were trying to organize the upcoming cataclysm of all events to their liking. Otis would say don't bother, if they asked. There was no way to steer a ship like this. They should all just make a run for it.

His question made even the mayor pause and look up from her papers. She was now going through prisons that could hold Otis if such an event ever came to fruition. Otis didn't care for such nasty talk. He had hinted that an exile on some tropical beach would serve him right.

The rumors said the man was some kind of vampire.

"An existential question, perhaps? Or should I give an answer detailing the parts I'm made of—like what kind of blood is pumping in my veins?" Dow offered.

"Whatever kind of answer rocks your boat." Otis was already bored with the conversation, to which his former self, imprisoned not so long ago and deprived of any interaction, told the present Otis, "*I quit. You are a complete selfish moron.*" Otis ignored such rumblings.

"Then I have to answer that I am what you see in front of you, like you, made of flesh and bones. If you want a more thorough answer, I'm afraid we don't have time for it." Dow got up and headed to the mayor, who quickly shifted her attention back to the papers she was scribing. Otis listened to the fountain pen scratch against the paper.

Otis shrugged and struggled out from between the two giants. He took a few laps around the couch to get the blood pumping again and disturb the others with his pacing. He finally settled to lean on the couch's backrest and peer outside the window. The Town Hall had once been an old manor which had been forgotten and deteriorated into a swamp. Someone had foolishly polished it clean and made it the center of the city as it was now. The other buildings stretched towards it. The weeping willows rose high around the building, occasionally clawing at the walls, trying to get in or perhaps doing what Petula was doing now: conveying a message. But that was too far-fetched even for Otis's imagination.

"Some sort of zombie apocalypse would cheer up this place. Don't you think, Mr. Emerson?" Otis asked, growing bored of the swamp view. "I could easily whip one up."

"Aren't you the funny one," Monty replied.

"Is this the start of a beautiful friendship?" Otis turned to face the man, not wanting to stare out of the window any longer. It was a depressing view. The whole Necropolis was depressing. It was no wonder he'd done everything in his power to get out in the first place. And holy corpse worm, he was going to do everything in his power to get out once again. That was a promise.

"I hope not, but I guess I'm stuck with you for now." The man flashed a smile.

Rugus glared at them. "Are you done?" the man asked.

"Quite. But I can't promise all the words won't come back."

"Is he going to be like that the whole time?" Rugus stated.

"No, if he knows what's good for him," Monty replied.

Otis smirked and crossed his arms.

The thing is that life has a funny way of wiping the smirk off one's face. It was one of those things that could last only for a second, and a wise person cherished that moment and didn't get stuck in the future or the past.[1] What wiped Otis's smirk off wasn't Rugus or the impending doom. It was an undead woman who shambled into the room without a thought of knocking and with a clear whiff of a desire for a zombie apocalypse.

---

1. Yep, that stuck thing again.

Everyone tensed up. Not Monty; he just shrugged as Mrs. Maybury walked in. Otis couldn't help but shudder at the sight of the undead and feel the acid taste in his mouth rise. He wondered if he should duck behind the couch. Mrs. Maybury had owned the corner shop in his childhood neighborhood. She still gave him the willies. It was like he was a kid again, and the woman was accusing him of stealing.

"That skinny kid is behind all this? I should have known he would amount to nothing good," Mrs. Maybury snorted.

"Afraid of being left out of all the fun then?" Otis retorted.

"No, that would mean I would have to enjoy your company. I highly doubt that," Mrs. Maybury stated. "And if anyone is interested, his lawyer is downstairs, demanding to see him."

"Aah, I see," Petula said, massaging her temples and then reaching for the small pot of tea on her desk to pour yet another cup. "Then someone better fetch the poor man."

If Otis had counted right, this was her fifth cup.

"Are you sure? Who knows who he's working for?" Mrs. Maybury stated.

Thank you, finally someone sane, Otis almost shouted. Yet he didn't. Aligning with Mrs. Maybury was all wrong.

"And denying his lawyer would be bad," Petula said.

"I'll go, ma'am," Rugus said, getting up from the couch, making it shift.

After that, nothing good followed. They went back to having serious conversations about boring matters. Otis was starting to feel like an invisible man. No one was paying attention to him. It didn't matter how many jokes he made. The mayor, Mr. Spurgeon, and Mrs. Maybury were having a lively conversation about Otis's lawyer and whether to throw Otis to the wolves, from the sound of it. All done in highly legal language, which was getting on Otis's nerves. The flesh fettle had found the coat rack and was examining it. Even the Gothic room was getting on Otis's nerves. Why couldn't there be more light in Necropolis?

It was high time he left this party behind and headed out on his own. Yes, he'd promised the mayor no funny business, but that had been then, and now he was thinking better of it. Especially as the entire legal process was all about him yet had nothing to do with him. This was about politics, rules, and setting a future example. Otis groaned and slid down the couch's backrest until his legs were in the air. That got their attention, especially the mayor's. The way she looked at him was like she was reading a book. Not the book of Otis. No. But the one that knew how to do the impossible with the mechanization of necromancy. Something Mrs. Maybury had pointed out a moment ago. She was even now ranting on about how the whole industrialization of Necropolis was ruining everything and Otis was to be blamed. Machines didn't have souls. And clearly, their makers didn't either.

Otis didn't like the undead at all. And if he had the stamina, he would argue that souls were nothing special. In a sense, they were not so different from metals and minerals. They served a function. The only thing that set them apart was you needed special equipment or a necromancer's well-tuned eye to detect them. There was nothing in the world that dictated a machine couldn't achieve that, a consciousness. Kraken shit, Otis was pretty sure he could get the glowing skulls to do just that.

Otis's hands itched from the mere thought. Then he remembered that a moment ago he'd planned to ditch all of this, and tampering with such matters would get him into more trouble.

"Mr. Thurston, it seems that everyone else has spoken, except you," Petula said, cutting the tension and making it worse. Otis knew why. He was the unpredictable element here. "I would like to hear what you think."

Ichor Pod arrived just in time to prevent Otis from having to participate in the charade. The undead cleared his throat from all the mothballs. "If I may, what my client is—"

That was as far as he got. The mayor silenced him with an ever-so-innocent glance. Then she turned her attention to Otis and his legs dangling over the couch's backrest. Otis slowly corrected his posture to sit up straight.

"If I may," Ichor Pod tried again. When Otis didn't show any sign of stopping him, the mayor let the undead lawyer go on. "It's only reasonable to hear my client's opinion, but he shouldn't have been transported without his lawyer present. Anything he might have said can't be used against him. He's not aware of the laws affecting his case, so I find it unreasonable for him to plead his case. However, I can consult with him if you give me a private room, and then we can come back with a full statement."

Ichor Pod was about to continue, but the mayor didn't let him. "I'm not one to protest the proper protocol. What I want to hear is what Mr. Thurston wants."

"To know how it took this long for my lawyer to get here," Otis let out. Not that he was that invested in what he'd said. The mayor tilted her head ever so slightly, looking at him as if she read his mind. It was in the empty space between them.

"Mr. Thurston, I highly doubt—" the lawyer started.

"Don't bother. I'm not that interested," Otis interrupted the man. "But to get back to the mayor's question. What I want is not to end up back in the Necromantic Council's custody. So, I give you free rein, Miss Mayor, to keep me out of there and stuff me into any prison you see fit, alive. It's painfully obvious that I won't get out of this as a free man, and if I do, it won't be for long, as from what I have gathered, I'm the most wanted man in the world. So, a cozy room, something to do, and three meals a day will do." Not that Otis was prepared to do that either, but it was what she wanted to hear.

"Mr. Thurston..." Ichor Pod started.

"You are fired..." Otis started

"That's unnecessary, Mr. Thurston," the mayor said. She stood up behind her desk. "Mr. Pod will continue to be your lawyer. You are a buffoon in need of a good one. You won't survive what is about to come without Mr. Pod. The Council won't hold any punches, and I can only act according to the law. You need someone who has no other agenda than your defense. I don't. The city comes first. So I'll give you two the room the lawyer requested. I'll even hand you the papers I have been writing so you can see what the city has to offer. But I'm afraid Mr. Emerson and Mr. Angerstein have to be present all the time. For protection, Mr. Pod, before you state otherwise. Do we agree?"

The undead nodded, dazed by the mayor.

"Good," Petula said and glanced at Otis.

He shrugged. He was hers for now, and if this was what she wanted, he would play house with Mr. Emerson and Mr. Angerstein while they watched the undead squirm.

"Sure, sure! Let's get this over with." Otis threw his hands in the air.

"Here," the lawyer stuttered. He reached for his briefcase and produced a thick folder. He pushed it into the mayor's hands.

"Thank you, Mr. Pod."

Life and its little occurrences made it somehow feel like every now and then you stepped out of bed and walked a mile in someone else's life. That it wasn't meant to be this way. Yet here you were. Percy was sure this wasn't his life. It was weird to be back up under the endless sky. Somehow, it was bigger and more intimidating now than it had ever been before. Like there were more possibilities behind the gray clouds and the pale sun.

The ghouls gathered around him and Philomena. Percy wanted to touch Philomena and draw her attention away from the city rising in front of them, but he just stood there like an idiot. He wanted more than that. He wanted to apologize for being him. He wanted to ask if she was in any danger being here in Necropolis. He could do none of that. Not when Gwerrusxh and her murder of ghouls were around them.

They'd surfaced on the outskirts of Necropolis, where a human was a rare sight. There were a couple of undeads whose alliance with the ghouls was as odd as those small fish cleaning the teeth of the great white shark, but that was it. There were plenty of Homo Nosferatu and Homo Lycanthropy, and others along those lines masquerading as officers. When Percy squinted, he saw gargoyles sitting on the rooftops, basking in the weak afternoon sun before going to do their night shift at the city's banks and other places where they were hired as surveillance.[2]

Percy let his attention linger on the rooftops of the residential buildings, searching for the Council's men, especially Laura. She wasn't there. He couldn't let that lull him into a false sense of security. The Council was set on removing Percy from this world, and nothing could stop that.

"Don't be nervous. They won't let anything happen to you," Philomena said as they moved along the street to meet Cruxh and his officers. The officers shifted from foot to foot, nervously glancing at the ghouls, the neighborhood, and then at him.

"I..." Percy began to protest that he wasn't nervous, but the ugly truth was that he was anxious. The control he'd built around him was slipping away, and he was experiencing helplessness for the first time in his adult life. He reinforced his wards as he looked at the police transportation with the city's insignia of a Kraken painted on it. The words "serve and protect" were transcribed underneath the symbol.

Cruxh clicked his tongue as they approached.

---

2. And no, no one ever saw them move. Not even the most enthusiastic gargoyle watcher with their little notebooks and binoculars. But the gargoyle watcher community had a bet going on, and Bob was sure he would win the miracle of the century.

"They have already started," Gwerrusxh let out. "Impatient, you lot," the ghoul sighed and let Cruxh usher her and the rest of them inside the carriage. Percy took a seat beside Philomena and Gwerrusxh. The remaining ghouls climbed on the roof and a few others hung on to the sides, making the carriage shake. Then they took off.

Percy wished he could see outside, but the only light coming in was from the door with bars on it. This felt like a trap. He was forced to sit inside like a blind octopus. He strengthened the hexes around him. There was a need to be in control. However, the illusion of control had become ever so clear in the past couple of days. Percy took a deep breath in and shut his eyes. He counted his breaths in and out and recalled what he was going to say at the Town Hall. The ghouls had instructed him to state the facts and nothing more or less. It suited him fine. The thing was that suddenly facts had become not facts at all. They seemed to have too many feelings included. Even the facts that Percy had held as objective truths. But there didn't seem to be an objective truth anymore, especially with human affairs.

Percy shifted his weight on the wooden seat, feeling the pressure on him. There had to have been a chance for all of this to go along another path. Not to the extent of simulations run simultaneously. But a different outcome nevertheless. Outcomes Percy couldn't figure out no matter how hard he mulled over it.

They arrived at the Town Hall with all their toes and arms attached. No attacks had been attempted, but they had been clocked. Their every move had been monitored ever since they'd arrived from the neighborhood where those belonging to the establishment didn't dare to enter, where the old laws of Necropolis were venerated. Not the laws of the strong, as some would think. No. More like the laws of mutual respect and words being kept when uttered all due to the horror of existing on the brink of society. So alien to anyone who thought grand illusions and a silver tongue were the surest way to win the game of life.

Percy followed Philomena and Gwerrusxh out. The yard was packed full of spectators, from common folk to the reporters and anyone else who had an interest in the verdict. Laura was there too. She stood next to the Town Hall's fountain with her men by her side. She still commanded the space despite all the onlookers. The fountain with its demons spewed water over Laura. She didn't seem to care that the water was splashing over her capotain hat. The hexer had her arms crossed, and she stared at Percy with murder in her eyes. He couldn't blame her. She had been marked by the imps. Laura was the only one who had eyes on him. The rest sighed as Gwerrusxh emerged from the carriage. This was the first time anyone had known the mother of all ghouls to come above. The event was more notable as Cruxh rushed beside his mother from his police transport. Everyone was watching the two of them.

Next to Cruxh stood Corporal Lawrence, according to his name tag. Percy looked in awe at the bugbear. They were usually enormous muscular creatures who could shift between the state of being and not being, wearing armor as if they were born with it. Corporal Lawrence was definitely one, yet he was like a mocking image of what their nature dictated. Scrawny, apologetic, yet as big as they came. It was like his existence was playing tricks on your perception. Percy had encountered a few bugbears in his life as a Monster Hunter and fought to banish them from ravaging remote villages; this was the first time he had faced one wearing a police uniform.

"Sir." The bugbear winked, making Percy shut his gaping mouth.

"Corporal Lawrence," a female voice said. The chief of police walked around the carriage to meet Gwerrusxh and Cruxh.

"Yes, ma'am." The bugbear saluted, hitting his heels together.

The sound echoed around the silent crowd, who were staring at them so intently that even a slight tremble of a finger could be detected.

"Go inside and announce our arrival," Hortensia Caster said. The chief of police was a tall, red-haired woman with freckles on her face. She was slim but toned.

"Yes, ma'am!" The bugbear blinked out of existence and reappeared at the Town Hall door, pushing it open. Percy followed his exit, noticing Laura and her men weren't there anymore. He cursed how he'd let them leave without marking it. Percy turned his attention back to the chief of police.

"Reverent…" the chief searched for the right word.

"Gwerrusxh is fine, Chief Caster," Gwerrusxh said and tilted her head ever so slightly. "I didn't expect you to come."

That made the chief's expression freeze. "That makes two of us. It's lovely to finally meet you, Gwerrusxh." Hortensia offered her hand to the ghoul.

The ghoul reached for it and tied her claw around the chief of police's long, bony fingers. Percy stared at the hand in the claw and smiled.

"Pleasure is all mine. I have heard only good things about you, despite you stealing away my ghouls and my son. But they say you hold the law in your heart. Is that true?" Gwerrusxh asked.

After another confused look, Hortensia Caster said, "I do my best, ma'am."

Percy was sure the woman would bow, but no, the chief held her stance. Percy was sure Gwerrusxh revered her more. The woman had earned the ghouls' and his respect for sure, if the stories were true. She'd weeded out the corruption at the Northnekton Bay station as a senior constable, and after a year the mayor had appointed her as the chief, taking out the rest of the bad coppers. She had been so efficient that the citizens had started turning back to the city's finest when they had any trouble. Now there was a station present in almost every neighborhood, and the police academy had been reinstated. The chief no longer handpicked trainees; nor was the program only six months. It took three and a half years of dedicated training, schooling, and work placements to become an officer of the law.

Still half what it took to become a witch or necromancer.

"Now, shall we?" Hortensia asked and gestured towards the door, where the bugbear had appeared again.

They followed the chief in, surrounded by her officers and the ghouls Gwerrusxh had taken with her.

Percy found a hand in his and looked at Philomena. She kept her gaze on the steps leading into the Town Hall. He squeezed her hand, and she returned the gesture without saying a word. If he survived this, he would ask about her history. That was for sure.

Laura and her men were inside. She sneered at him and mouthed something. Most likely, it was along the lines of, "*You are done.*" Or it could be a curse, but his hexes didn't react.

Having Philomena there and her hand in his had been a bad idea. He saw Laura clocking their closeness. Percy flinched but kept his hand in place. Laura and her revenge would have to wait. Whatever was happening inside the Town Hall's audience chamber was more pressing, and clearly, it was in full swing. No one could miss the hubbub.

The audience chamber doors drew open when they neared, and the shouting and hooting was making Percy grimace. Inside, everyone who was anyone in the city stood in their places, demanding to be heard. The only one seeming to enjoy the show was Otis. He sat smugly in his seat as people shouted about who should get to have him. An undead next to him had buried his head in his hands. On the opposite side of the table, the mayor tapped her pen against the desk ever so casually, letting the spectacle go on. The Council's representative, Wallace Crowen, was stating the laws that gave the Necromantic Council the right to decide over the necromancers. No one listened to him. The crowd roared and booed over the man's words.

Percy glanced at the mayor, who was letting all this happen. He wanted to shout at them all to stop and look at themselves in the mirror. He wanted to ask if a civilized person would act the way they did, but even if he dared to, he had no time. Gwerrusxh let out a low, loud growl.

The room fell silent and went very, very still.

The only one who wasn't fazed by the sudden noise was the mayor. She greeted them with a smile and stood up.

"Aah, finally," Petula said. "Now we can start, as everyone has gotten their rumblings out of the way. But before we do, let me first introduce the reverent Gwerrusxh, the representative of the ghouls."

The ghoul let out an incomprehensible noise, perhaps disagreeing with something. But then she said with a perfect Necropolitan accent, "Thank you, Petula, my good friend, for letting us attend this meeting," causing a stir and loud murmurs. "It has come to our attention that an unlikely machine has been made, and its legality is questionable. We, the ghouls, have come here to see if we can help decide the fate of such a machine and its maker."

The ghoul turned her black eyes on Otis, letting them linger there. Percy was glad to see some of the smugness melt away from the necromancer's face.

"Then you have arrived at the perfect time. The question of whether Mr. Thurston should be transferred from the Council's care into a state-run prison has taken a new turn. Mr. Thurston has offered to make the machine for anyone who wins the legal argument over his whereabouts and can offer him amicable accommodation. I don't see why the ghouls shouldn't weigh in on the matter. So please take a seat..." Petula took a deep breath in.

The crowd parted as the convoy made its way to the center of the chamber. Gwerrusxh sat down cross-legged on the floor in the middle of the auditorium circle. Percy felt uncomfortable to have all eyes on him.

"I can't help but notice that you have brought Mr. Allread with you. Do you happen to know where an inspector called Mr. Spooner might be?" the mayor asked when everyone had settled back into their seats.

"Mr. Spooner is willing to come and testify if his safety can be guaranteed," Gwerrusxh stated.

"That is unnecessary. I have his written testimony on my desk, produced by the defense. If and when his presence is needed, we can consider the matter again," Petula said. Percy couldn't help but notice that there was a flicker in the mayor's eyes. Something he didn't recognize, but something that Gwerrusxh did.

"Ith will beh so," the leader of the ghouls said.

"Good. Then we can proceed. If I'm correct, it is the Council's turn to state their arguments over the prison transfer. But this time, I demand silence from the audience," Petula said. She didn't raise her voice. She said it ever so casually, yet the whole room gawked at her as she sat down.

Percy's first thought when Petula had been appointed as the mayor was that she was too young. He thought she would be a pushover, and she would know nothing of the soul of this place and what it meant to be Necropolitan. Clearly, he was wrong about this and so many other things. Percy hoped that she would get it right. Whatever that right was. Of one thing he was sure: if necessary, he would stop the free market affair Mr. Thurston had turned the event into. Justice shouldn't be sold to the highest bidder.

There was a flicker behind the mayor's shoulder. As if a dark figure was standing behind her and holding on to her. The woman shivered, but then it passed. Percy looked around, but no one else had seen what he had seen. Or if they had, they could mask their astonishment.

"Yes, Mr. Allread?" Petula turned her attention to him as if she was prying into his mind.

Percy swallowed. Her silvery eyes had turned a darker shade.

He straightened his back and said, "I'm happy to be at the court's service."

"Then we better make this one." Petula smiled at him, and Percy felt again like she was inside his head.

CHAPTER TWENTY-NINE

FOR THE PIECE OF GOLD

The whole circus, as Petula saw it, settled into the audience chamber where everyone who was anyone had gathered to have their say in Otis's fate. Petula glanced over her shoulder, having an odd sensation that someone stood there, whispering into her ear. There was no one. She shook her head and returned her attention to the room.

Madam Sabine sat down, having shouted over Percy and the others to state a prayer for Otis's soul to resist. Resist what was unclear. The Council sulked on the other side of the table. Or more like puffed their chests out to let it be known that they weren't taking this—whatever this was—kindly. Then there were the judges called in to monitor the legality of the event, who looked as if their skin was itching, and they couldn't quite scratch the sensation away. Then, as the icing on the cake, the reporters had arrived, smelling blood. To Petula's surprise, R.E. Porter wasn't tightly gripping his pen amongst the others. But Lattice Burton was there, sitting behind the reporters as if to stand guard for truth and justice. Petula wondered whose truth.

The list didn't stop there. Petula shifted her attention to Kitty Worth-write. The banker held her head up high and sneered at Petula. Luckily, the banker didn't have her necromancer with her, or else she might use this opportunity to start a necromantic battle. But even Kitty wasn't that foolish.

That time would come later, when Petula was least expecting it. But the Council might try it. The necromancer helping Wallace Crowen to unload the files on his desk had pure, raw power. Anyone could see that. And who knew if she had been brought here as a last resort. Birthed and raised to take over when necessary. The woman had the posture for it. She had on a long black leather coat, and underneath that, she wore a black, high-neckline dress which looped around the back. She was convincing, stunning, noble, and tall. All of which Petula could never say about herself. It was often more persuasive than skill. The first line of defense in everything.

Petula glanced down at her own clothes. They weren't much. Maybe she shouldn't have insisted on wearing her knee-length wool walking skirt and the vest which looked like someone had forgotten it at the Town Hall. Petula reminded herself of what her Aunt Essie had said. It wasn't about what you wore. It was about how you wore it. This was her stage, and she could, for all anyone cared, look like something a cat dragged in. Yet in all honesty, it was not an easy stage to keep. Otis was ready to continue the charade he had ever so carelessly turned the event into, undermining everything they'd agreed on. The necromancer impatiently shifted his weight on his seat, preparing to draw the focus back to him. His lawyer had sunk his head into his hands and looked like he was willing to give up his afterlife.

There were too many moving parts for Petula's liking, all with headstrong determination that they were in the right. All willing to burn the city down to be victorious. The only sensible beings in the room were the ghouls. They were her ticket out of this. The leader of the ghouls was an unknown variable and a powerful one. Politicians and other self-serving twits don't much care for the words "unknown" and "powerful." They wanted lambs.

That was the thing with politics. If all you wished for was docile and simple creatures, then quality and the best solutions went out of the window. The concept of one policy, one mind, one opinion was death to change and possibilities. It was one reason Petula hated politics, especially as you always had to take a stance even when there was no clear point to declare. Somehow it wasn't okay for government representatives to say that there's no simple solution and sometimes no action is the best policy. Another thing Petula had noticed people forget was that the point of all this was to act for the common good.

Petula sighed and turned her attention to the political parties and their leaders: Sirixh, Mrs. Maybury, and Mr. Kilborn. But as far as they were concerned, they were waiting to see what side they should take. Politicians were too often concerned about how to keep oneself in power rather than the right thing to do. Perhaps that was too harsh a judgment for the three party leaders, yet behind them stood others waiting for the leaders to make one false move.

Dow and Mr. Colton were by her side. Whatever that meant. Trusting the loyalty of others was always touch and go. Who was to say that the hearts of men wouldn't sway when something new and shiny came along? And if this train wreck was going where Petula thought it was going, soon rights and laws would just be a pleasant memory of the good old days when things had been less brutish. There was a good chance that Necropolis would go back to the rule of the powerful,[1] where money or arms did the talking.

Everyone was waiting for her command to let them speak. A weaker person would enjoy this. Petula found herself to be weak. She needed this boost in stature to survive, and a tiny part of her died. The one who kept rebelling against all the social conventions. The one who'd chosen her clothes and spent a few precious moments in the wee hours in search of meaning through a microscope. That part got dissected and thrown out

---

1. Not that it wasn't now. But at least, here and now, those sitting in the deciding positions had to pretend to uphold the law.

every day, piece by piece. Some people might say that she sacrificed her life for the expectations of others, that there would come a time when she had nothing left but emptiness. Petula was well aware of what would follow.

"Good, now it seems everyone has settled in. But before I let anyone speak, we have to establish some rules. This is not your traditional court of law, and I, the ruler of Necropolis, will make a final judgment on the legality proposed by all parties. This is highly irregular and thus should be carefully considered. To assure the civility of procedures, I will give the floor to one party, and the rest shall respect the speaker with their silence." Petula gazed over all the parties.

Madam Sabine looked like she was about to explode. So did Kitty. They were sure she wouldn't let them get a word in. But that was not Petula's plan. She would make sure everyone could speak as much as they liked. Their inherent need to be seen and heard would make her goal easier.

"Are we in agreement?" Petula asked.

Some nodded their heads. Others tried to figure out a way to raise their voice without making an ass out of themselves. One who volunteered on behalf of everyone else was a reporter, who got a finger in his ribs courtesy of Lattice Burton. The woman most likely was thinking she had got one over on Petula. The reporter cleared his throat and looked around.

"Are we to expect no one else will be able to voice their concerns?" He stumbled on with every word, composing them so that even if Petula declined, it was her rather than him who would get the stink eye.

"Thank you, that was an important question to ask. As this has clearly become a public concern, I will also open the floor to the citizens. Mr. Thurston has made it clear that whoever wins the argument will get him and the machine. The trouble is that Mr. Thurston can't do that. Necropolis upholds its laws, and I'm not willing to throw them away at the command of a prisoner."

The reporter glanced behind him at Lattice Burton. The man was sweating and ready to disappear if anyone would be kind enough to curse him into doing so.

Petula kept her laughter from surfacing.

The reporter fell back into his seat, wanting to hide behind the notebook he pretended to write into.

"We will hear from the Necromantic Council first, then Mr. Allread. Mr. Thurston will follow, then I will open the floor for the audience. Lastly, we will hear our legal team, and then I will withdraw to decide. And no, Mr. Thurston, this is not an open forum for you to get someone to make the highest bid for your freedom," Petula said.

Otis had stood up, Monty and Rugus breathing down his neck, daring him to make one false move to end the debate once and for all.

"But—" Otis began.

"Sit down," Petula said. "I do have to insist."

The necromancer glowered but did as he was told.

"Now, Mr. Crowen, the floor is yours." Not that the Necromantic Council needed permission. Before Petula finished her sentence, the undead was speaking.

"Mr. Thurston's arrest was legal. I'm sure Mr. Allread will agree to that, even after having chosen to resign from the Necromantic Council," Mr. Crowen stated.

Petula noticed Mr. Allread stiffen.

"The city and the Council agreed that rule seventeen dash four grants the right for the Necromantic Council to arrest and pursue any necromancer overseas who has violated the necromantic laws as Mr. Thurston has done..." As Mr. Crowen spoke, Otis moaned loudly. "...That same clause also permitted us to imprison said offender and hold a trial for the members of the Necromantic Council's board to judge the allegations and see if they merit sentencing.

"Due to the nature of public interest towards Mr. Thurston and his imprisonment, the Necromantic Council saw fit to open the trial to the public so that everyone could witness that justice was done according to our customs and laws and that the Council has nothing to hide. It's a courtesy towards the Town Hall and other necromancers, something..." Mr. Crowen took back the words he was about to say. "Something we were happy to do to show that we are on the side of everyone and will do our best to aid the necromancers to fulfill their duties here and overseas.

"We are here to protect our profession and peace between its practitioners and the living world. The Council has the right to imprison and continue imprisoning Mr. Thurston. It was done for the good of Necropolis. Mr. Thurston's reckless behavior could have caused an international conflict or even a tear in our cosmos. But that's just a supposition until we hold a trial for his actions. The Council is willing to do just that if the city permits."

Wallace Crowen sat down.

Petula had hoped he would speak at length and say something to give her wiggle room out of handing Mr. Thurston back to them. She was unlucky in both. "Thank you, Mr. Crowen."

Mr. Thurston seethed. "Deliberation and permits..." Otis muttered very loudly. "I already said, whoever delivers me what I want will get the machine. It's as simple as that. Not about rule seventeen something..."

Petula had no time to oppose.

"Mayorrr," Gwerrusxh said, rising from the floor to her full height. The ghoul even managed to silence Otis. "Mayh I rrrrequest an opporrrtunity to speakh out of turn."

At the same time, the door to the audience chamber opened. Imogene and her entourage pushed in. The former secretary was dressed according to all the rules of witchery: lace, velvet, figure-hugging, and infamous. But she didn't fit inside the dress. Imogene squirmed like ants were crawling all over her body.

"Aah, Miss Granger, do step in," Petula said. "If I understand correctly, you are the acting Mother now."

The witch shot her a glance, having hoped to sneak in. Imogene's mother mouthed the words to demand respect but didn't speak.

"The Coven has come to witness the hearing," the woman said instead. Petula was sure Imogene's mother almost added that they had a right to be here. But that would have made it more of a plea rather than a statement.

"Then do take your seats. Gwerrusxh was about to speak, and I, for one, would like to hear what has made the ghouls request to speak out of turn," Petula said.

The witches took the first open seats near the center of the circular room. They sat just behind Madam Sabine and her followers. The head priestess of the Church squirmed on her chair. Not because of having a bunch of witches invade her personal place, but because the creatures that once had been seen as vermin now had their respect, and the Church had to wait for scraps.

Petula took a deep breath in as, again, the cacophony of everyone shouting at once took over the audience chamber. It was foolish of her to think the stubborn old Necropolitans could learn new tricks. Theater it was, then.

Petula raised her eyebrow and coughed loudly. Silence descended. Maybe more so as Petula had let out a static charge from the excess spirits hanging around. Not enough for anyone to suspect, but enough for them to feel it. "Now, do go on, reverent mother."

Gwerrusxh didn't hesitate. She smiled at Petula the way someone smiles when they know what you did.

"Mr. Allread came to ush in his hour of need, and the ghouls provided him and Mr. Spooner with sanctuary as requested. What hash come to our knowledge ish that a machine has been made that alters the states of nonexistence and existence with ease. Mr. Thurston ish correct that such a question should be addressed first rather than if he should be imprisoned and where..." Gwerrusxh growled over the others trying to speak and continued, "If I have understood correctly from what Mr. Allread has told us about the situation, there's no question that Mr. Thurston has violated the rules and laws of both the Council and Necropolis. He has put the world and peace between countries in jeopardy. Yet he has managed to create a machine unlike any other with the help of his friend, and the fate of such a machine is going to be decided here, as his co-creator perished in a fire. We want to understand the arguments for and against making such a machine and who if anyone should possess such power. Creating something out of nothingness, from the essence..."

The essence. Petula hung on to the word and could see the black liquid sparkling in her eyes. That was what had been at the tip of her tongue. The black liquid was what would make the machine work. It was the purest essence and maker of souls. The concentration and composition of it differed, making a variety. And as ghouls didn't traditionally come into existence the way other creatures birthed their offspring, they needed and used the pure essence to mold a new ghoul. Somehow Otis had found words to compose a formula to make that essence serve him through human souls.

Gwerrusxh had to have realized that. She was more than right. The most important subject in the room wasn't who got to have the machine, but whether it should exist in the first place. It was just not what the politics was about. Truth shouldn't be stated. It should be used for control or, better yet, monetized for the few. That was what Petula had learned. And it wasn't only here at the center of politics. It also infested other institutions. Even the ones she loved, like the university. Facts were hidden and ideas were masked with easy-to-sell reasons like security, health, and moral duty to ensure you got the major vote. Who could vote against security and health, no matter how absurd the cause was?

Now everyone waited for her to react. To see if she would open the floor for them to pursue the machine. The Council was surely against it. So far, they had been winning. Only Mr. Allread's testimony could sway the vote. Mr. Thurston was thrilled by what the ghoul had said. Next to the necromancer, Ichor Pod looked gravely ill. As far as Petula knew, the man had planned to go with an argument for abuse, giving Petula a cause to hold Mr. Thurston in her custody. Not that it would have been that simple.

She didn't have a way to stall this, or she did, but that would mean losing face. Doing such a thing even for the common good took more strength than Petula had. She had always thought more of herself. Just a human, after all. Petula wanted to be the better version of herself and do everything in her power so the machine and Otis would go where they should. The trouble was, there was no right answer as to where that might be. She only had a list of those she didn't want to have the machine: the Council, Kitty Worthwrite, or any independent entity in the city who could twist Necropolis into corporatocracy, Madam Sabine, and not the government either. She didn't trust the government to get it right. Not even herself. That left the ghouls. There was a thought.

"Thank you, Gwerrusxh, you made a valid point. The machine's fate and whether it should be made again is tied to this situation and where Otis Thurston should go. But, of course, this is all based on the premise that Mr. Thurston can make the machine." Petula saw Otis grimacing, and Ichor Pod stiffened next to him. Behind them, the reporters feverishly wrote down every word Petula said. No pressure, then.

Petula paused to take in a breath. All the tension she carried around her chest released. She noticed Dow watching her. He hadn't passed notes or whispered into her ear as he usually would. Instead, he had that praising look on his face when he was in teaching mode. This was the biggest conflict the city had seen since she'd stepped into power, and he thought he could sit on the sidelines. Or... Petula wanted to laugh. Or this could be her trial by fire, and he had organized it all to test what she was made of. But even he couldn't be that devious. What Otis had done had happened a long time ago, before he had her on his radar. Or... She locked eyes with him, and he gave one of his smiles. The kind that made people and wolves run out of his way. Yet a smile she associated with sympathy and encouragement.

"The Council has the legal right to hold on to Mr. Thurston," Petula said, keeping her focus solely on Dow. Otis roared, and the room exploded along with him.

"Shut up!" sounded over all the other noise.

But it wasn't Petula. She turned to face Mr. Allread, who stood by Gwerrusxh. Even the ghoul looked shocked.

"You cannot let the Council have him," Percy continued over everyone else. "They shouldn't have rights over our freedoms, nor should they be able to send men like me to kill others at their whim. Not here and not overseas. That's not what civilized countries do. I have seen their books. I have allocated money to assassins and payments to political parties to get what they want. That's not legal. That's not an entity that should decide the fate of Mr. Thurston or the machine—"

Petula lifted her hand to silence Mr. Allread and anyone else inclined to speak up.

"Thank you, Mr. Allread, for your candid comment, but it's unnecessary. While the Necromantic Council has the right to arrest and detain Mr. Thurston, the matter of the machine is another thing entirely and changes the situation. As Gwerrusxh pointed out, it possesses great power, and whoever owns it owns the markets and the city. They can dictate all our fates—"

"The Church..." Madam Sabine got up.

"This is not a market fair," Petula said over the priest. "The one who shouts the loudest and pays the most will not go home with the goods. What many of you haven't realized is the cost of the machine. There's necromancy involved, yes, and we know the price of our art. Breaking the boundaries between the living and the dead isn't exactly free. The question is what fuels the machine and what it needs once it's made." As Petula spoke, she noticed Mr. Colton leave her side and walk to Dow, who handed the man sheets of paper. The two men exchanged no more than a few words before Mr. Colton continued around the room. He lowered the papers into Wallace Crowen's hands.

"...And before you argue why the Town Hall should own such a machine, hear this. It's not ours to own or anyone else's to obtain. The easiest thing we could do is destroy it, but what would that mean for Otis Thurston? Death?"

Everyone held their breath, except for Wallace Crowen, who read the papers and gasped. He pushed them back to Mr. Colton as if they were tainted. He beckoned Mr. Colton to crouch lower and whispered something. Then Mr. Colton began to move, and instead of heading towards Dow, he headed to Petula.

"I'm not ready to sentence Mr. Thurston to death, nor am I willing to throw him into my cellars and torture him to give up his secrets. I know some of our citizens would see me finally taking my position seriously if I did such a thing. But Minta Stopford set our course for the new era of Necropolis, and I'm going to hold on to that. Because of her, we have had more discoveries, more economic growth, and a rise in happiness, if that's even possible in this godsforsaken place. Kraken is not exactly known for its cheer. And soon, we will witness the rise of other machines, which will shape our city into something none of us recognizes. So what we decide here is important. Especially as the cost of making this Bufonite is the cost of a living soul. Are you willing to sacrifice your children to feed it when we all know nothing is ever enough?"

Otis looked at her with astonishment.

"So here we are. Here I am, having to judge an impossible situation. And all you do is think of your bottom line, who has more power and popularity than you, and how others can serve you. All fine in the old Necropolis…"

Mr. Colton whispered into her ear. "The Council is willing to negotiate. They won't go against you if you don't reveal what is in the papers and make them look bad."

"What is in the paper?" She lowered her voice so only the man could hear.

"Oh, something Mr. Porter wrote about Mr. Crowen and his involvement with the Council. How he has ruled it for years, bribing and extorting the other board members to do his dirtywork. All of them are using the power of the Council to siphon money into their own projects. We have proof of Mr. Allread's accusations and more."

"I see," Petula said. The card that she had been planning to use if necessary, but fleshed out.

"Forgive me for this minor interruption." Petula addressed the whole room. "Key information has come to my attention, and we have to halt these proceedings."

Before the anger won over confusion, Petula added, "During that time, Mr. Thurston will be handed into the custody of the ghouls, who are monitored by the city's police force. Mr. Allread, who arrested him, will be his point handler." Only the very brave or foolhardy would try to get Otis from the ghouls.

"We will convene tomorrow. You are dismissed." Petula waited for someone to shout that you cannot do that, but they were still trying to process what she had said. She used that bewildered state to her advantage and hurried to meet Gwerrusxh.

"Will you?" she asked.

"Of course, Mayorrr. It will be our pleasurrre." Gwerrusxh bowed her head.

"You know what to do?" Petula whispered.

"Yesh, we will."

That was it. Petula oversaw the exchange from Monty and Rugus to the ghouls and Mr. Allread, who didn't look pleased to have the ticking bomb handed back to him. Hortensia Caster, Cruxh, and other officers guarded the ghouls as they hurried from the Town Hall. As Petula watched them and others leave, Dow appeared by her side.

"Get me a meeting with the Council," she said.

"Yes, ma'am."

"But before that, you will come clean about what you have been up to. I won't have it any other way."

It was like he had become an unliving thing. A concept. A clause. Not a human being. His life depended on rationalized arguing. Of course, he'd made some mistakes, but how many can say their mistakes created something beyond divine? Something which could put destiny in the hands of men rather than the rule of gods and chaos. And here they expected Otis to be ready to roll over and do as commanded, telling him there was no option to give him the life he wanted.

"If it's all the same, let's just get this over with. At least I know I have a bed waiting for me. I could use a night's rest," Otis interrupted Ichor's speech.

"Please, Mr. Thurston, you need to take this seriously. We have been given a moment to breathe, and we truly need to go over our legal defense…" Ichor glanced at Monty and Rugus, still towering by their side. The lawyer swallowed his words but gave him a gesture anyway. All of which Otis interpreted as a request for him to behave.

"You expect me to take this seriously when I'm being handed to the ghouls like some game piece to be moved around? Who knows what they will do to me? Hand me to whoever promises me freedom, and the machine is theirs. I'm done with this." Otis lifted his hand to silence the man, who was about to argue. "It's the only way we will dominate this farce."

"Mr. Thurston..." Ichor began but stopped in mid-sentence. They were already out of the doors, and Monty and Rugus were escorting them to the ghouls.

Otis wondered if he should point out that the ground shook as Rugus marched to the beat of his master. Otis bit his tongue. But the next thought was impossible to quash.

"Don't," Rugus warned him when Otis opened his mouth.

Otis raised his eyebrow as he watched the giant man.

"It's all over your ugly mug, and while I won't make it pretty for now, there will come a time when there's nothing to stop me. Understand?"

Ichor cleared his throat.

Rugus didn't back away.

"If you say so," Otis said. "But I have to say that with luck, there will be a time when we can make it into a dance. I have always liked the ones that do all the jumping. You know that thing where you jiggle your body?"

"Can I?" Rugus asked Monty.

"He's not worth it," the giant growled.

"Ouch, that really hurts," Otis countered.

"Mr. Thurston, must you?" Ichor Pod let out.

They walked outside, Otis trying to bait Rugus to react. The man refused to play along and kept his focus on the crowd and the ghouls already waiting for them. Otis noted that there were more than when he'd arrived. Hours ago. Hours, which now, as he saw, should have been spent eating and drinking and sleeping rather than listening to boring people going over all the clauses known to man. Especially now, because the crowd turned their cold, dead, and hungry eyes on him as soon as he emerged. Otis was sure he saw the flesh fettle at the edge of the crowd, giving him the shivers. But when he blinked, it was gone. He wondered if he was starting to lose his mind. The thing was, as far as he was aware, still locked in the mayor's office.

Otis shifted his attention to the ghouls, who stood solemnly, waiting for him to arrive. Mr. Allread was standing by their side, ready to serve as always. Otis glanced behind him, seeing the mayor there, her arms crossed. Otis thought it might be a good idea to mouth a sorry. What he'd done hadn't been personal, and he'd genuinely trusted that Petula would have protected him in the end. He'd reacted, and there was no taking it back. So he continued his march towards doom.

Rugus and Monty handed him to the ghouls. There was no need for cuffs. Just a nod of agreement and the two giants were gone. Not that it made breathing any easier for Otis. Ghouls were... they were. Let's just say that.

The undead lawyer followed Otis into the small carriage and sat next to them. Otis kept his eyes on Mr. Allread, who had taken his seat in front of him. The hexer didn't look happy at all. He looked like he was being tormented by all the nightmares in the world. Otis guessed why it was so and kept his mouth shut. He wasn't happy either.

The witch beside the Monster Hunter wrapped her fingers around the hexer's hand. Otis smirked but kept his silence. Mostly because Percy's eyes dared him to say anything. Otis was forced to mind his own business, which meant he had to entertain himself. He swung his hands behind his head and leaned against the wall, shutting his eyes. He wondered what the ghoul city looked like. While he hadn't been here when it was discovered, he'd heard the rumors even in Threebeanvalley. Brave lads and gals and everything in between had set up expeditions to enter the forbidden city. No one had returned. One thing was sure. There wouldn't be a sunny beach. Not under the dark, damp, forsaken Necropolis.

Otis was about to protest and demand that he should be taken to a nice five-star hotel instead of any corpse lairs, but the carriage came to a sudden halt, making Otis swing forward. The violent stop was accompanied by hasty words shouted outside and the door to the carriage being opened.

"Mother," Cruxh said, sounding apologetic.

"I heard. Let her have her say and then we will be on our way." Gwerrusxh stood up.

Otis hadn't heard anything but grumblings, yet he was ushered out, followed by Mr. Allread and Ichor Pod. Outside in the clammy night air, which seeped into his pores, a short, round woman, who swayed her hips from side to side, followed by the clink of her earrings and an entourage of Kraken followers in their usual robes with tentacles, stood eying Otis.

"Mr. Thurston, I presume," the woman said.

"Madam Sabine." Otis bowed, knowing her excellency from everywhere. While he had never been one for the cult or its teachings, the priest he believed in. The woman was a force to be reckoned with. He wasn't the only one to think so. The officer escorting them watched the woman and her followers' every move, ready to act. Madam Sabine took no notice. She only had her eyes on him.

Otis heard Mr. Allread shift his weight behind him, making the gravel grind against his boots.

Gwerrusxh interrupted the exchange. "Madam Sabine, we do this out of respect for you and your church. We will ask the same from you."

The head priestess tried to keep her annoyance off her face, but there it was. "Your reverence." Madam Sabine looked like she was about to bow, but then stopped herself.

"Mr. Thurston, it seems we don't have a lot of time, so I'll be blunt. If you announce Kraken to have a claim over your soul, then the Church has a say in where you should be. Think about it, Mr. Thurston. The Church can be your friend. Kraken already is. It loves all who are clever and twisted." Madam Sabine smiled.

"Then let me be as blunt, your excellency," Otis began. Ichor Pod seized his arm, but he ignored the lawyer. "What's in it for me?"

Madam Sabine laughed. It was one of those laughs that was round and warm, and it took the receiver into its embrace. "Blessed be you and your dark soul. Freedom inside the Church and a sainthood. Who knows, maybe you will rise to the position of a pastor or even a chaplain. The Church is always looking for new places to spread its word."

"Madam Sabine," Cruxh warned the priestess. His men readied themselves.

Madam Sabine held her ground, letting her colorful dress with its pink, green, and blue metallic fabrics have its effect, fortified by her followers with their robes and tentacles.

Otis laughed. He couldn't help himself. This was beautiful. He had no illusions about Kraken. But the thing was that even with sainthood, churches often meant you had to follow and serve, and he wasn't that good with following and serving. Then again, he would be the center of attention and not hidden in a basement.

Next to him, Ichor Pod muttered that Otis was toying with his soul. Otis groaned at the stupidity of the words of men who dared not take risks. Risks were what made Otis push further. They were why he could make the glowing skulls be more than they were, and it was why he could make the Bufonite again. He didn't need Levi Perri's glorious box. He could make the great machine inside a skull. Any skull. And make it more Necropolitan and make everyone fall in love with him.

Madam Sabine coughed. Otis noticed that everyone was looking at him; that he had been silent for a while.

"Thanks for the sainthood and everything. I'll think about it," Otis said, more because of the way the ghoul looked at him. Not intimidatingly, no. More with a curious, concerned head tilt done in the ghoul way, which was a lot scarier than if the ghoul had bared its teeth. Gwerrusxh was sizing him up, and he had the odd sensation that he didn't want to disappoint the woman.

"But—" Madam Sabine started.

They were drawing a crowd. Necropolitans could always smell blood, and they knew that afterwards, there were bodies to be looted and bodies to be taken as spare parts. Then there was the shadow again. The one that Otis had seen in the Town Hall crowd.

"Thank you, your excellency," Gwerrusxh warned the head priestess.

Madam Sabine's followers didn't look kindly on the leader of the ghouls.

"Madam Sabine," Cruxh beckoned, making Otis blink. The flesh fettle was gone.

"We will meet again," the head priestess said and retreated with her followers.

Otis was hurried back into the carriage and then, in no time, ushered into a small cellar entrance inside a pitiful house in the bad part of town in a smelly alley.

"This is where I have to leave you, Mr. Thurston," Ichor Pod said, looking at the blackness opening underneath them.

Otis couldn't blame the lawyer for not wanting to follow them into the ghouls' lair. Still, he was disappointed. Not out of wanting the company, far from it, but at where the man drew the line of duty.

"Suit yourself," Otis stated.

"You really can't help yourself," Mr. Allread let out.

"What did I say?" Otis wrinkled his nose.

"Not a thing, not a thing." The lawyer intercepted the conversation. "I will be back tomorrow. When I know what the Town Hall has decided."

CHAPTER THIRTY

APOCALYPSE ASSESSING ITS PREY

I t would be nice to think Petula had slept two hours straight in her office after the declaration she'd made and woke rested and functional when Dow came to get her to deliver justice.[1] Dow woke her twelve minutes after the weeping willows had broken in. Dow only had to raise his eyebrow to make them leave and shut the windows behind them. Petula was oblivious to any raised eyebrows. She woke to Dow coughing loudly.

She kept her eyes closed. "Tell me you have assassinated them all, and I can continue my sleep. I was having a perfectly lovely nightmare."

"They seem to want you instead of me."

"Just as you like it."

"You got me there."

Petula snapped her eyes open and looked at Dow. Then she snarled. "You did that on purpose."

"I cannot say, ma'am."

"So, what is it?" Petula pushed herself up. Her head felt wobbly as she

---

1. Not that she or anyone thought she should do that. She was a politician and not a judge, but it goes to show that politics had invaded areas where they didn't belong. Okay, policy making and forming new laws were up their alley, and granting pardons, but messing with the actual legal process... Yes, Petula would be more than happy to sleep through the next week and see if Necropolis was still standing when she woke up.

did.

Dow looked at her with concern.

"Madam Sabine is going to declare the Bufonite to be an abomination, thus belonging to the Cult of Kraken as a divine instrument. Mr. Thurston will be seen as a saint and given the Church's protection."

"Are you being serious?" Petula asked. She had thought her little rest between all of this would have given some clarity. Clearly, it hadn't.

"Quite."

"I thought her to be more sensible."

"I think she is. The Church is stronger and growing by the minute. The troubles with our economic situation and with the new inventions coming from places like Threebeanvalley are making everything uncertain, and people are turning to the Church to find reason."

"I thought we were already done with this nonsense."

"It's your generation, ma'am. The younger ones have gone back to fortune-telling and predicting things from the stars and tea leaves, and through the octopus the Church has in their apse. It's drawing crowds in."

Petula sighed. Madam Sabine was a clever head priestess. The octopus had been brought in a year ago, and ever since, there had been whispers about it and its predictive powers. The newspapers posted all the predictions that came through on their front pages, making it impossible to escape the creature and its sway on the city. No wonder people saw it as important. It was made important. Petula had nothing against octopuses. Wonderful creatures altogether. But they knew nothing of the future. Not when the gods themselves were as clueless about it as the next fellow.

"And..."

"And what?" Petula held her breath.

"I was told that Madam Sabine contacted Mr. Thurston on his way to the ghouls, offering him sainthood."

"And?"

"He's still with the ghouls, but who knows for how long."

"And the Council?"

"Waiting outside for you to summon them in."

"And you?"

"Me, ma'am?"

"Don't play with me, Dow. Not today."

"I acquired the information needed as leverage with the Council, ma'am," Dow replied.

"Something I already knew, and you would know that if you had been around." Petula narrowed her eyes.

"Mine comes with a credible witness and files to back them up," Dow said.

"Files?"

"Yes, ma'am." Dow produced a thick brown folder with papers sticking out of it from under his long black jacket, which reached his ankles.

Petula took the folder and laid it open on her knees. In it were the scattered documents of Mr. Crowen's life as an undead and his climb to dominate the Council. That wasn't all. There were the names of all the board members and their misdeeds. There was old Mr. Wicks, who was Agatha's father. Wicks had used the Council to make policies to influence the markets. He'd made a fortune with all his speculations. Then there was Mrs. Kelvin, who was the mother of Lord Kelvin. A man Petula had hired to install the new voting system in the Town Hall: buttons with nay and yea connected to a skull through copper wires. Old Mrs. Kelvin was a bitter old woman who used the Council to influence her family's wealth by obtaining land deals from unfortunate dying clients. She had also secured the national herb contracts both overseas and in Necropolis through the Council.

Petula took a deep breath in and continued reading. The next name was daft old Mr. Cummings. Everyone knew the man. He was an aristocrat who had to be invited to every social event the city held. The man was one deck short of a fellow, but he was evidently in the Council to be bribed and bought by others to act as they wanted. The documents also revealed the old rumor to be true. The man was the illegitimate son of Oliver the Great. He was greedy and a bit of a pervert. Petula wondered why the last remarks had been added, but then she read onward and wished she hadn't.

Petula sighed and wondered if she should read the rest. She did. Miss Dankworth had risen to her position in the Council from being an excellent necromancer. She'd wanted to shape the Council to be the servant of the city and its necromancers, but she was quickly put in her place. If she didn't behave, they would have her removed, and not in the good old retiring way. She had a drinking problem, and she used the Council's necromancers, witches, and other members as her personal staff to deliver revenge to those whom she thought had wronged her.

Mr. Luckinbill was the son of a great warrior necromancer who'd fought in the necromantic wars. He thought he was as great as his father, but truthfully he had never held a sword or uttered a spell to vanquish his enemies. That didn't stop him from trying to make a war out of every conflict the Council got into so he could be the hero he wanted to be. Petula looked at the image of the gray-bearded man with a soft, round belly.

The last name on the file was Mr. Ord. Quiet was underlined in the file several times. The man was half deaf. He was an arms dealer, selling illegal necromantic talismans, potions, and weapons overseas to anyone willing to buy. Things that were even forbidden in Necropolis. He also owned several workhouses, where he employed those who couldn't pay the Council for their resurrection bills. "More cunning than he seems" had been written in the margins, along with "others don't take him seriously as he can't hear and seldom says anything, but he sees everything and remembers everything and uses it to make more money."

Lastly, there was an article by R.E. Porter exposing everything with a flair that would make the city riot.

So that was that, then. "Where's Mr. Crowen's personal history?"

"There's none. He has been an undead longer than the records remember. And he made darn sure there's nothing of who he was left."

"Why didn't Minta do anything about him and this?" Petula gestured towards the files.

"No proof, no opportunity or reason. We were busy elsewhere."

"And you had the opportunity now?"

Dow smiled. "Commodious."

"I see. What else are you leaving out? What else did you dig out from that den of dead speakers?"

Dow raised his eyebrow.

"I'm tired, so do forgive me for my choice of words."

"I have done all I must for us to survive."

Petula handed back the folder. "Then you better summon the Council here and we can get this over with."

Back when she didn't wear the heavy crown or have friends, she would never have done anything like this. She would have done the correct thing, whatever the cost and whatever her emotions said. Now, she lied to herself that there was no other choice than to use the papers. But the annoying, unfortunate thing was there was always another choice. Maybe not an easy one. Nevertheless, it was there to be considered if you cared to dig around. Of course, she could tell herself you didn't survive in Necropolis if you didn't play games. So why should she be the only sucker following the letter of the law or upholding inner moral guidelines? The basic game theory stated that she should play the selfish game when others chose it as their strategy. Tit for tat, and here was the tit to keep her crown shining if she ever wanted to keep her head and retire.

"As you wish, ma'am." Dow took his exit.

Petula had enough time to brush her clothes smooth and arrange her hair so that it didn't look like she had slept. As she got ready, Mr. Colton came in, taking his position at the windowsill, barely saying anything to state his presence. Petula was used to that. He was always there. Even in her awkward moments.

When she was ready enough and had circled behind her desk, there came a quiet knock on the door. Mr. Crowen came alone. There was no sign of that tall necromancer who'd lurked at the meeting beside the undead. There was just Dow with him.

"Do come in," Petula said.

"What can we do, Mr. Crowen, or can I call you Wallace?" Petula asked, seeing the man stiffen.

"Mr... Wallace is fine, Mayor," he replied.

"Then Petula works well, too," Petula countered.

"Petula."

"There, not so hard," Petula said, again causing that light discomfort in the man. "So, Wallace, we seem to be at an impasse with our Mr. Thurston. I hope you have come to help me figure out the right thing to do." That threw the man even more off kilter.

"Yes, ma... Petula, the Council has come to aid you as best it can."

"Good. Take a seat." Petula circled behind her desk and sat down. "Do you mind if Mr. Spurgeon takes the minutes?"

The Council's administrator hesitated and then shook his head. He reached for one of the chairs in front of Petula's desk, making its legs screech against the floor.

Her saw the noise as an invitation to materialize out of nowhere and jump onto Petula's lap. It peered over the table at the undead.

Dow sighed. Not in a way the other man would have noticed. No. But Petula had become good at detecting the changes in her secretary's mood. The man produced a notebook and a pen from his jacket and positioned himself behind Petula on a small stool.

Petula petted the cat and knew that she would get the stink-eye from her maids at getting her walking skirt covered with cat hair once again.

The Council's head administrator was staring at her in stunned silence, searching for how to reply. Or so Petula deciphered the silence, making her rebuke her inner voice for jumping to conclusions and running with them without stopping to consult reality. You know, the stupid old reality one has to obey. A reality where you can't slip through the cracks into fictional dimensions with less of everything that makes life that much harder.

"Mayor..." Wallace Crowen began.

"I thought we agreed on Petula."

"Yes, do forgive me. Petula. I will be frank with you. The Council would like to keep the article out of the papers. Of course, it will damage the reputation of said persons, but it will also undermine the whole system, and who knows what kind of chaos it will bring. We would like to handle the matter personally and have time to make the necessary changes before rumors start to circulate." Wallace glanced behind him at Mr. Colton.

"The Town Hall doesn't find it necessary to spread any rumors, but what we need to see are big changes. We feel that it's high time the city modernizes its policies towards resurrection services and the process of making laws to govern the necromancers," Petula said.

"The Necromantic Council is there for a reason," Mr. Crowen warned.

"Yes, and it will continue to perform its function, but that function needs to be reassessed. Some of the tasks the Necromantic Council has taken upon itself will have to be transferred to the government. Others need close monitoring by said government, meaning the allowances handed to the Council will have to be recalculated as well."

The undead snarled.

"Let me be frank with you..." Petula looked the undead directly in his eyes. "Did you think this would go as it has gone with the previous rulers? I bet you tried to find dirt on me. But I don't mess around..." She wanted to add graphic details but didn't. "But you get to stay. So does the board. I like to know who I'm dealing with. And I will attend every meeting from now on, or someone from my government will."

"But—"

"There's no buts, Mr. Crowen. We don't have time for them. We have other important matters to discuss, and one of them is Mr. Thurston. The Council isn't in the wrong to detain him, and we both know that the machine can't fall into the wrong hands. But you haven't won any favors by imprisoning him. And I won't either if I send him back to you. Then there's the fact that others have already made their plays to obtain him and the machine, and they won't stop—"

"He has to die. The machine can't be made. It will throw everything out of balance. It will make anyone holding it a tyrant, a god, and it will destroy them and the rest of us. The Council never wanted the machine or Mr. Thurston," the undead said.

Petula curled her lips.

"Don't look at me like that, girl. I'm not some evil mastermind trying to destroy the world by trying to own it."

Dow coughed.

"I'm sorry, Mayor. I spoke out of line," Wallace Crowen hurried to add. "What I meant to say is that you do what you see as necessary, and the Council will back you up as long as Madam Sabine or some other fool won't get Mr. Thurston and the machine."

"And what about Mrs. Culpepper?" Petula asked.

"Any misunderstanding can be clarified and true justice, whatever it is, will take its course so we can go back to normal."

"Yes, normal. What a funny word. I have never understood if such a thing can even exist when things keep changing with every action we take, shifting ever so slightly away from that initial point and ending up in a new state until the process starts again." Petula stroked Her.

"General state of being then, ma'am," the undead offered.

"Around and about," Petula countered and grimaced.

"Then we agree?" the man asked.

Dow tensed up next to her, and Mr. Colton shifted his attention fully to her. "It seems we must," Petula said.

The man nodded and stood up. "Indeed..." the undead paused and then added, "Heavy is the crown."

"That can't be given away," Petula said.

Wallace Crowen smiled. "I am at your disposal anytime, Mayor. The Council is here to serve the city. And one more fact at your disposal. Imogene Granger is Wesley Epith's illegitimate daughter. Imogene's mother poisoned Mr. Epith."

Petula watched the man take his exit after the declaration. Then she collapsed against the back of her chair and shut her eyes before Dow started his little speech about how she'd done everything horribly wrong. All Petula could think about was Otis and the machine of grief. How could such a beautiful concept of opulence out of nothingness cause this much pain and sorrow? It made Petula doubt the whole thing about humans being sentient.

Dow coughed, cuing her to open her eyes. Petula didn't want to, not yet. She needed the moment to exist without any action needing to be taken. But such moments never lasted. Petula opened her eyes and gave Dow permission to speak.

"What do you want to do with Mr. Thurston?" Dow asked.

"What I want is to lock myself into my mansion and never venture out," Petula sighed.

"You can always do that and let Madam Sabine or better yet Mrs. Worthwrite have the necromancer and his cursed machine," Mr. Colton stated. He swung his legs down and stood up from the windowsill, ready to be commanded at will. "It would buy you good faith and get them off your back. There's talk in the town that Mrs. Worthwrite has hired a woman called Mara Strout to assassinate you. She's good. A former Monster Hunter."

Dow glanced at the bodyguard.

The man lifted his hands up and said, "Just playing Kraken's advocate. It would certainly set Petula free and remove the target from her back."

Dow glowered. His eyes turned slightly more yellow.

"Do forgive me. I know nothing of running a state." The man went back to sitting on the windowsill, opening the window to let in the night air.

Dow exchanged glances with Mr. Colton but said nothing. The moment passed, and Dow put his hands behind his back as he circled in front of Petula's desk. He stood there like a priest of the apocalypse, assessing his prey.

"Dow?" Petula asked.

"You know what to do," Dow said.

"You can't be serious," Petula snorted. "Until now, you have advised me on everything that I say and do, and now you say I know what to do?"

"Yes," Dow said.

"You want me to kill Otis?"

"Yes," the secretary said.

The next thing Otis noticed after arriving in the ghoul city was that more than a day had passed since the cursed mayor had cast him out here. Not that Otis wasn't glad to be rid of the Council and the Town Hall's goons, Rugus and Monty, and the charade at the hearing. It was just that having the ghouls looming over him was disconcerting, especially as Percy had clearly become one. The man was always there at his side, monitoring him, checking on him, and trying to ease him into living in the ghoul city by introducing rules and information about the ghouls. None of which Otis cared about. He just wanted to be free.

Being trapped in this demonic pit would be easier to manage if there was an end date, but no. No one told him what was going on. Ichor Pod had come to visit him more than once, but he came without news of what was going on at the Council, the Town Hall, or with Madam Sabine or anyone else offering him his freedom. The dry, moth-eaten lawyer just wanted to go over his legal defense. Otis couldn't take another clause even if his life depended on it.

Otis had started to seriously contemplate the doomed priestess's sainthood. It was better than the limbo here. The ghouls didn't seem to mind the situation at all. They shrugged every time he asked if there was any news. Some of them even answered that you can't force the future. Otis caught Percy doing the same more than once. The banal man Otis had known on the ship had achieved a new level of annoying. Something Otis would have found hard to believe back then. And he hated to find out how restricted his imagination was. He had always thought it was possible to consider all the possibilities, small and large. Maybe there was some truth to the uncontrollable future. But that was some shit the ghouls tried to brainwash him into believing.

There came a cough at the door. Percy and the witch doctor, who seemed to hang around the man everywhere he went, were there with a tray.

"Leave it," Otis said.

"How are you doing?" Philomena asked.

"Perfectly fine." Otis glowered. She was referring to the feeling of suffocation under several tons of rock. At first, he hadn't noticed it, but after three days, the sensation had snuck in and had grown stronger with every second he spent here. He'd turned his restlessness into a quest to find a skull. You would think a lair full of ghouls would be stacked with bones, but no. Just weird art and bunny statues.

"Are you sure?" Percy asked. "The ghouls have ways to alleviate any condition."

"No, thank you, I won't have them messing with my head." Otis knew he was sulking, but it was the only control he had over his destiny, and he was reserving his right to be in any mood and make any decision he could. Another thing that messed with him was that he'd expected the ghouls to ask him to make the machine. But no. They only wanted to know his philosophical positions on the universe, right and wrong, the rarity of life, and his postulations about the purpose of life. The ghouls made him experience the worst headache of his life. No one could blame him.

Nevertheless, he'd started to build the machine anyway. Surprisingly, no one restricted his attempts. They let them have all the materials he needed, except souls. But that could be solved by offing Percy or Philomena, depending on who irked him the most. Or the small fellow he had once met, Mr. Spooner. It was just that he was sure the ghouls' laissez-faire philosophy wouldn't extend so far.

Percy lowered the tray next to the scattered mechanical parts. The gears, plates, screws, all his tools were there, and even the uptight Percy said nothing.

"Thank you. I'll get to it as soon as I finish attaching the gears," Otis said.

Percy didn't comment. Otis kept a forced smile on his lips as the man stood there, watching him turn the gears in his hand to appear busy. He hoped that Percy wouldn't notice the mechanics weren't really attached inside the machine. Otis had made residual spirit energy keep them in place. It had been hard to come by, as the ghouls rebelled against the dead, but there was always something dying in the caves. All sorts of critters, he'd drawn power from. It was like that little spark you got on a dry, cold day when even a slight touch on something metallic made a zap. Enough, but not enough to do anything significant. Otis wished he'd paid more attention to what Levi had done. He had some rudimentary knowledge as a material engineer, but he was more used to working with bones. Maybe the machine could be made of such rather than metal. Still, there were no bones, and there was the question of the cocktail Levi had used inside the machine. It was the one thing that had made the ground souls tap into the creation of things.

Otis's stomach growled from the smell of the soup Percy had brought. Next to it were freshly baked bread slices and real butter. While he had been fed well at the prison, butter was a rare luxury. Lard was the most common substitute, and while the damp, cold air of Necropolis burned it off, it didn't leave Otis feeling well.

"We are going to go star-watching when it gets dark above. You have been permitted to come with us if you wish," Percy said.

"Yeah, sure," Otis said.

Percy understood to leave him alone. Otis waited for the door to shut behind them before he drew the tray closer and gulped down the vegetable soup with cauliflower. Just like Nana had made it. When Otis was done eating, he went back to tinkering with the plates, letting the spiritual residue float the gears into some sort of order and keep the metal plates attached to each other.

His mind wasn't in it. Every opportunity it got, it went back to figuring out how to escape. This limbo, this golden prison, was not what his life should look like. He desperately needed his freedom, and he wasn't willing to trade it for servitude as so many were. It was no freedom if you jumped and did as you were told. Nothing equal about that.

But equality was a tricky beast, mixing itself with loyalty, respect, and a sense of duty, care, and love. It was also questionable whether there could ever be pure freedom, especially when it was impossible to avoid other people and their needs and desires and the constraints of the environment. But maybe there could be a workable equilibrium, where the gains and losses evened out, and the one who had to be the sucker changed every now and then. Maybe. Equality was a utopia, difficult to fit into reality. Perhaps he was just restless, especially as the ghouls were making him think all the things he would rather not. They had said that he was restless, and nothing would satisfy him as long as he was. The key, according to them, wasn't something beyond. It was here, now, and inside oneself.

Nonsense.

Otis would play along. He was going to be a good boy until... Until when? That was the big question. The ghouls were everywhere. He was pretty sure they noticed when he was using his necromantic skills and shapeshifting abilities. After the first day of transforming into one of them and trying to walk out, he'd learned his lesson. There had been a cough behind him and a gentle nudge to go back. Plus, he was pretty sure there was something nasty lurking in the cave system.

Still, if the mayor thought she was going to forget him in this basement, she had another think coming. He didn't know what that other think might be. He had only done what anyone in his shoes would have done. This was unfair.

He was getting his usual headache. Otis moved to the bed beside his work desk, leaving the machine's skeleton to mend on its own. When he shut his eyes and fell asleep, the machine kept assembling itself. The thing was, when you give someone or something life, they go on despite your desires and pursue survival with the parts you have given them. They are not your puppet. Okay, they might be if you have twisted their sense of self with yours. But even if you do, they keep a separate kindle alive just because. So the compound of critters went on, searching for a meaning in its existence beyond the command Otis had given it.

Outside the room, the ghouls sniffed the events unfolding, but they weren't ones to stop new life from occurring, not now, at least, when it hadn't reached a critical mass. It was Otis's creation. It was up to him to teach it a thing or two about the world, the universe, and what it meant to have consciousness of it.

One of the ghouls sighed. "Pity the creature who knows to have a mind. Especially the one lurking in the tunnels. Someone really needs to go talk to it."

The other one sighed as well. "It's his duty. It's his life that is keeping it alive. It will follow him to the end of the world."

The first one nodded, and nothing else needed to be added.

Chapter Thirty-One

All the Nastiness Aside

A king without clothes or the bureaucrat with endless tasks? Petula wasn't sure what she had become. A few days had passed since Petula had given Otis to the ghouls to keep. She had suffered ever since from a nauseating ulcer resulting from dealing with everything. It felt like it was growing, but nothing was new there. Petula concentrated, trying not to swing her legs like a child in the oversized chair as she waited for an audience at the Council's headquarters to see the undead man and his board. She had been here every day since the fiasco at the Town Hall.

Monty and Rugus stood stiffly next to her. Mr. Colton couldn't be with her, which was a shame. His appearance didn't immediately scare people away like Monty and Rugus's did. But she'd sent Mr. Colton to the needlepoint group's trial. Petula had wanted to go, but it couldn't be helped. For now, she just had to keep her dignity and not act like a little girl just because she had a shorter stature than the chair allowed for. Meanwhile, the Council's employees were running around in the building like someone had set it on fire. When they saw her, they froze like she'd caught them deep in her flowerbeds, stealing her elderberries. She hadn't quite decided if the hurry was because of her visit or because rats tended to jump ship when the storm came.

Petula looked at Monty and Rugus.

Monty gestured with a slight head jerk that he agreed. He stretched his hands above his head and said loudly, "I'll go and ask what the hold-up is." The man glanced at Rugus, ensuring he knew that she was not to be let out of sight.

Petula watched the huge man walk past the necromancer, witches, and all sorts of clerks from dead to alive, causing them to scurry aside just at the sight of him. Petula shifted her attention to the spirit world around her to sniff out what from the bottom of the ocean was going on. There weren't any laws against her summoning a ghost even in the middle of the Cult of Kraken ceremony, so why should there be any in here? The trouble was that she wasn't so keen on snooping. A moral line, one could argue. But more so the finding out part. Once you knew, it was hard to get rid of the duty of knowledge. "*I didn't know*" was always a bad line of defense, especially coming from the representative of the people. And she was supposed to be just that.

This was what leaders did. They found out even the uncomfortable information and did something about it. But the thing was that this was about people, and she was not that keen on figuring out the realities formed inside minds. She preferred mathematical puzzles or something as foolhardy as solving the mechanics of photosynthesis by putting ten pandas inside a boat and watching what they did rather than figuring out the minds of men. Of course, there were theories to help her understand. Still, she'd found that the silly buggers refused to play along, coming up with statistical deviations and whatnots, throwing off the well-formed doctrines about human behavior and cooperation. There was no denying that the mushy problem-solving organ wrapped inside a bone cocoon was faulty and leaky, yet it did amazing things like creating the institution she was sitting in, in all its glory and horror. So Petula scratched her forehead as she quietly muttered a command for the nearest spirit to come to her.

The hallway exploded with dead souls, drawn towards her call, eager to finally have an appointment with a necromancer.[1] Crit, Petula thought. She'd overreached. She had been so long out of the day-to-day business that she'd made the rookie mistake of not being specific. Now, she would have to somehow satisfy the deads' curiosity if she didn't want to be haunted for the next decade.

"Crit," Petula said aloud. She heard someone snicker at the other end of the corridor. The woman bore the usual signs of a necromancer without dressing in all crosses and bones. It was in the way she held herself; the great beyond held no terror. The woman approached her, her heels clicking against the marble floor while Petula commanded the spirits to their liminal existence.

The woman coughed when she reached them.

"Yes," Petula said, still preoccupied trying to prevent a spirit infestation from mushrooming. Petula turned around to face the woman, narrowing her eyes, and dared the woman to say anything.

The woman's somewhat superior expression melted away as Rugus made his presence known. The woman took a quick glance behind her, as

---

1. THE NECROMANCER. Also, it would be easy to think that in a building full of necromancers, you would swiftly get your soul shipped to the afterlife of your choosing or to a new lovely body with all ten toes intact, but that was a misconception. The Council's necromancers were too busy planning the future for the living by writing memos about all the possible actions with an appendix included. To the Council, the spirits were a bloody nuisance keeping the necromancers from doing their job—so what if the concentrated spiritual energy inside the building might collapse the space-time continuum? It was not their problem. They would suffer the mild headache happily as long as they didn't have to deal with other people's shit.

if trying to choose which devil she should deal with.[2] She chose Petula to be the lesser evil as she stood her ground.

"Your grace." She bowed.

"Petula will do," Petula said, causing that constipated look on the woman's face that always appeared when she insisted people call her by her first name. Or it could be that Rugus straightened his back, or there was a chance it was the woman's usual expression. The latter was not that far-fetched after being trapped inside the Council's headquarters. It would strain even the strongest contender. There was nothing like shifting papers and pretending it was somehow significant to kill a soul. You know. Especially as the woman was a necromancer and meant to tamper with the lines between the living and the dead. Then again, there was no great difference between Petula and the woman if she really stripped off all the fancy titles and looked at the day-to-day actions. Petula also made papers spin.

"Papers spin," a spirit whispered into her ear. A sneaky one who had gotten past her defenses into her consciousness.

She evicted it with a simple phrase, "Leave."

The woman raised an eyebrow but said instead, "Mr. Crowen and the board are ready to see you. Could you please follow me?"

Petula let a deep breath out and hopped off the chair, pushing the remaining spirits back with a command.

Petula and Rugus followed the woman down the hallway.

"It seems we have been guided to the wrong place since the beginning."

"Accidentally," the necromancer clarified.

---

2. Petula or her boss. She had already selected the devil she worshiped, and no, it wasn't Kraken. It was the manifestation of pure terror people experienced when they first realized the world and their parents were imperfect, and they had to deal with it on their own. A church of similar souls met every Tuesday on North Ekton Street. Aunt Conney always brought her famous lemon cake to cheer up the otherwise dreary morning.

Accidents had kept happening every time Petula had been here, along with the boardroom moving around the building. Still, Petula let it be. If this was the best they could do, then she didn't have anything to complain about.

Monty found them before they headed down.

"Everything alright?" Petula asked.

"Yes, ma'am," Monty replied.

They were taken to the lower floors, to a small corridor filled with mothballs, dust, and spiders to remind Petula that this was done to mess with her. They were to wait behind two huge mahogany doors. That part, at least, they got right. Something she expected from the Council and its board members.

Mr. Crowen pushed the doors open, letting them in. Petula couldn't help but notice that the undead looked gravely ill by the standards of the dead, meaning he had been skipping his taxidermy appointments. She said nothing. She followed the man in, Monty and Rugus staying close by. The necromancer who had come to get them was gestured to leave, denied permission to see the board. The woman made a loud sigh. Rats indeed, Petula thought.

"Wait," Petula said.

The woman stopped in her tracks. Petula produced a small business card out of her pocket and handed it to the bewildered necromancer. "Make an appointment," Petula said.

That got a rise out of the undead bureaucrat, whose silence said it all. That wonderful passive-aggressive thing that makes the hair on your neck rise. Petula ignored the sensation and marched back into the boardroom. She expected to see the usual crowd, the ones from her files and ones she had been seeing the past couple of days, but Agatha Wicks sat in the middle of five other necromancers. Agatha's father was missing.

Petula tensed her whole body so as not to show the Council had done their homework and gotten under her skin.

"Good evening," she said and took the seat offered by Mr. Crowen. Rugus and Monty positioned themselves behind her, showing everyone they were willing and able to hurt anyone.

Mr. Crowen glanced at the two men but kept his silence.

Petula stared past the undead straight into Agatha's milky white eyes. She still remembered vividly how the woman had lost her sight. The woman shifted her gaze to meet Petula's. She could see through her spirits. Those eyes of hers made Petula's heart do funny things inside her chest. She didn't like the feeling at all.

As always, Agatha was as beautiful as she could be. Composed to perfection even in her plain Church clothes. She didn't wear tentacles like the others did, but Kraken was embroidered at the collar of her black dress. Her long white hair, drained of color by the same mishap that had blinded her, was tied behind her back in a loose knot. A few curls framed her face.

"Ma'am," Mr. Crowen said. Petula barely heard the man.

Petula let go of the past and returned to the present. "Good, we can start. We have a long list to go over, and we are already behind schedule." She plucked cat hair off her skirt.

"Yes, of course, ma'am."

"She prefers Petula," Agatha interrupted.

"Yes, Miss Wicks. Petula has always felt more approachable." Petula once again met her classmate's milky white eyes. "How is the Church treating you?" she asked, knowing she had delivered a punch, regretting it instantly. If all the rumors were true, Agatha was gaining popularity inside the Church, causing friction between her and Madam Sabine.

"Fine. Madam Sabine has offered me a position to go abroad and do missionary work. I'm to leave in six months. Until then, I'm helping my father with his duties. He's not doing so well," Agatha said. The usual lighthearted tone of hers was gone.

"I'm sorry to hear that. I hope he gets well soon. If there's anything I can do to help, let me know."

Agatha exchanged looks with Mr. Crowen.

Petula wondered what the undead had over her or her father to make her compliant. Agatha had always been friendly but strong-willed enough not to let anyone push her over. But this was not about Agatha. This was about the city.

Mr. Crowen settled near Petula by the oblong table. He was acting as secretary, making Petula conclude that old habits died hard.

"Petula," the undead managed to say. "Your proposal for the Council's future is—"

Never interrupt, Petula heard Dow say inside her head, but even he knew it had its uses.

"We can get to the proposal later. What I want is your accounts. I have been going over the payments you have received from the city, and I cannot find in the public records where the money goes."

The board looked startled. Agatha included.

"Mayor, we are a private entity in the city and use our money as we see fit to fund our operations. We are tasked to protect, educate, and keep peace in all necromantic matters. And I'm leaving out the resurrection services and licenses we provide," Miss Dankworth interjected.

"Yes, Miss Dankworth, you are quite right about your duties, but you are not and have never been a private entity. From the first contract to the latest, it has been clearly stated that you are an extension of the city's authority. More so now, as we are going to change how things are organized inside these walls. We have already established that the Council will be tied to the Public Resurrection Ministration, and the joint task force will be named Necromantic Affairs." Petula took a deep breath in to give her a second to think and watch the board's shocked expressions.

"The name can be negotiated, but unfortunately, not the merger.

Necropolis cannot keep financing both. Another option is to cut funding to the Council and strip the granted legal rights away. That means no overseas operations, no resurrection licenses, and no implementing rules for the necromantic community. You can advocate necromancers' rights to the Town Hall, and the Town Hall will consider them, but that's all.

"Another thing that the Town Hall has discussed is the current necromancer loaning programs. They are very strict and closely monitored by the Council. Their popularity and use have been limited. Necropolis has received many international complaints. From now on, necromancers have the right to practice outside Necropolis. The kinks in preventing megalomania have yet to be worked out. But these are the Town Hall's terms. Another thing is that Necromantic Affairs will be working closely with the Witches' Council. The name has yet to be finalized, but the witches will become a fully fledged part of Necropolis. I will leave the papers drawn by my legal team for you to look over, along with the old contracts with highlighted sections. You can have a look at them and get back to me."

On cue, Rugus produced a folder from the satchel he had been carrying for her and handed the papers to Petula.

Petula pushed them towards Mr. Crowen. The man was having a million tiny conversations inside his head. Petula felt sorry for putting him in this position, but it had to happen. His free rein had to end.

"Now, I will leave you to look them over with your lawyers. I have another meeting to attend, for which I'm already late." Petula rose. "And Miss Wicks, do come and see me before you leave. It's always so nice to chat with you. I do hope your father gets well soon."

She left, giving no opportunity for the board to argue back or use Agatha as they had intended. Dow had once said to her that great leaders weren't all-seeing and knowing, but they prepared even for the most unlikely events. It made sense. But it also meant that you had to be able to step into the shoes of others and view the world from their perspective, and that messed with one's head. An open mind was a curse and a gift that often left you stranded in the middle of a stormy sea.

Another thing a great leader has is compassion. Without compassion, you didn't know the hearts of men, and you made a poor substitute for cultivation. That was what cities, nations, and empires were for. To cultivate, both lands and men. Petula felt sorry for what she'd done, but it seemed leaders had to consider the suffering of the many rather than the few. In the long run, she hoped taking control of the Council would lead to less misfortune than now. A hope or a prediction based on current facts was the best she could do. All anyone could do.

With any luck, this would be the end of it all. Petula could go back to her home and rest. But there was no rest for her if she wanted to steal a moment to do what her heart wanted. Not even when she hadn't had time to eat anything today since breakfast. Petula's stomach was aching, and she was still jittery after seeing Agatha. But that should be the least of her worries. There was a line of diplomats waiting at the Town Hall to discuss Otis and the machine. Also, Dow had insisted they have alone time to go over all that had been set in motion. Then there was a meeting with Mrs. Maybury, Sirixh, and Frederick Kilborn, wanting to hear updates on how it had gone with the Council and to figure out the Town Hall end of it.

Also, Mrs. Maybury had, in the middle of all this, gotten her committee on modern technology working. They were now stipulating what all the new technology pouring in would mean to Necropolis's economy, culture, and day-to-day life. There was also a stack of articles on Petula's desk about what the rise of new technology meant to Necropolis's position in global politics. The committee seemed to think it was imperative they opened up necromancy and other forms of dead control and witchery for all nations—controlled and taught by Necropolis, of course.

Petula had dreamed of such freedom as a student, and now it could happen. Petula pushed all the state business away. Now, she would have that one thing she needed the most. That was to meet Henrietta and see that the witch was alive and okay.

Petula's coach came to a halt at the Necro Botanical Gardens' gates. The iron fences with their stone walls towered in front of her. Petula could feel a flutter inside her stomach, yet she got out of the coach and took a long stride into the gardens. The witches' extra security measures were sniffing around her. She could sense it as a chatter, pulling and pushing her. They made sure she knew she wasn't welcome here. The witches blamed her for everything that had gone down. The papers had written as much. Petula concentrated on every pebble at the sole of her heel, how they moved, listening as they ground together, twisting together with the way the leaves rustled in the wind and the scent of soil and flowerbeds. Petula needed time to stop just for a moment. But time didn't stop for anyone, not even for the gods.

Petula glanced at the main house, but she decided to go to the greenhouse where she and the needlepoint group always met. She was right. Henrietta was already deep in the flowerbed. Her husband hovered around her along with other witches, who looked unsure what to make of it. Imogene was nowhere to be seen.

"Henrietta." Petula cleared her throat.

The witches around Mother took a stance around the old woman.

The old witch looked up and pushed to her knees. She glanced at Monty and Rugus, hovering beside her. "It's okay," she said.

The witches didn't move.

"Everything will be alright," she added. That made the witches around her relax, yet none of them let their guard down.

"Did you arrange this?" Henrietta asked, clutching her trowel.

"The Council made their decision, and the judge..." Petula shook her head.

"You shouldn't have. But thank you anyway," Henrietta said, pushing past her witches, who still kept a wall between Petula and the woman. They let her through. Henrietta wiped her hands on her trousers, leaving a thick soil print, and clutched Petula, hugging her tight.

Petula stiffened. She kept her hands straight down and tried not to breathe.

Monty coughed, and the witch let go.

"The others?" Petula gasped.

"Home and trying to recuperate. All this is quite a change from prison life." Henrietta took a step back, giving Petula breathing room. The old witch offered a smile, looking Petula deep in her eyes.

Petula didn't know quite what to do with it. "It must be. I wanted to come and see how you were doing. I would have been at the trial, but you know how things are in the city."

"Yes, don't worry about it. We will change all that." The old witch gave her another smile. This one looked more forced and tired than the other one.

Petula wanted to ask why. She didn't. "You will. Witches will be granted a seat in the government. All the papers have been drawn and actions set in motion, but..." Petula didn't want to say that it all depended on Henrietta, who ran the Coven, and how the meeting to finalize it would go.

"You have been busy." The witch's features turned softer, the rigidness around her eyes and mouth melting away. She faced her husband and said, "Did you say Judika had made some sort of cake?"

"I'll fetch it for you, and some tea," Eurof said, ushering the other witches out with him. They left reluctantly.

"So, all is back to usual now?" Petula dared to ask.

"It would seem so. Though it's still undecided what happens to me, there are rumors floating around about Ruby's involvement with Wesley

Epith's death, which might affect Imogene's leadership. How about at your end?"

Petula wasn't sure if the old witch cared one way or another. Petula did. From her reports, Ruby Granger or her daughter wasn't someone she wanted to lead the witches into a new era. But it was Henrietta's battle to win if she decided so.

"I'm still alive; there's that. However, one thing is sure: there will be more attempts on my life as I go forth assimilating the Council into the government. There already have been."

Henrietta pushed her trowel into the flowerbed near them and sighed. "You don't have to do this alone. You have a friend to help you with that," Henrietta took a long pause.

Petula gave the woman that. It was what she owed to the old witch.

Henrietta continued, "Don't get me wrong, when we first met, I was willing to sell your trust, but not anymore. I don't care about the machine or the Council or the city's politics. Not beyond securing the gardens and the Coven and what we do to help witches. Especially now, as reports about persecutions around the world have peaked. If you and I can work together to make this all function, then... I'll do everything I can. Who knows, if we bitch and moan together, maybe it won't be as bad. Maybe we can keep each other in check."

Petula's first instinct was to let out a snarky comment. But saying something sincere would mean surrendering control to the woman. All Petula managed was, "Thank you."

She was saved by Eurof, who came in with a tea tray and lemon meringue cake. He set them on the metal garden table then withdrew, giving an awkward smile to Henrietta, who shook her head to signal something. What it was, it was between them. Petula couldn't even begin to imagine all the silent conversations couples had.

"Don't worry about it. I was lousy at this human-to-human thing before

I met Eurof. He taught me a thing or two. It's him who made it possible for me to be *Mother*. I would have done a terrible job otherwise. It all boils down to human relations, really. It's what politics and really anything is about. But let's not dwell. Let's eat cake and drink tea. A lot more fun when sharing it with someone." Henrietta winked.

Petula had never seen her make such a move. She couldn't help but laugh. Of course, it wasn't a spectacular laugh. More like a dry chuckle. Still, it was better than nothing, and it made Petula's chest feel all warm and wrong.

She took her seat opposite Henrietta, who was already pouring tea into the delicate porcelain cups. This time Petula even ate the cake and found it actually pleasant.

"What about the needlepoint group?" Henrietta asked.

"I don't see why we can't continue our meetings. Someone needs to talk to Lattice and see if we can do something about her predicament. I don't think she meant to harm us. And she made everything smoother when Ida and Annabella got into one of their debates. We need her."

Henrietta hesitated. "Yes, we can try again with her if you think it's wise."

"Better the demon we know than an unknown monster in the shadows. At least we can try to befriend it."

"What next?"

"I need to go and kill Mr. Thurston. I can't stall the inevitable."

Chapter Thirty-Two

THEY'LL WALK THROUGH PAIN AND SORROW TO OBTAIN IT

D awns were something different. They came with expectations, yet there was hope for the new and different. Mornings in the ghoul city were always busy. It was like the city needed everyone to contribute to make it glow and move. Yet there was another paradox. No one hurried around, no one ever felt like they needed to run to fulfill their duties. The tasks got done, and if they didn't, there was suddenly no need for them. Percy had grown not to question it. He liked his new routines. He woke up early, devoted his days to accounting, and shared a meal with Philomena and Elmer and occasionally with Otis. Then he attended public debates about philosophy, art, and politics or went to bed to read. Mostly he monitored Otis, seeing the man several times a day. His least favorite task, but the necromancer had started to grow on him. Percy also noticed that Elmer thrived even more than he did in the ghoul city. The man even took part in the debates about morality and took lessons from Cruxh to hone his skills as an investigator. It was infectious how ghouls took things to the next level. Percy had become better with numbers and all the forces governing them. All highly disconcerting.

Percy didn't know if they still needed the sanctuary, but Percy had his task to monitor Otis set by the mayor herself. So there was no leaving.

Elmer had applied for full citizenship, never planning to go back up. He said things like no one here laughs at me, and this is what a real society looks like.

"Hey, you," Philomena said, startling him.

Percy sat outside on the porch, waiting for her to come out.

"Are you ready?" she asked.

"Yeah," he said and joined her to get Otis. The necromancer had finally agreed to come stargazing to ease the pressure of having an enormous bedrock over his head. The same sensation that had plagued Percy and Elmer in the first days. It still sometimes did. Though Elmer now found it somehow reassuring, as if the extra gravity kept him more securely on the planet. Percy had concluded it meant he welcomed the possibility of being thrown out into space without the laws of physics there to catch him.

They walked in awkward silence. It was always there. Percy had noticed, but he didn't know how to make it go away.

"Percy," Philomena started, as if to ask his permission to speak, yet she gave him no time to let her. "I like spending time with you."

"Yes, I enjoy it too." Percy felt a shiver run all over his body. He had been taught never to say such things. He couldn't remember if anyone in his family had ever said the big word aloud. Not at least his grandma or his mother.

"I don't mean it that way."

"Me either."

"Oh."

They continued all the way to Otis's place without saying more.

Otis wasn't ready, as Percy had expected. The man was, as usual, tinkering with the machine and cursing Kraken to the bottomless pit of eternal damnation. Percy had learned to ignore the man's blasphemy. The necromancer meant nothing by it. And what did Kraken care of Otis or his machine? Or him, for that matter? They were all insignificant. The men's destiny barely registered in the vibrations of the universe. He was wrong there, but how was he to know that some men had ways to make the gods notice? Nevertheless, Percy had come to accept his insignificance a long time ago. He had never had grand plans for himself or thoughts of importance. He had always done his duty with the least amount of harm possible. But now there could be hope.

Percy glanced at Philomena. He left such thoughts for those private moments and focused on Otis. "It's time," he said from the door, half expecting the man to refuse, but Otis shoved the gears out of his hand and got up.

"Let me get my coat," he said.

Percy watched as Otis walked to his closet. The man looked different and more at ease with himself. He had softer features, and he looked more androgynous compared to when he had been brought here. The scars from the fire were gone.

"What are you staring at?" Otis let out when he drew the coat on.

"Nothing, just thinking about things." Percy was sure his cheeks were getting red.

Otis let out a wide grin. "If it's nothing, then I'm fine with that. But if it was my body, then I don't mind you looking. I'm quite pleased with how it turned out. I think I'll keep this one longer."

Percy's breath was caught in his throat. Otis enjoyed it.

"It suits you." Percy defused the situation.

Otis shrugged it off, and they headed out to the tunnels. It was a long, complicated trek to the shoreline caves where the lair came to meet the sea. Philomena could navigate the path with ease. Percy was sure she took extra turns and loops to make the journey harder and avoid giving Otis any bright ideas.

But all such worries got wiped away as the beach opened in front of them. There was no place to flee safely. The only escape was through the freezing cold water, and it didn't look welcoming with its dark, rough rocks peeking out. No ship could land here, and only a foolhardy person would attempt swimming in these waters.

The moon was high, and the air was crisp, making the stars shine brighter. Next to Percy, Otis shivered, but he was sure it was not from the cold but from seeing the open sky. It was all twisted and odd after being under the stones for so long. Otis refused to say anything, but he took a position on a rock near the shore and sat down. Percy and Philomena gave him space to be on his own. They sat down closer to the cave entrance, keeping the worst chill away. However, Percy could feel the same shivers that had passed over Otis shaking him as well.

"It takes a long time to get used to it. Even I sometimes miss the sky so much that it aches," Philomena said, taking his hand.

This time he didn't flinch. He drew their entangled hands closer to his stomach and put his free hand over them, holding tight.

"I will get it."

She laughed softly. "You will."

They sat there watching the stars, and he occasionally glanced at Otis. But the necromancer was not in any hurry to escape.

After a while, he came to sit with them.

"You know, I cannot make the machine," Otis said when they let him have his space. "It was always Levi who made it work. I just stripped the souls to their bare essence and made them manageable. Levi infused them into his cocktail and made the mechanical parts work with it all. I have tried and tried, but there's something I don't get. I have even tried to put my spin on the concept by using a mouse's skull I found and the dead critter energy in the caves, but that's not the key. I managed to tap into the markets above and do some banking, but what good is a fortune if I'm stuck here? At least I got the beach part I wanted."

"I'm sorry," Percy said.

"Me too. Think about all the trouble I have caused. It's silly if you think about it. How one apparatus or even an idea of it can make the whole city spin out of control." Otis laughed.

Percy couldn't help but join him. The man was right. It was absurd. Terrifyingly so.

"I'm kind of glad Levi is dead and the prototype was destroyed," Otis said.

"What now, then?" Philomena asked.

"They won't leave me alone. They will come calling one day when they have sorted out the initial blowout upstairs. The machine is too promising. They'll walk through pain and sorrow to obtain it." Otis shook his head.

Percy squeezed Philomena's hand.

"Elmer told me there have already been attempts. He has been tracking them down with the ghouls." Philomena hesitated as she said it. She glanced at Otis and then at Percy.

"As expected," Otis said. Then he laughed. "Percy, it seems like you and I'll be stuck together for a long time. You are not as bad as you were back then, but that doesn't mean you are not infuriating. I don't think we mix well together."

Percy snorted. "No, we don't. I should have let you die and saved all the trouble."

Otis laughed. "You should."

"You can't say that," Philomena protested.

"Yes, he can. It's the truth."

"What will the mayor do?" Philomena changed the subject.

Otis massaged the back of his neck. "She seems like a reasonable person, and she never was that keen on getting the machine. But I did screw her over."

"It's just that she can't keep hiding you here forever. And they might send you with him." Philomena sighed, looking Percy deep in his eyes.

Percy held her hand tightly and said nothing. There was no controlling the future. He had to believe the universe would provide whatever it provided for now. He just hoped it let him keep some of the newfound happiness that he'd stumbled upon.

There has to be a resolution. It can't be any other way. The mind yearns for it. And a little bit of peace and quiet, not all the hassle of running around like a headless bird with the ancestors that once ruled the world.

Henrietta stared at the ceiling above her bed. It felt odd to be in her own bed. She traced the lines between the tiles. They reminded her of the web fungus made underground. The same web everything was made of. There was now a line between her and Petula, the young necromancer, an unlikely ally. There was an even stronger one between her and Eurof. Eurof, who let out a quiet snore next to her. She loved him more than anything. She would have to disappoint him.

Outside, birds were calling for warmer winds to come through the seas. She listened to their caws while letting the lines guide her in the right direction. Not that she needed any fortune-telling. Henrietta already knew what she needed to do, consequences be damned.

She carefully got up and placed her feet on the floor. There was no light coming from the windows. Everything was still dark, and any decent being would be sound asleep. Henrietta had never been decent. Her only chance was to become so in her old days. When she had been young, she had been one of those wild children unable to stay still, toe the line, and not ask silly questions.

Henrietta brushed her hair with her fingers. The knots in her bed hair reminded her how she had never combed it as a child. "*A bird will make a nest there,*" she heard her mother say. Her mother had loved her, but

440K.A. ASHCOMB

Henrietta hadn't made it easy for her. She wondered if her teacher of a mother would be proud of her now. The only thing remaining from that child was the soil under her fingernails and the dirty clothes by her bed.

Henrietta closed her eyes, seeing yesterday unfold in front of her, hearing the gavel bang against the wood as the judge had decided the charges against them were dropped. Petula had arranged Theodora Lycwell as their judge. That much was sure. Henrietta saw the judge's narrow yellow eyes looking at her and winking. Another wink. How had the mayor known she and the judge had been best friends as kids? And the mayor had trusted them not to sell her out. Henrietta was sure it hadn't even crossed Petula's mind.[1]

The judge's eyes hadn't been the only eyes upon her. Imogene had looked at Henrietta with astonishment and fear, and something else, which Henrietta couldn't name. But there had been vast numbness between them as Henrietta had arrived in the gardens, Ruby standing beside her daughter, sneering at Henrietta with accusations and contempt, demanding that nothing needed to change.

Henrietta opened her eyes and let them adjust to the darkness. She got up from the bed and tied the robe around her, which she'd left lying on the armchair in the corner of the room. The morning robe was made from the finest silk. It had little leaves painted on the green fabric. A gift from Eurof.

Everything smelled like lilacs. Even Eurof had when he'd embraced her in the courtroom after the charges had been dropped. Henrietta still remembered the pitiful state the courtroom had been in. While the police functioned in the city, there was a lot to be desired for the city's legal system. No one used it. There were easier ways to get justice in Necropolis.

"Mistress of nature," Henrietta whispered as she tiptoed around the bed and headed to the door. The wood felt soothing under her soles.

---

1. There, she was wrong, but Petula would never let her know that she had taken a chance with them and won.

"*Let's go home*," Eurof had whispered into her ear then. He had held her tight, not letting go even at the judge's request. Now he slept soundly on the bed, letting out scuffs of air as he turned to his right side.

Yes, home, Henrietta thought. She carefully closed the door behind her and turned to face the empty corridor. No one seemed to be awake. The halls of the Coven were quiet. Only the walls moaned as the temperature changed with the arrival of the early dawn.

Henrietta made her way to the basement, moving slowly down the flight of stairs. She clutched the pouch dangling from her neck. She was glad to notice it was still there. No one had stolen it while she slept. Henrietta had filled the pouch with the garden's soil when she'd arrived at the Coven. It was the first thing she'd done. Henrietta pushed the basement door open. She snapped her fingers, and the dark basement came to life. The candles mounted in iron candlesticks swelled to full flames. Everything glowed warm orange. There in the middle of the basement was a summoning circle, drawn on the stony floor. Henrietta tiptoed down the two steps and took her place in the middle of the circle. She sat down, letting her robes drape over her knees. Henrietta was there to wait and see.

She would know what to do if she was any witch at all.

Henrietta was right. Imogene stepped in through the door after only a short wait.

"Let her," Henrietta said to the roots she'd tied into the door frame and the two wooden steps to guard her from Ruby and her like. But Ruby was a coward, unlike her daughter.

Imogene bowed her head. "Mother," she said. The girl was alone. She knew the customs, unlike her mother. Too arrogant, that one.

"Mother," Henrietta repeated, bowing her head. She was still sitting in the middle of the circle, her feet crossed. Henrietta could not help but observe the dark circles under Imogene's eyes. She looked like she had been crying.

"Couldn't sleep?" Henrietta asked.

"Not even a wink," Imogene said. "May I?" the younger witch gestured to the boundary of the circle.

Henrietta nodded, and Imogene stepped over the threshold. She knelt in front of her, keeping a space between them. The young witch shifted her nightgown so that it hung loosely beside her feet. She was barefoot, as was Henrietta, wearing a white nightgown, as was Henrietta.

"So, how do you want to do this?" Henrietta asked, smiling at her former secretary.

"I think by spells is the custom. You with your roots, and I with my blood." Imogene showed the cuts on her arms.

"You finally found magic to call your own."

Imogene scoffed. "It has always been with me. I just dared to use it."

"Against me?" Henrietta asked, astonished. She'd expected the attempt on her life to be made by someone else. Not Imogene. She was too soft for that.

The young girl nodded, the color fleeing from her face.

"I see. I underestimated you. I shouldn't have," Henrietta said.

"Everyone does. It wasn't only my mother who wanted me to lead the Coven. I sold you out."

"And?"

"And I thought I could take care of things better than you, but..."

"It's like herding cats."

"Yes," Imogene snorted.

"You have to make them think it's their idea, whatever you decide. You will never get the credit. Not with this lot. They are too proud and stubborn for that," Henrietta said.

The witch looked up with a hopeful expression. "Yes," she stuttered.

"So you want to learn?" Henrietta asked.

The young witch dared to nod, biting her lower lip.

"Then no one has to die."

"She will never accept—"

"Leave your mother to me," Henrietta interrupted Imogene.

The young witch bowed deeply, pressing her forehead to the ground. "Yes, Mother."

"Get up. Nothing of that sort."

Imogene lifted her head, and Henrietta saw that the young witch's eyes were swollen from tears.

Henrietta leaned forward and wiped the tears away. "Judika should be up already. I think she can whip us up a breakfast. I don't know about you, but I am famished. It's all this dead and dying business. But we will change that. You and I. This city of ours should celebrate the bloom of life and not decay." Henrietta tied her hands around the younger witch's shoulders and guided her up and out of the basement.

"I'm so sorry, Henrietta. I should never have..." Imogene let out a long, stifled sob.

"None of us should have. We humans seem to be faulty like that." Henrietta squeezed the younger witch harder.

Chapter Thirty-Three

And on the Death Rattles

W as it truth or harmony that needed to win? Raul wasn't sure what he should root for any longer. He had written the truth. A part of it, at least. Yet, nothing. They hadn't exactly told him not to say anything, but here he was sitting in his office, exonerated from the murder charges, not having written a single word about what he'd found out about the Council.

The charges had wrecked his reputation inside the newspaper. He hadn't gotten new assignments since. His exoneration was all due to there being no body, but Sandy kept spreading lies that he had, in fact, killed someone, and the only reason he was free was because someone was protecting him.

Everyone at the office avoided his company. To top it all, he got to read Sandy's reporting about Otis Thurston and how his exile to the ghoul city was going. You couldn't call it reporting. Fluff, the worst kind. And Sandy seemed to be at a loss. Lattice Burton wasn't there to keep everyone in line. So it was all down to the writer's conscience what to report.

That wouldn't last. Not in Necropolis. The Council would... Raul wasn't sure if they would win. Petula had gotten the better of them, or so his sources said. Not that Sandy said any such thing. She still seemed to write for the Council, painting their mayor as irresponsible for handing the necromancer to the ghouls, but there was no coherence in her pieces. They all sounded a tad paranoid, yet they were fluff full of adjectives, speculations, and grand claims, simply emotive manipulation. Just to get people all stirred up without having to lay down any information at all.

Raul drew his typewriter closer but then pushed it back. He didn't feel like writing. Truth had no say nowadays.

They were transporting Otis today.

Raul took the jacket from the backrest of his chair and took his new hat off the table. He opened one of his drawers and took a whiskey bottle out. He walked straight out of the office, making sure everyone saw him leaving with the bottle, his editor included. Raul dared to glance towards Sandy, seeing the self-righteous look on her face. Good, Raul thought.

He flinched as he stepped out. There were still red stains on the cobblestones where the woman had been killed. He still didn't know why the creature had killed the woman and why it had led him into the Council's headquarters. Though he could guess.

Raul walked past the spot and handed the bottle to the first drunkard on the street he could find. He didn't have to walk far. There was always someone hanging around in front of the local pub, even when the day hadn't gotten past noon.

"Here you go." Raul thrust the bottle into the man's arms. In return, he didn't get a thanks, just stink-eye. But Raul didn't care. He moved on, heading to the Town Hall to call in a favor from his friend. When he arrived there, he slipped in through the servants' entrance and found Elvira at her desk. Raul coughed, and the woman cocked her head at him. She wrinkled her nose, drawing her whole face into an angry line, making her look like a hawk.

"Hello, doomsayer," Elvira said.

"Elvira," Raul greeted.

"What do you want?"

"Access—"

"No interviews, and no, I won't tell you anything. Go away, doomsayer," Elvira interrupted him.

"Just a peek. All I need is clarity."

Elvira scratched her head, then narrowed her eyes. She seemed to look past Raul and straight into him simultaneously. As if she saw the future, his and the world's, unfolding in front of her. She snorted and then nodded. Without saying a word, the woman returned to the papers on her desk. Raul stood there, stunned. He had been ready to offer her a bribe or even demand this as payment for getting the city's crime statistic down to the neighborhood level to her, but nothing. The woman let out another snort, meaning if he was going to have that peek, he had better do it quickly. Raul hurried up the stairs, slowing down only when someone was coming down. No one questioned his presence. Not when he'd gotten past Elvira.

Raul made his way to the mayor's office. Every creak he heard made him jump. He waited for the two giant men to appear at any time and force him out, or worse. That much he had gathered already, that he had been a tool for the mayor. And while Rugus and Monty seemed like sensible people, sensible people didn't care for their master being spied on.

The hallway to the mayor's office was quiet. The eerie kind of quiet that makes the hair on the back of your neck stand up. Raul pressed himself behind the first crude statue he found. It was some sort of nightmare horror with enough eyes to share with the blind. Raul took a breath in and tried to gather the courage to march into the mayor's office and demand an explanation. But the silence was still there.

Raul leaned deeper against the wall, waiting for the moment to happen. What he got was the floor creaking. Ever so slightly. Just enough for a paranoid person to hear. Raul remained in place, hoping that the statue was big enough to hide him. He dared to peek just enough to see the hem of a black skirt gliding down the hallway. Kraken shit, Raul thought and pressed his head back against the statue. It wasn't Petula. Of that much he was sure. Whoever she was, she was taller than the mayor. And that someone knocked on the mayor's door.

Raul heard Petula shout, "Enter."

But the someone didn't do that; they waited at the door, expecting something.

The door opened after a while. "Yes?" It was Dow's voice.

Then there was silence, and the door closed.

Raul dared to peer just enough to see Dow and a mystery woman standing in the hallway. She looked familiar. Raul was sure he had seen her somewhere. That she held significance. She was dressed in all black, which wasn't strange in Necropolis. A requirement, in fact. She wore a fedora with peacock feathers attached to it. Not a requirement. More like a personality trying to seep in.

"Not here," Dow said.

"You owe me. I let you kill one of my lives for your goals..." the woman purred.

"Go to my office and make sure no one sees you," Dow commanded.

Raul withdrew behind the statue, listening as the woman left and Dow went back into the mayor's office and then came back out. When they were gone, Raul got out from behind the statue. He stood there in the hallway, at a loss for what to do, smelling the woman's perfume. It made him feel sick and his heart race as if someone was trying to kill him. He clutched his chest. Everything was spinning, and his mouth felt dry as paper. He needed a drink.

"Mr. Porter, do come in before you get yourself killed." Petula's voice pinned him down in the moment.

His heart was still racing, but the rest of his body followed the command, opening the closed door.

"Don't look so startled," Petula said when he entered the office. "And close the door. We don't want others to know. Do we?"

Raul pushed the door closed and lingered there.

"Don't worry, Dow won't be back. Whoever pulled him out, it sounded highly urgent. Something clearly not meant for my ears and eyes," Petula said. She was sitting behind her desk with the map of the city laid out in front of her. Raul had heard that the Church of Kraken was planning to attack the convoy transferring Otis. So were Threebeanvalley, Leporidae Lop, and a few other nations. Not to mention the International Shipping Corporation, Ministry of Truth—not Necropolis's, but there were places in the world that thought such a bureau would make a fun addition to the society—and the Bank of Necropolis. There had to be a few others whose names Raul didn't recognize. Not all of them were trying to obtain Mr. Thurston. Some were trying to kill him. Otis would emerge from underground at Mess, where the undead and their like lived. It was the easiest place to secure. Hortensia Caster and her men, along with Cruxh, had been busy all morning, making the place survivable. Or so Sandy had stated to the whole newspaper and Necropolis.

Raul couldn't help but notice Petula was unlike he had seen her before. She was fully dressed to Necropolis standards, wearing a top hat, her white hair curled. She also wore tails over a formal short black dress. She looked like she was born to lead the city of the dead, with all the coffins, skulls, and bones embroidered into the top hat and on the collar of her dress.

Staring at her made the spinning stop, and Raul's eyes focused back on reality. Raul gasped for breath.

"I know," Petula said. "I'm going to meet Mr. Thurston publicly today, and I was told to dress the part. They wouldn't have it any other way. They even insisted on me wearing makeup, but I had to draw a line somewhere."

"But..." Raul managed to say.

"You came to see me, or so I gather," Petula said when he didn't add anything coherent after his but. She lifted an orange tabby off her lap and placed the thing on the map. The cat curled up in the middle of it, and before it pressed its head to its paws, the cat cast a judging glance towards Raul, deeming him irrelevant.

"I..." Raul glanced at the door.

"There are no answers, Mr. Porter. If I had any, I wouldn't be dressed like this."

"But..." Raul was starting to hate how pathetic he sounded.

"Books, Mr. Porter. I recommend you write one, and then maybe the clever ones will read it and know the truth. Isn't that what you seek? Truth, I mean."

Raul was sure his mouth was hanging open.

"If it's money and status keeping you in the newspaper rather than the truth, then go to the university. They have all sorts of positions open, and they pay, and you can write. They like it when people write. The rest of the world, not so much. Not if it isn't in the form of the fluff your newspapers seem to spew out." Petula narrowed her eyes, and for a second, Raul was sure they went all black.

He stepped back and blinked his eyes. A dark, tall man stood behind the mayor, his hand on her shoulder. But when he blinked again, there was just an empty space where the man had been.

"Once again, Mr. Porter, books are your answer." Petula's voice sounded hollow. "Now you'd better leave. Dow is coming back, and I don't think you being here is in his plans."

"What's happening?" Raul spat out.

"I'm going to see Mr. Thurston, and I will make it all go away," Petula said in her usual melancholic voice.

"But..."

"I mean it, Raul. Books and leave."

Raul hurried out, looking back as he closed the door behind him. The shadow of a man was there.

"Be careful," he said as he closed the door. Raul hid behind the statue once again as Dow came up the stairs. He waited for the secretary to enter the mayor's office.

He fled the building and hurried home. He still saw the stranger's eyes peering into his soul and smelled the perfume the woman had worn. Raul felt like he'd escaped death as he slumped into his unmade bed. The room started to spin again but in another way. This time something seemed to click inside him. Maybe the mayor was right. Then again, maybe not. The news was there for a reason. And he wanted to tell the news with his integrity intact. He needed to find another avenue. Raul just didn't know what that was. Maybe he should go to the town square and shout what he knew; at least there the public could question him.

There's no escaping the fact that death waits for everyone. If there's such a creature as Death, only the dying are privileged to know. But it isn't a privilege the living care for. Otis would attest to that. His heart was beating fast as he was escorted to Necropolis through the underground tunnels. He had been summoned. He'd protested this was unconstitutional torture. That they should have let him stay with the ghouls. No one seemed to agree with him, least of all his lawyer. There was mutual agreement with others that Otis couldn't stay with the ghouls. Some might argue for a good reason, as Otis had come up with a perfectly good plan to win the trust of the ghouls and then escape. But Miss Kraken Shit Mayor thought better of it.

What he'd read was that she was no longer Necropolis's sweetheart. Good, she deserved everything coming to her. Otis pressed forward despite wanting to turn around and flee. There was no fleeing. The ghouls were by his side in the glowing tunnels. That was another thing that irked him.

This place shouldn't exist. The ghoul city was full of masterpieces humans would kill to obtain, but they were locked here in the basement with the monsters.

Otis frowned at Percy, Elmer, and Philomena's quiet murmurs. He was sure that the banal man and his friends were chatting about how glad they were to get rid of him. Otis had thought Percy had changed, but no, he was still an obedient little boy, marching to the beat of his master's rules. Rules that oppressed the masses and made the rich free of guilt. There was no ounce of original thought in Percy's tall frame.

Otis knew he was being extra harsh and rude, but it was a shame to waste a good sulk, especially on such a day. And if, as a bonus, he made others' lives miserable, then even better.[1] However, it could be argued that if he paid more attention, he might start seeing the opportunities left for him. No one had shackled him. The ghouls weren't looking that closely. Percy had eyes only for Philomena. And Elmer was mostly deep in his own thoughts. But all he saw was doom and gloom, so doom and gloom was all there was. You couldn't help some people.

They emerged out of the tunnels into the streets of Necropolis, surrounded by wooden shanties pretending to be three-story houses. Behind the shacks, the early January light shone cold and bright, making Otis shudder. Otis wanted to crawl back into the tunnels away from the gathered onlookers. He hated the feeling of suddenly having too much space around him. But this time the ghouls were looking, and his jerking movements were clocked. One of the ghouls laid a claw on his back, making Otis flinch. The ghoul withdrew his claw and muttered an apology.

Otis grunted, "No worries," in response, and he actually meant it. Not that he cared to elaborate on that. He kept eying the roads packed full of people. The police officers in their blue uniforms and custodian helmets

---

1. And no, he didn't see anything wrong with that.

tried to keep people out of the square, but it wasn't easy. Everyone wanted to see him. There were little kids waving their homemade banners with I love Otis written on them. But Otis didn't see those. All he saw was the adults and the hate on their faces. He waited for the moment they would break free and then... No more Otis.

The crowds roared his name in unison, accompanied with a storm of flashes as amateurs and professionals memorized the moment. Otis flinched at every light powder used. The ghouls beside him weren't happy. They said nothing. They did nothing. But Otis felt the change in their mood. He couldn't blame them. The entrance to their home was compromised, and there was no telling what the huge, careless Necropolitan mob might get into their shared heads. There was a possibility of violence, and the ghouls hated violence.

That was what Otis liked about them. They were docile monsters that could have taken over the world if they saw fit. But they hadn't. They wanted their own version of Otis's dream of a life of leisure and gaiety without duty and death, though with a heavy set of responsibilities and a lot more thinking. The last two Otis would prefer to live without. But he had been born into an academic family, one that saw idleness as rude and glee as overrated. His mother would be proud now. There was no glee or idleness in his cards.

In the middle of all the fuss stood a single prison cart with two huge black horses meant for him, taking him either to the gallows or some brutal labor camp. If they thought it could keep him secure and alive, they were fools.

Otis grimaced.

The flashes surged again and then died for a fleeting moment, as if the crowd, the ghouls, and the rest of them took a fraction of a second to breathe. Then, the silence turned into a roar, cheering Otis's name, and the flashes returned. The banners waved in the air, making the susurrus of life even louder.

Otis drew his hands against his ears. The ghoul city had been alive but not loud. Not hungry. He wanted to flee. The irony of it all was this was what he'd yearned for when imprisoned by the Council: recognition of his excellency. Now there was no excellency. He was nothing more than a glorified skull spinner and not some great machinist for the crowds. Their hope to escape the poverty of being slaves to the whims of others wasn't in him.

Otis hurried to match his steps with the ghouls and the rest of his escort. They were speeding towards the cart, more than willing to get rid of him. Otis couldn't blame them. He was a ticking bomb just one false move away from detonation. The ghouls gave their little nods and exchanges with the officers. Otis let two undead police aid him inside the cart while the crowd continued roaring. Otis wondered if they wanted his freedom or downfall. Then again, it might not be an either-or question.

The door shut behind him, and he heard Percy whisper, "Don't worry. This is not the end." But then the man got pushed away, and Otis couldn't reply. He sat down and leaned against the wall, his whole body feeling heavy. From the small window on the door, he saw the ghouls leaving.

Otis dug his fingers into the wooden bench, squeezing it so hard that the tips of his fingers were getting numb from the pain. The cart nudged forward, and Otis held his breath. *To the gallows*, he thought. The cart moved again, but this time the whole cart began rocking. Otis latched on to the bench tighter. To keep from falling, he swung his legs onto the bench and braced them against it, growing his limbs longer in the process to get the full effect.

The roar outside was definitely no longer a cheer.

Something slammed against the cart, making it shake as the horses tried to pull free. Otis swung off the bench with full force, hitting his head against the wall. He tried to pull himself up, but his hands couldn't find a hold. He leaned against the wall a little longer, and when he got his breath back, he touched his forehead, finding something wet and sticky there. The wound had to wait. The cart rocked violently again, and Otis fell to his side.

"From the bottom of the miserable ocean," he wailed.

The rocking stopped, and he curled into a ball at the back of the cart. His sides ached, and the blood from his forehead kept dripping onto the wood. Otis knew he should move, do something to escape, but he didn't have time to form a coherent thought. The door to the cart was ripped open. Otis expected to see a mob or the officers reaching in, but what he got was dead energy. A spirit. Then another and another pushing in.

Otis quickly drew protective wards around himself before the spirits reached him. Time seemed to slow down as he stared at their twisted mouths and angry gazes hovering at the brink of his wards. They were sent to kill him. There was no doubt about that. Otis was grateful that the ghouls hadn't used the Council's iron cuffs to restrict his talents, otherwise the spirits would have bitten into his flesh and consumed him. Otis shuddered. Whoever was behind the attack was bold enough to let the spirits loose in the middle of Necropolis.

The spirits roared at him. Otis took in the hatred. That was what his university education had prepared him for. And nothing much else. He listened to their hatred spewing over the rising panic outside. Otis cast out another spell to dismantle the subtle attack coming from his left. It only angered the spirit who had attempted to kill him. It and the rest of them hissed at Otis as they swayed against the wards. Words like pathetic were thrown around. The spirits should have known better. Otis was pretty used to hearing such words. They were far less hurtful than what his mother had said to him whenever he failed the experiments she'd set. Far less.

Still, the spirits were nasty little things, and they should be shown that it was polite to shut up if you didn't have anything nice to say. This was why you never let the dead leave behind unfinished business. You burned their doilies and smashed their woodwork and took apart their art. And you let the dying confess their absolution and made damn sure to listen. Otherwise, they turned sour.

Otis didn't care for spirits. Never had. Deteriorated dead energy was easier to use than conscious spirits. The only spirit he liked to work with was a cooperative one. The angry gave him the willies. The last time he'd dealt with angry spirits had been in Threebeanvalley. It had been a fluke that he'd gotten so many under his control. Otis was sure they would have turned against him in the end. He didn't believe in being a master. The unequal distribution of power always got you one way or another. Luckily Percy had been there, or he would surely be dead.

The spirits lashed out again, crawling all over him. Otis drew his hands over his head, feeling their hatred make his clothes flutter. He felt nauseous at the smell of his own sweat and blood.

"Go away," he snapped at the spirits.

They didn't make a move. Instead, they waited for him to drop his guard, screeching every time they failed. Otis regretted the day he'd followed his mother's footsteps to become a necromancer. Not that he was ever given a choice. He had been admitted to the university based on recommendation.

The roar was getting louder, and more spirits were seeping in through the walls. At least the first ones had been decent enough to hold their beliefs about doors after death. He cursed at the blood still oozing out of the wound. He didn't have any desire to be trapped inside this hole when the reaper came calling. Otis let out a command for the spirits to back off. Whoever controlled them had a greater hold than he could ever possess. Still, the wards made sure they wouldn't be able to touch him.

Otis hesitated but let go of his head and pushed up. The spirits were frozen at the edge of his wards, watching his every move for a mistake. The door behind them was ajar. Why hadn't the ghouls come to his rescue? Part

of him wanted to shout that if this was how they treated him, they could...
He wasn't sure how to threaten a ghoul. Still, they were being rude to toss
him aside like this. Where was their sense of responsibility or doing what
was morally right?

Otis wanted to curl back into the fetal position and be done with the
world. The world didn't want it that way. The flesh fettle he'd made dashed
through the door, pushing against the spirits and taking hold of Otis's
collar. It dragged Otis out of the cart. All Otis could do was watch the
creature, astonished. It wore an oversized long black raincoat and a hat with
a wide rim to hide its deformed face that had become more solid and less
rancid.

Otis expected it to be raining outside to give that last dramatic effect the
situation called for, but it was still dry and cold. However, the darkened
clouds had gathered over the square, ready to rain down on the command
of someone powerful enough.

Otis lay tangled in the flesh fettle's arms as the spirits attacked him.
When they couldn't get to him, they tore into the flesh of the fettle, making
it scream in agony. But it didn't let go. It kept its grip on Otis.

Outside, people were running to safety. Someone had unleashed enough
spirits to invade the whole city, attacking everything and everyone moving, concentrated mostly around the tumbled cart. Past that, Otis saw
the Monster Hunters and others fighting not only the spirits but other
creatures undoubtedly sent for him. No one could be foolish enough to
open the gates to the afterlife, letting the dead flood out of their own free
will. You couldn't control the hungry and the desperate.

Otis shouted a command over the roaring spirits and the crowd to
extend his wards around the flesh fettle. The spirits lashed in rage as they
came into effect. Otis wasn't sure how long he could keep them up. He
was starting to lose his concentration. His whole body trembled after every
command he made, which didn't bode well. He would give himself ten

minutes at most.

Around them, the camera obscuras still flashed on. Miraculously, the spirits left the reporters and their photographers alone, making the first steps towards the invention of war photography. Some reporters were already considering stitching the word "press" into their clothes as talismans against misfortune, snipers, and shrapnel. They had no clue what these last two were, but both the reporters and the photographers felt it highly important to have a guard against them too.

Just past him and the flesh fettle, Percy and the ghouls were surrounded by the loose spirits. They were fighting them off, but they wouldn't last long either. There was an excess supply of the dead here on this soil. Wave after wave crashed against the ghouls. Seeing Percy and the ghouls under pressure made Otis's whole body feel all weird. This wasn't his fault. People made their own mistakes. But Otis couldn't help but be reminded of what had happened in Threebeanvalley. It was exactly the same. Only this time he wasn't the one who'd sent the spirits against the hexer.

"Let's go," Otis commanded the flesh fettle, turning his gaze away from the hexer and the ghouls and the others. It was foolish to feel affection towards anyone. Stupid on so many levels. Early on, Otis had learned that attachment only led to disappointment and hurt. So there was no need for him to intervene. Percy and the ghouls would survive. They would protect Philomena and the small goblin man, Elmer. It was all right if he escaped. He didn't owe anything to Percy or anyone for that matter. Not even one wasted thought.

This was stupid.

"Stop," Otis murmured.

The flesh fettle stopped.

"We need to go back," Otis sighed, indicating towards Percy and the ghouls.

Beyond them, the crowds were starting to clear off, leaving only the ghosts and the officers, the hunters, and those who were still trying to get to Otis. There were hoods with tentacles involved and other more conspicuous outfits from the hired help with enough cunning and mass not to be seen. Though it didn't matter. Otis saw none of that. He had his full attention on the hexer.

The flesh fettle dragged Otis towards Percy despite letting out complaints and moans as the spirits got tenser around them the closer they got to the ghouls. Something was wrong. The spirits didn't feel right. And Percy seemed to be pushing more spirits out of him than towards him. The ones getting away swirled around them, dashing towards the fleeing crowd.

Otis dropped some of his guards, and the spirits that got to him felt—he wasn't sure what they felt—maybe wrong.

Percy saw them coming. "Go," he mouthed.

Otis shook his head. "I can't."

"Yes, you can. We did this for you," Percy said. "Now leave!"

Otis's mouth hung open, and he swallowed hard, frozen in the moment. The flesh fettle wasn't stunned. He didn't wait for a command from Otis. He dragged the necromancer with him, but they didn't get too far. They were stopped by a man approaching in a top hat. He whistled as he walked through the spirits. He was gray and lifeless, wearing tails with coffins, skulls, and bones stitched into them. His eyes were pitch black. He wore the usual signs of the death spinners. He dragged not only spirits but also mindless zombies with him. A sight Otis never thought he would see in the light of day. A wet dream most necromancers joked about when they had had a drink or two.

The flesh fettle stopped in its tracks, dropping Otis to the ground. The spirits fled around them as the man kept coming, still whistling the haunting tune. Otis knew death when it came, and this was it. Or maybe this was the monster the Council hid in their basements. There were rumors about secret necromantic testing and weapons. Or maybe it was the dark lord himself. Otis had never given a thought to such superstition. Now it seemed like he should.

"Old Man Death," he let out, bowing deep.

There came a chuckle, filling up the open space around them. The spirits had fled. There was just stillness around them, the flashes still going on.

Otis backed away as the man didn't stop. Otis commanded the flesh fettle to attack him, and the fettle followed the command, lunging at the man. But when it reached him, Old Man Death tore it apart with one swift hand movement. The corpse fell in two halves on the ground. The man wiped his red hand against the hem of his jacket and turned his full attention back to Otis.

Otis crawled away, but the god didn't stop there. It walked over the dead body. Otis hurried to his feet, mumbling incantations to wake the spirits to aid him, but none came.

The man was close enough to grab Otis by his throat. All he did was laugh. It sounded all wrong. It sounded light yet dry, hollow and commanding, and mocking and kind.

"Don't bother," the man said. The voice was all wrong too. It sounded familiar.

Otis couldn't decipher it.

Not that there was a point. The man unleashed his spirits and zombies on him, commanding them to devour him. Otis saw it. They bit into his flesh, tearing it apart, eating his liver and heart. Yet he stood there unharmed. Like the flesh fettle did, holding on to the rim of his hat and nodding as it took its exit. Otis felt it letting go of the bond between them. He could force it to stay, fortifying the bond. He didn't.

"Don't move or do anything, and you will have your second life," the man whispered, sounding a lot like the mayor.

Otis panicked. He let out the incantation he'd formed, and the excess spirits around him surged against the god. But something heavy dropped on the back of his head, and Otis lost consciousness.

Chapter Thirty-Four

ALL THIS BUSINESS MADE FROM DEATH AND DYING

Henrietta was kneeling down in the garden at the Necropolis Reformatory for the Criminally Insane and Other Offenders. The prison gates rose over the garden, reminding her that they were meant to keep people in. She had her hands in the soil, and the faint sun shone through the clouds. The early spring birds cawed at the trees shielding the garden from the direct sun. Somewhere behind her, Imogene was chatting with the warden. She could hear their quiet voices. Henrietta had come today even though Imogene could manage on her own. All the bad blood between them was gone, and they understood these things happened. That was Necropolis politics for you. There was no day someone wasn't contemplating killing you.

She continued weeding the patch, occasionally brushing her forehead.

A shadow landed across the garden and over Henrietta, accompanied by Imogene saying, "Mother."

"Is it time?" Henrietta let out.

"Yes. You have a little time to clean up before we have to be at the Town Hall."

Henrietta brushed her knees as she got up. It would be a spectacle if she went in looking like this to the first-ever Town Hall meeting where witches were allowed.

"Everything is set here for the next month. The warden will see the weeding is done, and they can start to sow. I have drawn a detailed plan for them of where the new vegetable patches should go, so you don't need to worry." Imogene handed her a handkerchief.

Henrietta wiped her forehead and cheeks and pushed the not-so-white cloth into her apron pocket. December was well past, and the spring had surprised them all. Mostly due to the fact that they were still alive.

Henrietta unwillingly left the prison garden behind. This had been a special visit. Henrietta no longer had time for anything other than the city's politics. The plan to go home to Amanita with Eurof had been postponed. Yet eventually, they would go home. That much she had promised Eurof. She gave him a few hours of uninterrupted time before they went to bed. It had brought them closer and made Eurof less restless.

Imogene pushed a parcel into Henrietta's hand on her way to the Coven. The girl had packed a lunch for her. Henrietta unwrapped the brown paper folded over the incredible sandwich Judika had made. She bit into the sandwich, tasting the magic only Judika knew how to do.

At the Coven, Henrietta washed quickly as Imogene laid out an outfit for her.

"You don't need to do that for me anymore," she said.

"I don't mind. I truly don't."

Henrietta had started to prepare Imogene for the future to come. She would make a fine Mother someday. Imogene just had to unlearn her bad upbringing: all the lies her mother told her about witchery and what to pursue in life. Imogene was ready to hear her, unlike before.

"Imogene," Henrietta said as the witch tightened the corset's laces around her waist.

"Yes, Mother?"

"I want you to take the floor today at the Town Hall. Give them a detailed account of how the Coven will be an integral part of the city's economy. I'll do the opening, but you'll handle the details about how many inquiries we receive overseas to study under us, how many refugees we take in, our international program plans and what kind of revenue that brings in with taxes."

"But..."

"You know the numbers." Henrietta refused to hear any further objections. She finished dressing and wondered if this was the last time Imogene would be there to help her. She would have to find another witch to run the day-to-day errands. Imogene was already too busy for that.

There came a knock on the bedroom door as they were heading out.

"Everyone decent enough?" Eurof asked.

Imogene let Eurof in. "I'll leave you two alone and get the papers." Imogene ducked her head as she pushed past Eurof.

"Everything alright?" Eurof asked, looking after Imogene.

"She will someday accept that you don't hate her," Henrietta said.

"But I do a little. I can't help myself," Eurof admitted.

"No one is asking you not to," Henrietta said, and then she went on to change the subject. "I'm glad you suggested going to the prison." She walked to him and let him embrace her. "It did the trick," she whispered as she pressed her head against his shoulder. It was home.

He held her. "I'm glad. Weeding always makes you happy."

"I just wanted to come and say good luck," he said after a while.

She just kept her head on his shoulder, existing solely in the peaceful bliss of his arms. When it was time, she let Eurof escort her out to the coach. Imogene was already waiting for her, not showing any worry about her running late. She just smiled at them as Eurof let go of Henrietta's hand when she got inside.

Once the coach took off, Imogene nervously went over the papers and muttered all the numbers aloud. Henrietta let her do whatever she needed to do to get ready. She instead focused on looking out of the window. Maybe a witch could lead the city one day, or who knew, perhaps a ghoul or even a vampire or a werewolf. Not to mention a ghost. Henrietta chuckled. That would be a day worth seeing.

When they reached the Town Hall, the spectators had arrived. The camera obscuras preserved the moment of Henrietta and Imogene standing on the Town Hall steps and bearing the Coven's crest. Henrietta forced a smile on her face, hating the cameras. She found it disconcerting to see her own face in the papers. The superstitious part of her believed that gradually her soul was being snatched away. And who knew if such an apparatus might send the entire nation spiraling into a dark pit of self-hatred and depression with a whole lot of obsession over trivial things.

Henrietta politely answered the reporters' questions about how joyous this occasion was; how finally the Coven would be represented at the Town Hall; how this would bring the Necropolitans closer together.

"Mother." A ghoul appeared next to them, bowing her head and letting Henrietta escape. "I will escort you in." The ghoul pushed a path into the Town Hall, making everyone hop aside. The situation inside wasn't any better. All the members of all the political parties in the city were present, even those who usually slacked off. Everyone had come with their full army of assistants. There was barely room to breathe or move inside the foyer. But it seemed like the Town Hall had hired ghouls to organize everything. They showed everyone where they should go and sent away people deemed to be extras. Everyone who was anyone was already there, even Kitty Worthwrite. Henrietta had read from the papers that the woman had made herself the head of the commerce coalition to secure her place at the Town Hall meetings forever. The previous leader had died in unfortunate circumstances. Something about swallowing poison accidentally.

Mr. Crowen was there too. The Council had been assimilated into the government. Henrietta wasn't sure how Petula had managed that. Whenever she asked about it, the mayor made an excuse to change the subject. Another thing the mayor refused to speak about was the bizarre death of Mr. Thurston and the appearance of Old Man Death. The thought of the... god—she didn't want to use that word—gave Henrietta the shivers.

The whole thing had to be a mass hallucination provoked by Otis unleashing spirits to escape, which, in the end, turned against their master. That was one of the explanations. Henrietta couldn't keep track of how many other theories floated around the city. Some said Petula had orchestrated the whole thing and hidden Otis somewhere to make her the machine. Others said the Church of Kraken had kidnapped the necromancer using a mirage. Every single explanation ended up sounding like a conspiracy theory.

Henrietta and Imogene followed their ghoul guide to the audience chamber. Petula had reserved them the best seats. Henrietta dared to glance at the mayor. She gave a weak smile in response. The necromancer looked fatigued, as if multiple stories were running inside her head and she was trying to figure out which was the one being played out in front of her. One thing was for sure, Petula didn't look happy. Henrietta wondered how many objections or political plays against the witches joining the Town Hall she had countered today. Even the newspapers questioned Petula's decision. What use were witches in a land formed by necromancy?

Petula rose up from her seat, and the buzz in the room quieted down.

"Good afternoon. I'm glad to see so many of you could attend today's Town Hall meeting. So many new faces..."

Henrietta was sure the last remark was sarcastic, yet the mayor delivered it as a compliment.

"We have three items on the agenda for today. First, we have to decide if we should allocate funds to washing and restoring the city's..." Petula glanced at her papers. "...One thousand and thirty-seven statues."

Henrietta was sure the woman grimaced. She'd seen the numbers, and the money and hours required to maintain the historically significant statues were mindbogglingly high.

"After that, we must choose a retirement plan for the Town Hall members." Petula hurried through that statement.

Henrietta was sure that hadn't been on the docket she'd received.

"And lastly, we will vote on whether the Coven should become part of the government... Let me see... Yes, the first speaker for today should be Helaine Peabody from the Historical Society. The floor is yours." Petula sat down, drawing the papers she'd opened on the table closer to her and grabbing a pen to make notes.

A tallish woman with high cheekbones and a nose to match them, dressed in businesslike clothes, took the podium near the huge windows. Light filtered in through the painted glass, portraying skeletal figures among dead trees. The woman coughed and ignored the commotion coming from the impatient politicians. She took her notes out, laying them on the podium.

"Ladies and gentlemen," she began. Henrietta tuned out. So did most of the audience, but not Petula. No one noticed that because they were too busy wanting to stab their ears with their pens, having to listen to the monotonic ramblings of the historical society representative. But Petula persevered. No detail was too minuscule for her attention. Especially if she was to grant a major portion of the taxpayers' money to the project.

The same thing happened with the second item on the agenda. The Town Hall members barely registered the subject, in a hurry to get to the main attraction. Someone might argue that Petula had planned that, taking a step towards being able to retire alive from her position. Some couldn't even fathom why a retirement plan was necessary. They were planning to run the government until the last bone in their body gave out. The only ones who noticed her move were Henrietta and Mrs. Maybury. However, getting out of the position alive was still far from Petula's reach.

Necropolitans liked their leaders strong and bloody. Henrietta was sure that if anyone could get out alive, it would be Petula. Thus far, the young necromancer had fended off the multiple assassination attempts and duels that had increased in frequency as the Council had become part of the government.

"Now, that's settled then." Petula cleared her throat as the room murmured about this and that, waiting for the main entertainment to start. "Last on the docket is voting for the Coven to join the government. Before the ballot, we'll hear from Henrietta Culpepper, and then we will open the floor for questions. So Mother, if you please." Petula showed the utmost respect, bowing her head. She didn't have to, but she did it anyway.

Henrietta rose from her seat, feeling the movement in her stiff knees. They ached and told her that she had been sitting too long. The room felt smaller as she climbed to the top of the podium. There you could look down on the attendees. This had to be the reason why most religions had their priests standing over the masses. One step away from being gods themselves.

"The Coven is grateful to have this opportunity, and we don't take it lightly," Henrietta started. "We are ready to build a new future for Necropolis, where witches play an important role in securing the prosperity and unity of all. Not only as the managers of the most visited attraction in the city but also by creating jobs for future generations. We already have an overflow of witches coming from all over the world to study and visit us. By expanding this program, we can bring more revenue into the city. Imogene Granger has prepared the statistics and our plans to make the Coven a vibrant part of Necropolis and the Town Hall. We carry with us the knowledge of nature and minds to be bent for our use..."

Henrietta let her mouth do the talking, drifting away from what she said. The last part, *to be bent for our use*, made her uneasy. She had to offer it for Necropolis, which wanted more than tea and cakes to nourish their souls.

"...The Coven would choose who is best to represent them... But now I will step down and let Miss Granger go over the details. With the numbers, you will see why the Coven should be an integral part of the Town Hall and how it can transform the city we all love. The witches can help take the business of death and dying to a new level." With those words, Henrietta let Imogene take her place.

She saw that the younger witch's hands shook and heard her mutter her prepared statements as she moved to the podium.

"Thank you, Mother. Now, if I may show you the current number of applicants and the actual requests we get..." Imogene stuttered her first words, but soon she got so immersed in the numbers that her words began to take on a life of their own, boring some but making Petula Upwood smile.

Imogene kept speaking and speaking, and finally, when it was time for questions and opinions, everyone in the room was too exhausted to make a real objection. Henrietta would take the credit for that if someone ever asked, but truthfully it had been a fluke, an afterthought. Though Imogene had always had a fondness for statistics and clauses.

Mr. Crowen coughed when Imogene stopped. "The Council sees that the witches are a wonderful addition to our policymaking, but maybe as a sub-commission. We find it concerning to spread the city's deciding power too thin..."

"No power should ever lie with only one party," Kitty Worthwrite snarled, removing any need for the Coven to intervene. A cynical person would think such a statement wasn't made out of altruism but to give the banker more room to get her point across by playing different parties against each other. Money was money, and it could buy power and popularity. Such was the nature of a democratic system. Not incorruptible even from the get-go. Buying one voter had just shifted to mass-marketing and lobbying.[1] But you had to be really jaded to think that. Or possibly aware of those who played the resource game with a very twisted sense of how to win.

Petula silenced Mr. Crowen when he looked like he might argue. "We have heard all the arguments. You will find two colored bone fragments in front of you..." The mayor gestured at the desks in front of them.

Henrietta found two finger bones wired to the desk. One was indigo and the other as white as bones came. Copper lines led out of both of them. Henrietta followed the wires as Petula went on.

"You are to vote through them. I was assured that this new voting system will work." Petula gestured at the skull behind her inside a glass box. The copper wires led to its eye sockets. "The skull it is attached to will calculate the nays and yeas. Now, if you can please refrain from touching them while I explain." A few hands and claws had already reached for the bones. "The dyed bone is yea, and the uncolored one is nay. You are to hold your chosen appendix on the bone until it vibrates, and then your vote has been secured. I will give the go-ahead when you can touch it."

As Petula spoke, a lanky, bearded young man stepped up next to the glass box and laid a hand on it. The man looked like one of those new waves of people who wore plain suits instead of stylish necromantic velvet and leather clothes. Nevertheless, he was a necromancer. It was the eyes.

"Is everything ready, Lord Kelvin?" Petula asked.

The lanky man nodded.

"Now, please do choose. Uncolored bone as nay and blue as yea."

Petula laid her hand on her desk and chose one. It was impossible to see what she picked because the side of her desk rose high.

Henrietta laid her hand on the blue one, holding her forefinger on the polished bone. When it finally vibrated, she withdrew quickly. It felt like

---

1. The beauty creative minds can come up with.

lightning in a bottle. Around her, the Town Hall members let out odd noises. Some of them laughed. Others screeched. Then there were the dead silent ones, who you could feel thinking.

"All the votes are in, ma'am," Lord Kelvin said in his lifeless tone.

"Let the skull speak then," Petula let out.

The skull rattled as the necromancer laid his hand over the glass box. "Seventy-three percent for the yeas and twenty-seven for the nays."

"Thank you, Lord Kelvin. It seems like we have our vote. The Coven will join the Town Hall."

Second chances. That's what it was all about. How was one supposed to get it right from the get-go? Otis opened his eyes. Everything was too hazy at first. The room and the faces staring at him were spinning. But he wasn't dead. His body ached too much for that. He was lying on something soft. Based on the firmness of the thing, most probably a couch. Then, when he could focus, he saw Philomena's face. The witch smiled at him.

"Welcome back," she said.

"Good, he's awake," another voice said. It was the mayor, standing behind the witch.

Behind her stood the all-feared Dow Spurgeon.

Otis searched for Percy and Elmer or any of the ghouls, but they were nowhere to be seen.

Otis groaned as he pushed up to his elbows. Philomena hurried to help him up.

"What's going on?" he groaned again.

"A second life," Petula said. "But only if you agree to our terms. Otherwise, it's some miserable dungeon Mr. Spurgeon can find for you."

It was hard to read if she was joking or not. It didn't feel or sound like a threat. Just a statement of facts. Still, none of it made sense. Not what had happened, how he'd gotten here, or why the mayor... why the mayor... he couldn't grasp the last part his brain was trying to tell him.

"That's not an explanation," Otis groaned again. He managed to drag himself upright, not letting Philomena fuss over every tiny thing that could go wrong. He looked around. The room he was in was stacked with books and papers on every surface, including the divan he was lying on. There was a small stack of books at the foot of it, next to it, and if he looked down, underneath it as well. Even the fireplace in the middle of the room was buried behind a pile of books.

They were in the mayor's study. Somehow it looked even more ransacked than it had after Wicks' attack. Otis focused his gaze on the flames heating the room.

"Why didn't you just kill me?" he asked. Making noise kept him firmly secured in the here and now. If he went on and let the silence take over, there would be a flood of murmurs in his head about the future and the past, all catastrophic. He didn't like when his mind talked back. It never had anything good to say. Just mindless babble that tended to disturb even the cleverest minds.

"I promised that you would survive if you worked with me. You didn't, but I still kept my end of the deal." Petula crossed her arms.

"I see. That's not an explanation, though," Otis said more out of habit than to get under the mayor's skin.

Petula looked away from him to the witch. "Is Mr. Thurston fit enough to have a discussion?"

"He should be fine. I can find nothing wrong with him. Just light bruising at the back of his neck, but that will go away. Whoever hit him knew what they were doing." Philomena added the last sentence with a careful, questioning tone.

"Thank you, Mistress Lace. You may leave now. I take that your silence is a given."

Philomena bowed her head to the mayor. "Of course. I keep my word. Mr. Thurston is dead." Then she turned to face Otis and said, "Good luck, and it was nice knowing you."

Otis swallowed and then stammered, "You too." That was all he could manage when Philomena took her exit accompanied by Mr. Spurgeon.

Petula used the opportunity to sit next to him on the couch. Otis felt as if he should shift farther away from her. He stood his ground, which meant nothing. There weren't many places he could escape, except maybe the enormous new ornamental red rug in the middle of the room. Even that was littered with books. But there was a space in the middle of it, and he could picture the mayor sitting there, reading all day long. Or hoping she could.

"Mr. Thurston, I know you must be confused. But as I said before, this is a chance for you. I'll keep that promise. Only before I can help you, I need you to do a few things for me." Petula tapped the book pile at the end of the couch.

Otis recognized them. They were his notebooks. The last time he'd seen them, they had been securely tucked inside the undead man's briefcase. Some of them were even from before his imprisonment, when he was making the skulls.

"They were a fascinating read. It's clever how you made the skulls. So interesting, in fact, that I might attempt to make one. More special than the machine you and Levi Perri made. The one that made the whole city go crazy. The Church of Kraken is adamant about finding your soul and having you resurrected. So are the banks. But they won't find you. To think, all this, and you have nothing to give them." Petula shrugged.

Otis was sure he had written all the information about the machine in code, but she had somehow cracked it. Somehow the mayor made him feel highly self-conscious. He could usually joke around the discomfort or even propose that he could turn himself into anything she could dream of. All he managed was, "I see."

"I guess you want your explanation," Petula sighed as if he'd failed some test.

Otis nodded.

"I have a new identity for you and a ticket out of Necropolis to a lovely island with enough sun and leisure for you to be content with for the rest of your life. But you can never return, never attempt to make the machine again, and never be Otis Thurston again. Preferably, you should find a more suitable profession to occupy your time. I can't force you not to practice necromancy, but it might be wise for your own safety not to. It will draw attention. They'll never stop searching for you, dead or alive." Petula got up. She took the notebooks with her, walked to the fireplace, and dropped them in.

Otis screamed. He hadn't meant to, but it came out. The animalistic agony. It was like she'd dropped him in there, erasing his existence. The mayor let him scream. So did all the others in the house: Dow, Mr. Colton, and Monty and Rugus. Otis was ignorant that he was being watched, that he wasn't actually alone in the room with Petula. It was just as well. The scream turned into a suffocating pressure in his chest, making just a wheeze come out.

"It's a shame, I know. You have worked marvels to advance our profession. Mechanizing necromancy. But we are not ready for that. Not when we are still fighting about who gets to sit in the big seat. I would love nothing more than for your machines to see the light of day. They could solve so many things. It's just as well that you cannot make one, and that your partner died in that fire.

"Don't get me wrong, I'm not doing this with a light heart, and I fear that I'm making a mistake here, to be honest. Yet here we are." Petula took a poker off the rack next to the fireplace and stirred the fire.

Otis couldn't find words to reply. He was surprised that something so primal had come out of him. He hadn't thought he cared. It had always been this great big game for him; to see if he could take a concept further, any concept, really. But he had never cared. It had been just to pass his time until he could go out and drink and preferably find some company to spend the night with. He wasn't that particular about what kind of company. He had always thought nothing mattered. Life and everything boiled down to the question: "What would amuse me next?"

And here she was offering all he had ever wanted. He would be a fool not to accept. This just felt wrong. He should be dead now or rotting away in prison. Yet here he was, feeling moderately warm and watching everything he had been being burned into oblivion. Otis snorted.

"Okay, I accept, but I want a good life," he said. "Not some shitty thing where I need to work my ass off. One with a servant or two to take care of my needs, and a pretty view out of my window... and good company. Not some remote place where there's no civilization. I want to be a gentleman of leisure. That's my price for silence and disappearing for good."

"You are not in any position to bargain, Mr. Thurston. You owe your life to us. Several assassination plans were targeted for the exchange, not to mention kidnappings. So, we gave them a show to remember, a divine justice. It's a good thing to have a bit of religion in the city other than Kraken, and thanks to you, Old Man Death is alive and kicking." Petula put the poker down in its stand and turned to face Otis. She didn't seem that convinced by her little speech.

Otis let it go and gave a faint smile. "Were they real? The zombies, the spirits? You?"

"Some of them. But mostly, they were there to tell a story."

Otis said nothing. He was pretty sure she wouldn't tell him how. How could she command and control so many at once and give herself that appearance? Let alone have zombies with her. He hadn't seen proper zombies, controlled ones, ever. Accidental zombies, yes, while at the university, but not the real deal.

Petula tilted her head and then straightened it. She took a deep breath in. Before she could say anything, Otis cut her short. "So, did they buy it? This Old Man Death?"

Petula smiled. "That's another thing you need to forget. Rumors are floating around that you crossed the gods with your stunts. You are going to be a legend. I would say a living one, but I'm afraid that's not the case."

"Oh well, at least Otis Thurston amounted to something. So what's my new name going to be?" Otis leaned on his knees, feeling a lot better. The banging at the back of his head was gone, and he was past that sickening state where you are sure you are condemned for good.

"Fred Orgel, a man of moderate fortune, will arrive in New Monster-rata to monitor the National Trust for Wildlife. Mostly the role consists of throwing parties and acquiring money from the wealthy. That said, I wouldn't make myself too known if I were you. There's only so much protection I can give." Petula walked to a bookcase, picking up a parcel. She handed it to Otis.

He opened it, finding legal documents concerning Fred Orgel and his small fortune. He frowned. "Why wildlife?"

"You might as well do something good," Petula answered immediately, as if she had the answer ready.

"Why Fred Orgel? Couldn't it be Jonathan Osborne or something else?" Otis fiddled with his new identity card.

"Sorry, it has to be Mr. Orgel from now on. He fits your description and build, and those scars on your face..." Petula nodded towards the imp claw marks and the burned flesh from that fateful night back in Threebean-valley. Otis automatically reached for them, cursing himself for letting his shapeshifted form collapse.

Petula continued, "They can be explained by the accident you suffered on the way there. Mr. Orgel drowned not two days ago, to the dismay of none. He had no living relatives, no personal acquaintances, no one to miss him."

"It's sad to be him," Otis said. He stared at the picture of the man. He could make him more handsome.

"He was a lord. You get to be one too."

Otis must have smiled, as Petula added, "This is not a reward, Mr. Orgel. It may seem like one. But if I had my say, you would rot in prison. I know how you made your machine work. You used souls as energy. You stripped their personality and history for your use, and I condemn that to the highest degree. For any other leader, capital punishment would be serving justice, but..." The mayor shook her head.

Otis had to look away. He wanted to say that he felt sorry about it all. That he had done it because it had been the best option back then. That if he could correct his past, he would. He wasn't proud. He could still see his victims' faces. The realization they would be gone. Gone, gone, gone, echoed inside Otis. He scratched his forehead, where the burn marks were the deepest.

"Here we are," Petula said in a lighter tone when Otis kept his gaze on his hands. "Maybe use your next life more carefully. Maybe let Fred Orgel care about wildlife and New Monsterrata and its peculiar fauna. It's like a mini-Necropolis, but with more sun and, as I have gathered, it is more easy-going."

"Sounds like my kind of place," Otis said, lifting his eyes to meet Petula's.

"You won't ever be Otis again. No machines. Skulls only if necessary and with Necropolis's approval. There will be reports, so I can see that you keep your word. I'll drag you back here if necessary, and there won't be a trial, just sentencing."

"Fred Orgel won't let you down. Where Mr. Thurston was a notorious machinist who brought the gods down to deliver divine justice, Mr. Orgel finds tea parties and strolls around the gardens fulfilling. It is his life's mission to guard wildlife and enjoy a laugh or two. Such is Mr. Orgel."

As he said that, Otis shaped his appearance to meet the name. His features were slightly more angular than his usual narrow structure but still regal. The scars were there but not as prominent. He altered his green eyes to be brown to match his new hair. He touched up the appearance with a hauntingly poetic look, narrow mouth, and almond eyes. But he didn't make himself too pretty. Just enough to counter the scars he was to carry.

"Then we agree, Mr. Orgel. You are to leave tonight. All your belongings will be provided for you."

"At your service, ma'am." Otis stood up and bowed like a lord would. "It's my duty to guard your interests in New Monsterrata."

EPILOGUE

U nlike the sea in New Monsterrata, this one roared against the cliffs violently, making whitewater splash over the top. Again and again, the waves hit the shore as if trying to smash it to pieces. The wind howled, and there was no hint of that beautiful sunset Otis had seen. Not here. Here, darkness swallowed the landscape under the watchful eye of Kraken.

The sea god had risen from the depths. There beyond the cliffs on a private beach, the Church of Kraken, led by Madam Sabine, prayed for the god, sending offerings its way. They asked for the machine; they asked for the inventor's soul; they asked for the city to be theirs.

Kraken hadn't risen for them. Instead, there was a new belief in the city, a whisper that was the seed for the creation of a god. It had always been there, dormant, waiting for just one more push to become. Now was the time. Its acolyte stood on the cliffs as the sea chipped them away one pebble at a time. The city whispered of Old Man Death. Death had never needed gods. It had just existed. The unavoidable condition. A force the Necropolitans had found a loophole around, but eventually, even a soul and dead body would follow the second law of existence.

The man, the acolyte, stood there thinking he'd won. But you couldn't control the gods. You could only hope they cooperated, or you ended up having to chop off their heads. And if you didn't do it the right way, the head would grow back. Kraken's life was far from any chopping block.

Necropolis belonged to Kraken; it existed as long as there was belief. Thus far, it hadn't cared what the mortals did, but now... now it sank the gifts meant for it and sent its tentacles forward as a sign that it had heard their prayers. Beyond its sea, the mortal man the Church sought was alive, watched by the other gods. Gods that played games with souls.

Kraken withdrew its tentacles. The message had been sent. But what they made of its sign was not Kraken's concern. It sank under the waves, letting the sea swallow it. Before its head was fully submerged in the water, it saw the acolyte turn away and walk back into the city, where the heart of all Necropolitans lay.

Otis swung his legs down off the hammock and pressed his feet deep into the white sand. He looked up and saw a wave gently rolling up the beach, only to retreat to the ocean before hitting his toes. The sun had already set for the day, yet it was still warm outside. Lying here and listening to the bird calls and the sea was a ritual he'd begun at the end of every day if there was no party to throw. But of course, there was almost always a party to throw. Last night had left him nauseated, so here he was, enjoying the peaceful moment in paradise.

If this was his punishment, then the gods and the mayor had a funny way of delivering justice. Running New Monsterrata's National Trust for Wildlife was a cakewalk. He could do it in his sleep. All people wanted was for him to give speeches about how preserving nature and its fauna and flora was imperative. He gave those speeches at parties serving food and drinks to the rich. Most of whom were colonists or tourists in this Shangri-La. He wasn't quite sure where all the money he acquired went or how much there was. Others in the trust took care of that, and whenever he asked after the money, they suggested that maybe he should plan an extravagant event to raise more awareness for their vital cause. Events that drew crowds from all over the world. Otis was pretty sure not all was right in paradise. But he wasn't convinced it was his battle to fight.

Oh, sometimes he fancied maybe he was sent here because something was amiss. The natives, the colonists, and the reservation didn't seem to go well together. Then, of course, there were the parties, but that was all the trust did, except open new nature walking paths or commission paintings of rare flowers and birds.

Otis scratched his head. This was not his headache to have. He'd earned a nice, cozy retirement.

Otis left the hammock behind him and headed down the narrow passage in the middle of the tall trees. The porch of his mansion and the National Trust for Wildlife headquarters was already being lit by the servants not too far from the beach.

"Sir," they greeted him and bowed their heads as he walked past them.

He sometimes forgot that he was now a sir, Fred Orgel, living on his inheritance with no care in the world. Sometimes he wondered how the real Fred Orgel would be. Would he care about the money that seemed to float through their hands and disappear somewhere? Would he care that the Necropolitans ran the place rather than those whose ancestral lands these were? And if he would care, why?

Otis made his way upstairs, where his living quarters were. He had the third floor entirely to himself. A place where he was expected to live with his family. A romance would look good, his advisers said, especially when he asked too many questions. They presented suitable partners at the balls he threw. Too easy. Too mundane.

He passed his drawing rooms and other useless spaces and headed into his bedroom with its massive wooden bed and see-through canopy. But he wasn't yet ready to retire. Not alone, at least. He opened his closet, shut the door behind him, and pushed a panel behind his suits. The panel slid open.

Behind the secret wall, he had built a small working space where he had his skulls, copper wire, and necromantic shards and tools. The row of skulls on the shelf glowed in all colors, from blue to orange. They were doing banking all over the world, especially in Necropolis, speculating with the future and hedging bets on everything that was going on. Otis had made a fortune betting on the Council being assimilated into the government. He had full trust in the mayor. This was his way of connecting to the land of the living dead. It made him feel like he hadn't been forgotten.

Otis took a new skull from the box next to his work desk. It had been quite an adventure to secure as many as he had. Grave robbing had been involved, along with sneaking out and shapeshifting to change his appearance.

This new skull wasn't going to tap into Necropolis's markets. He meant it for New Monsterrata. He was going to see what flowed in and out of the place and, most importantly, who. He didn't have to, but somehow the idleness he'd yearned for stopped being fun after a few months. Otis assured himself that he was just dabbling to pass the time. That he was doing this for the flora and fauna. Just a peek to satisfy his curiosity. After all, he was meant to stay away from anything that would draw too much attention.

He hummed as he drew lines on the skull with a needle-sharp metallic carving tool. He was just killing time.

Petula stood in the night air, watching the city from high above. The usual mist hanging around Necropolis stubbornly covered most of the houses and streets. Only the tall buildings with pointy rooftops and gargoyle infestations rose above the mist. So this was going to be her home from now on. A city that never slept; a city full of monsters. Petula was more concerned about being stuck with the humans. Their restless tendencies

K.A. ASHCOMB

and egoistic natures combined with their fleeting lives made them dangerous, mainly because their need for energy never subsided. She was one of
them, but sometimes she wished she had been born as a bat or, better yet,
one of those giant beasts she sometimes saw diving in Necropolis's waters:
blue whales. What kind of dreams did they dream? What kind of world did
they see?

"Miss Upwood," came a voice behind her. A voice she had been expecting.

"Cruxh." Petula turned around to face the officer. She had the tabby on
her lap.

The ghoul bowed his head, and she nodded in return.

"You wanted to see me?" Cruxh stated, not with his usual friendly tone,
gesturing to the strange surroundings. They'd met and socialized several
times. Petula had had dinners with him and Mrs. Maybury. But this time,
she'd asked him to meet her here in a secluded place, just the two of them.
She had barely been able to shake off her guards. She was sure they were
looking for her somewhere, pissed off and panicking. Not here, though.
Petula had set up spirits to scope the place, and here on the hilltops where
the ancient ritual places lay, there was no living soul other than Cruxh
and her. After tonight, she would have to find another way than astral
projection to fool her escorts and... Dow. She still felt drained.

"Yes, I have something for you." Petula took the vial full of ghoul essence
out of her vest pocket with her free hand. It was slightly less full, but she
hadn't wasted a single drop.

Cruxh took the vial without saying a word. He waited, and she would
deliver. So it went. So it always went. Life sought answers the universe gave
only to the most curious and tenacious seekers.

"It's beautiful. It truly is. You and your kind are made of the cosmos. The
pureness of it. That force that ties all of us together. If you look through
a microscope, you can see tiny stars and planets being born and more.

If I'm right, it's the thing Mr. Thurston sought when grinding souls for his machine. But human souls don't come close to what yours is. Maybe you have another purpose than hiding in your caves? Who knows?" Petula sighed.

"How?" Cruxh asked carefully.

"That I don't know. Maybe by intelligent design. Perhaps by an accident, or just because it could happen. I don't know. We have our gods, but I gather you don't."

Cruxh shook his head.

Petula had to look away. There was that sadness and yearning he'd had when he'd handed the vial to her. But the divinity and birth of the universe were beyond her reach. Death and energy she could understand.

"Thank you, Petula. You have done more than you can imagine for our kind. And if there is—" Cruxh bowed as he said all that but looked sharply up as Petula interrupted him.

"There's something you can do."

The ghoul narrowed his black, lifeless eyes.

"I need you to find out who Dow is."

The ghoul's free claw curled into a tight fist. "If that is what you want, then I will do my best, ma'am."

"Not for the mayor, Cruxh. For me. I have and will continue to put my life and future in his hands. He's not a bad man, but I need to know more. All that he does..." Petula couldn't finish that sentence. Everyone knew what Dow did. He was just there, and things happened. Not the things others thought were at stake. No. Something grander. Something only the man could see. He could see past the charade and see the notes that composed it. Information seemed to float to him and let him use it to shape the world. Some said that information was all there was. That it was how everything came to be. But would it mean there was no matter, no now, future, or past, or actuality? Petula wasn't ready to throw matter out of the window, yet she wasn't prepared to disregard those notes that made everything have a meaning.

"Can't you—"

"I have asked, but he keeps his guard up."

"I'll do my best." Cruxh reached for her shoulder and laid his claw there.

Petula put her hand over Cruxh's claw pressing softly against her shoulder and smiled. This was a lonesome game. She hadn't realized how lonely she felt. It was so easy to get caught up in what she had to do. And for that, it was imperative to forget the person inside. But underneath the skin of any leader, there was a being that remembered and yearned to be heard, understood, and loved. But of course, some forgot such things, ignoring their basic needs, caught up in the desperate hunger to lead.

"Thank you," Petula said.

"Shall we?" He looked down the path where he had come up.

"We'll stay just a little longer."

His silence said it all.

"Don't worry, I'll be fine. No one will harm me when Her is with me."

Cruxh left them alone.

As Petula turned to face the city once again, something moved inside her. Something she didn't recognize. If anyone had seen her, they would have seen a man standing in her place. The last thing Petula heard as she left was an echo, "Old Man Death." It seemed to echo in her. It seemed to say that she was there to give the city a god to believe in.

"You need a name," Petula whispered. "How about Amity?" she asked and petted the cat.

Somewhere, a small egg pulsed inside a green knapsack. It was a machine unlike anyone had ever seen. It had traveled wide and far, giving something to those who had nothing, like a miracle that could never stay still. It belonged to a girl and a boy and their pet rabbit.

ACKNOWLEDGMENTS

A special thanking are needed for those who helped me to complete this book. Writing The Council Of The Dead and publishing it wouldn't have been possible without their support. Foremost, thank you for my husband, Henri, who carried me through my father's death and helped me to write this book, who never let me give up. He always pushes me to be the best version of myself. Special thanks to my beta readers, Raymond St. Elmo and the rest. They pointed out the book's weaknesses and strengths, giving me hope that publishing this book makes sense. Thank you, Emily Nemchick for editing, she scrutinized my text and made it better. And thank you for all my friends who were patient with me and my scattered writing brain.

AUTHOR'S NOTE

Thank you for reading my book! I'm so happy that I got this one into your hands. It was touch and go, as writing this book took a year longer than I expected. The shape of the book changed a lot during the writing process. At the beginning of the book, I knew that I wanted to write about bureaucracy and the Necromantic Council, but then the witches and the reporter snuck in, and it became about more than the Council and Petula Upwood. I had to write about truth, friendship, and injustice, about needlepoint and revolutions, because everyone knows revolutions and needlepoint go together.

That wasn't the only reason writing this book took so long. I lost my father in the middle of the writing process. He died suddenly, and I had to find strength to go on. At first, I tried to write every day as I usually do, but then the grief got too much, and I had to take a break and try to... I still don't know what I had to do to get back to being functional. This book wouldn't have come about without the constant help and support from my husband, Henri. He patiently listened to me and read my book several times, giving me the needed feedback.

So here we are. The book is now what it was meant to be, shaped by the process and everything that went on while I wrote it. I'm happy that Henrietta Culpepper took her part in the narrative. I loved writing about her love for nature, her care for the witches, and the struggle of being a leader. She's the leader I would love to have. With Raul, I gave hope to all those who have lost the meaning of life. The bottle isn't the answer, but it isn't blind obsession either. Who knows what the answer is and how intense it has to be? Then there are Cruxh, Elmer, and Percy. They all want to uphold the law and do the right thing in a chaotic, self-serving world. It's not such an easy thing to do, especially with people like Otis running around with their mad inventions.

Otis, what can I say about him? He is what he is and what he is meant to be. The machine of his is another thing entirely. I tried to solve the problem of the Bufonite and what such a machine would do to our world. I would love to be an optimist and say that such a machine would be a blessing, bringing happiness and prosperity for all. Yet I fear that the history of humankind has shown otherwise. Even now, the inequality is mind-boggling—something Petula would note, too.

Petula was written to try her best in the system she inherited from her predecessors. I feel bad that she is being destroyed in the process. The thing with power is that it is all fun and games if you don't have a conscience. As soon as you start to connect with the little fellow and don't see people as numbers, you will struggle. But how can you make decisions and guard the bigger picture if you feel for every granny and lost child? Then again, what kind of society doesn't?

That's one thing I can't wrap my head around. We breathe these societies of ours, and they seem to collapse at one point or another. I keep searching for an answer to satisfy my curiosity about how societies and communities should be organized and what it means to exist in society as a person. That fuels my writing. That is why this book is here in your hands. See you in the next one! And thank you once again for reading this one. It means a lot to me. Now, if you could leave a review, I would appreciate it. It helps.

Sincerely,

K.A. Ashcomb

ABOUT THE AUTHOR

K.A. Ashcomb grew up reading books by Terry Pratchett and other comical fantasy authors. After acquiring her MA in Comparative Religion, spiced with Social Psychology and Sociology, she found herself working behind a bookshop's counter. With tons of free time on her hands, she began to create stories about gods, unfortunate heroes, and other jerks to amuse herself. The stories grew bigger and bigger, and she had to put them on paper, and so her first book Worth Of Luck was born, then Penny For Your Soul and Mechanics Of The Past, and now The Council Of The Dead is here.

When she isn't writing and reading books, you can find her in the local forest reservation, roaming there while trying to find her way back to her keyboard, beloved books, her two mischievous cats, and her husband. She is also an avid outdoor boulderer, nature photographer, and could forever ponder about human behavior and societal structures and the mystery of atoms. She works as a part time occupational therapist, helping kids with autism, sensomotor problems, and emotional regulation difficulties.

COMING NEXT FROM K.A. ASHCOMB

Skulls are taking over Necropolis. They already command banking. Penny Lock has been working on them for years in a small factory, perfecting her trade. But she makes one mistake, getting her in trouble with those who want to control the skull market behind the scenes.

Cruxh is sure there is something odd going on in the city. He can sense it. It can sense it, too, and it is determined to get the inspector out of its way and out of his job. But who would be foolish enough to attack the ghoul?

Made in the USA
Columbia, SC
16 November 2024

46723234R00295